STRAWBERRY MARSHMALLOW

ICHIGO MASHIMARO

Strawberry Marshmallow Vol. 5
Created by Barasui

Translation - Emi Onishi
English Adaptation - Nathan Johnson
Retouch and Lettering - Star Print Brokers
Production Artist - Courtney Geter
Graphic Designer - James Lee

Editor - Peter Ahlstrom
Digital Imaging Manager - Chris Buford
Pre-Production Supervisor - Lucas Rivera
Production Manager - Elisabeth Brizzi
Managing Editor - Vy Nguyen
Creative Director - Anne Marie Horne
Editor-in-Chief - Rob Tokar
Publisher - Mike Kiley
President and C.O.O. - John Parker
C.E.O. and Chief Creative Officer - Stu Levy

A  Manga

TOKYOPOP and 🐢 are trademarks or registered trademarks of TOKYOPOP Inc.

TOKYOPOP Inc.
5900 Wilshire Blvd. Suite 2000
Los Angeles, CA 90036

E-mail: info@TOKYOPOP.com
Come visit us online at www.TOKYOPOP.com

ISBN: 978-1-4278-0469-3

First TOKYOPOP printing: June 2008
10 9 8 7 6 5 4 3 2 1
Printed in the USA

STRAWBERRY MARSHMALLOW

ICHIGO MASHIMARO

VOL. 5

BY Barasui

HAMBURG // LONDON // LOS ANGELES // TOKYO

CUTE GIRLS ARE BACK IN TOWN

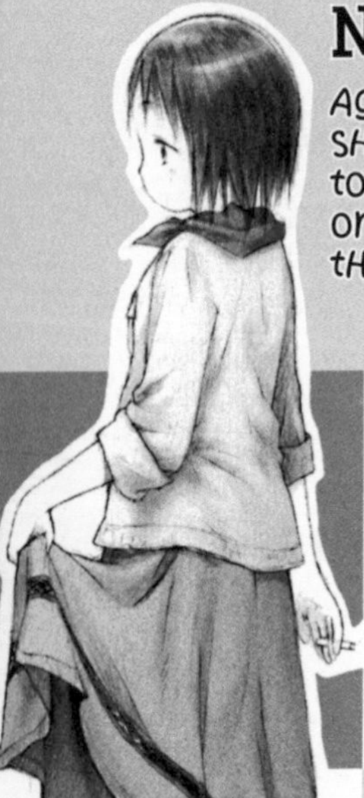

Nobue Ito

Age 16. The oldest of the bunch, she has as an irrepressible addiction to nicotine. When she's not puffing on a cig, she's teasing the girls through any means possible.

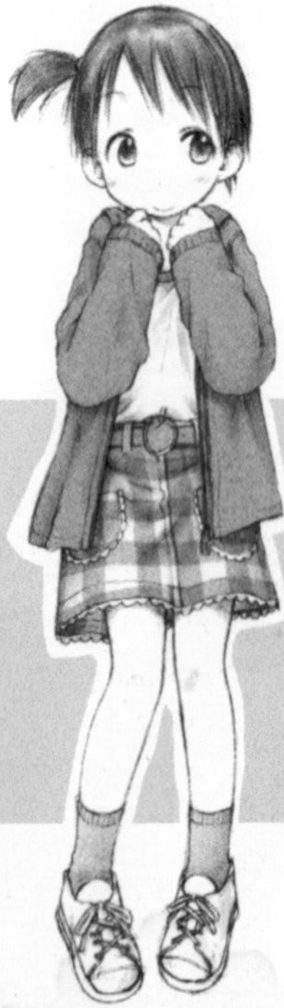

Chika Ito

Age 12. Nobue's little sister--and complete opposite. She tends to play the victim to the other girls' antics.

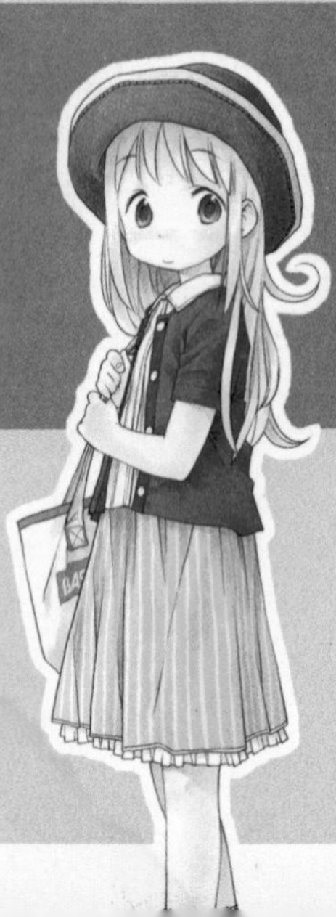

Ana Coppola

Age 11. The new student in Matsuri's class. She's from England, but she's been living in Japan so long that her English is terrible. She doesn't want anyone else at school to know she's fluent in Japanese.

Miu Matsuoka

Age 12. The cutest of the cute, this spazztastic ball of energy lives next door to Chika and Nobue, and will never pass up the opportunity to bring a little mayhem to their lives.

Matsuri Sakuragi

Age 11. Also known as "Mats," Matsuri is timid, a crybaby, and completely lost when it comes to sports. She's also often teased by the girls for her mysterious white hair.

John

Matsuri's pet ferret.

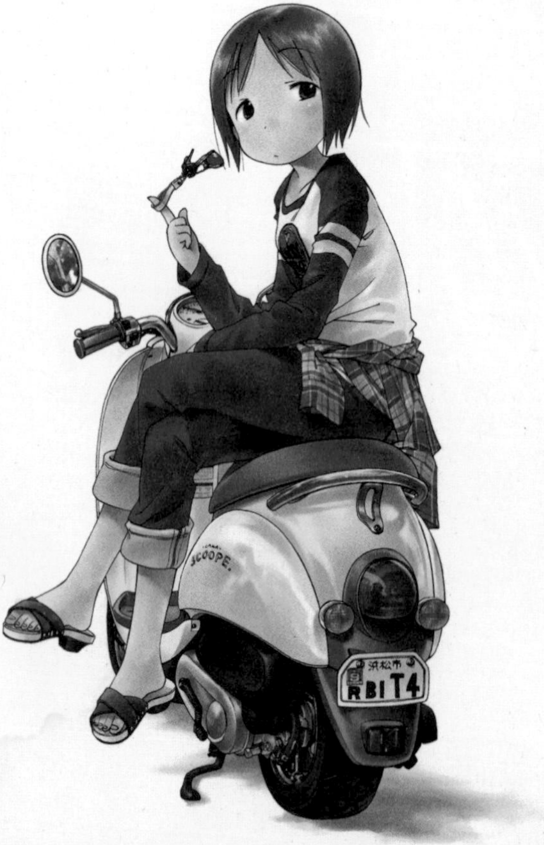
SCOOPE.
浜松市
RBI T4

STRAWBERRY MARSHMALLOW

ICHIGO MASHIMARO

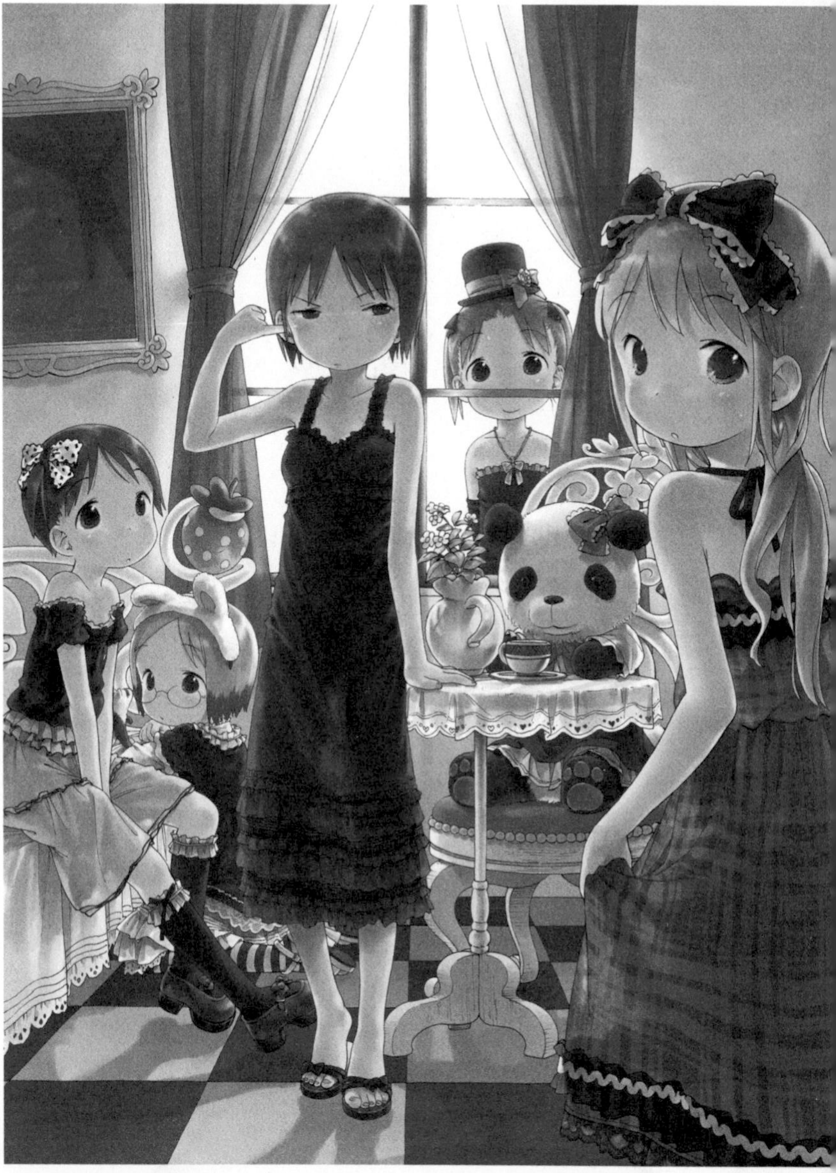

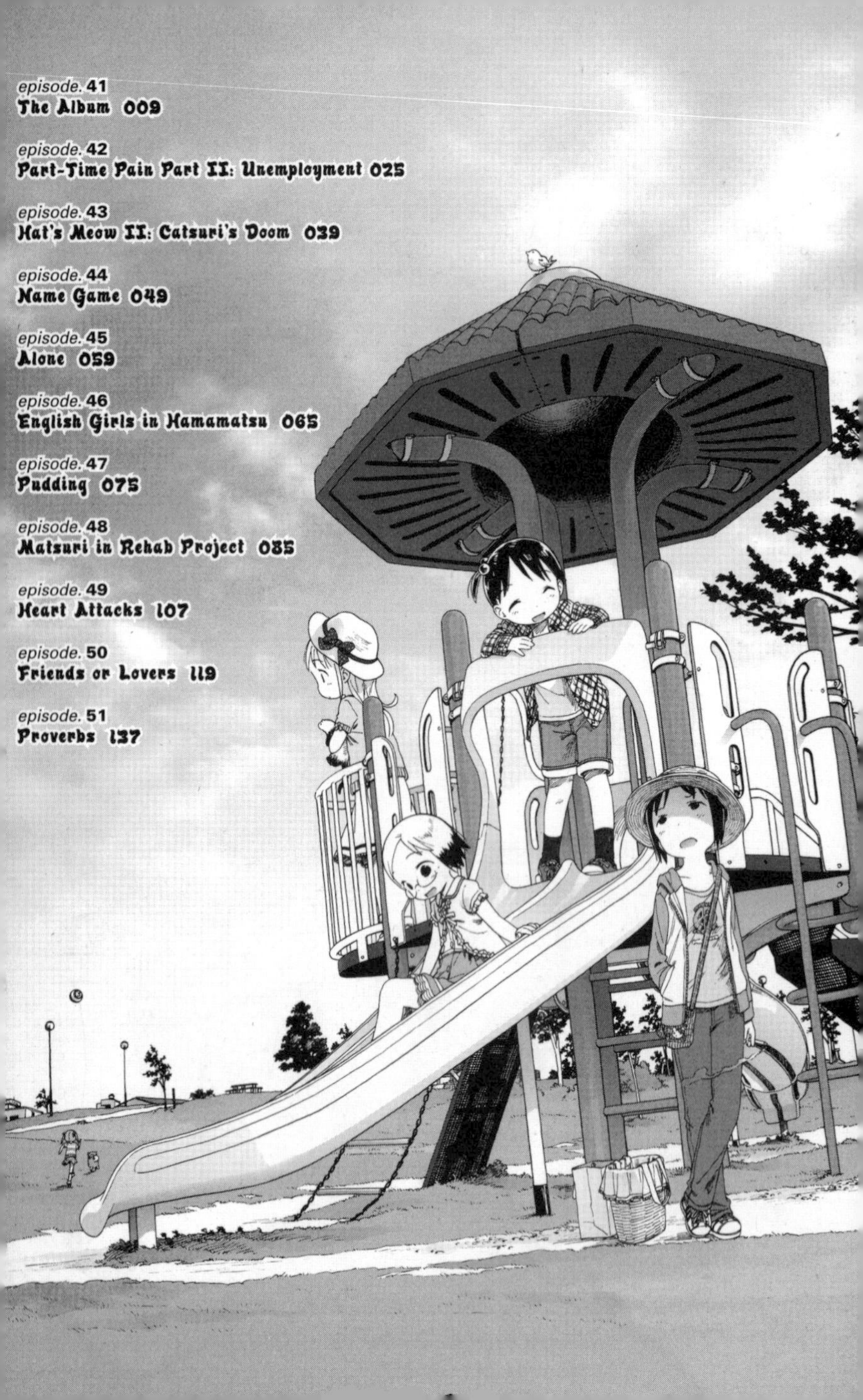

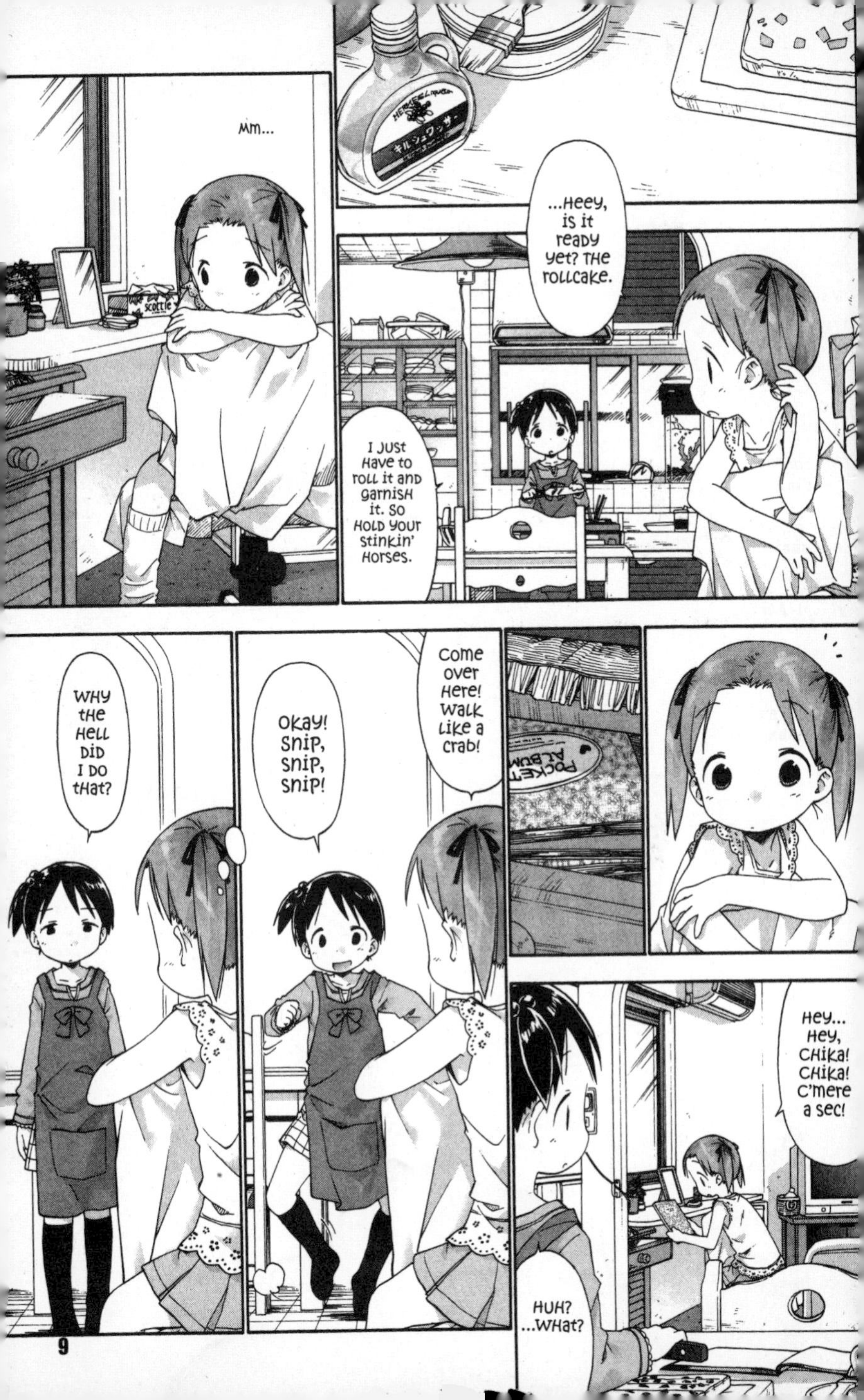
キルシュワッサー
...Heey, is it ready yet? The rollcake.
I just have to roll it and garnish it. So hold your stinkin' horses.
Mm...
POCKET ALBUM
Hey... Hey, Chika! Chika! C'mere a sec!
Huh? ...What?
Come over here! Walk like a crab!
Okay! Snip, snip, snip!
Why the hell did I do that?

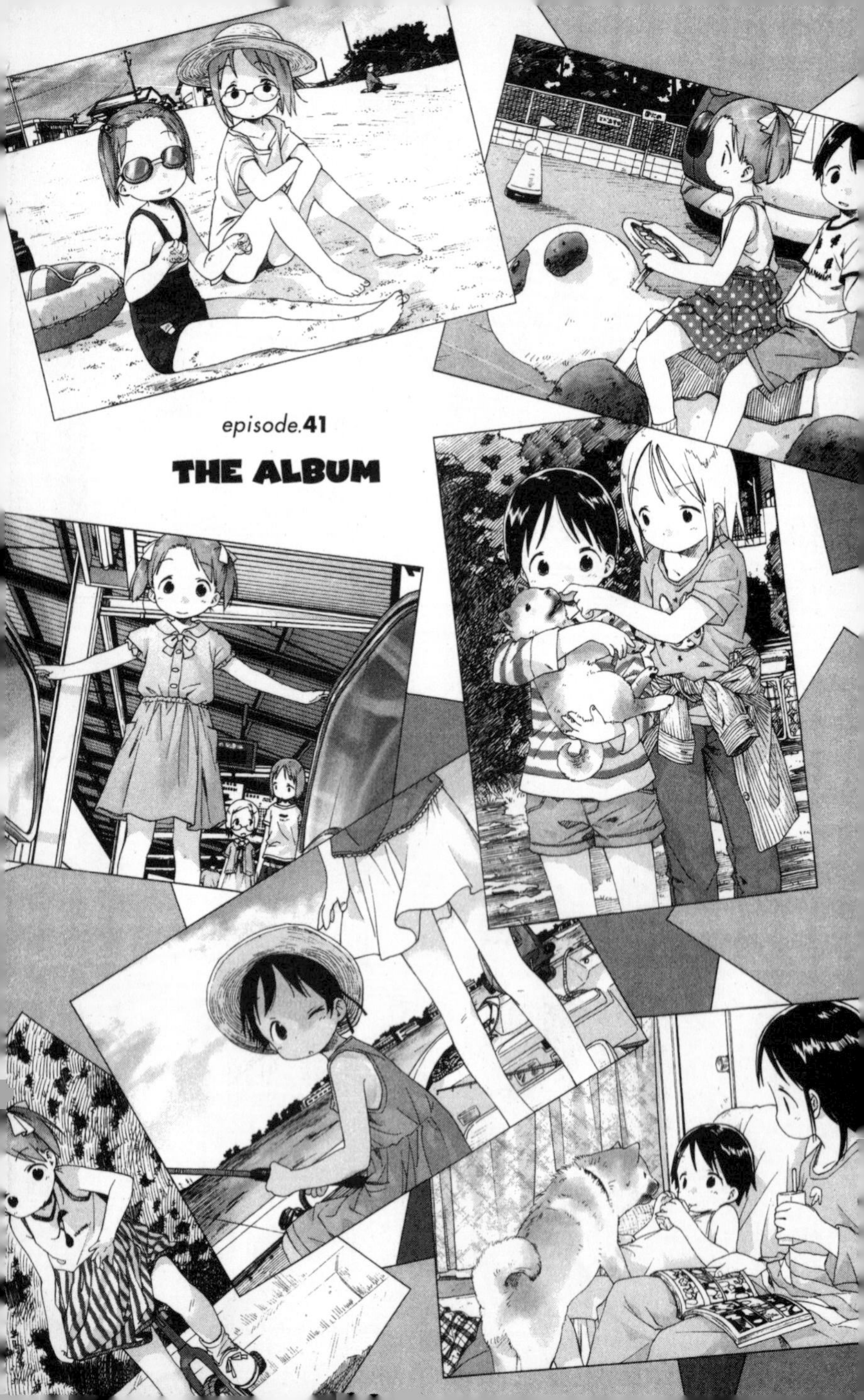
episode.41
THE ALBUM

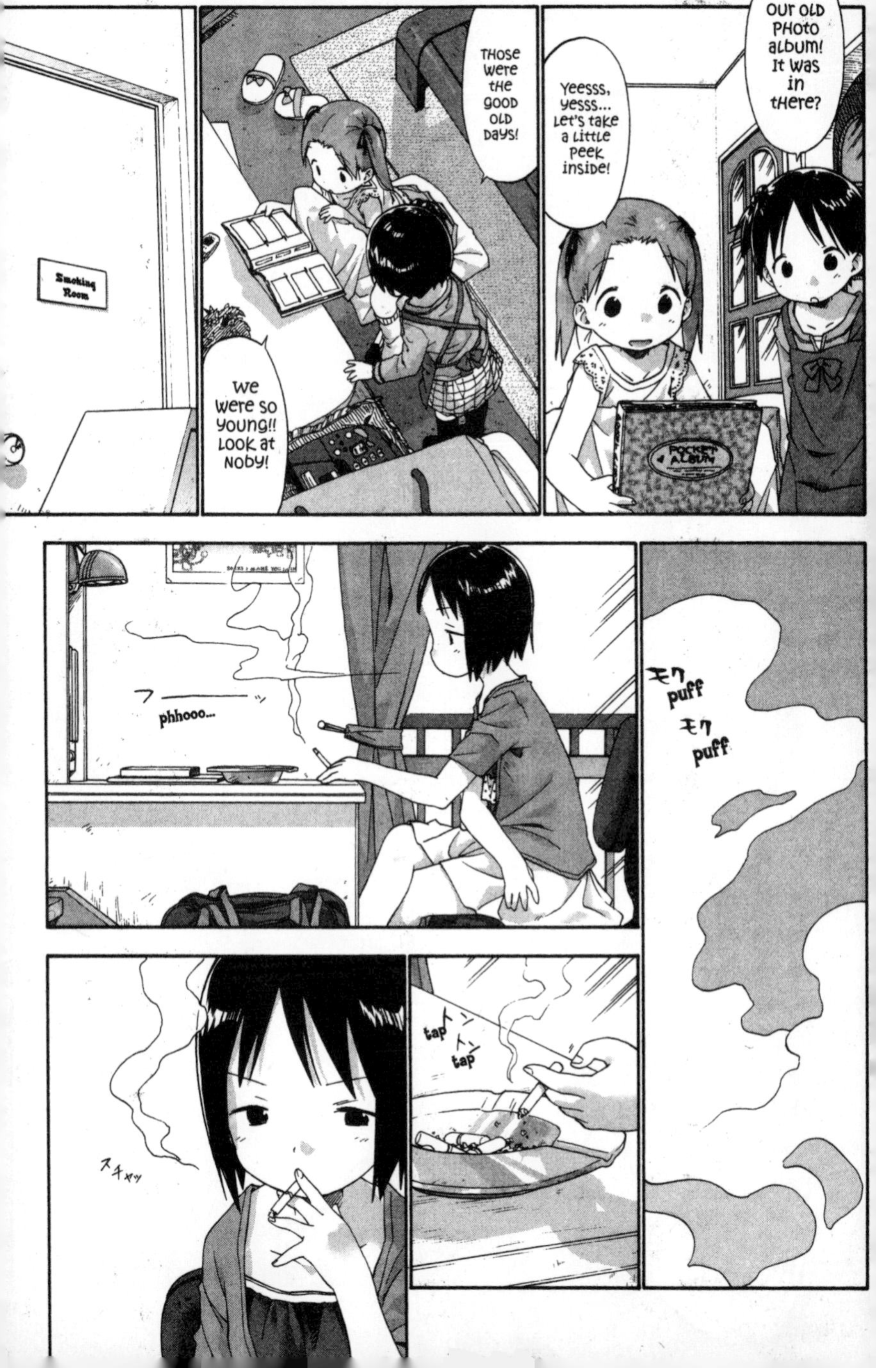
Our old photo album! It was in there?
Yeesss, yesss... let's take a little peek inside!
Those were the good old days!
We were so young!! Look at Noby!
Smoking Room
モク puff
モク puff
フーーッ
phhooo...
トン tap
トン tap

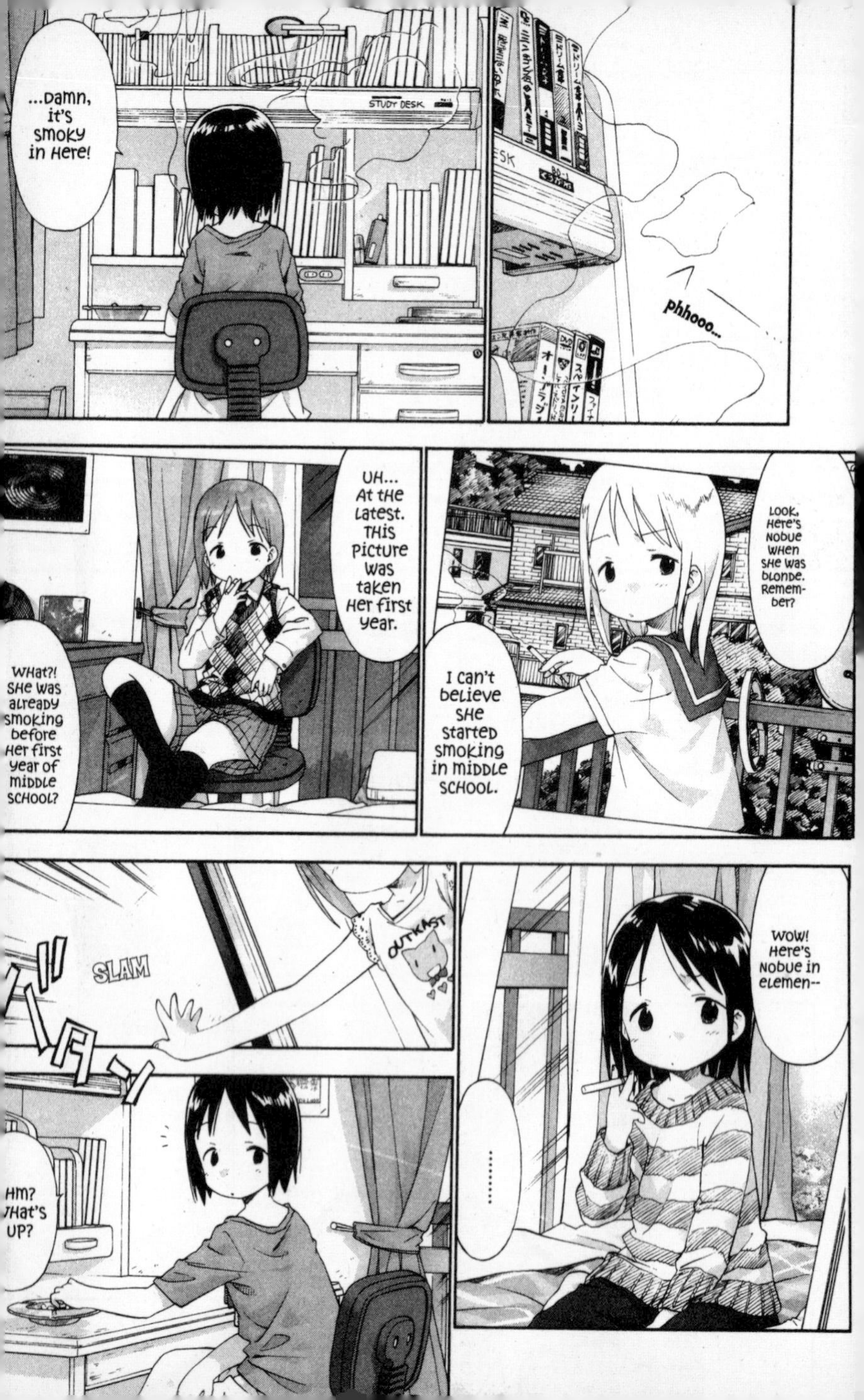
phhooo...
...Damn, it's smoky in here!
Look, here's Nobue when she was blonde. Remember?
I can't believe she started smoking in middle school.
Uh... at the latest. This picture was taken her first year.
What?! She was already smoking before her first year of middle school?
Wow! Here's Nobue in elemen--
....
SLAM
OUTKAST
Hm? What's up?

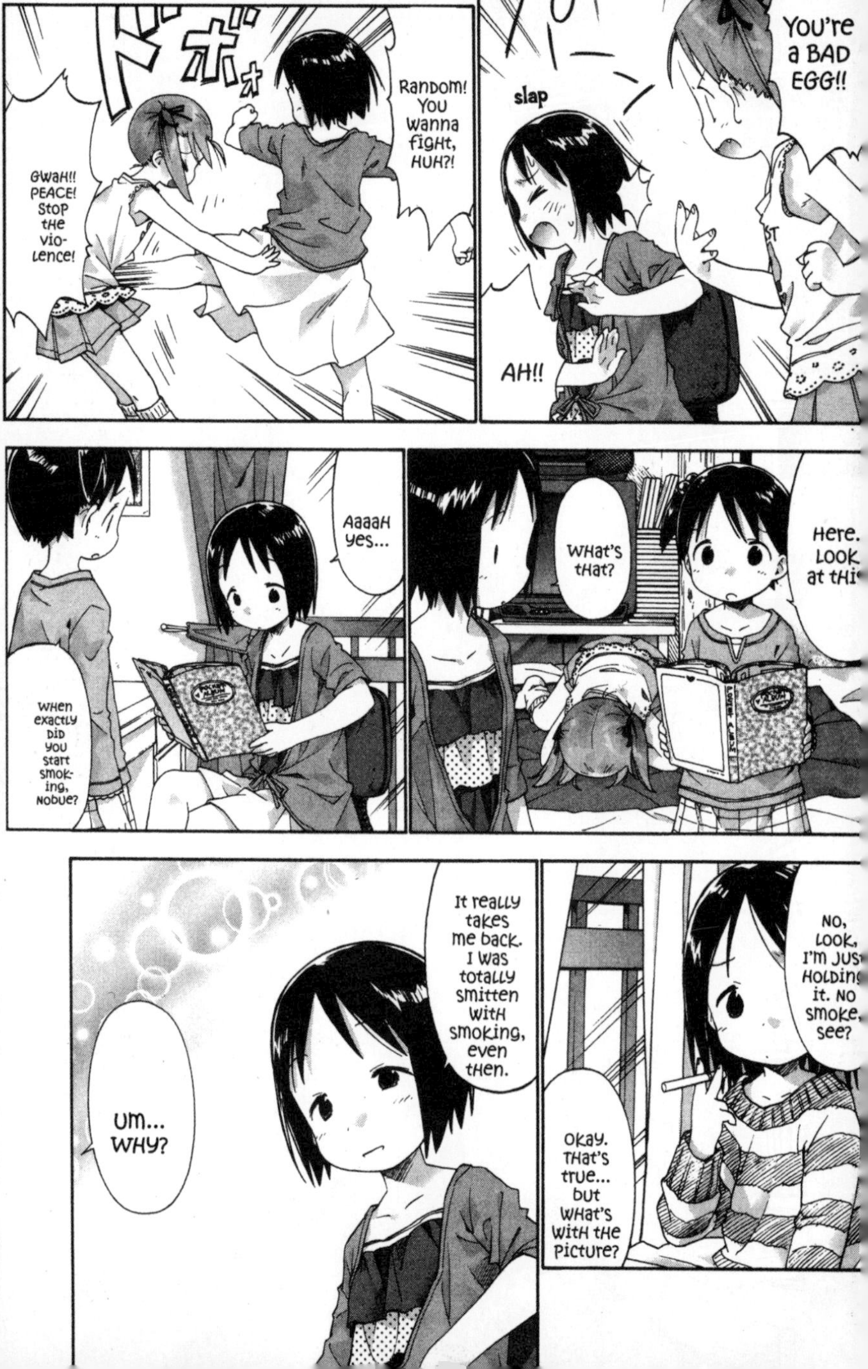
You're a BAD EGG!!
slap
AH!!
Random! You wanna fight, HUH?!
GWAH!! PEACE! Stop the vio-lence!
Here. Look at thi
What's that?
Aaaah yes...
When exactly did you start smok-ing, Nobue?
No, look, I'm jus holding it. No smoke, see?
Okay. That's true... but what's with the picture?
It really takes me back. I was totally smitten with smoking, even then.
Um... why?

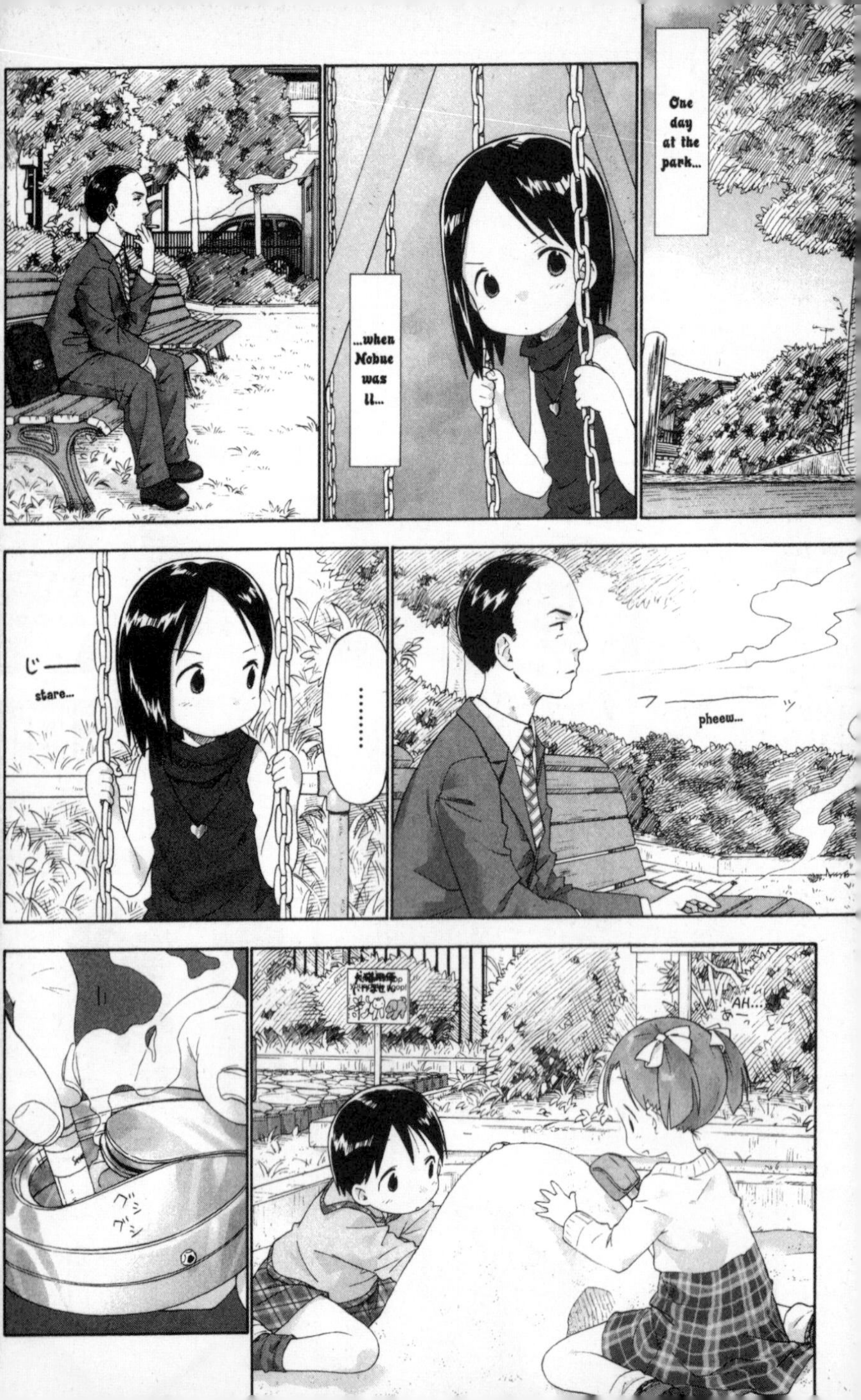
One day at the park...
...when Nobue was 11...
フーーーッ
pheew...
じーー
stare...
....
AH...
あー
グシグシ

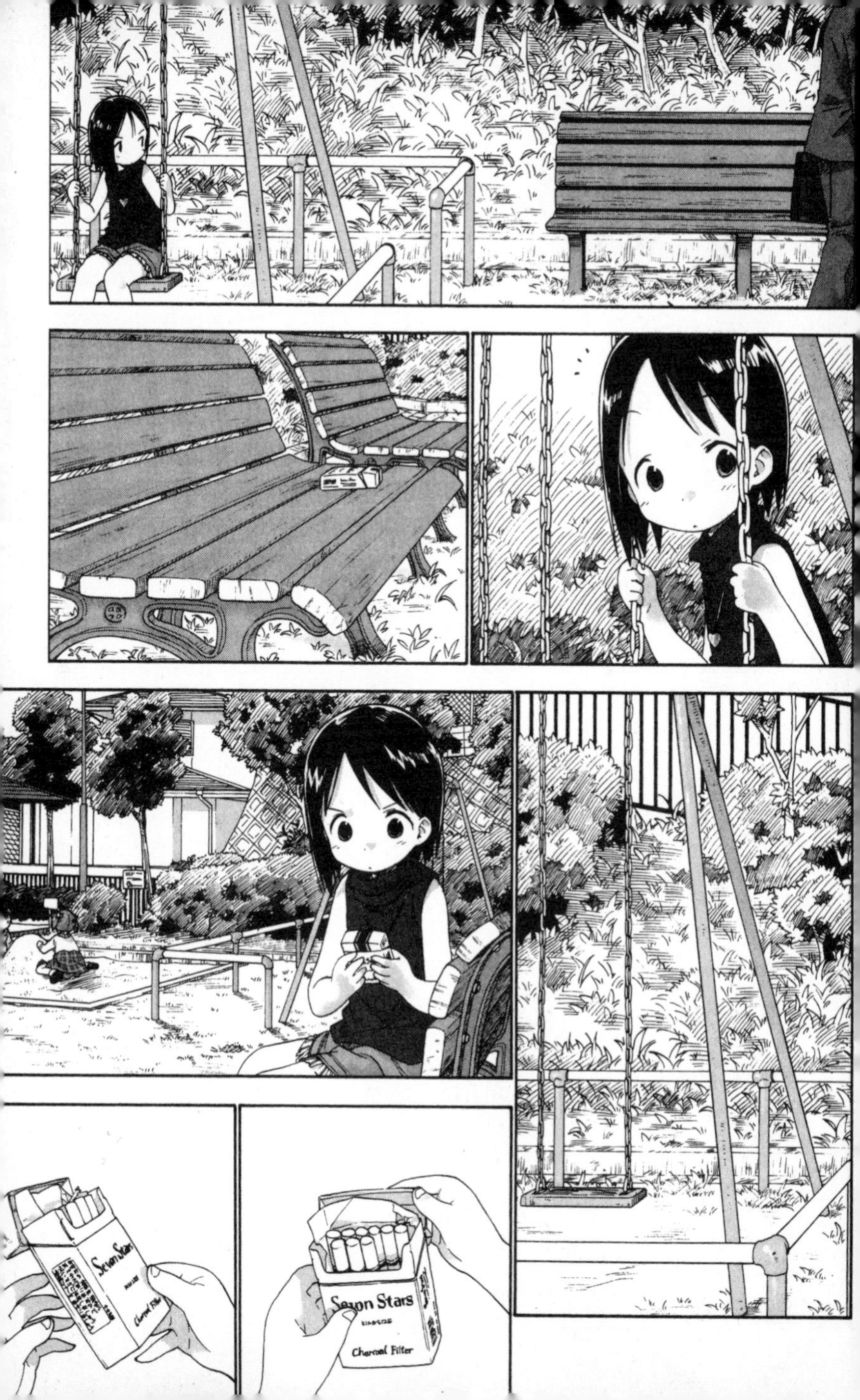
Seven Stars
Charcoal Filter
Seven Stars
Charcoal Filter

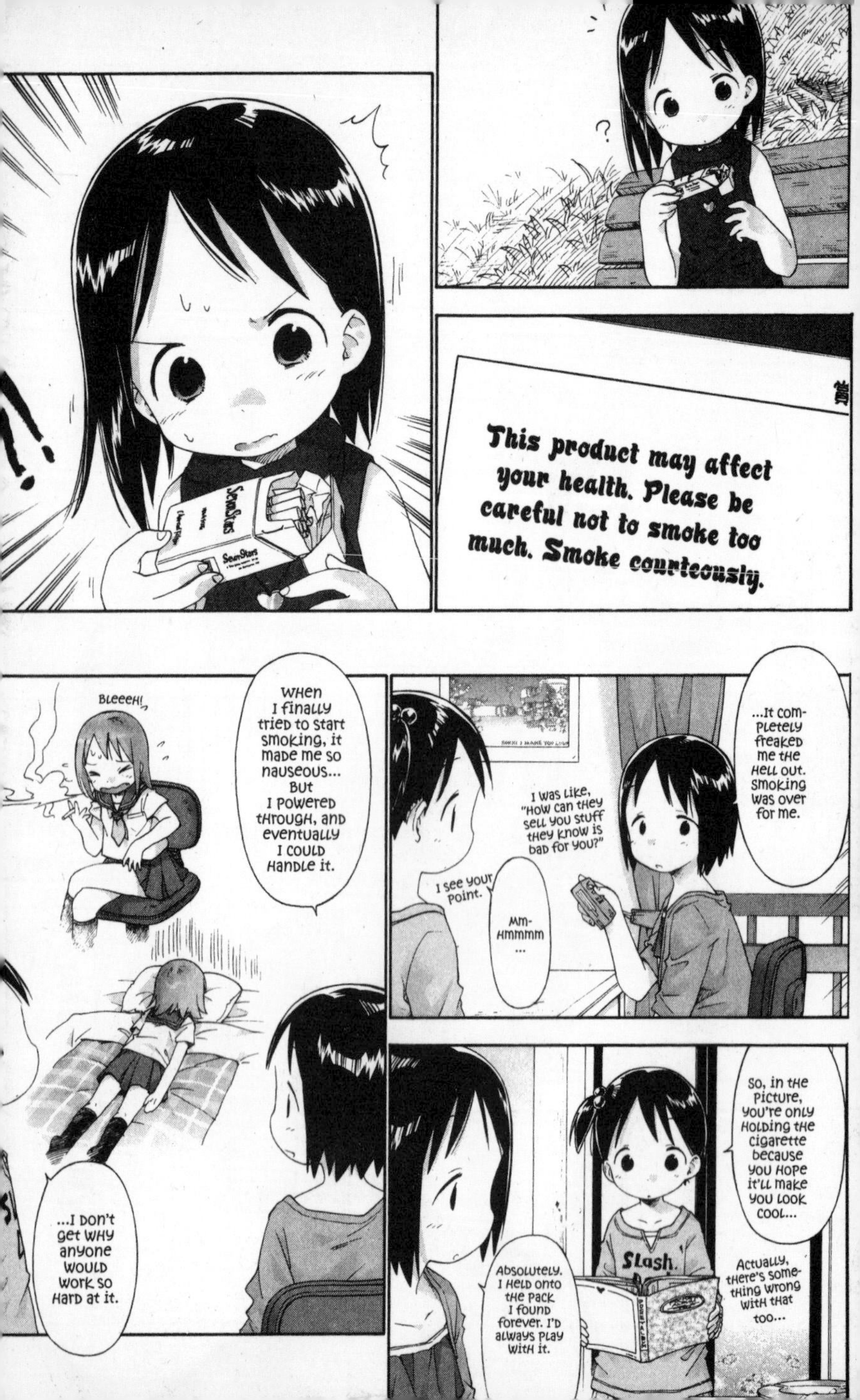
?
This product may affect your health. Please be careful not to smoke too much. Smoke courteously.
!!
...It com-pletely freaked me the hell out. Smoking was over for me.
I was like, "How can they sell you stuff they know is bad for you?"
I see your point.
Mm-hmmmm...
So, in the picture, you're only holding the cigarette because you hope it'll make you look cool...
Actually, there's some-thing wrong with that too...
Absolutely. I held onto the pack I found forever. I'd always play with it.
When I finally tried to start smoking, it made me so nauseous... But I powered through, and eventually I could handle it.
Bleeeh!
...I don't get why anyone would work so hard at it.

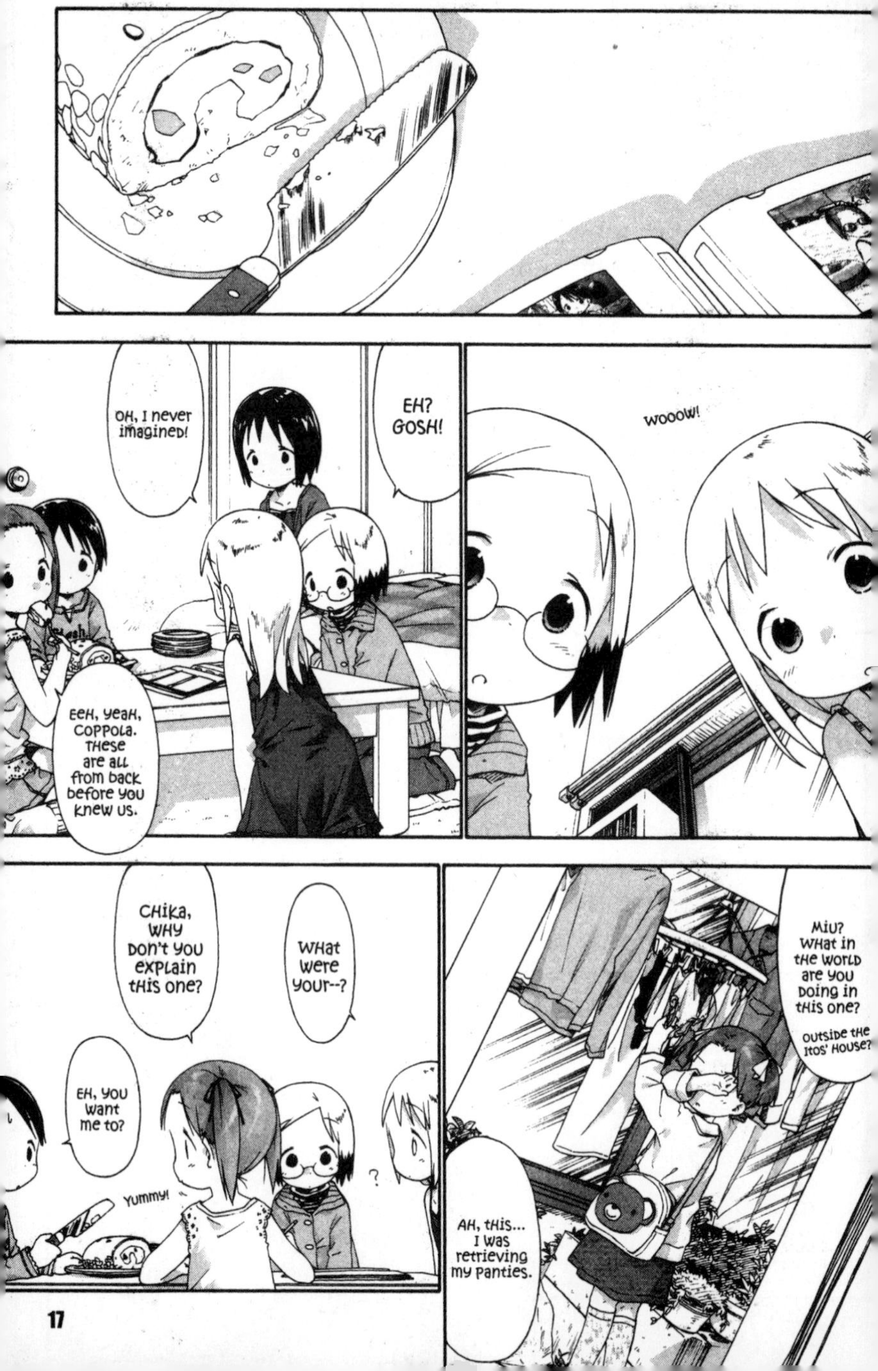
WOOOW!
EH? GOSH!
OH, I never imagined!
EEH, YEAH, COPPOLA. THESE are all from back before YOU knew us.
MIU? WHAT in THE WORLD are YOU DOING in THIS one?
OUTSIDE THE ITOS' HOUSE?
AH, THIS... I WAS retrieving my panties.
WHAT were your--?
CHIKA, WHY Don't YOU explain THIS one?
EH, YOU want me to?
?
YUMMY!

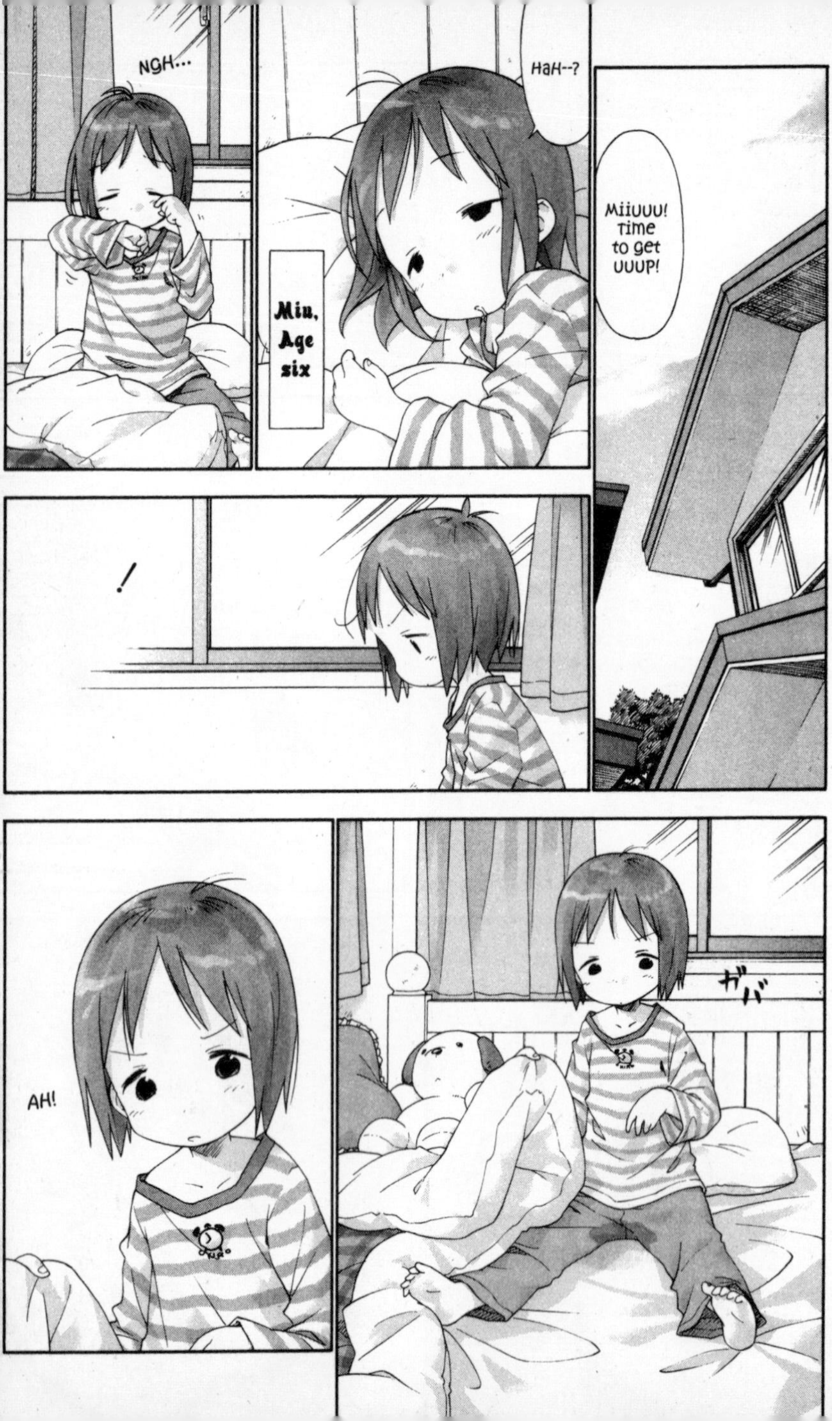
Miiuuu! Time to get UUUP!
HaH--?
Miu, Age six
NGH...
!
ガバ
AH!

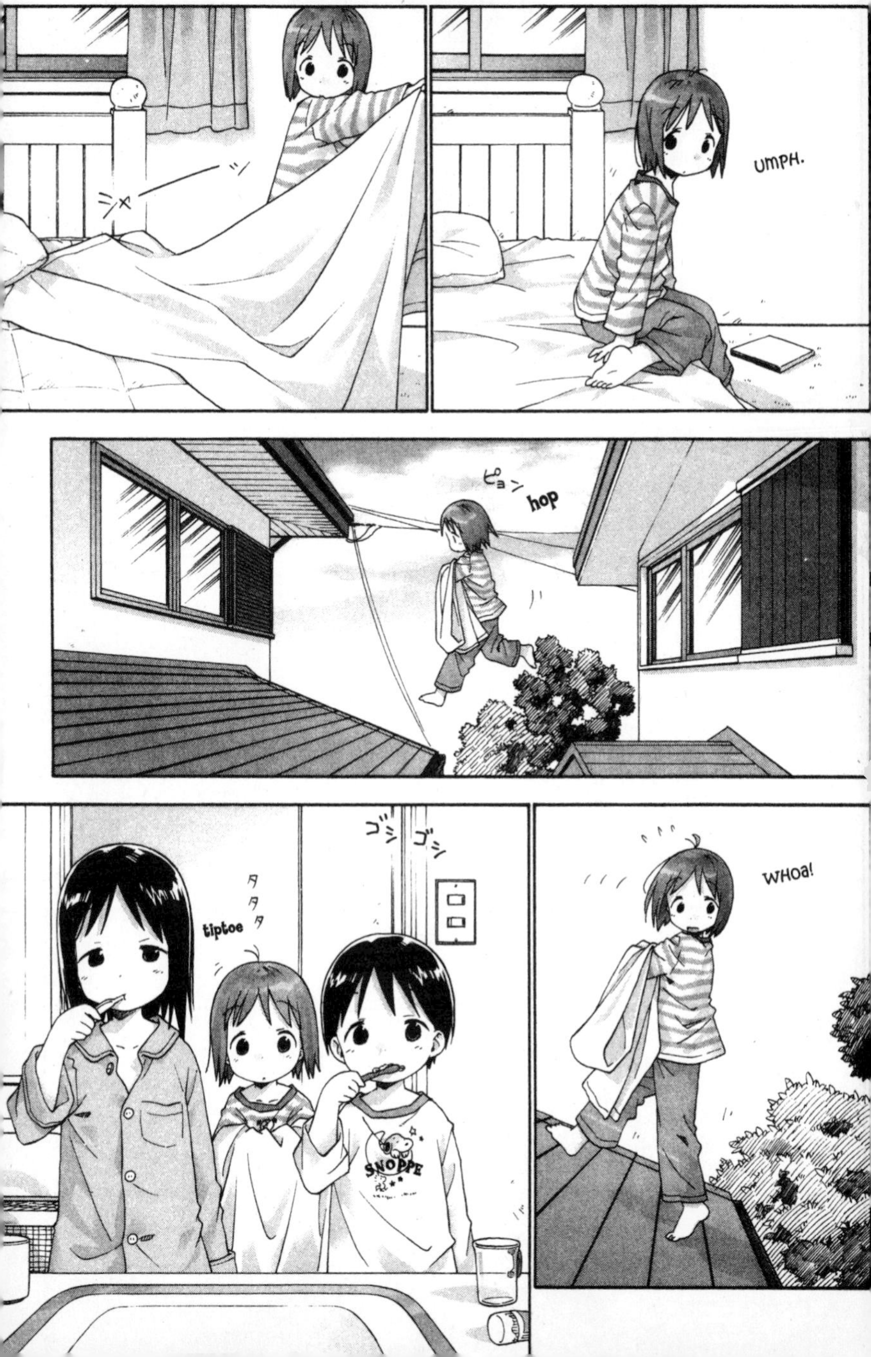
UMPH.
ピョン
hop
WHOa!
ゴシ ゴシ
タタタ
tiptoe
SNOPPE

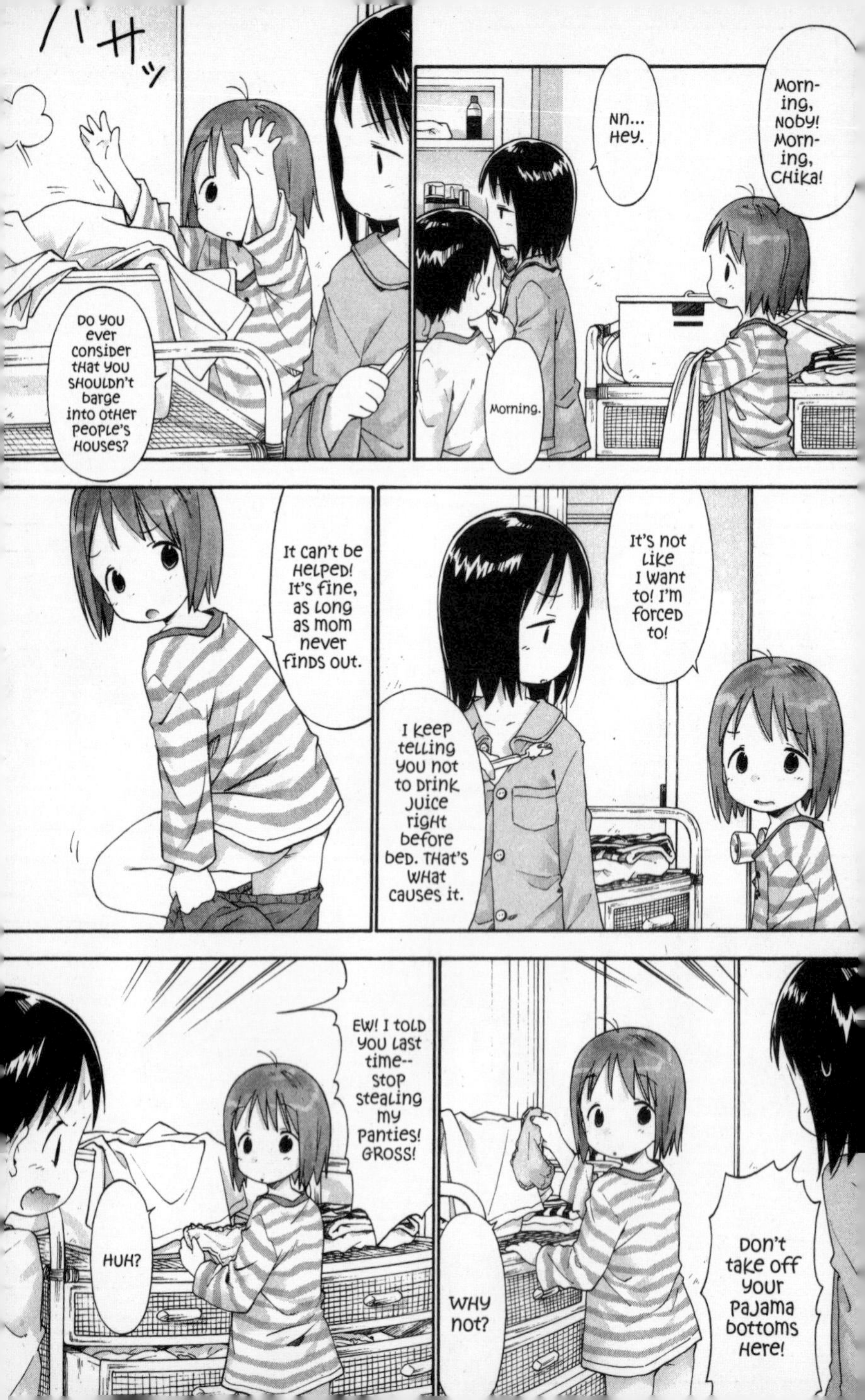
Morning, Noby! Morning, Chika!
Nn... Hey.
Morning.
バサッ
Do you ever consider that you shouldn't barge into other people's houses?
It's not like I want to! I'm forced to!
I keep telling you not to drink juice right before bed. That's what causes it.
It can't be helped! It's fine, as long as mom never finds out.
Don't take off your pajama bottoms here!
Why not?
Ew! I told you last time-- stop stealing my panties! GROSS!
Huh?

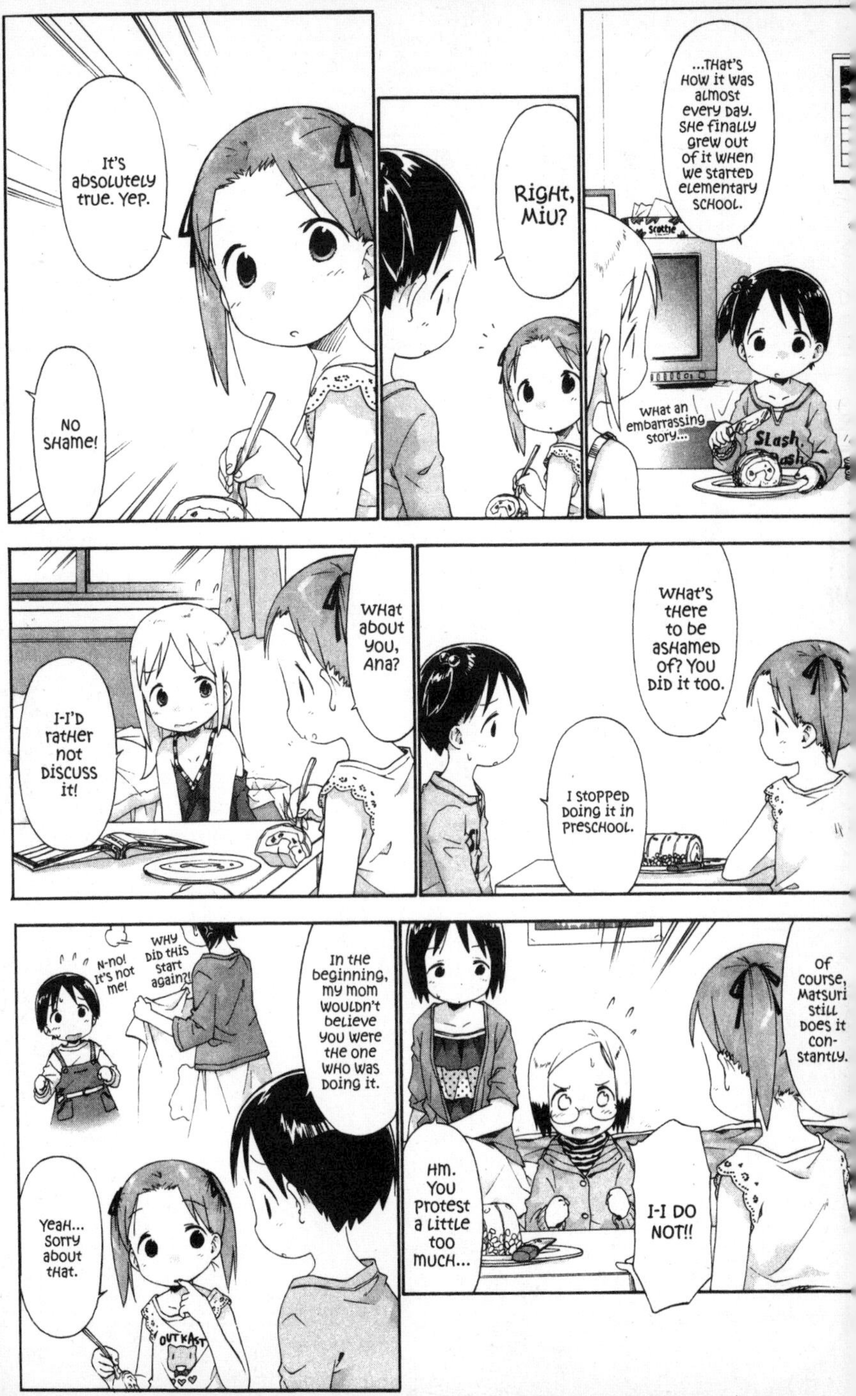
...That's how it was almost every day. She finally grew out of it when we started elementary school.
Scottie
What an embarrassing story...
Right, Miu?
It's absolutely true. Yep.
No shame!
What's there to be ashamed of? You did it too.
I stopped doing it in preschool.
What about you, Ana?
I-I'd rather not discuss it!
Of course, Matsuri still does it constantly.
I-I do not!!
Hm. You protest a little too much...
In the beginning, my mom wouldn't believe you were the one who was doing it.
Why did this start again?!
N-no! It's not me!
Yeah... sorry about that.
OUT KAST

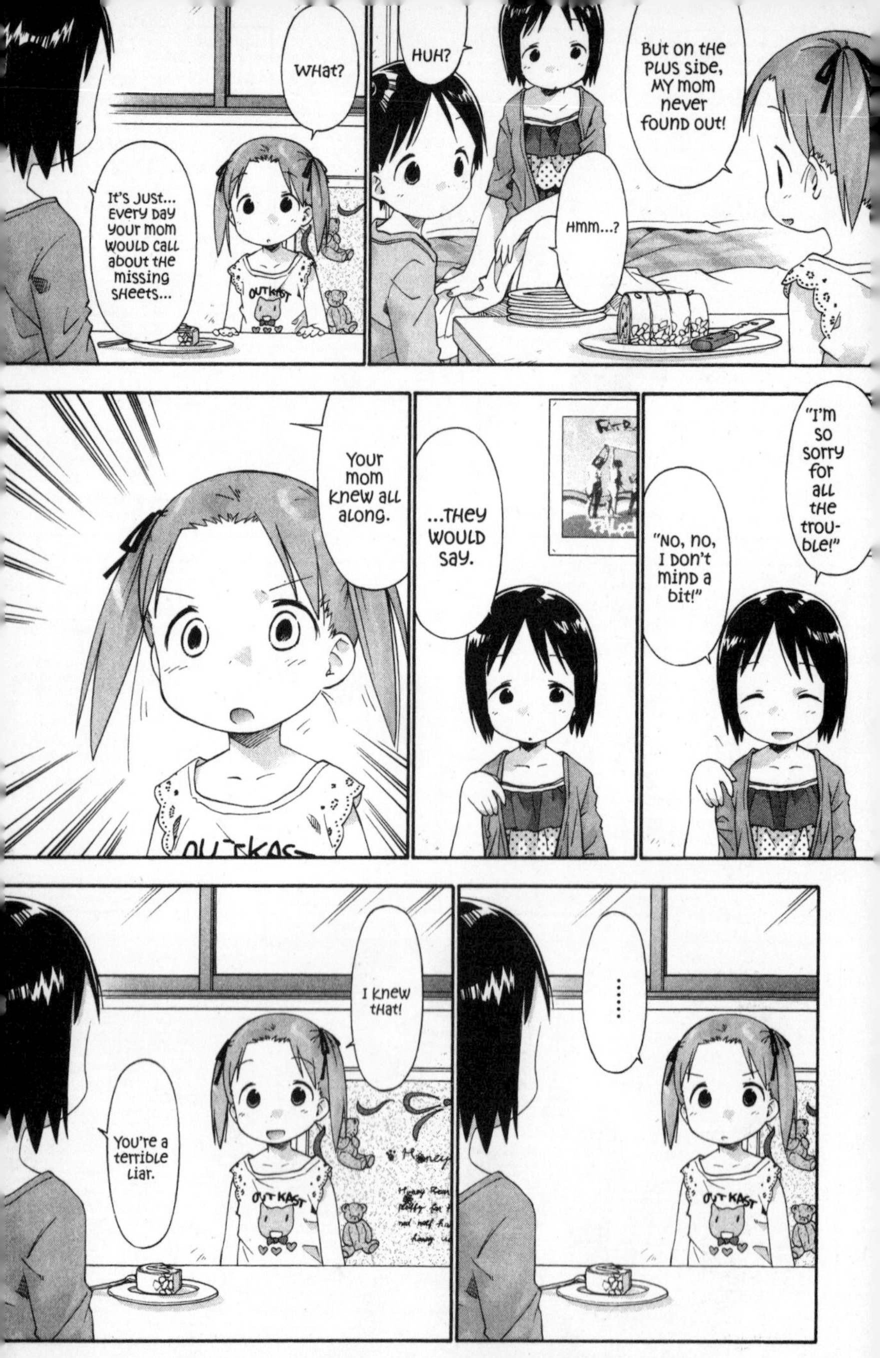
But on the plus side, my mom never found out!
Huh?
Hmm...?
What?
It's just... every day your mom would call about the missing sheets...
"I'm so sorry for all the trouble!"
"No, no, I don't mind a bit!"
...They would say.
Your mom knew all along.
......
I knew that!
You're a terrible liar.

Spring —— Chika

Miu

Summer

Matsuri

Autumn

Ana

Winter

Nobue

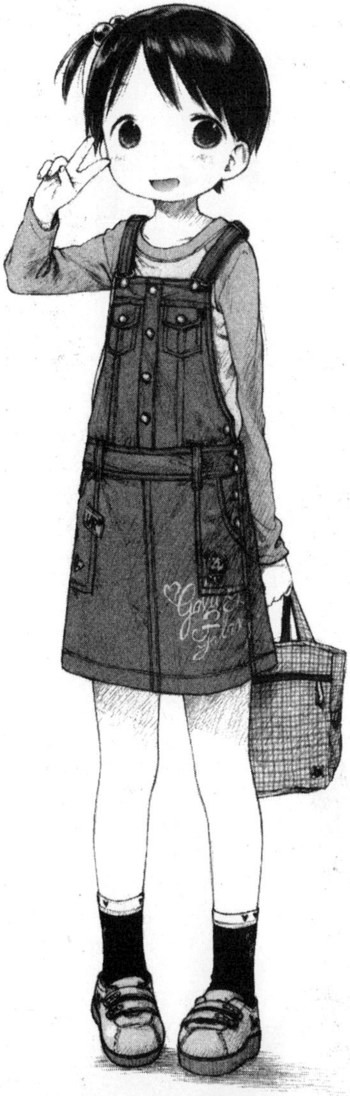

Spring	Chika
Summer	Miu
Autumn	Matsuri
Winter	Ana
	Nobue

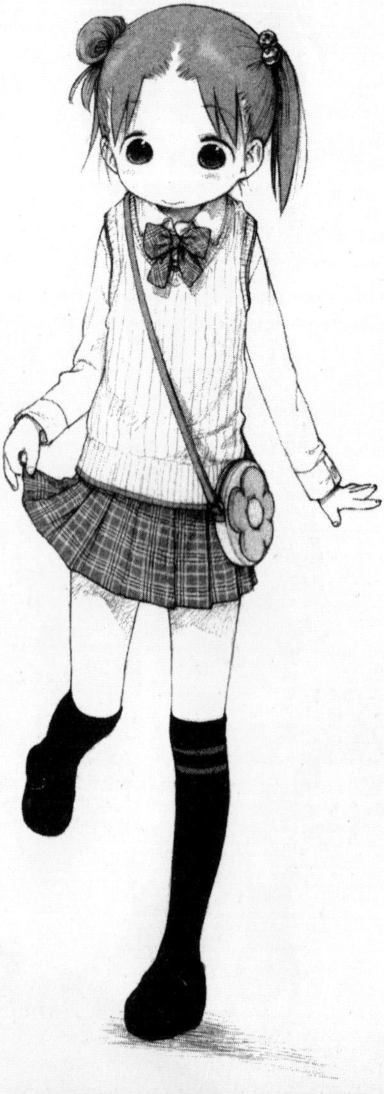

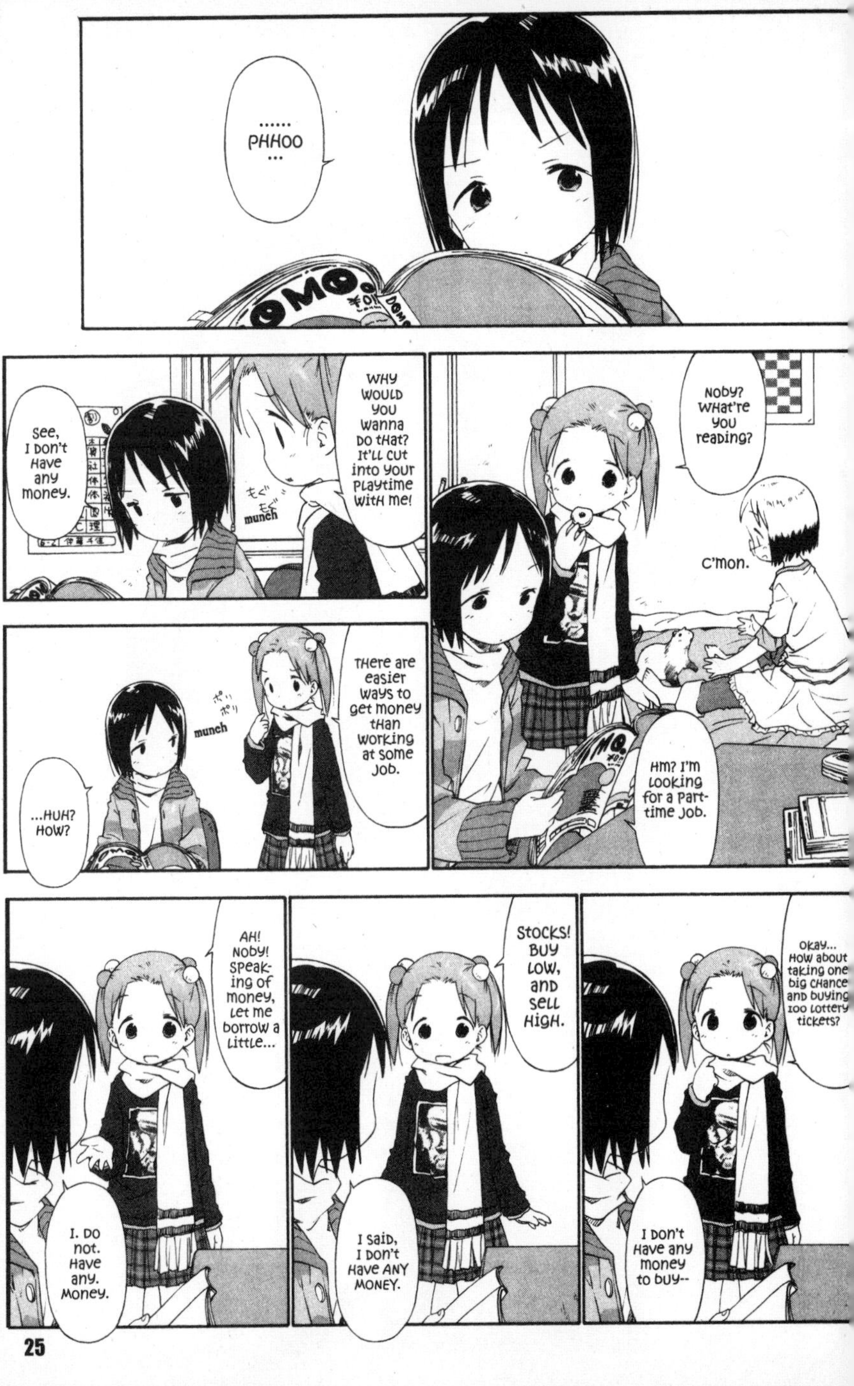

...... PHHOO ...
Noby? What're you reading?
C'mon.
Hm? I'm looking for a part-time job.
Why would you wanna do that? It'll cut into your playtime with me!
もぐ もぐ
munch
See, I don't have any money.
There are easier ways to get money than working at some job.
ポリ ポリ
munch
...Huh? How?
Okay... How about taking one big chance and buying 100 lottery tickets?
I don't have any money to buy--
Stocks! Buy low, and sell high.
I said, I don't have ANY MONEY.
Ah! Noby! Speaking of money, let me borrow a little...
I. Do not. Have any. Money.

episode.42

PART-TIME PAIN PART II: UNEMPLOYMENT

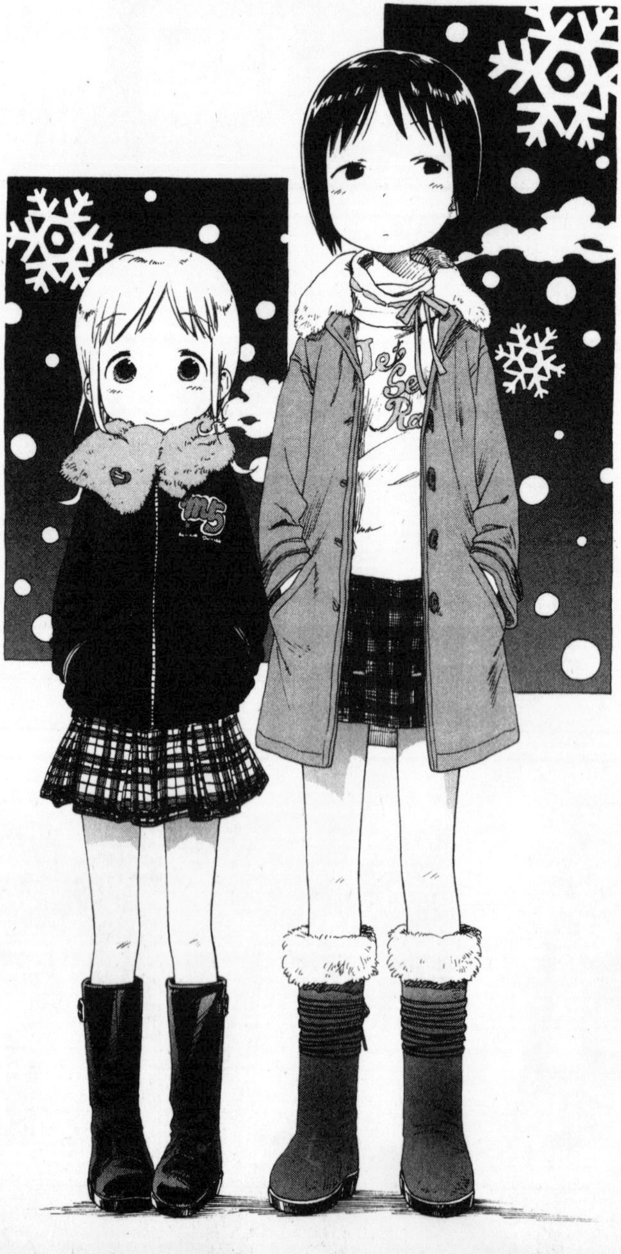

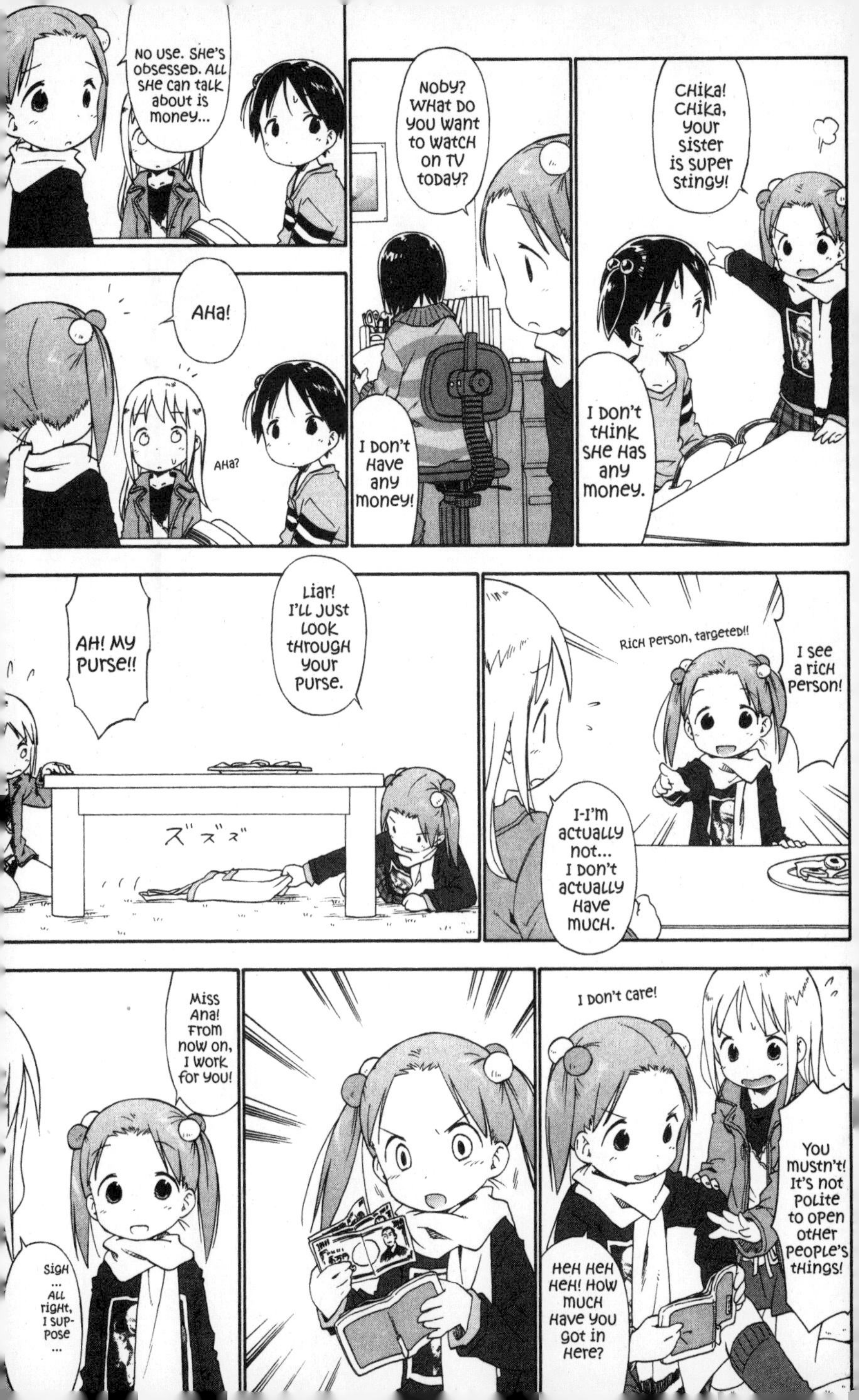
CHIKA! CHIKA, YOUR SISTER IS SUPER STINGY!
I DON'T THINK SHE HAS ANY MONEY.
NOBY? WHAT DO YOU WANT TO WATCH ON TV TODAY?
I DON'T HAVE ANY MONEY!
NO USE. SHE'S OBSESSED. ALL SHE CAN TALK ABOUT IS MONEY...
AHA!
AHA?
I SEE A RICH PERSON!
RICH PERSON, TARGETED!!
I-I'M ACTUALLY NOT... I DON'T ACTUALLY HAVE MUCH.
LIAR! I'LL JUST LOOK THROUGH YOUR PURSE.
AH! MY PURSE!!
ズズズ
HEH HEH HEH! HOW MUCH HAVE YOU GOT IN HERE?
YOU MUSTN'T! IT'S NOT POLITE TO OPEN OTHER PEOPLE'S THINGS!
I DON'T CARE!
MISS ANA! FROM NOW ON, I WORK FOR YOU!
SIGH... ALL RIGHT, I SUPPOSE...

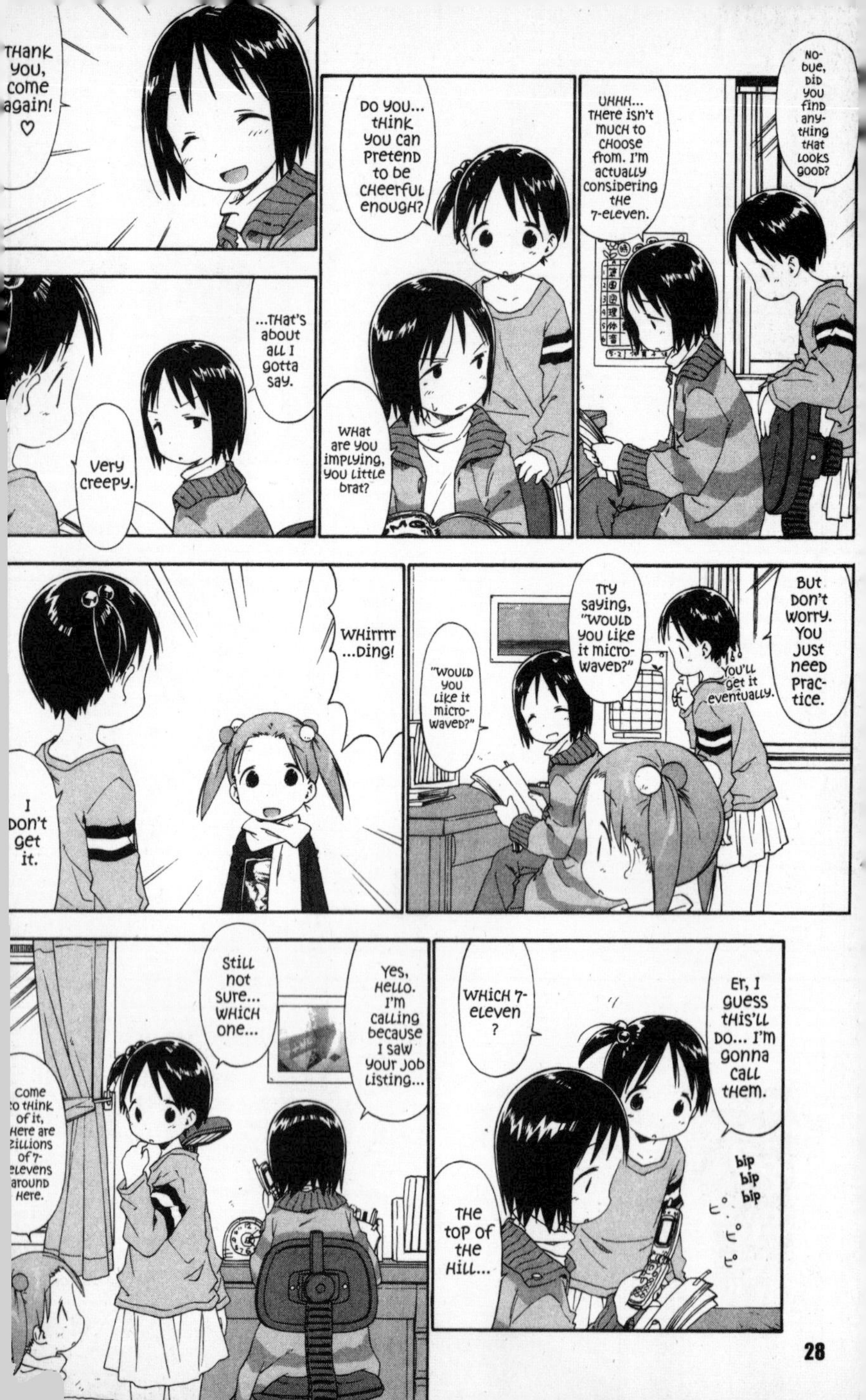
No-bue, did you find any-thing that looks good?
Uhhh... There isn't much to choose from. I'm actually considering the 7-Eleven.
Do you... think you can pretend to be cheerful enough?
What are you implying, you little brat?
Thank you, come again! ♡
...That's about all I gotta say.
Very creepy.
But don't worry. You just need prac-tice.
You'll get it eventually.
Try saying, "Would you like it micro-waved?"
"Would you like it micro-waved?"
Whirrrr ...ding!
I don't get it.
Er, I guess this'll do... I'm gonna call them.
bip bip bip
ピ ピ ピ
Which 7-Eleven?
The top of the hill...
Yes, hello. I'm calling because I saw your job listing...
Still not sure... which one...
Come to think of it, here are zillions of 7-elevens around here.

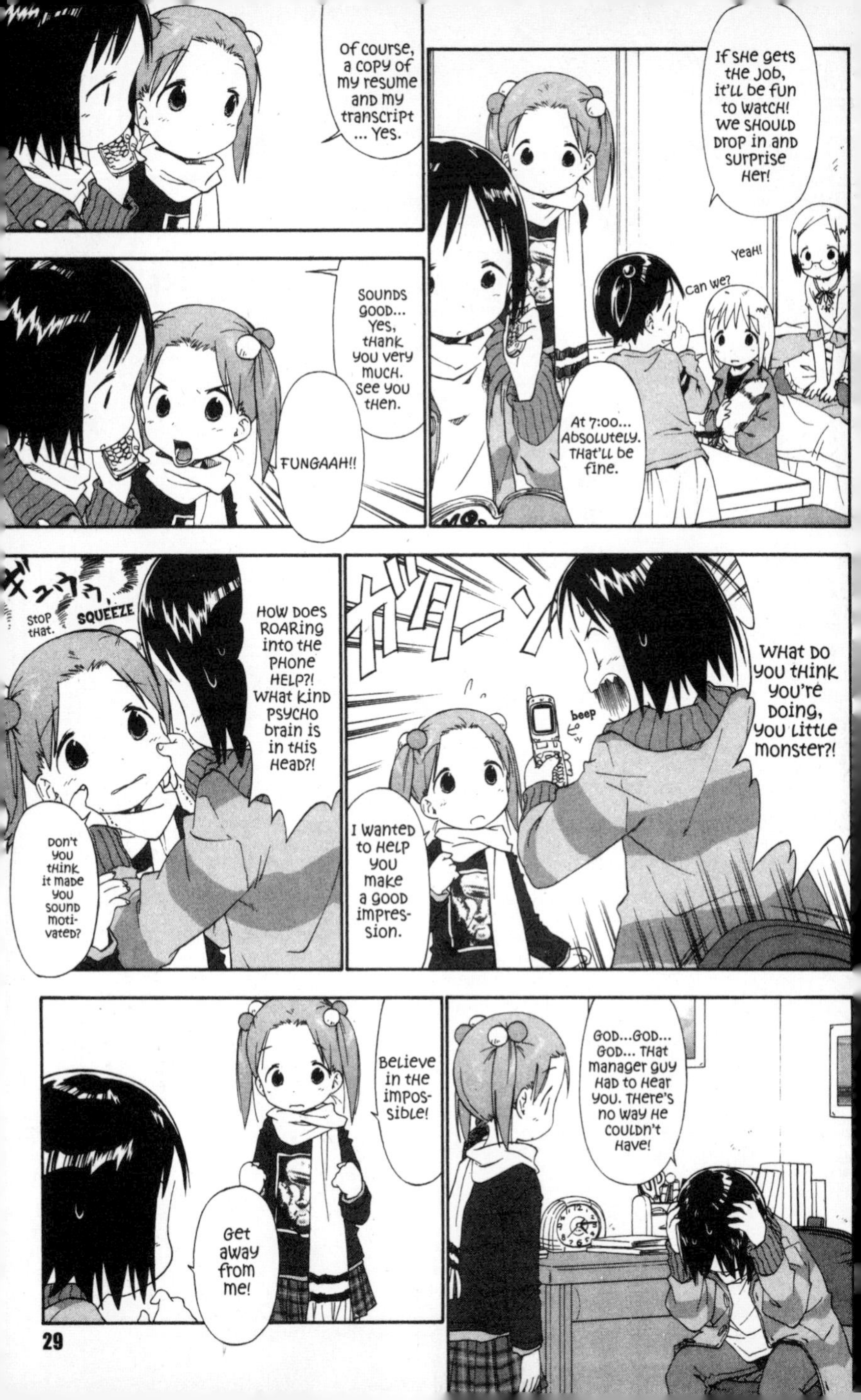
If she gets the job, it'll be fun to watch! We should drop in and surprise her!
Yeah!
Can we?
At 7:00... Absolutely. That'll be fine.
Of course, a copy of my resume and my transcript ... Yes.
Sounds good... Yes, thank you very much. See you then.
FUNGAAH!!
What do you think you're doing, you little monster?!
beep
I wanted to help you make a good impression.
SQUEEZE
How does roaring into the phone help?! What kind psycho brain is in this head?!
Stop that.
Don't you think it made you sound moti-vated?
God...God... God... That manager guy had to hear you. There's no way he couldn't have!
Believe in the impos-sible!
Get away from me!

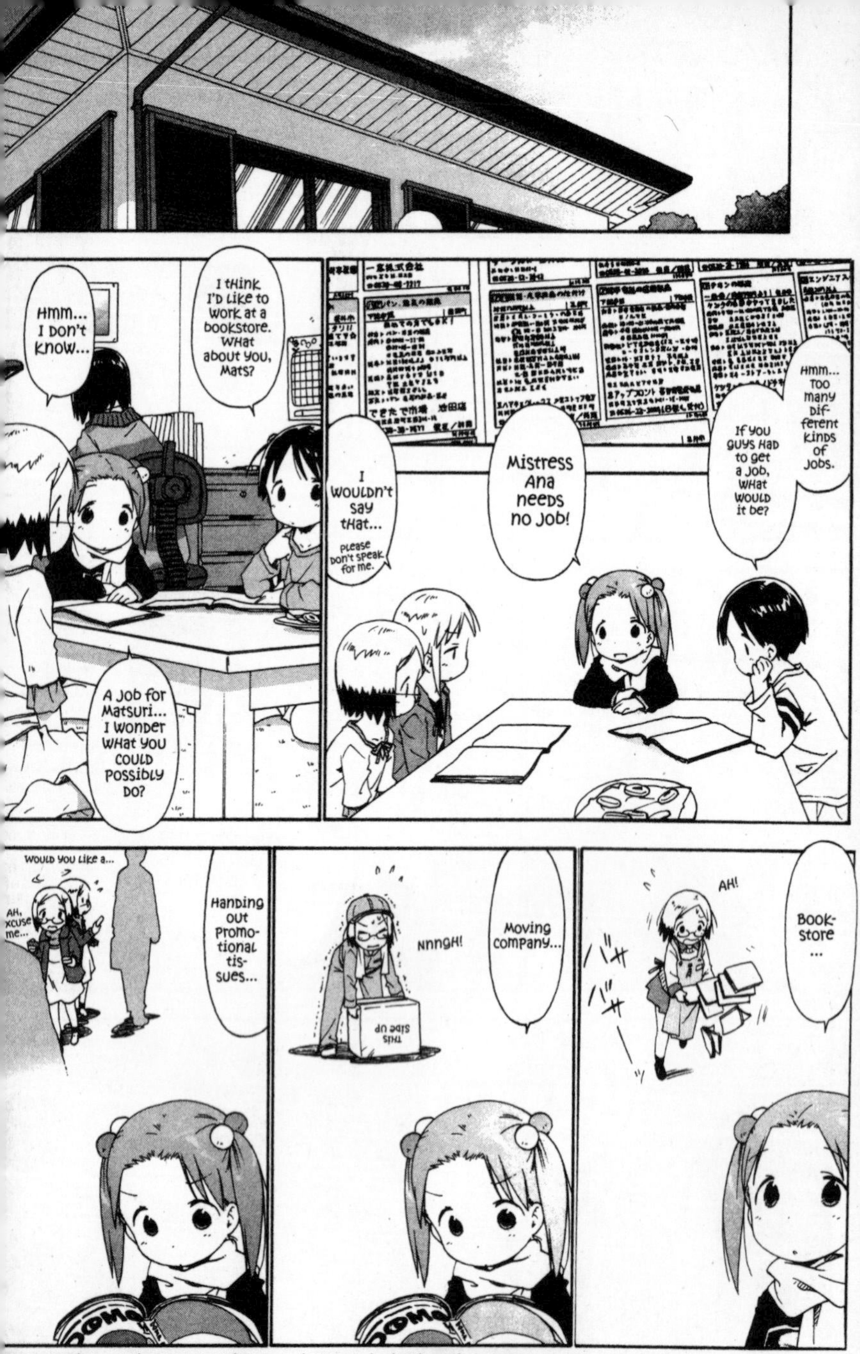
Hmm... Too many different kinds of jobs.
If you guys had to get a job, what would it be?
Mistress Ana needs no job!
I wouldn't say that...
Please don't speak for me.
I think I'd like to work at a bookstore. What about you, Mats?
Hmm... I don't know...
A job for Matsuri... I wonder what you could possibly do?
Bookstore...
AH!
Moving company...
NNNGH!
THIS SIDE UP
Handing out promotional tissues...
Would you like a...
AH, XCUSE me...

Note: passing out tissue packs with advertisements inside is a widespread marketing practice in Japan.

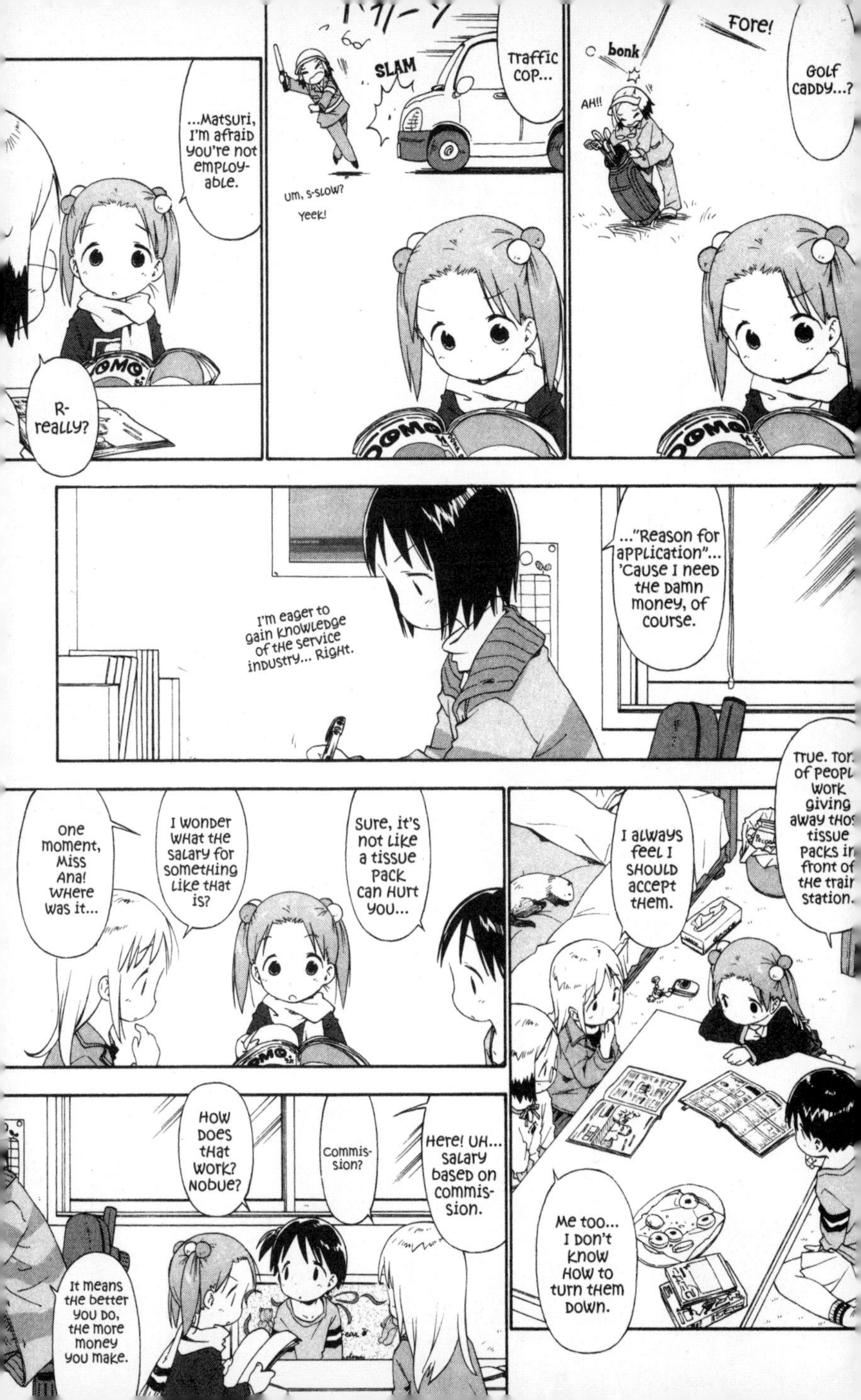

Fore!
bonk
AH!!
Golf caddy...?
Traffic cop...
SLAM
Um, s-slow?
Yeek!
...Matsuri, I'm afraid you're not employ-able.
R-really?
..."Reason for application"... 'Cause I need the damn money, of course.
I'm eager to gain knowledge of the service industry... Right.
True. Tor of peopl work giving away thos tissue packs in front of the trai station.
I always feel I should accept them.
Me too... I don't know how to turn them down.
Sure, it's not like a tissue pack can hurt you...
I wonder what the salary for something like that is?
One moment, Miss Ana! Where was it...
Here! Uh... salary based on commis-sion.
Commis-sion?
How does that work? Nobue?
It means the better you do, the more money you make.

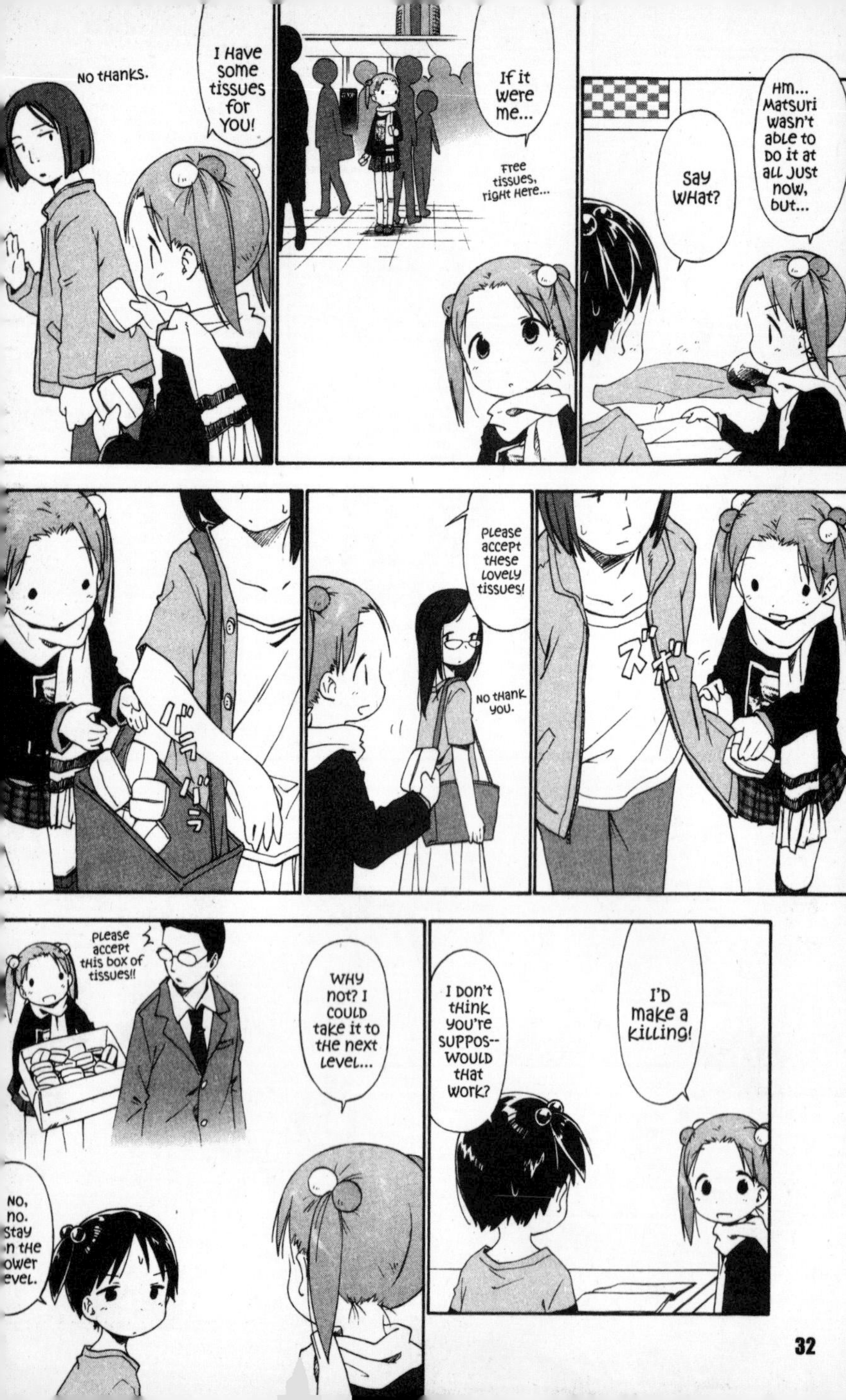
Hm... Matsuri wasn't able to do it at all just now, but...
Say what?
If it were me...
Free tissues, right here...
I have some tissues for you!
No thanks.
Please accept these lovely tissues!
No thank you.
I'd make a killing!
I don't think you're suppos-- would that work?
Why not? I could take it to the next level...
Please accept this box of tissues!!
No, no. Stay n the ower evel.

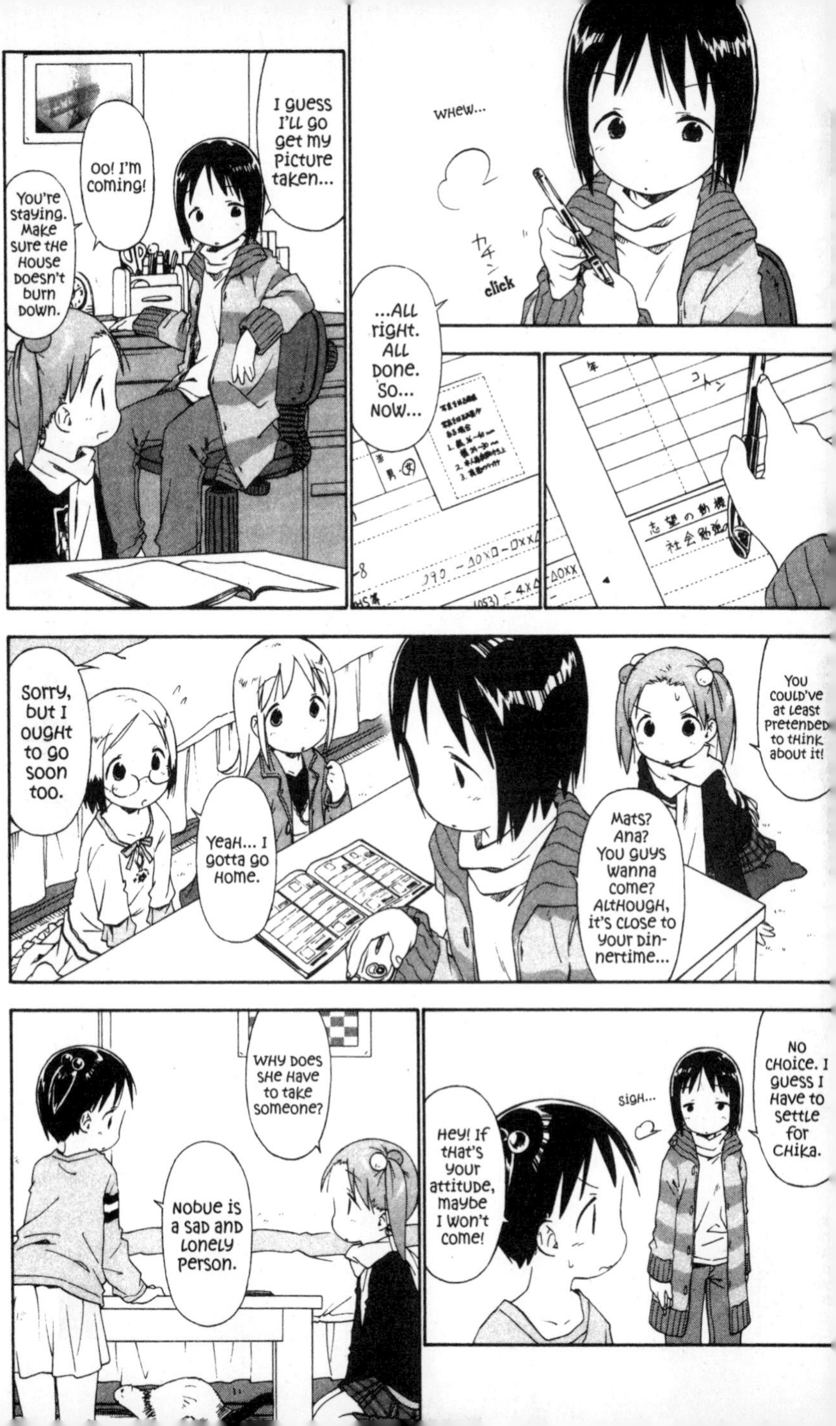

WHEW...
カチン
click
...ALL RIGHT. ALL DONE. SO... NOW...
I GUESS I'LL GO GET MY PICTURE TAKEN...
OO! I'M COMING!
YOU'RE STAYING. MAKE SURE THE HOUSE DOESN'T BURN DOWN.
YOU COULD'VE AT LEAST PRETENDED TO THINK ABOUT IT!
MATS? ANA? YOU GUYS WANNA COME? ALTHOUGH, IT'S CLOSE TO YOUR DIN-NERTIME...
YEAH... I GOTTA GO HOME.
SORRY, BUT I OUGHT TO GO SOON TOO.
NO CHOICE. I GUESS I HAVE TO SETTLE FOR CHIKA.
SIGH...
HEY! IF THAT'S YOUR ATTITUDE, MAYBE I WON'T COME!
WHY DOES SHE HAVE TO TAKE SOMEONE?
NOBUE IS A SAD AND LONELY PERSON.

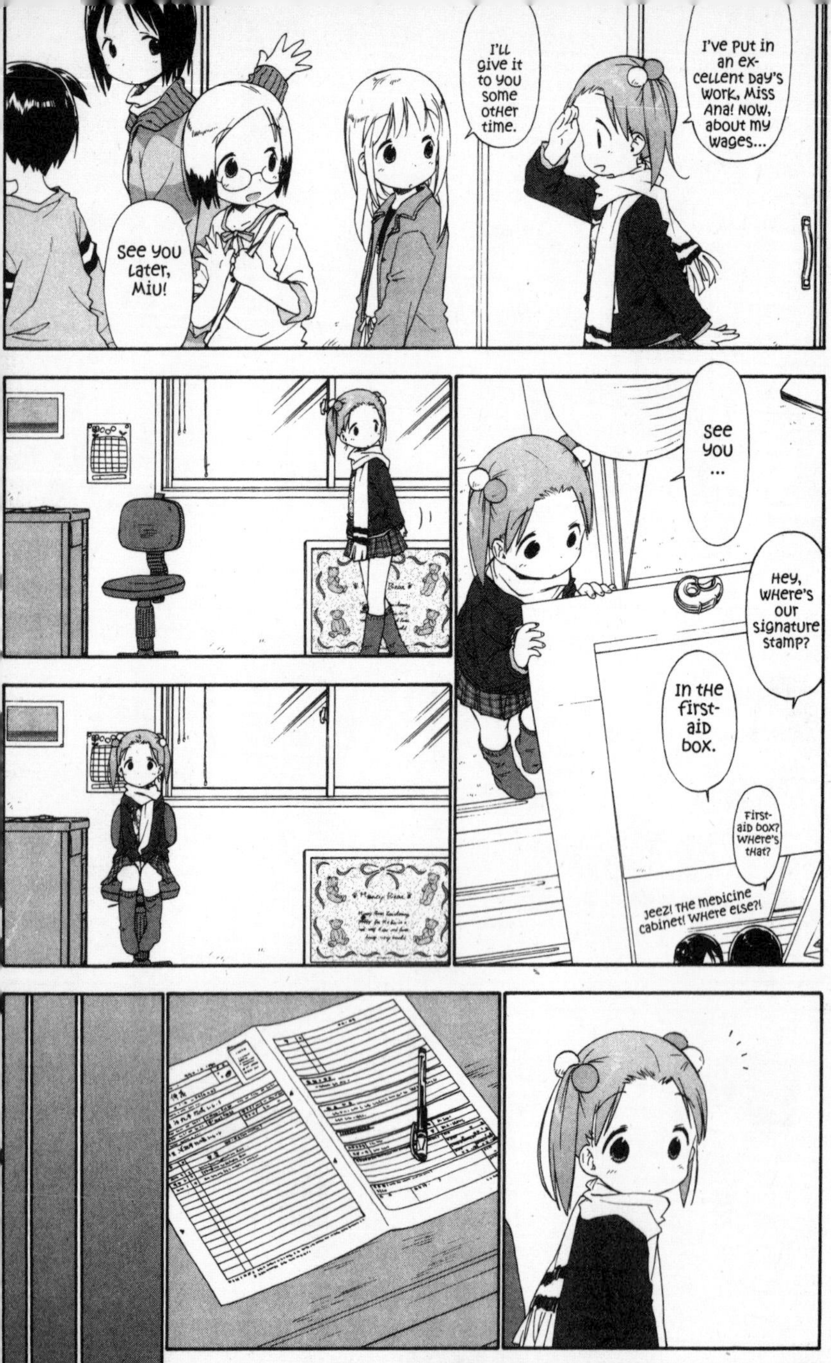
I've put in an ex-cellent day's work, Miss Ana! Now, about my wages...
I'll give it to you some other time.
See you later, Miu!
See you ...
Hey, where's our signature stamp?
In the first-aid box.
First-aid box? Where's that?
Jeez! The medicine cabinet! Where else?!

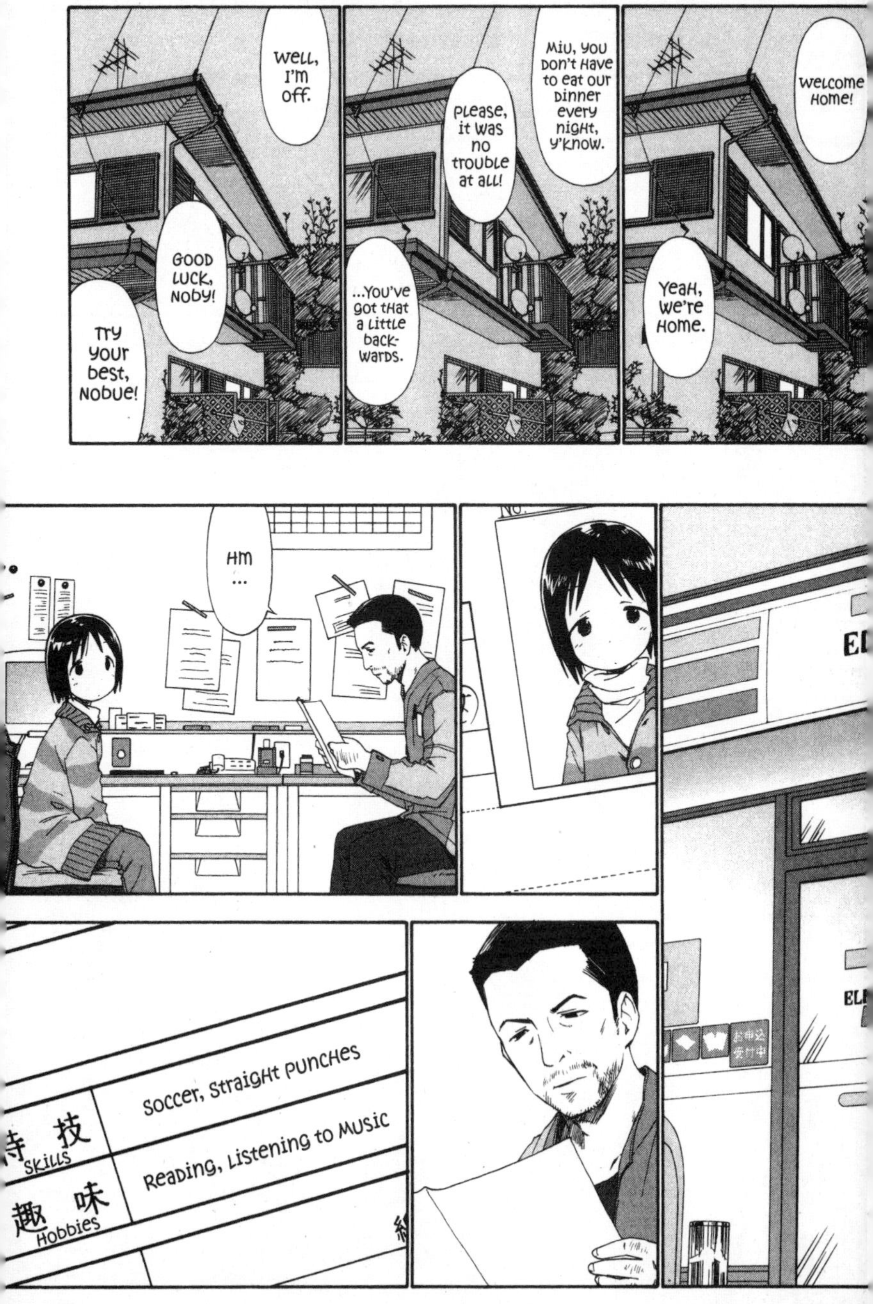
Welcome home!
Yeah, we're home.
Miu, you don't have to eat our dinner every night, y'know.
Please, it was no trouble at all!
...You've got that a little back-wards.
Well, I'm off.
Good luck, Noby!
Try your best, Nobue!
Hm ...
Soccer, straight punches
技
Skills
Reading, listening to music
趣 味
Hobbies

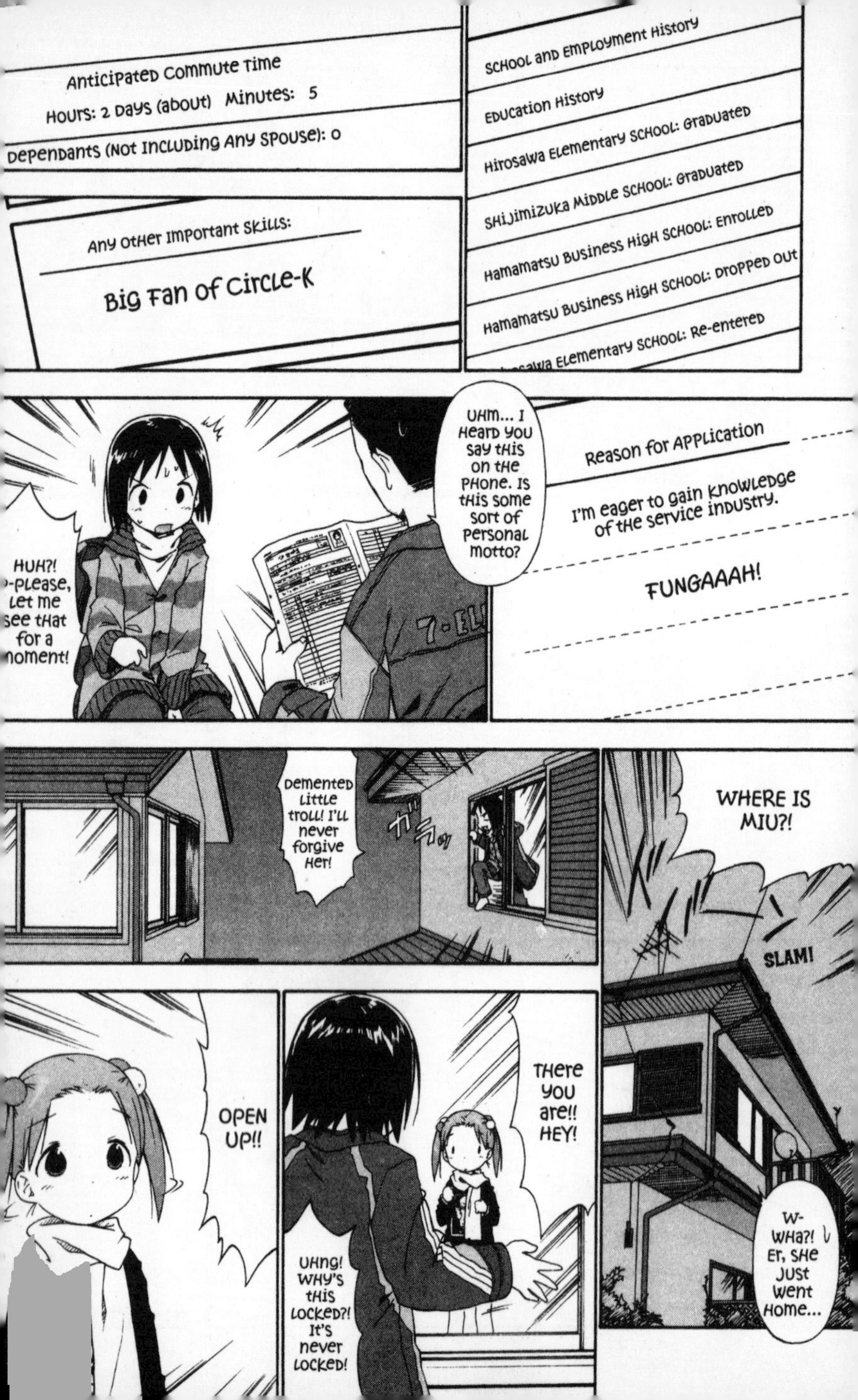
School and Employment History
Education History
Hirosawa Elementary School: Graduated
Shijimizuka Middle School: Graduated
Hamamatsu Business High School: Enrolled
Hamamatsu Business High School: Dropped Out
Elementary School: Re-entered
Anticipated Commute Time
Hours: 2 Days (about) Minutes: 5
Dependants (Not Including Any Spouse): 0
Any Other Important Skills:
Big Fan of Circle-K
Reason for Application
I'm eager to gain knowledge of the service industry.
FUNGAAAH!
UHM... I heard you say this on the phone. Is this some sort of personal motto?
7-EL
HUH?! -please, let me see that for a oment!
WHERE IS MIU?!
SLAM!
W-WHA?! Er, she just went home...
Demented little troll! I'll never forgive her!
ガラッ
There you are!! HEY!
Uhng! Why's this locked?! It's never locked!
OPEN UP!!

Spring	Chika
Summer	Miu
Autumn	Matsuri
Winter	Ana
	Nobue

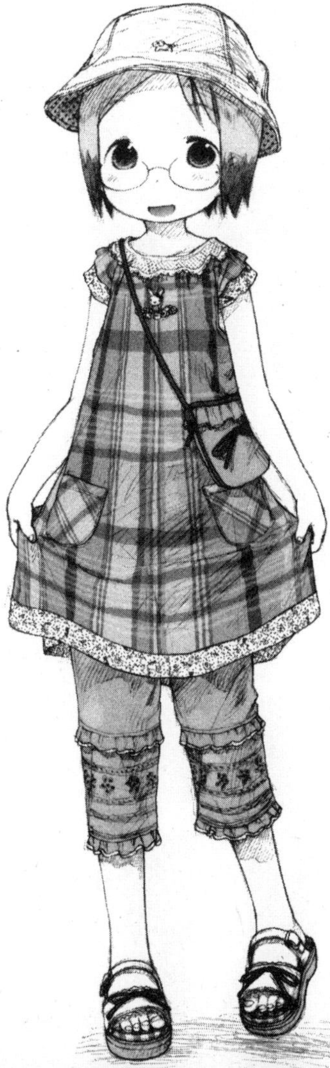

Spring	Chika
Summer	Miu
Autumn	Matsuri
Winter	Ana
	Nobue

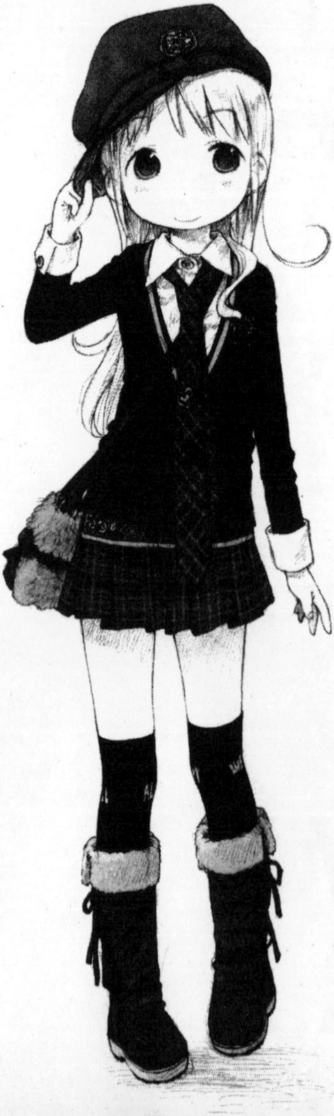

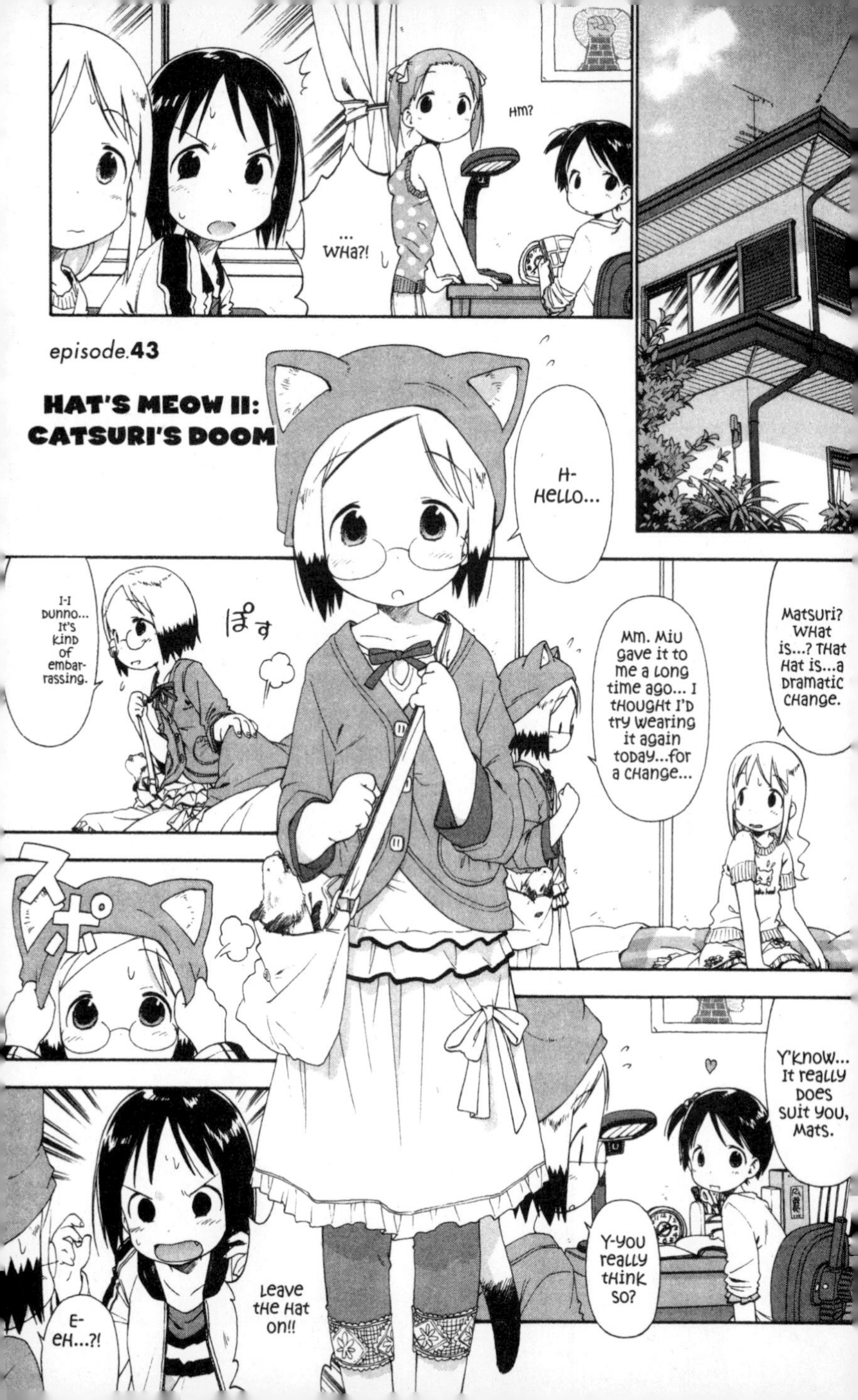
Hm?
... Wha?!
episode.43
HAT'S MEOW II: CATSURI'S DOOM
H- Hello...
Matsuri? What is...? That hat is...a dramatic change.
Mm. Miu gave it to me a long time ago... I thought I'd try wearing it again today...for a change...
I-I dunno... It's kind of embar-rassing.
ぽす
スポ
Y'know... It really does suit you, Mats.
Y-you really think so?
Leave the hat on!!
E-eh...?!

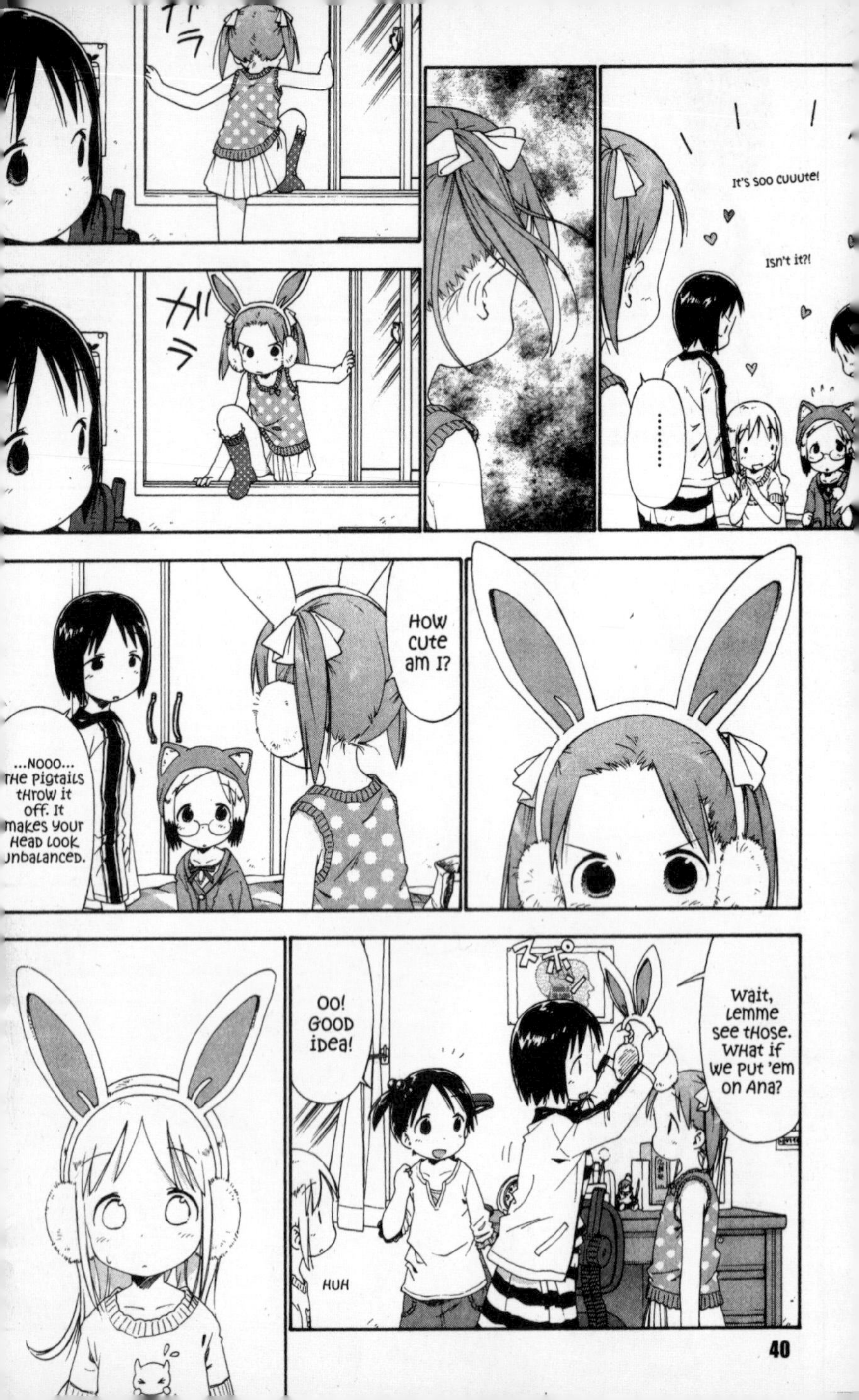
It's soo cuuute!
Isn't it?!
......
ガラ
ガラ
HOW cute am I?
...NOOO... THE PIGTAILS THROW IT OFF. IT MAKES YOUR HEAD LOOK UNBALANCED.
スポン
Wait, lemme see those. WHAT if we put 'em on Ana?
OO! GOOD idea!
HUH

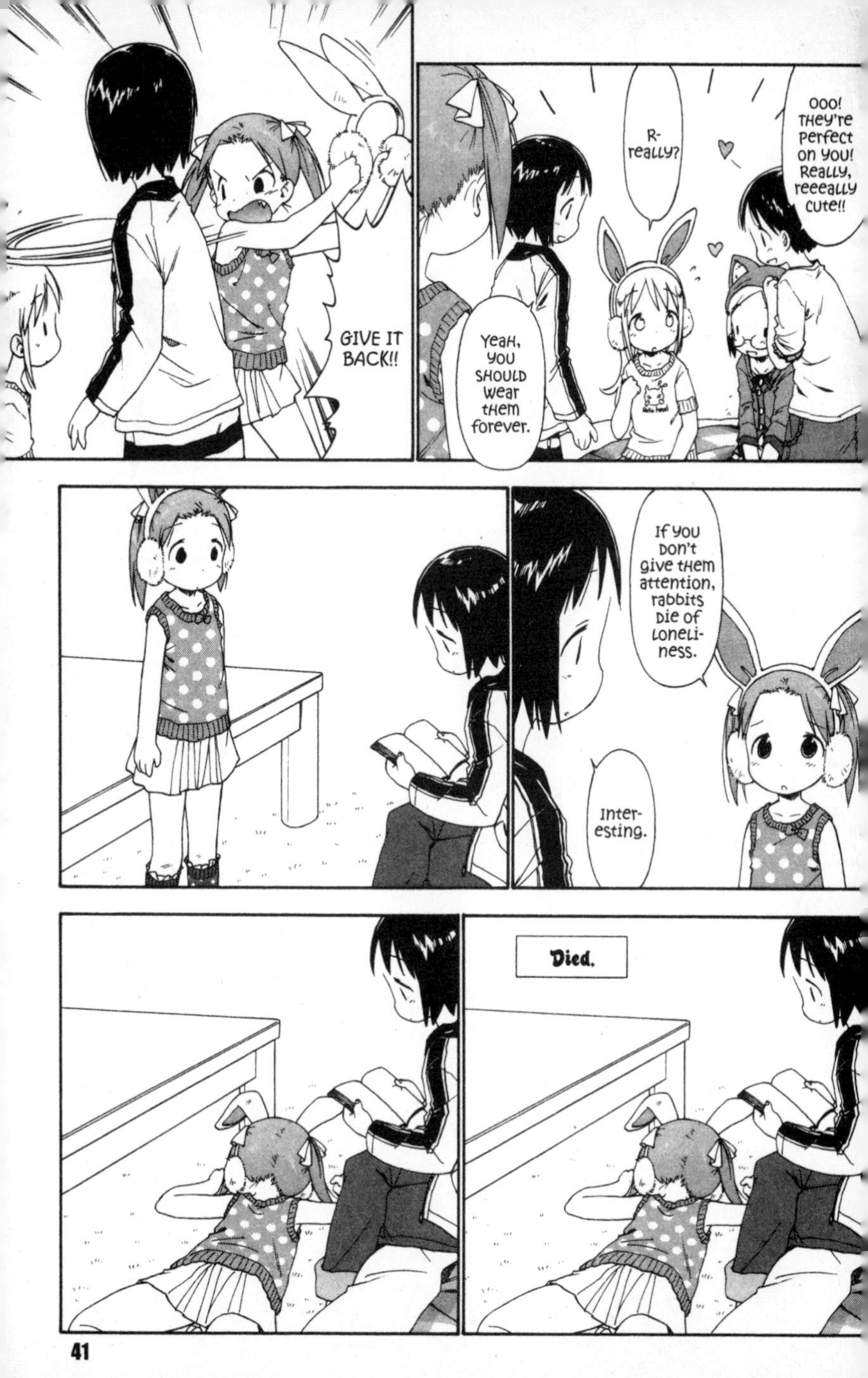
Ooo! They're perfect on you! Really, reeeally cute!!
R-really?
Yeah, you should wear them forever.
GIVE IT BACK!!
If you don't give them attention, rabbits die of loneliness.
Inter-esting.
Died.

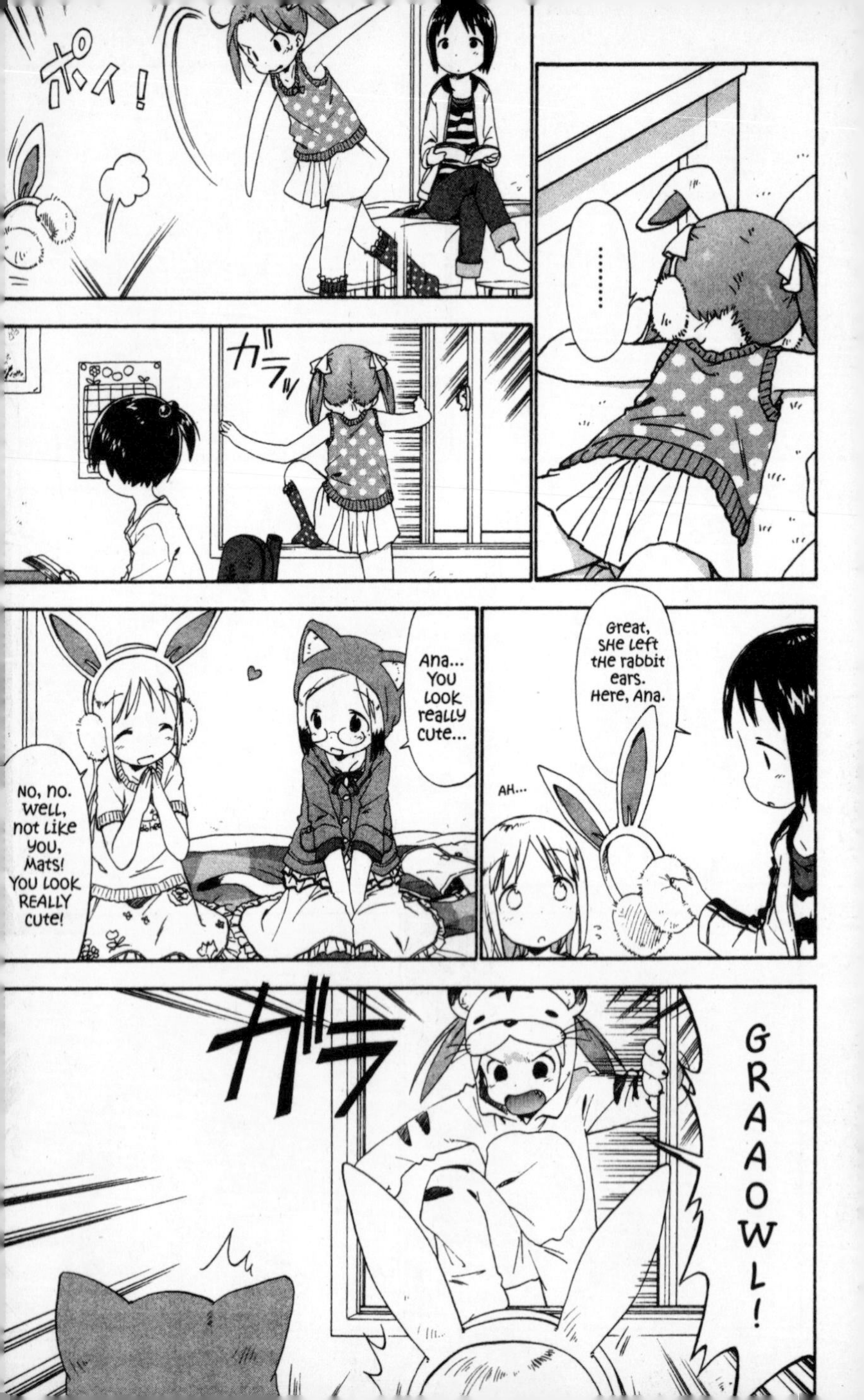
……
ポイ！
ガラッ
Great, she left the rabbit ears. Here, Ana.
Ah…
Ana… You look really cute…
No, no. Well, not like you, Mats! You look REALLY cute!
ガラ
GRAAOWL!

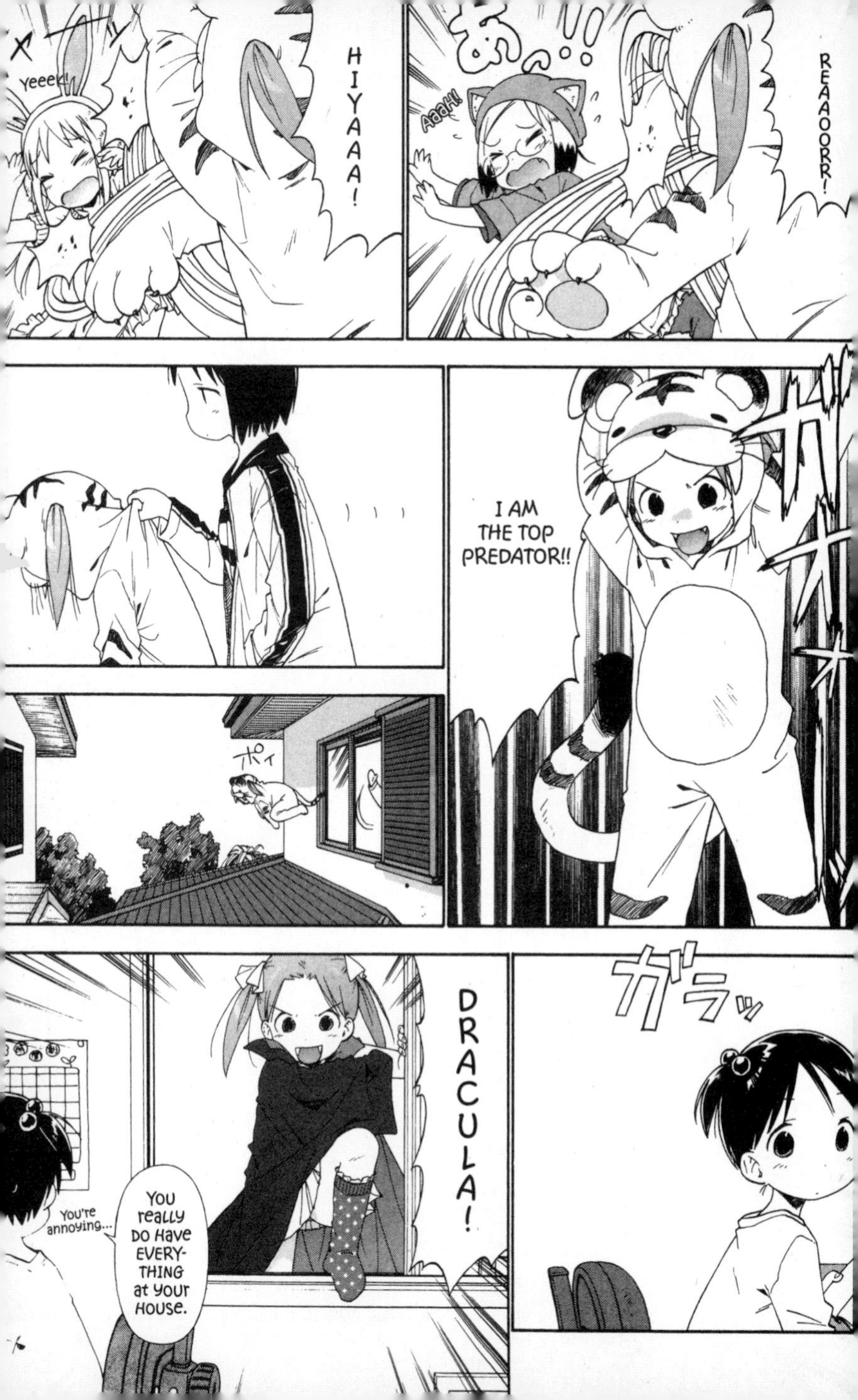
REAAAOORR!
AAAH!
HIYAAAA!
YEEEK!
I AM THE TOP PREDATOR!!
ガオオ
...
ポイ
ガラッ
DRACULA!
You really Do Have EVERY-THING at your House.
You're annoying...

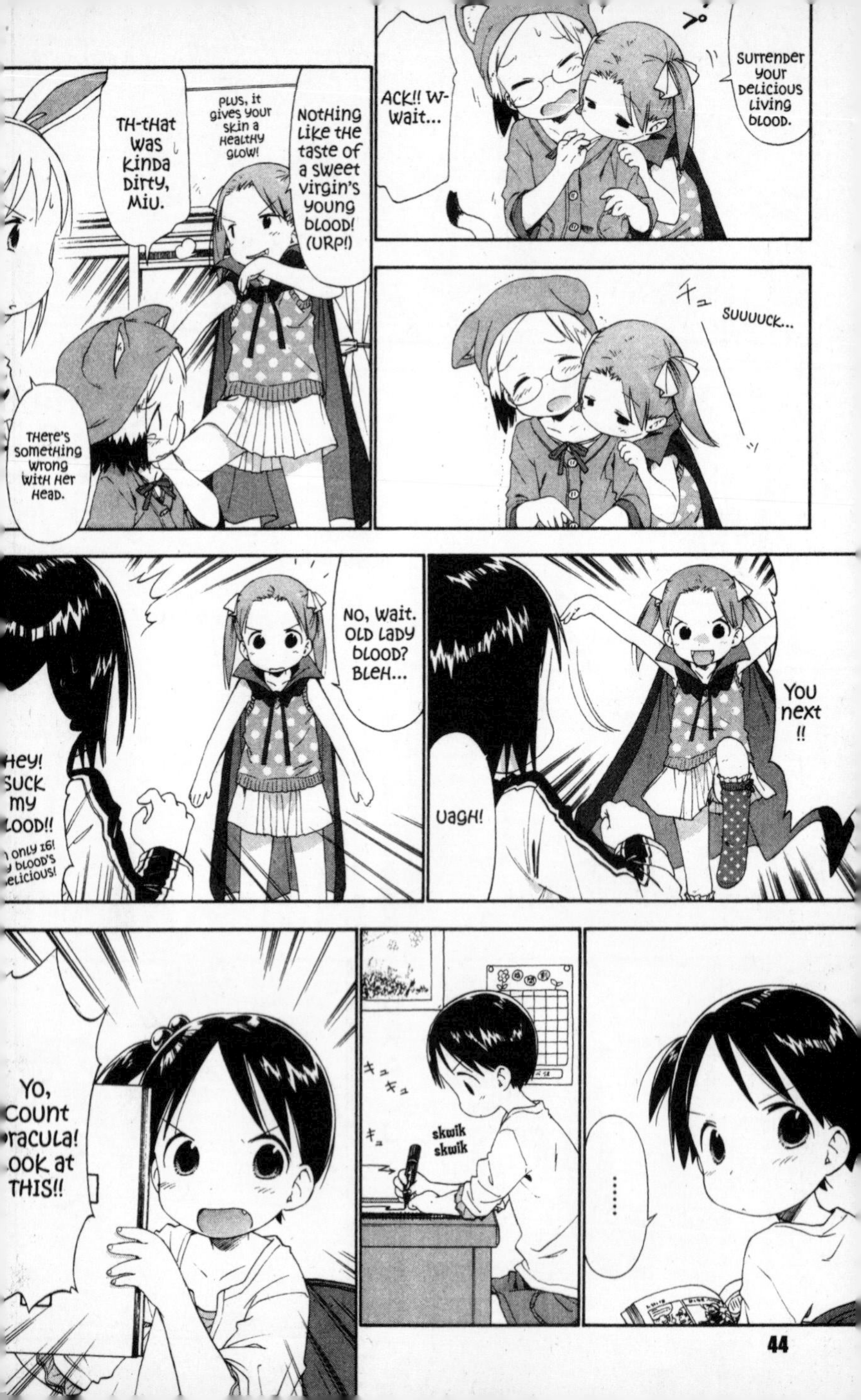
Surrender your delicious living blood.
ACK!! W-wait...
チュ
SUUUUCK...
ッ
Nothing like the taste of a sweet virgin's young blood! (URP!)
Plus, it gives your skin a healthy glow!
Th-that was kinda dirty, Miu.
There's something wrong with her head.
You next !!
Uagh!
No, wait. Old lady blood? Bleh...
Hey! Suck my lood!!
n only 16! y blood's elicious!
......
キュ キュ
キュ
skwik skwik
Yo, Count racula! ook at THIS!!

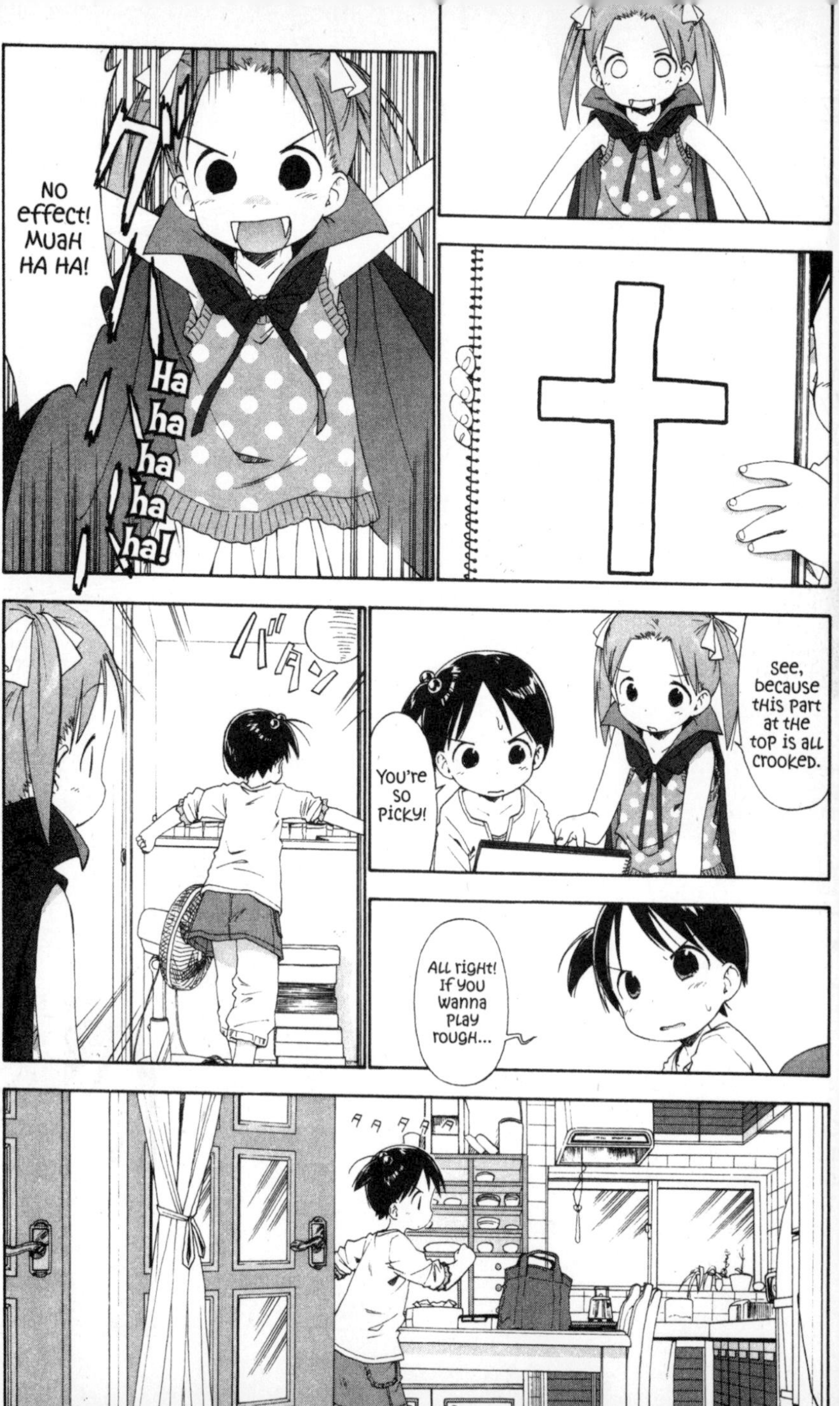
NO effect! MUAH HA HA!
Ha ha ha ha ha!
See, because this part at the top is all crooked.
You're so picky!
All right! If you wanna play rough...
バタン

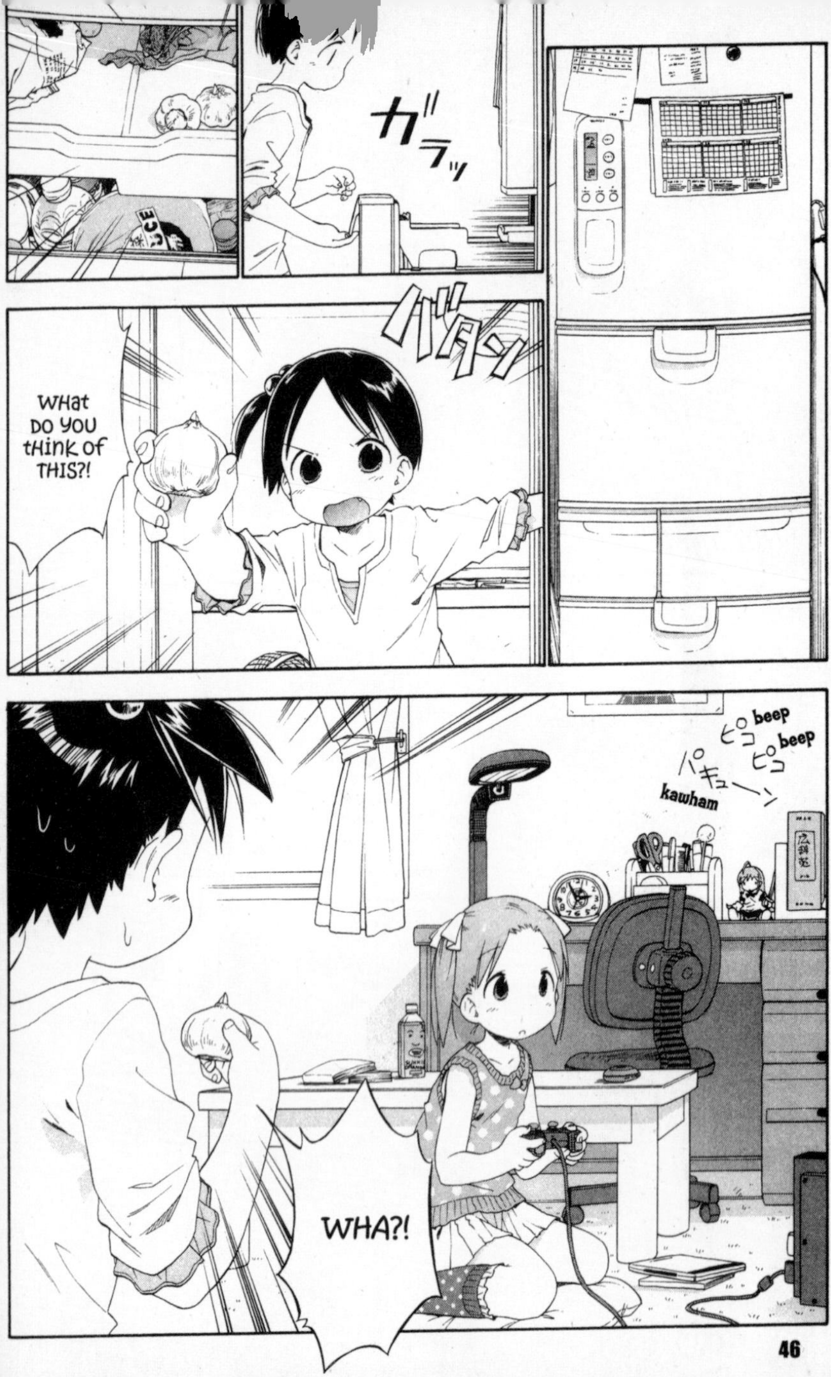
ガラッ
バタン
WHAT DO YOU THINK OF THIS?!
ピコ beep
ピコ beep
パキューン kawham
WHA?!

Spring	Chika
Summer	Miu
Autumn	Matsuri
Winter	Ana
	Nobue

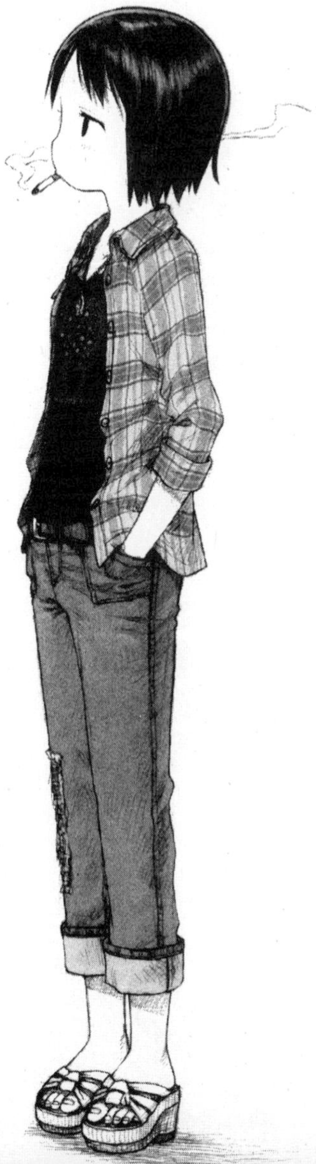

Spring	Chika
Summer	Miu
Autumn	Matsuri
Winter	Ana
	Nobue

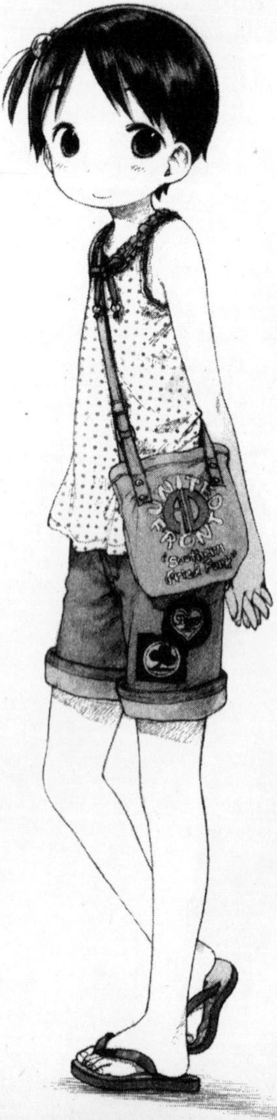

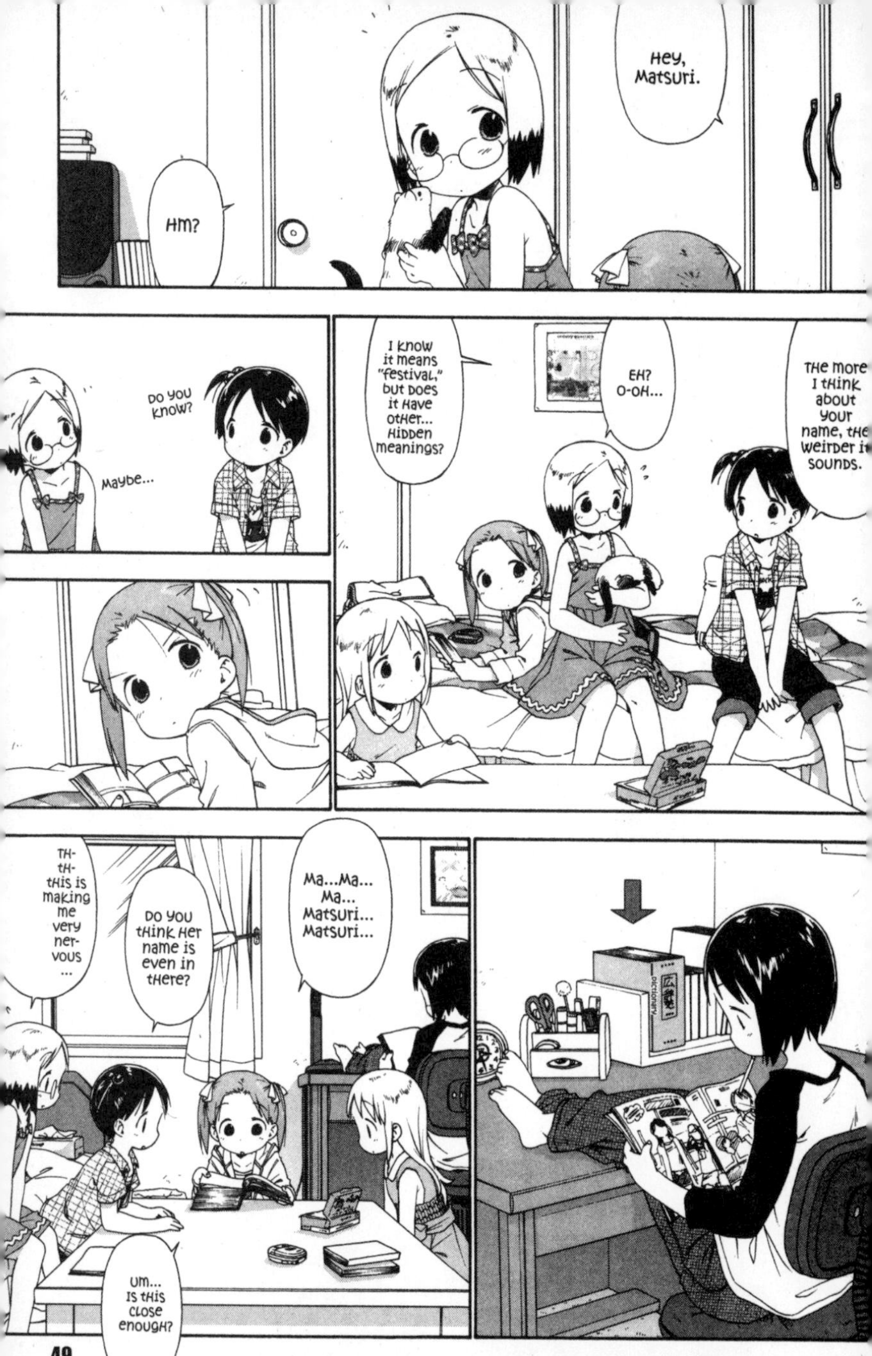
Hey, Matsuri.
Hm?
The more I think about your name, the weirder i
sounds.
Eh? O-oh...
I know it means "festival," but does it have other... hidden meanings?
Do you know?
Maybe...
Ma...Ma... Ma... Matsuri... Matsuri...
Do you think her name is even in there?
Th-th-this is making me very ner-vous...
Um... is this close enough?

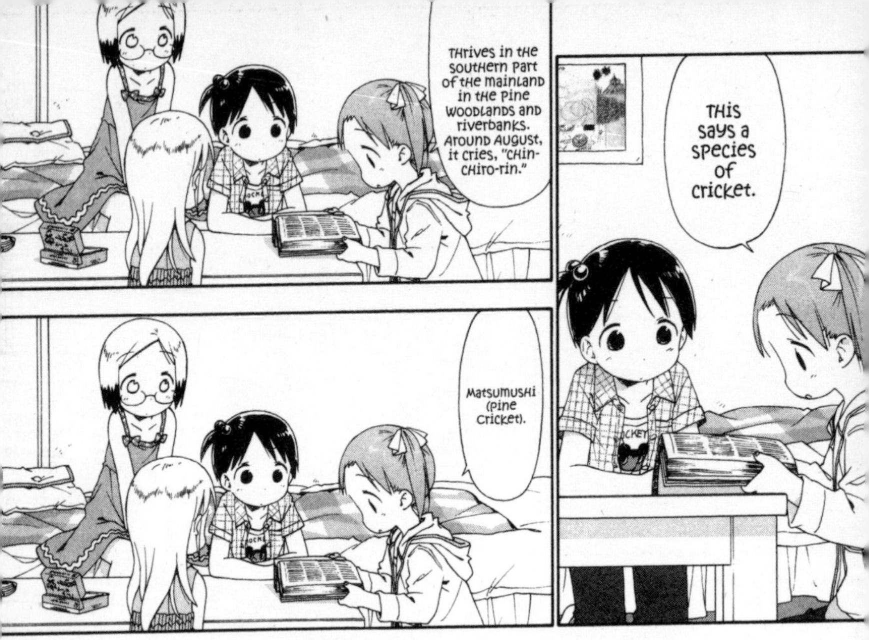
This says a species of cricket.
Thrives in the southern part of the mainland in the pine woodlands and riverbanks. Around August, it cries, "Chin-chiro-rin."
Matsumushi (pine cricket).

episode.44

NAME GAME

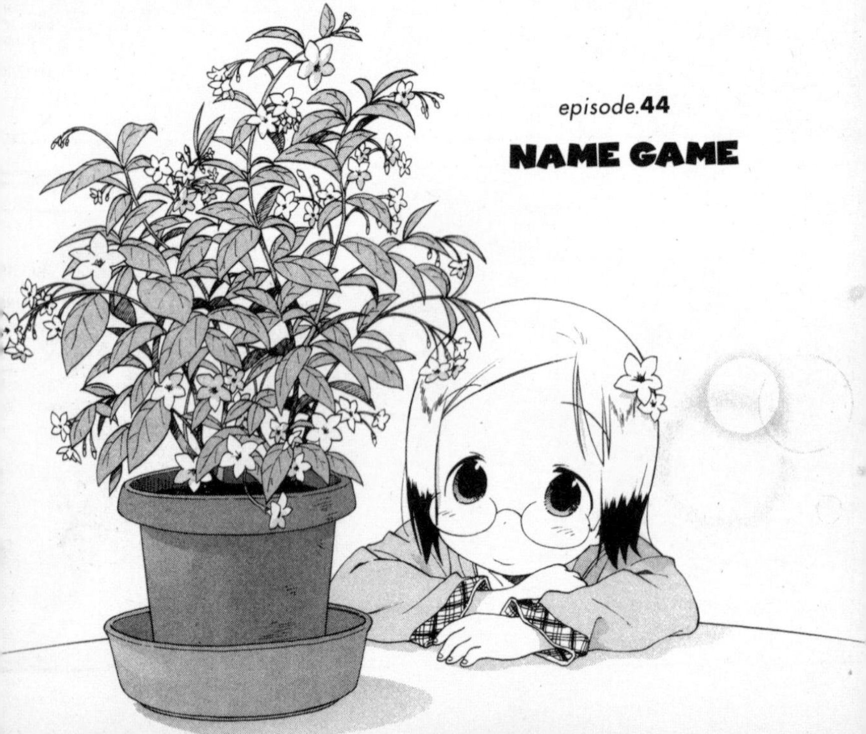

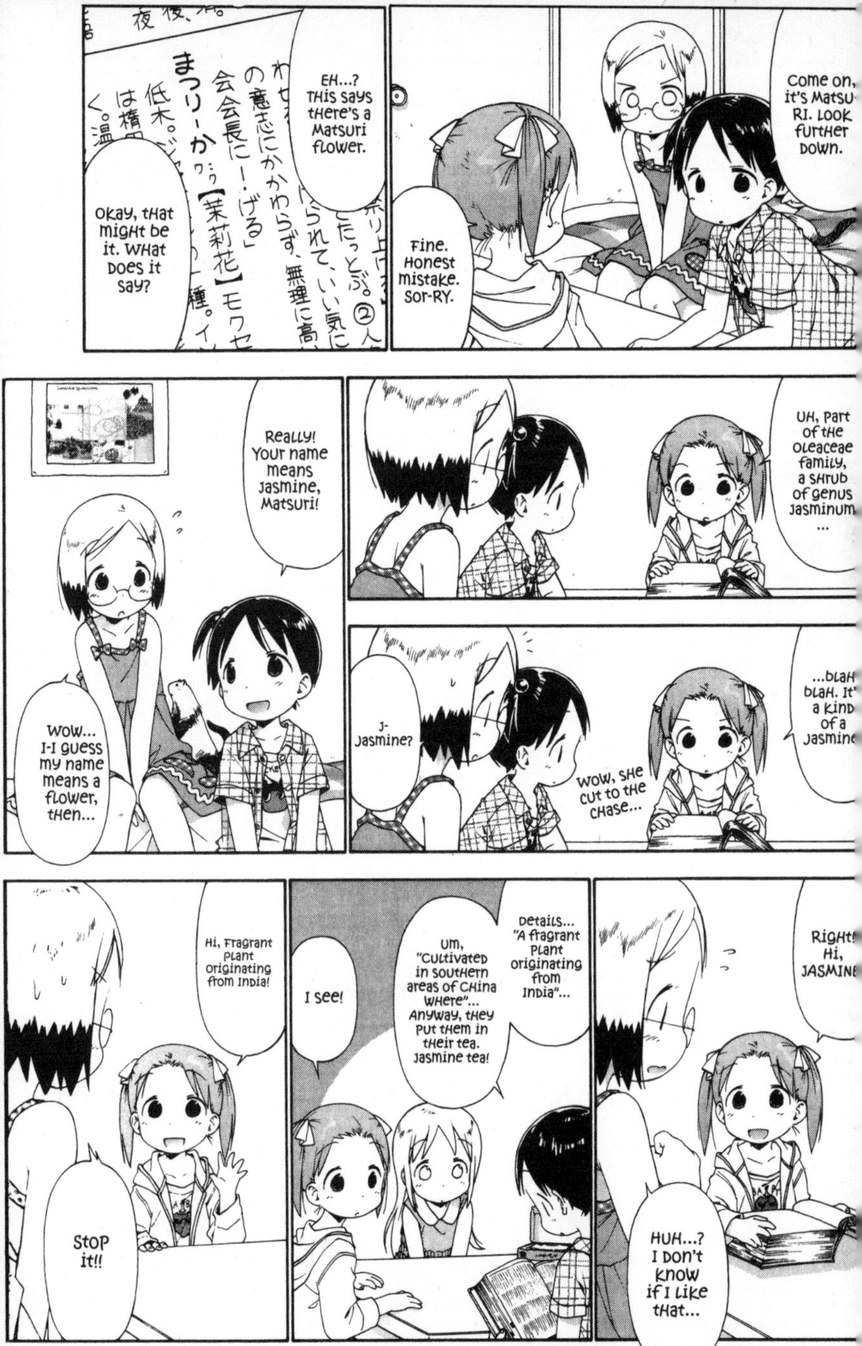
Come on, it's Matsu-ri. Look further down.
Fine. Honest mistake. Sor-RY.
EH...? This says there's a Matsuri flower.
Okay, that might be it. What does it say?
Uh, part of the Oleaceae family, a shrub of genus Jasminum...
...blah blah. It' a kind of a Jasmine
J-Jasmine?
Wow, she cut to the chase...
Really! Your name means Jasmine, Matsuri!
Wow... I-I guess my name means a flower, then...
Right! Hi, JASMINE
Huh...? I don't know if I like that...
Details... "A fragrant plant originating from India"...
Um, "Cultivated in southern areas of China where"... Anyway, they put them in their tea. Jasmine tea!
I see!
Hi, Fragrant plant originating from India!
Stop it!!

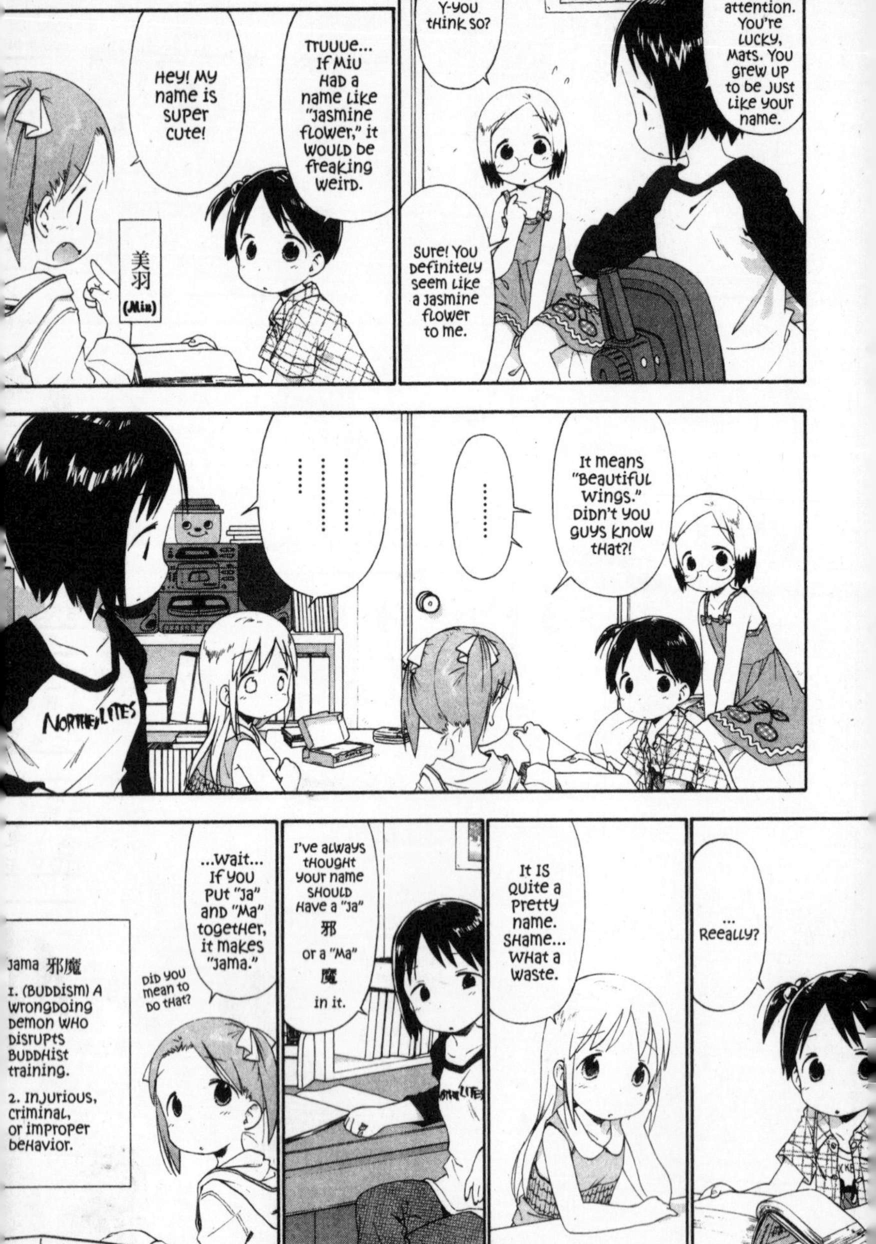
Pay no attention. You're lucky, Mats. You grew up to be just like your name.
Y-you think so?
Sure! You definitely seem like a jasmine flower to me.
Truuue... If Miu had a name like "jasmine flower," it would be freaking weird.
Hey! My name is super cute!
美羽 (Miu)
It means "Beautiful Wings." Didn't you guys know that?!
......
....
... Reeally?
It IS quite a pretty name. Shame... What a waste.
I've always thought your name should have a "Ja" 邪 or a "Ma" 魔 in it.
...Wait... If you put "Ja" and "Ma" together, it makes "Jama."
Did you mean to do that?
Jama 邪魔
1. (Buddism) A wrongdoing demon who disrupts Buddhist training.
2. Injurious, criminal, or improper behavior.

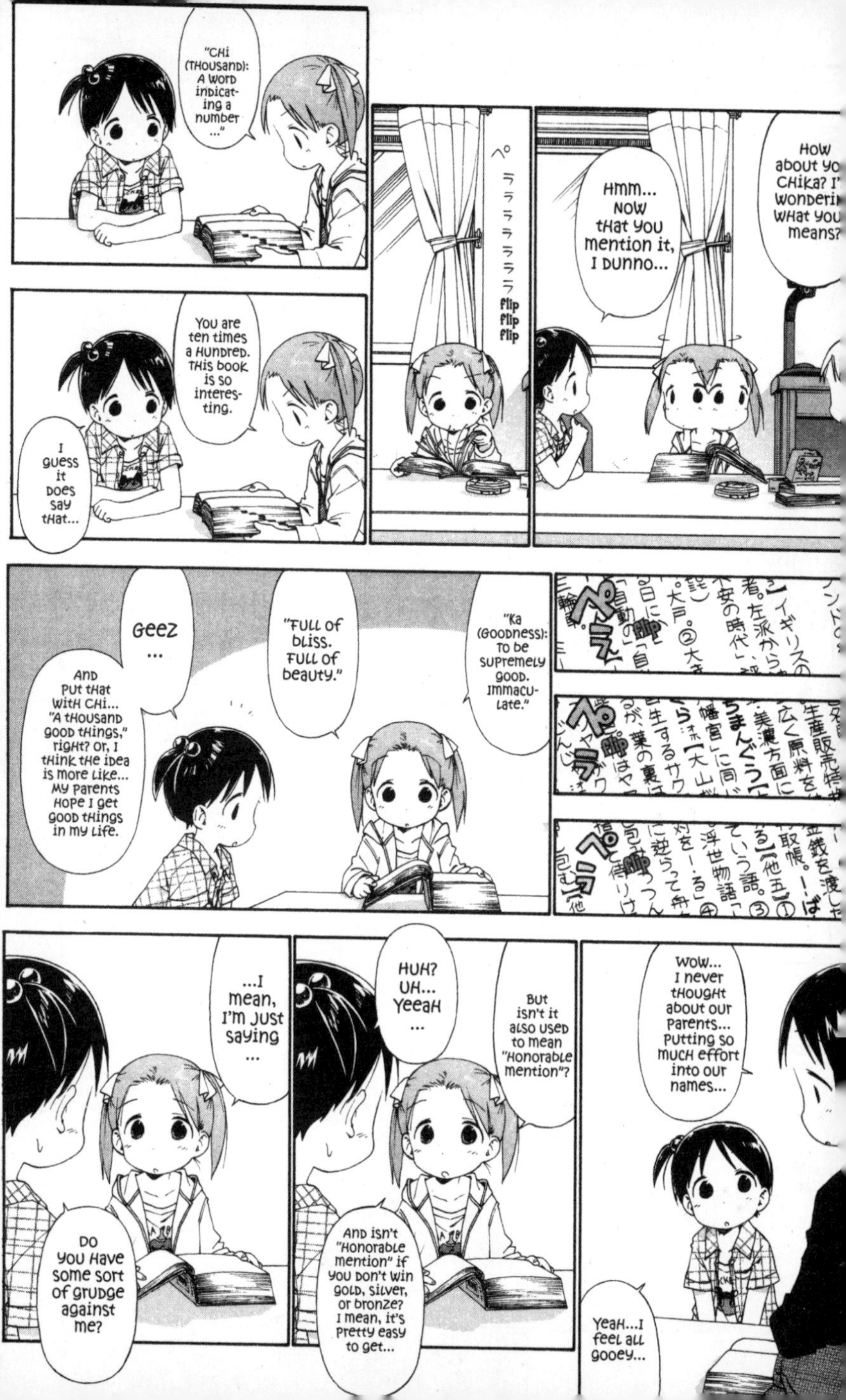
How about yo
Chika? I'
wonderi
what you
means?
Hmm... Now that you mention it, I dunno...
ペラララララ
flip flip flip
"Chi (thousand): A word indicating a number..."
You are ten times a hundred. This book is so interesting.
I guess it does say that...
ペラ
ペラ
ペラ
"Ka (goodness): To be supremely good. Immaculate."
"Full of bliss. Full of beauty."
Geez...
And put that with Chi... "A thousand good things," right? Or, I think the idea is more like... my parents hope I get good things in my life.
Wow... I never thought about our parents... putting so much effort into our names...
Yeah...I feel all gooey...
But isn't it also used to mean "Honorable mention"?
Huh? Uh... Yeeah...
And isn't "Honorable mention" if you don't win gold, silver, or bronze? I mean, it's pretty easy to get...
...I mean, I'm just saying...
Do you have some sort of grudge against me?

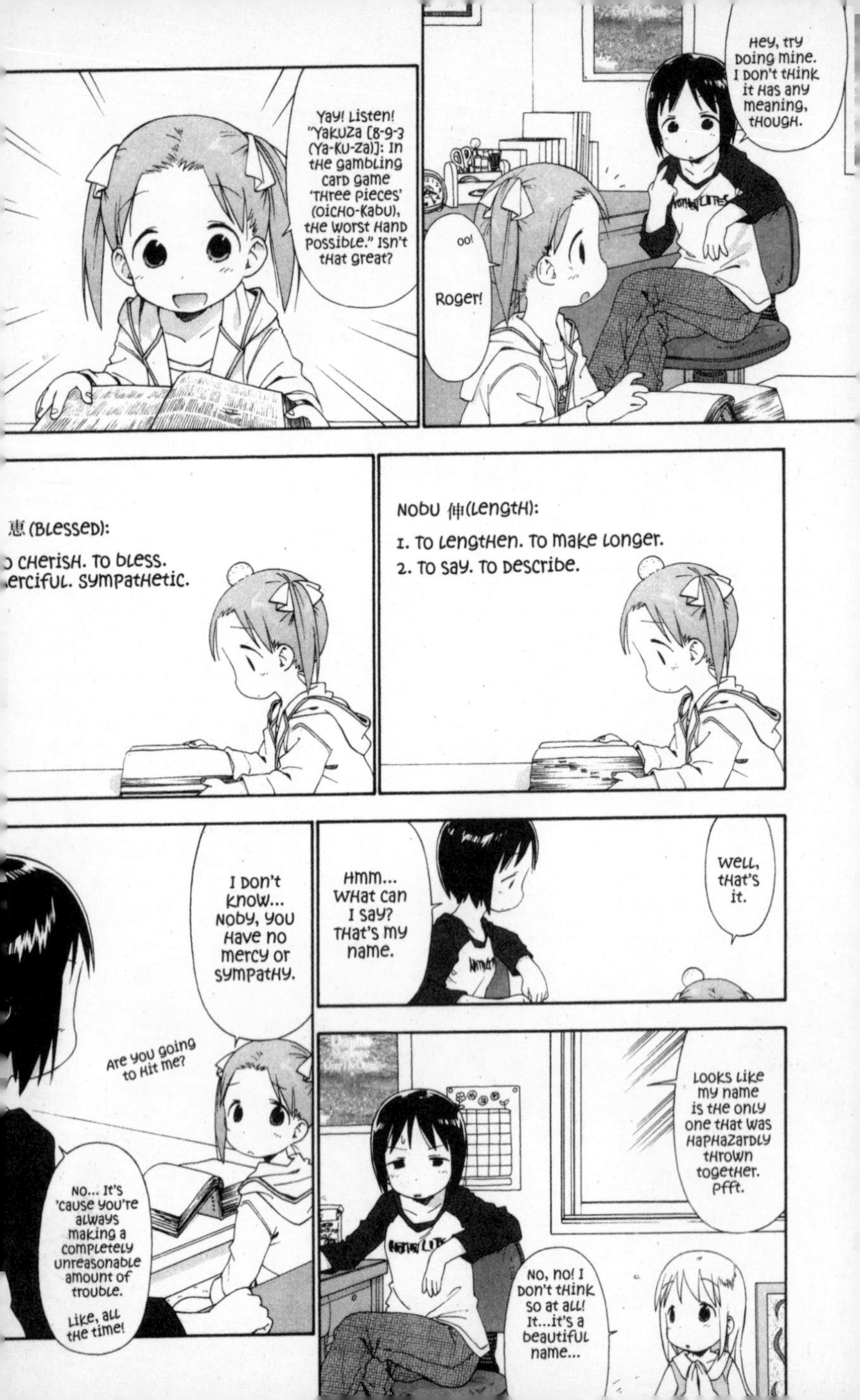
Hey, try doing mine. I don't think it has any meaning, though.
Oo!
Roger!
Yay! Listen! "Yakuza [8-9-3 (Ya-Ku-Za)]: In the gambling card game 'Three Pieces' (Oicho-Kabu), the worst hand possible." Isn't that great?
Nobu 伸(Length):
1. To lengthen. To make longer.
2. To say. To describe.
恵 (Blessed):
o cherish. To bless.
erciful. Sympathetic.
Well, that's it.
Hmm... What can I say? That's my name.
Looks like my name is the only one that was haphazardly thrown together. Pfft.
No, no! I don't think so at all! It...it's a beautiful name...
I don't know... Noby, you have no mercy or sympathy.
Are you going to hit me?
No... It's 'cause you're always making a completely unreasonable amount of trouble.
Like, all the time!

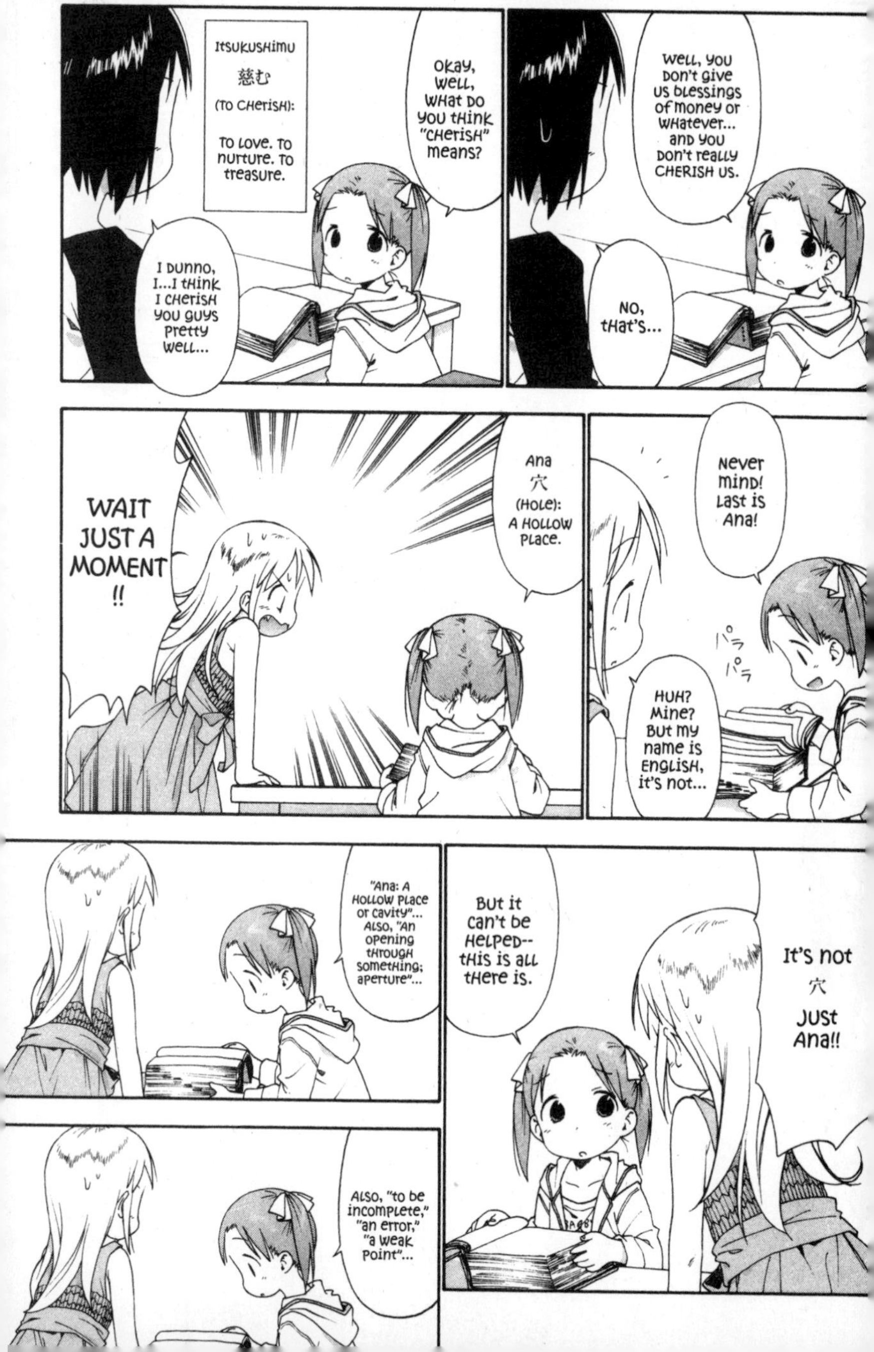

Well, you don't give us blessings of money or whatever... and you don't really cherish us.
No, that's...
Okay, well, what do you think "cherish" means?
Itsukushimu 慈む (to cherish): To love. To nurture. To treasure.
I dunno, I...I think I cherish you guys pretty well...
Never mind! Last is Ana!
パラ パラ
Huh? Mine? But my name is English, it's not...
Ana 穴 (hole): A hollow place.
WAIT JUST A MOMENT !!
It's not 穴 just Ana!!
But it can't be helped--this is all there is.
"Ana: A hollow place or cavity"... Also, "An opening through something; aperture"...
Also, "to be incomplete," "an error," "a weak point"...

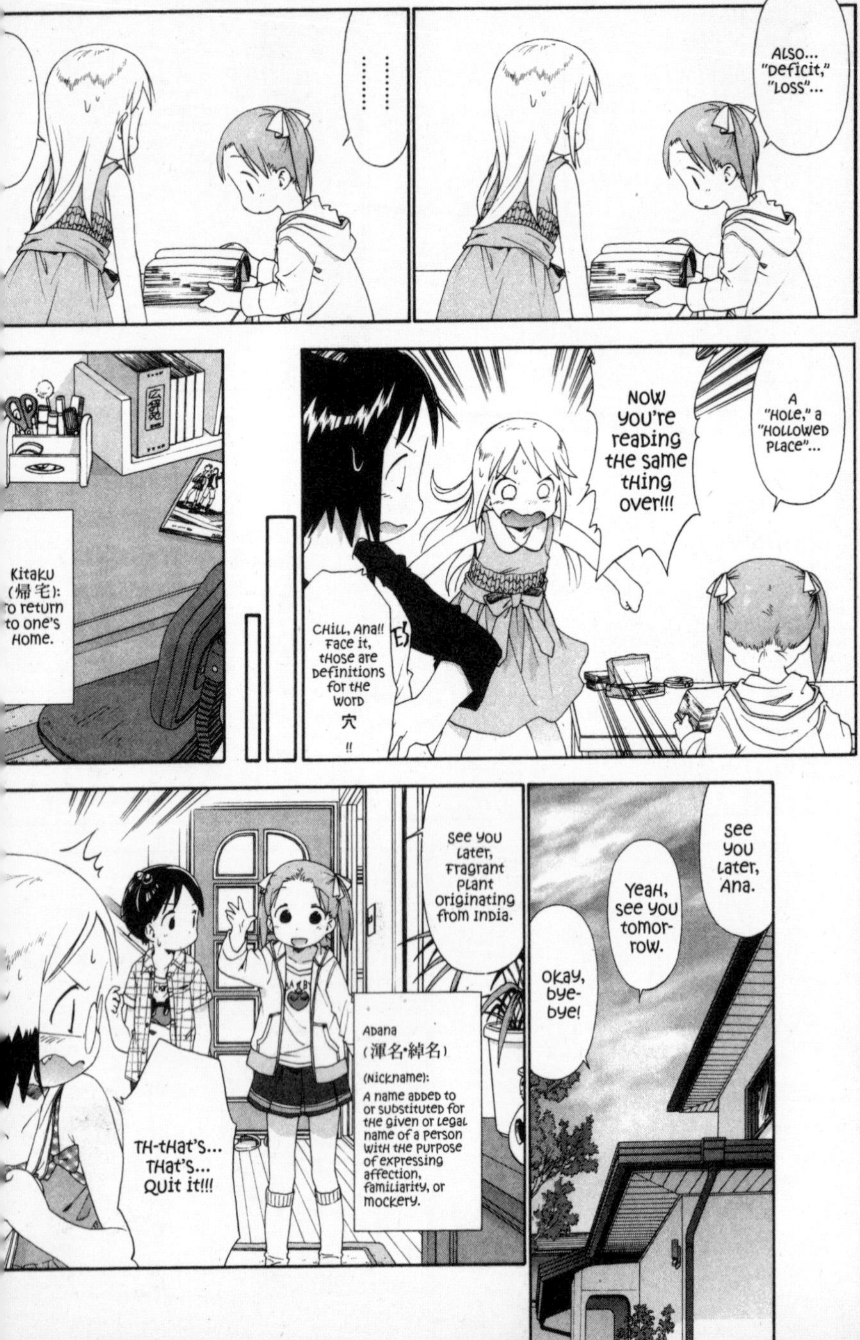
Also... "Deficit," "Loss"...
......
A "Hole," a "Hollowed place"...
Now you're reading the same thing over!!!
Chill, Ana!! Face it, those are definitions for the word 穴 !!
Kitaku (帰宅): to return to one's home.
See you later, Ana.
Yeah, see you tomorrow.
Okay, bye-bye!
See you later, Fragrant plant originating from India.
Adana (渾名·綽名) (Nickname): A name added to or substituted for the given or legal name of a person with the purpose of expressing affection, familiarity, or mockery.
Th-that's... That's... Quit it!!!

Spring Chika

Summer — Miu

Matsuri

Autumn

Ana

Winter Nobue

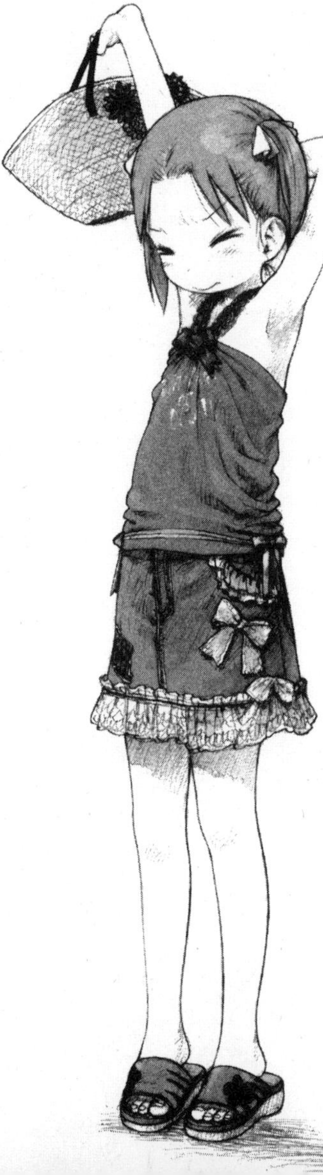

Spring Chika

Miu

Summer — Matsuri

Autumn Ana

Winter Nobue

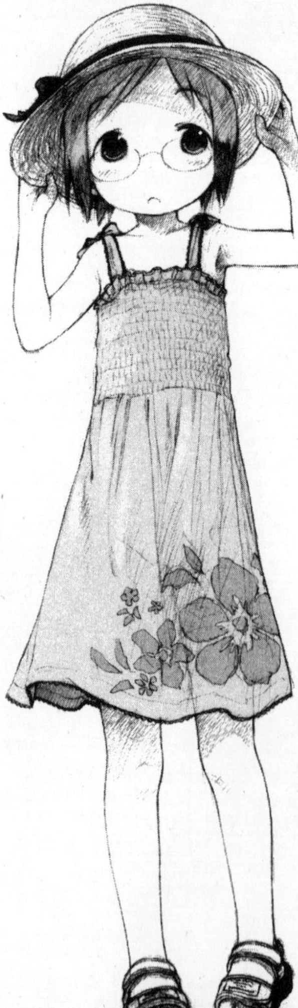

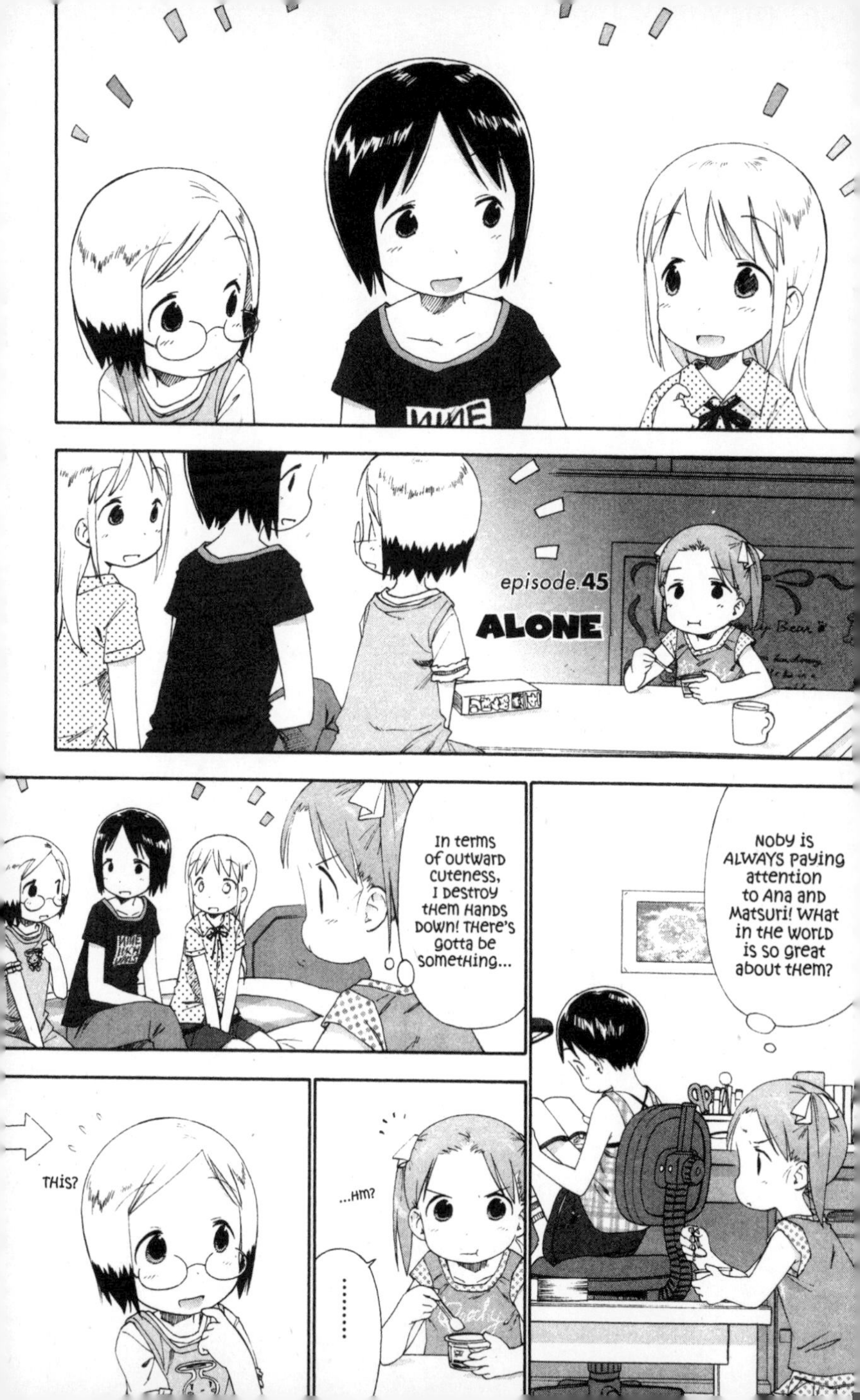
episode.45
ALONE
Noby is ALWAYS paying attention to Ana and Matsuri! What in the world is so great about them?
In terms of outward cuteness, I destroy them hands down! There's gotta be something...
...Hm?
......
THIS?

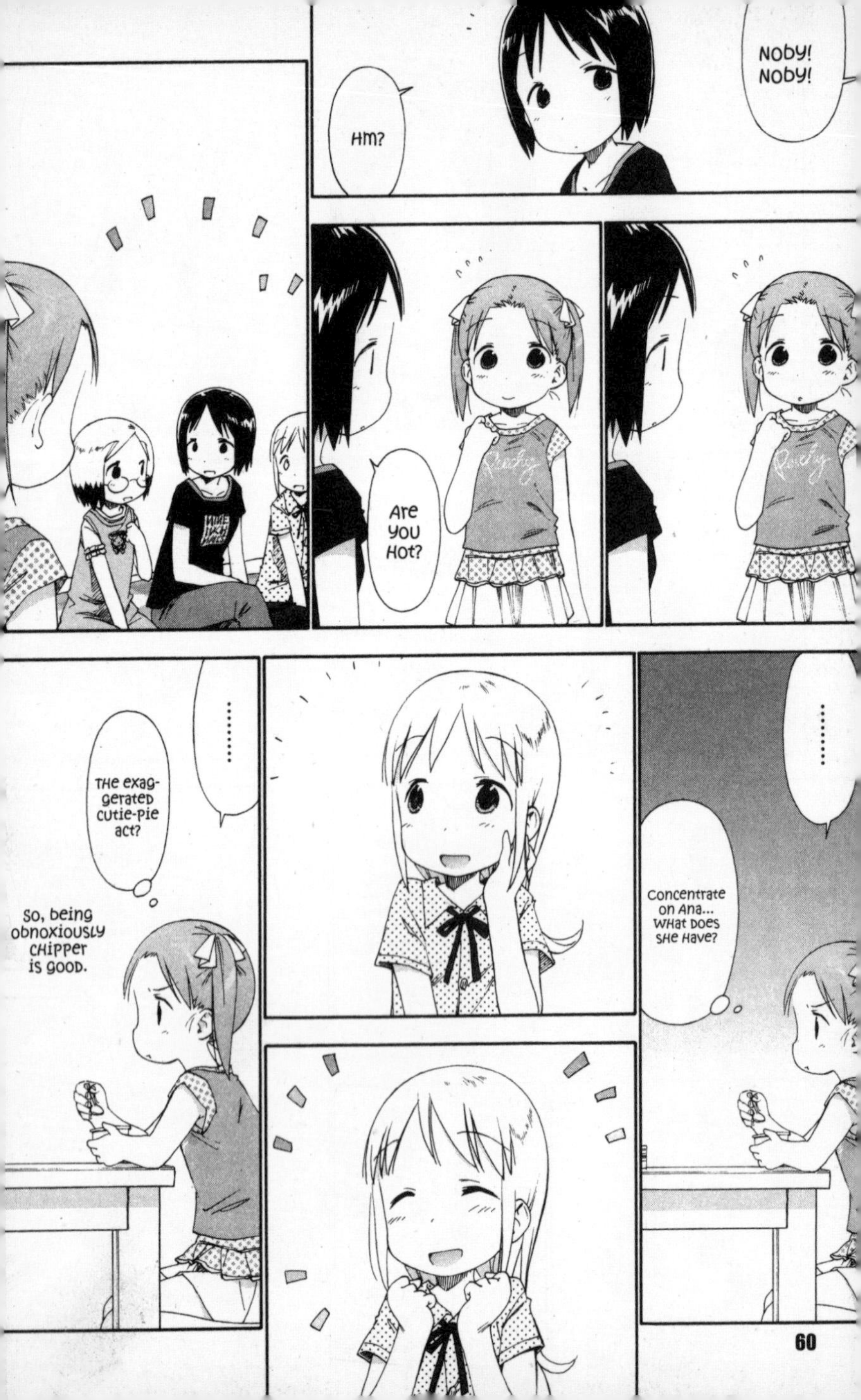

Noby! Noby!
Hm?
Are you hot?
....
Concentrate on Ana... What does she have?
....
The exag-gerated cutie-pie act?
So, being obnoxiously chipper is good.

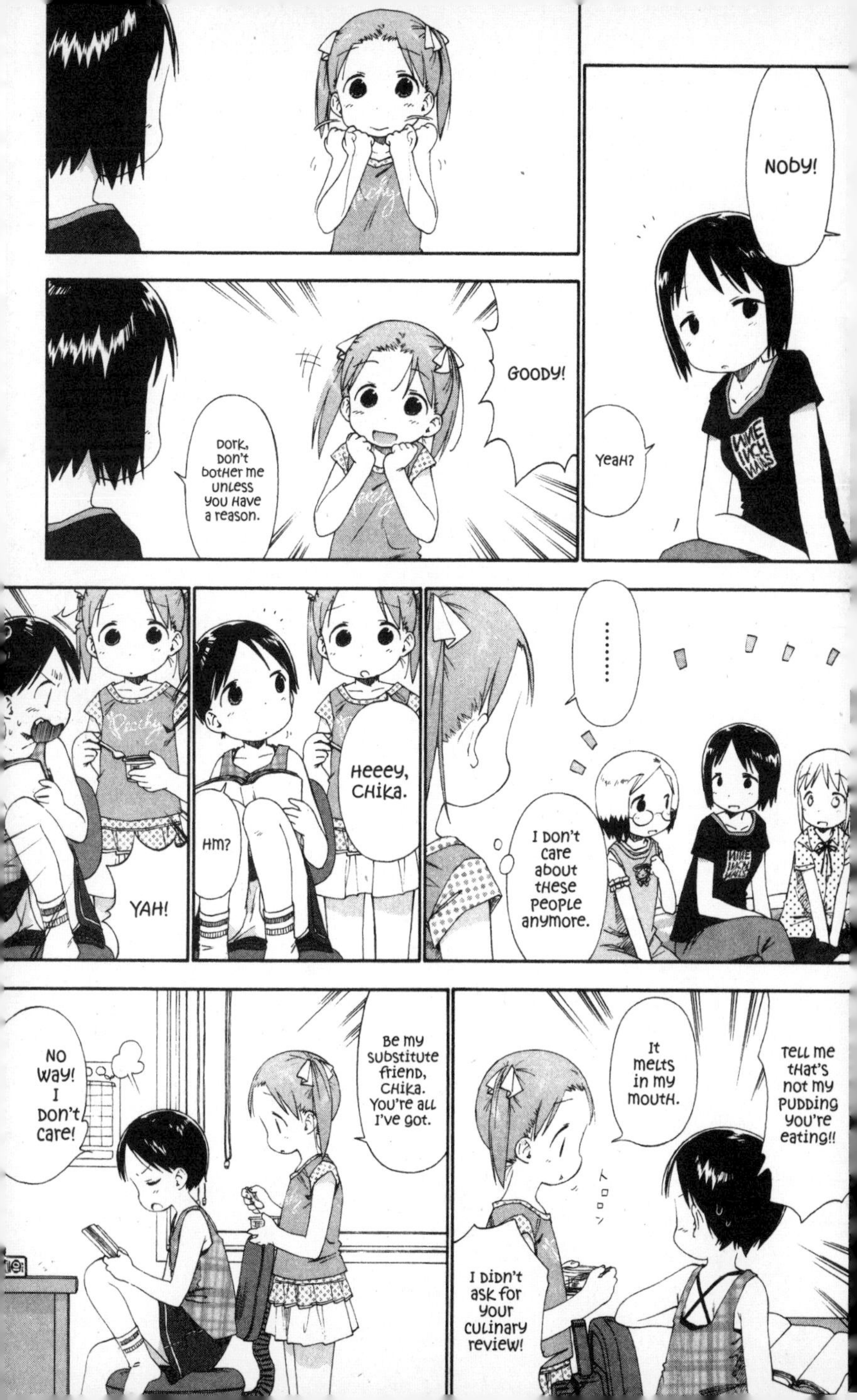
NOBY!
YEAH?
GOODY!
DORK, DON'T BOTHER ME UNLESS YOU HAVE A REASON.
......
I DON'T CARE ABOUT THESE PEOPLE ANYMORE.
HEEEY, CHIKA.
HM?
YAH!
TELL ME THAT'S NOT MY PUDDING YOU'RE EATING!!
IT MELTS IN MY MOUTH.
I DIDN'T ASK FOR YOUR CULINARY REVIEW!
BE MY SUBSTITUTE FRIEND, CHIKA. YOU'RE ALL I'VE GOT.
NO WAY! I DON'T CARE!

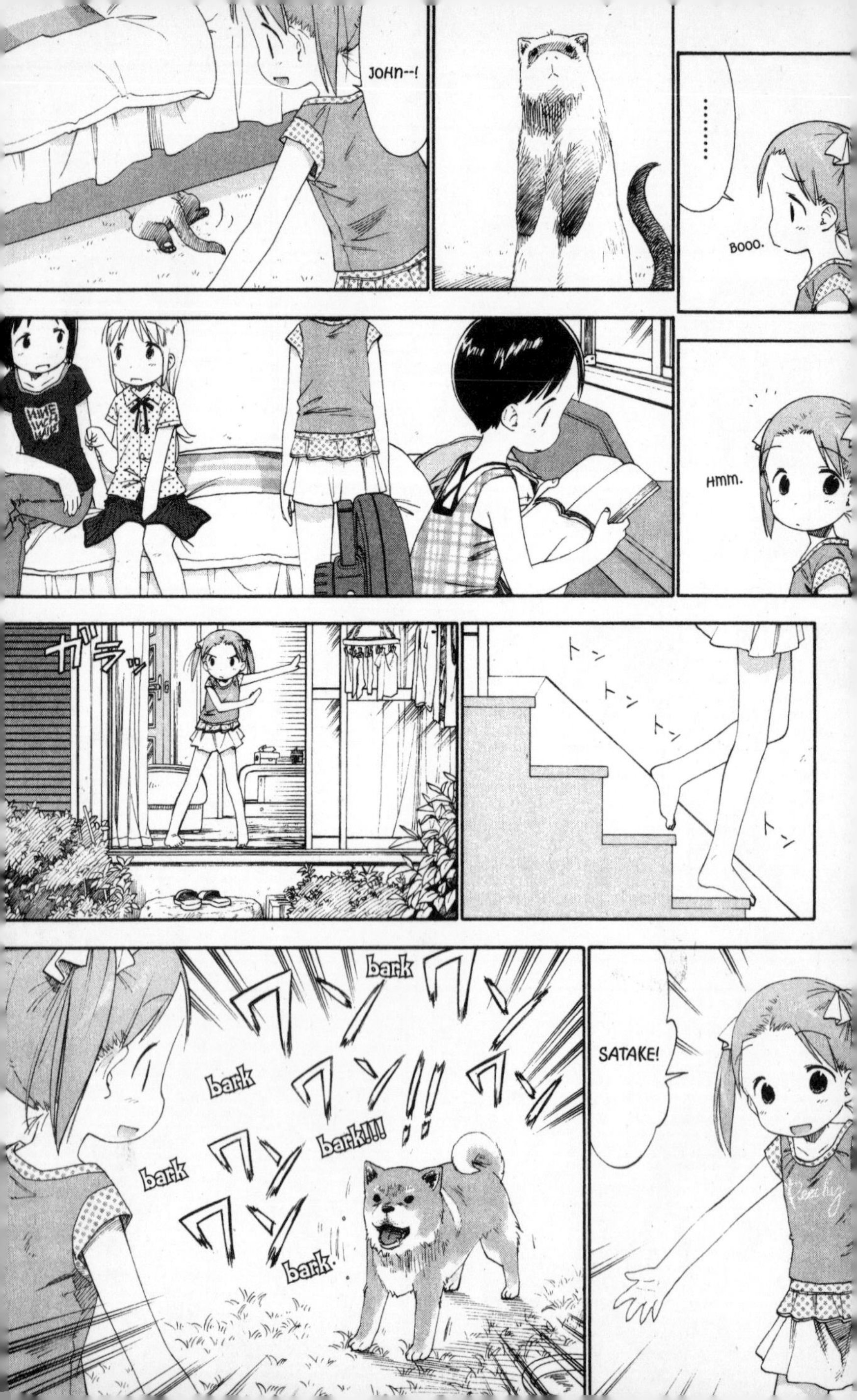
......
BOOO.
JOHN--!
HMM.
トン
トン
トン
トン
ガラッ
SATAKE!
bark
ワン
bark
ワン!!
ワン
bark!!!
bark
ワン
ワン
bark.

Spring	Chika
Summer	Miu
Autumn	Matsuri
Winter	Ana
	Nobue

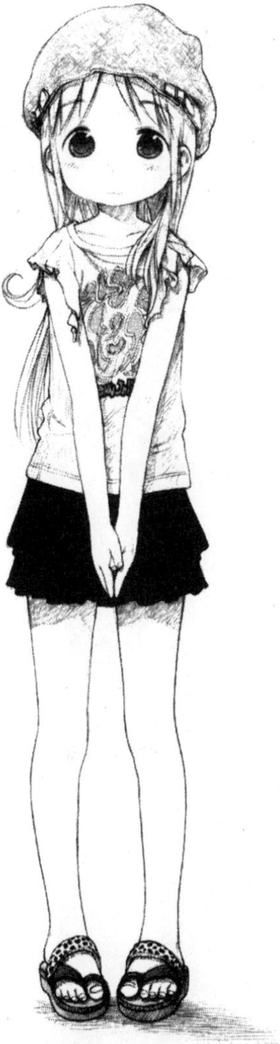

Spring
Summer
Autumn
Winter

Chika
Miu
Matsuri
Ana
Nobue

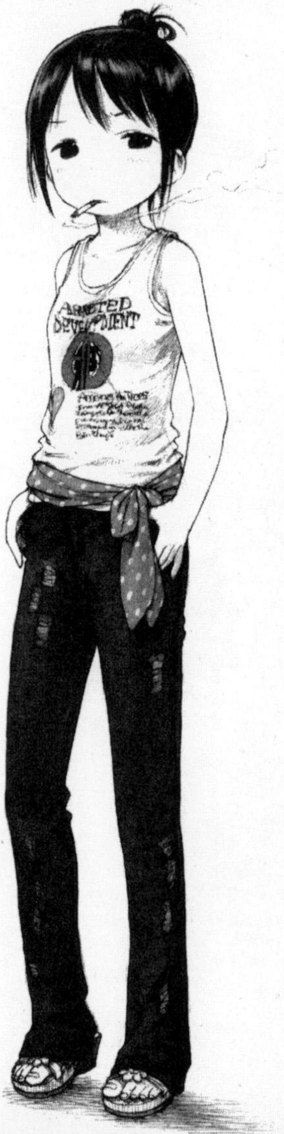

episode.46

ENGLISH GIRLS IN HAMAMATSU

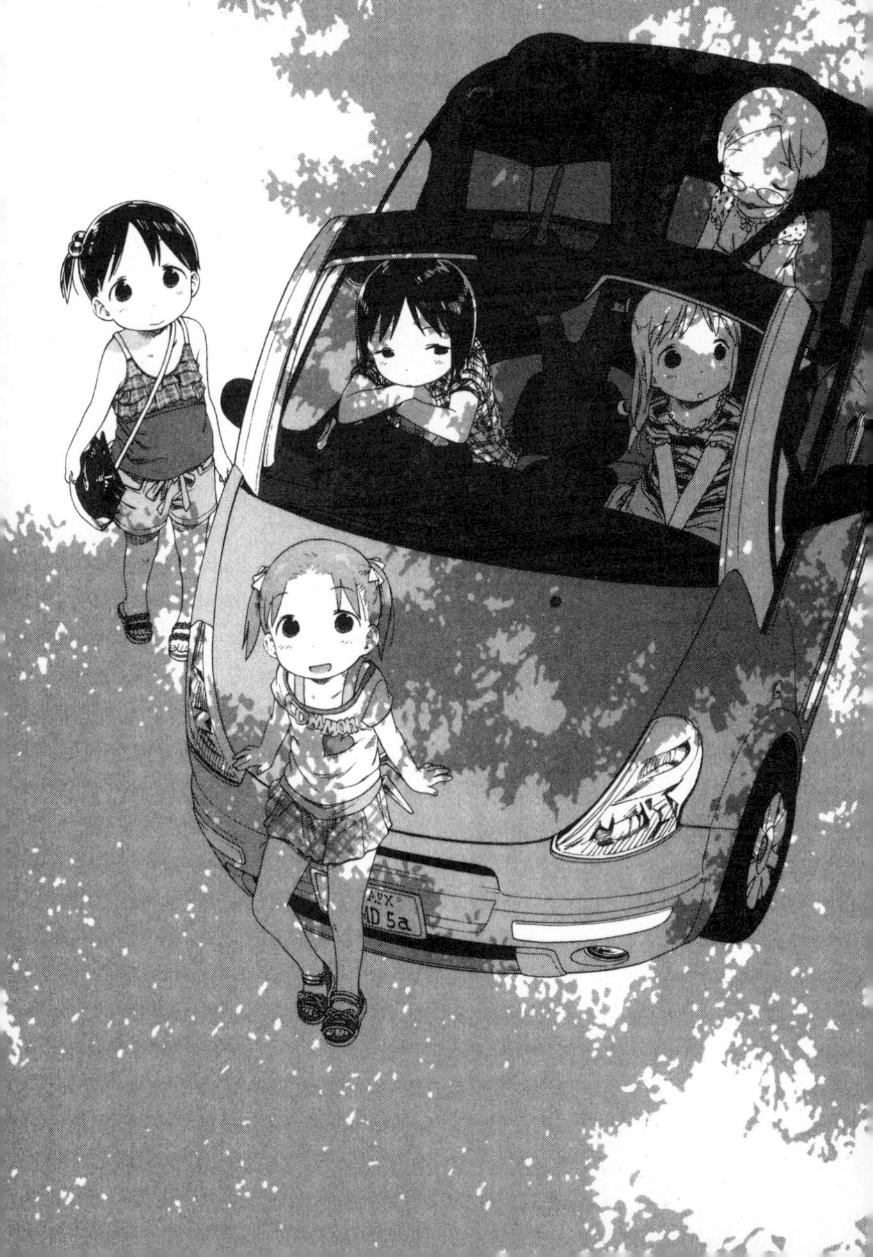

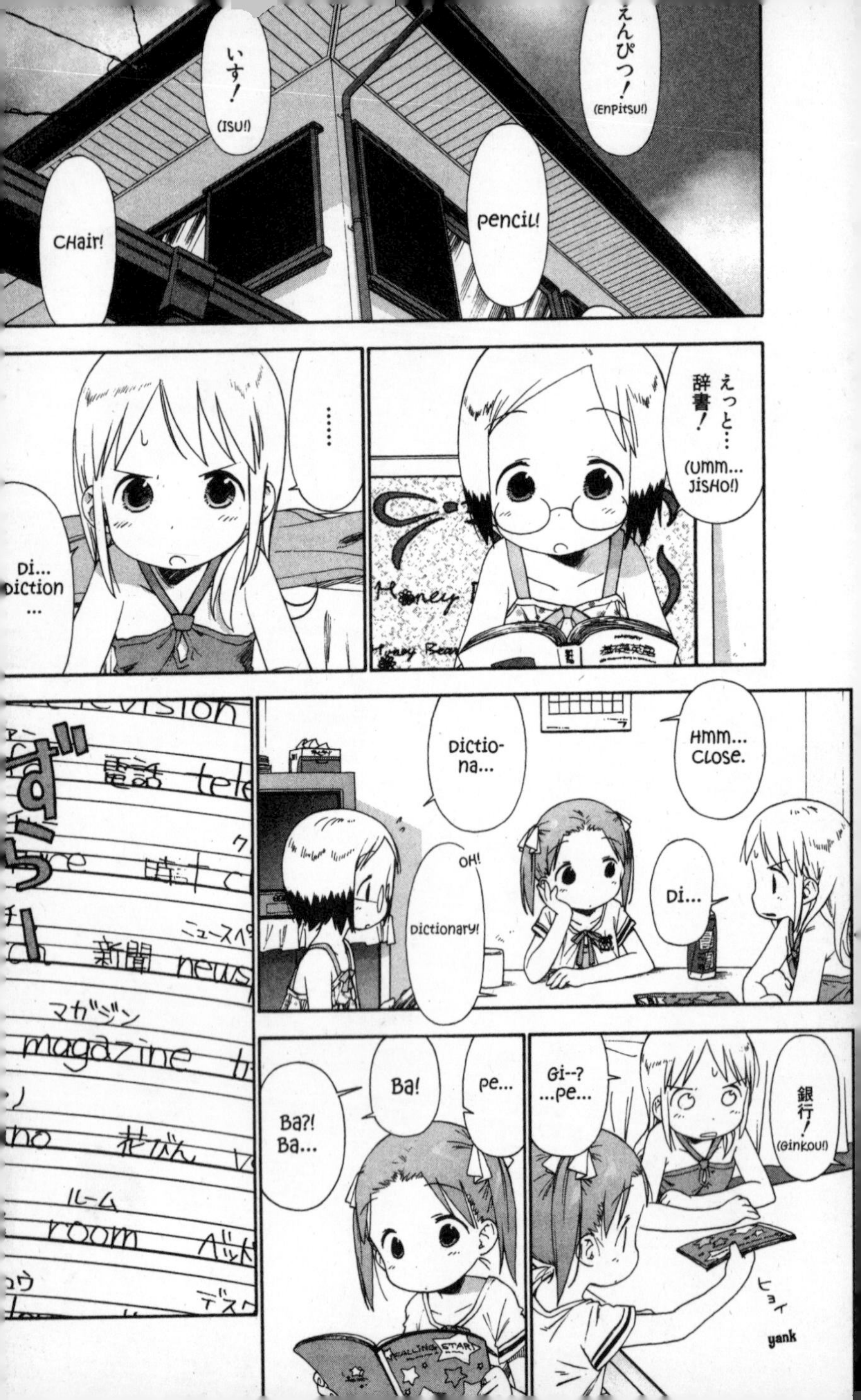
えんぴつ！
(Enpitsu!)
Pencil!
いす！
(Isu!)
Chair!
えっと…辞書！
(Umm... Jisho!)
……
Di... Diction...
Hmm... Close.
Dictio-na...
Di...
Oh! Dictionary!
銀行！
(Ginkou!)
Gi--? ...pe...
ヒョイ
yank
pe...
Ba!
Ba?! Ba...
電話 tele
ニュースペ
新聞 news
マガジン
magazine
花びん
ルーム
room

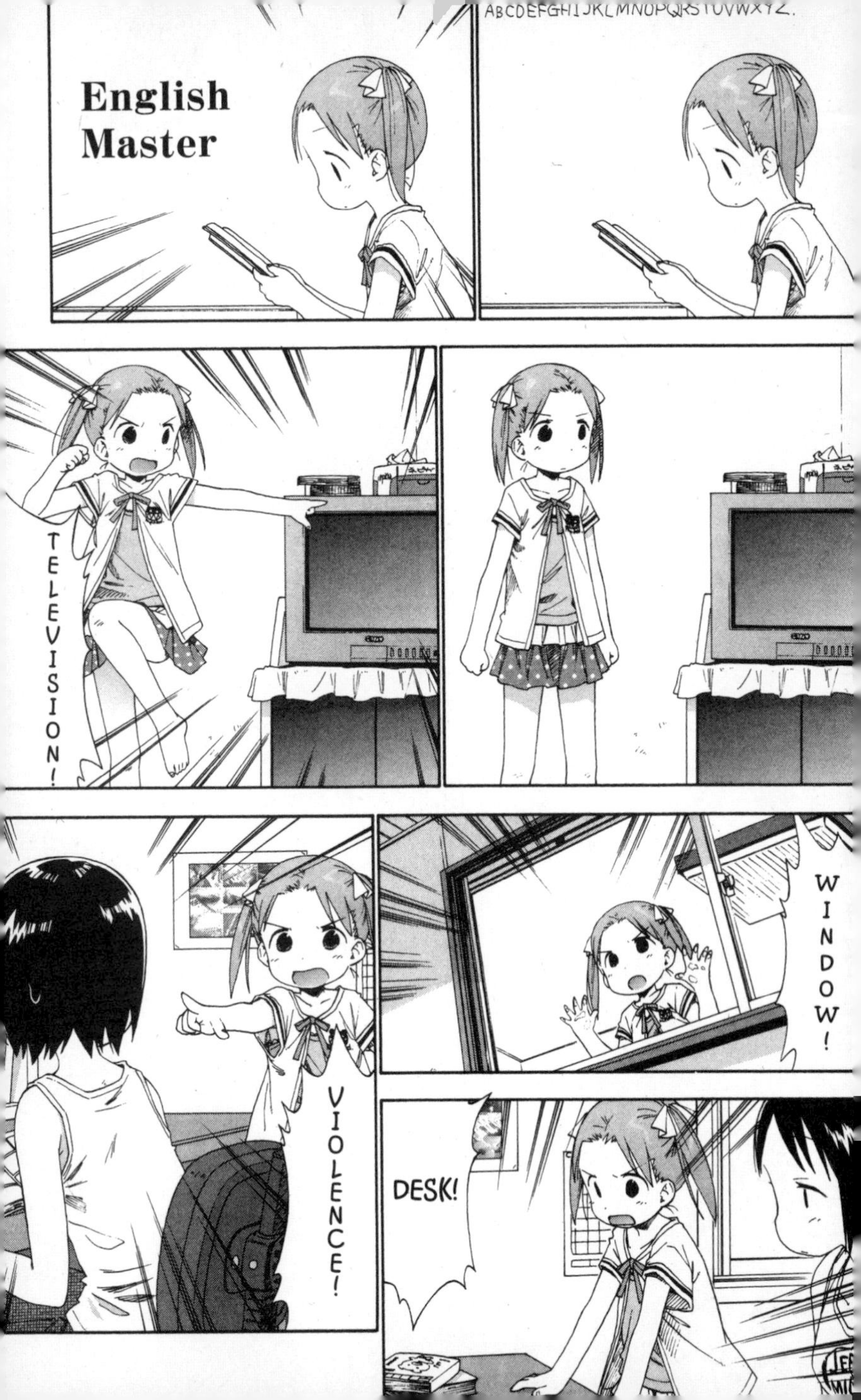
ABCDEFGHIJKLMNOPQRSTUVWXYZ.
English Master
TELEVISION!
WINDOW!
DESK!
VIOLENCE!

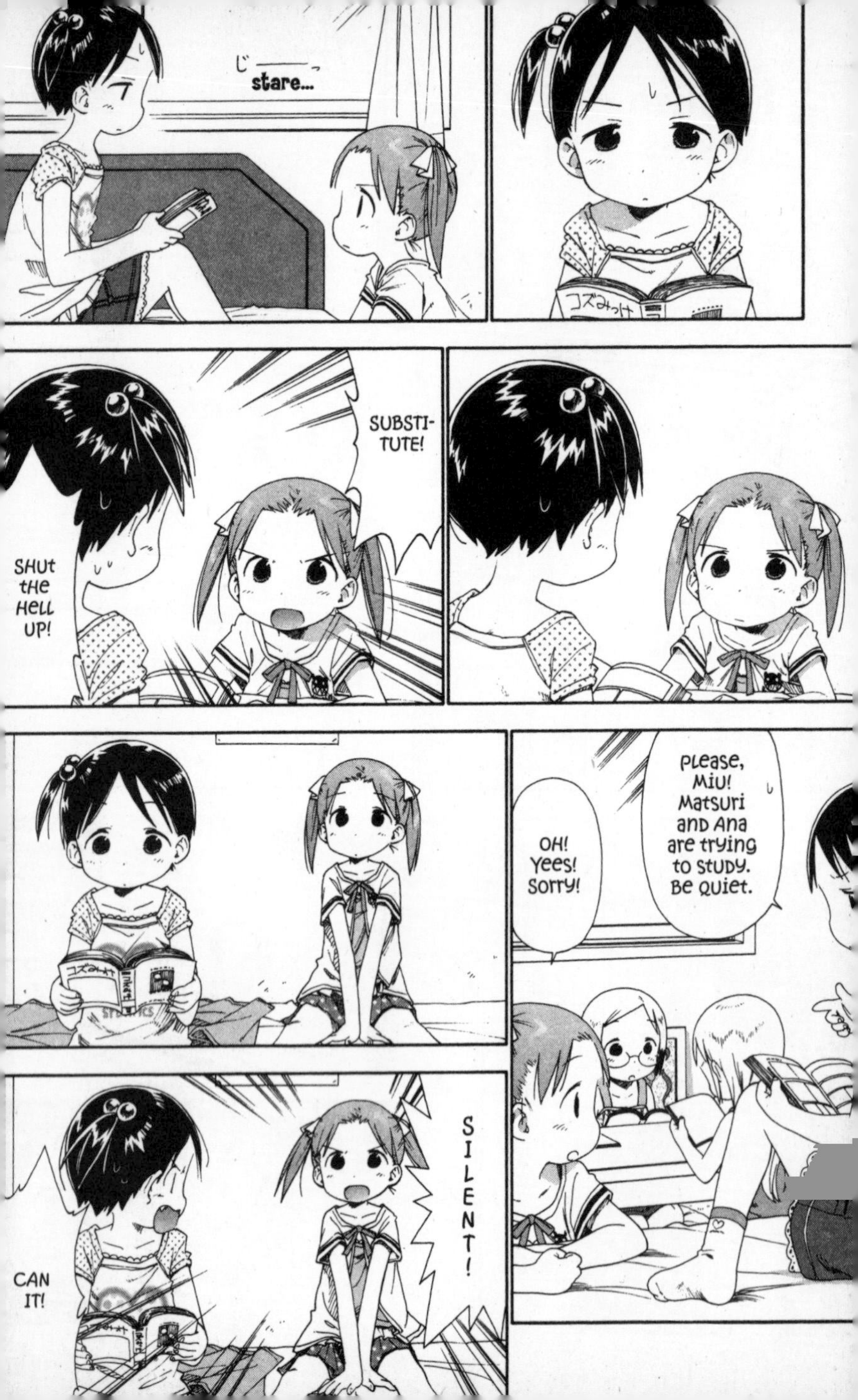

じーっ
stare...
SUBSTI-TUTE!
SHUt tHe HeLL UP!
PLease, Miu! Matsuri and Ana are trying to study. Be quiet.
OH! Yees! Sorry!
SILENT!
CAN IT!

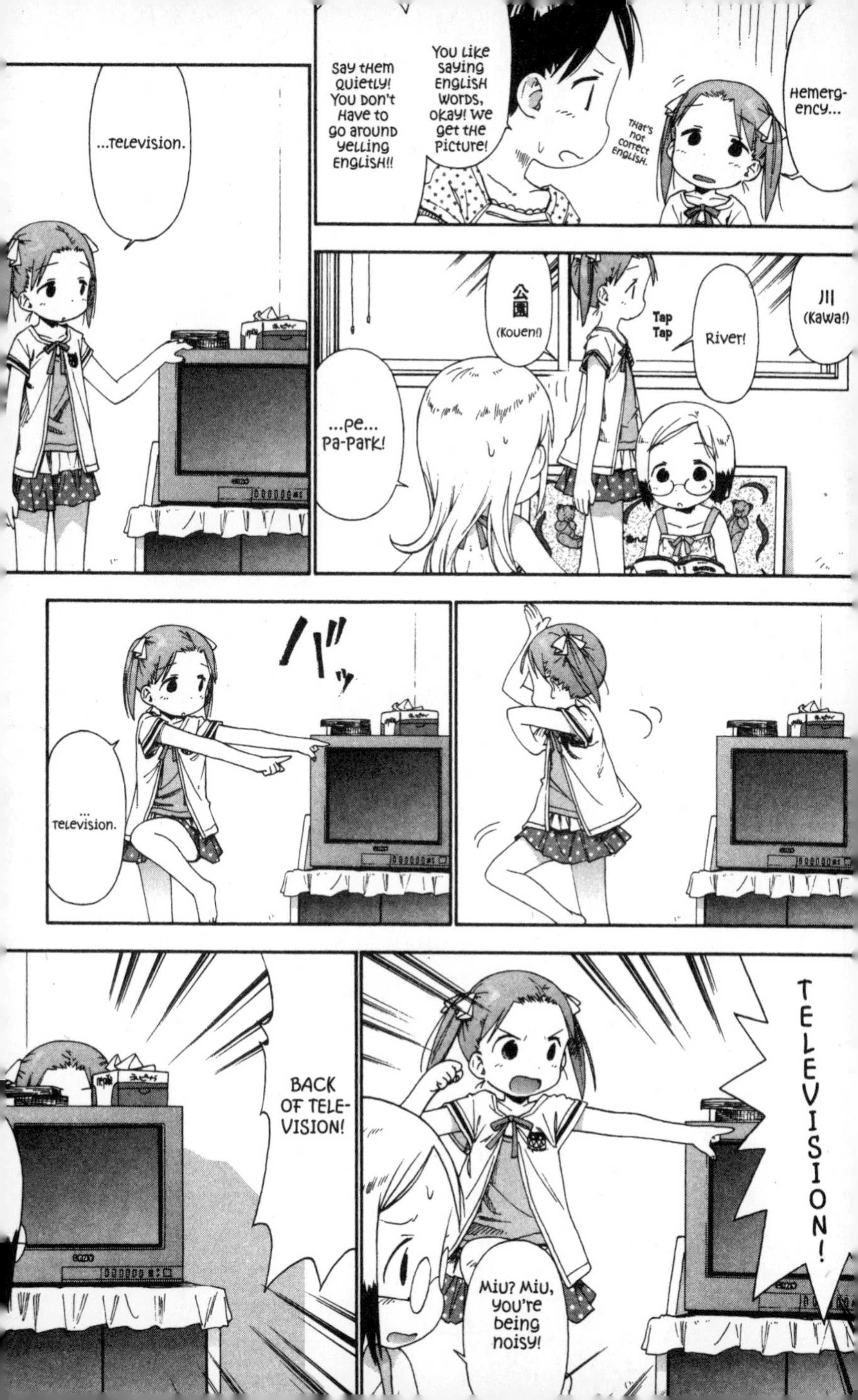
Hemerg-
ency...
That's not correct English.
You like saying English words, okay! We get the picture!
Say them quietly! You don't have to go around yelling English!!
川
(Kawa!)
Tap Tap
River!
公園
(Kouen!)
...pe... Pa-park!
...television.
バッ
... television.
TELEVISION!
Miu? Miu, you're being noisy!
BACK OF TELE-VISION!

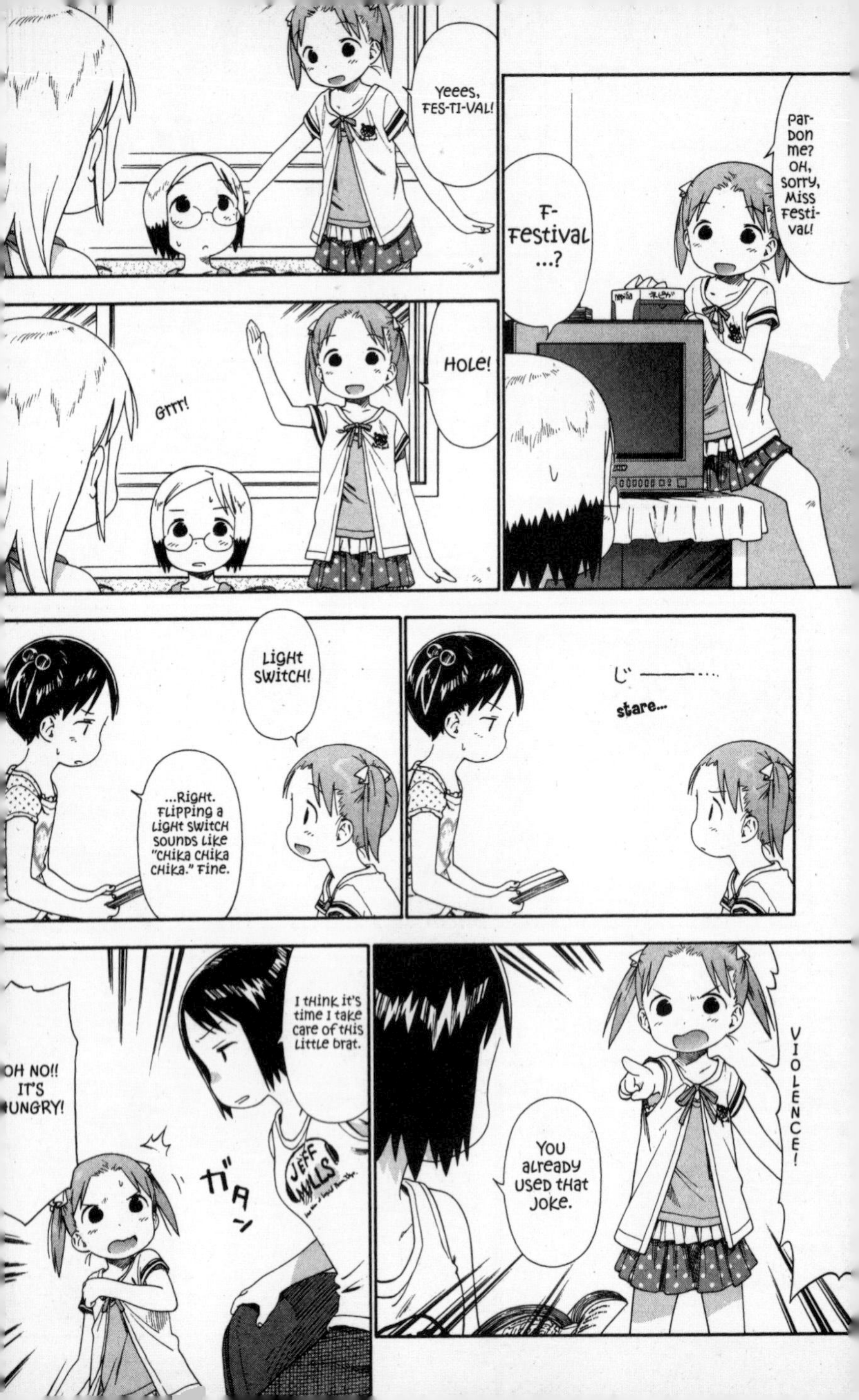
Pardon me? Oh, sorry, Miss Festival!
F-Festival ...?
Yeees, FES-TI-VAL!
HOLE!
Grrr!
じ——…
stare...
Light switch!
...Right. Flipping a light switch sounds like "chika chika chika." Fine.
VIOLENCE!
You already used that joke.
I think it's time I take care of this little brat.
JEFF MILLS
OH NO!! IT'S UNGRY!

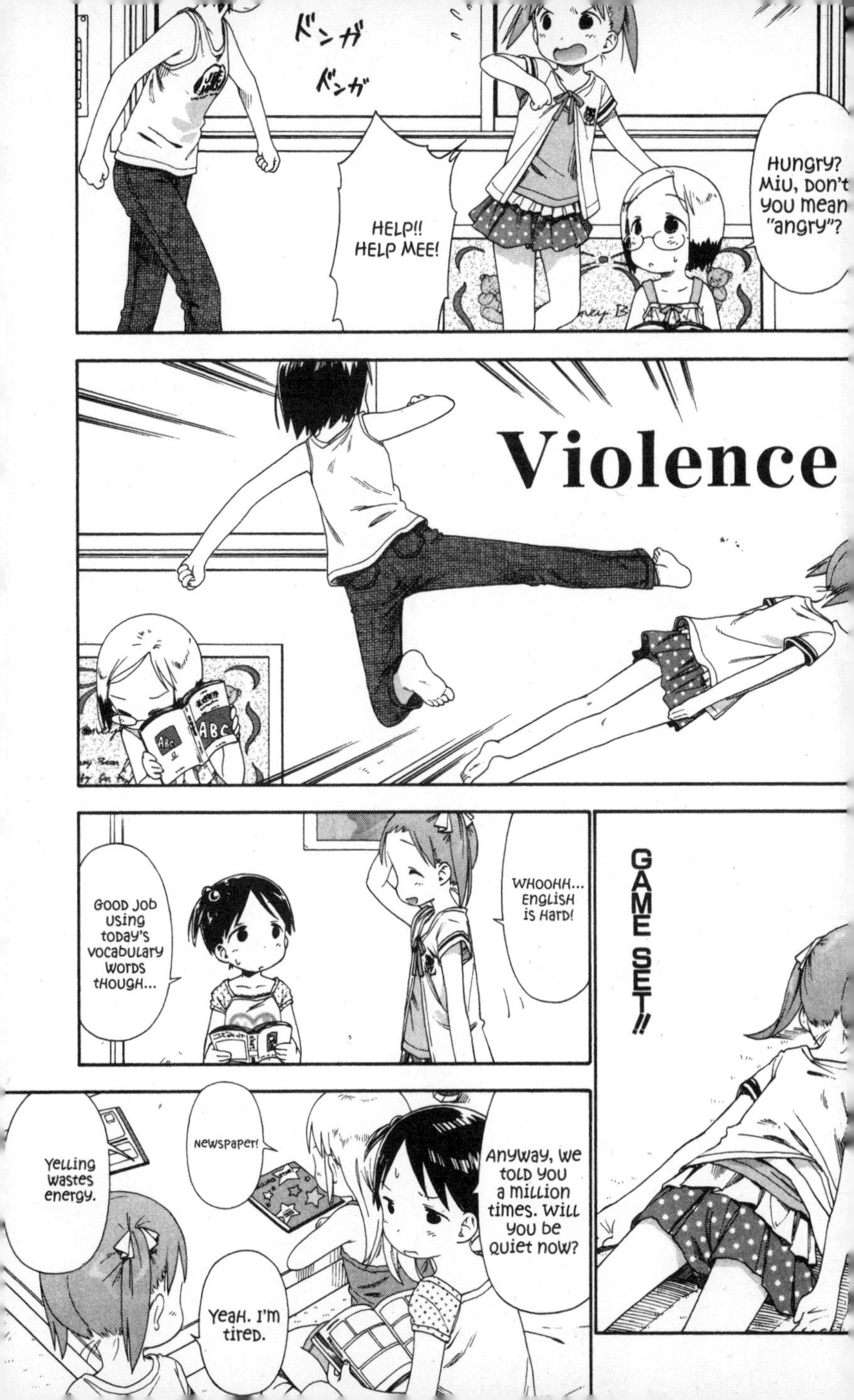
Hungry? Miu, don't you mean "angry"?
ドンガ
ドンガ
HELP!! HELP MEE!
Violence
GAME SET!!
WHOOHH... English is hard!
Good job using today's vocabulary words though...
Anyway, we told you a million times. Will you be quiet now?
Newspaper!
Yelling wastes energy.
Yeah. I'm tired.

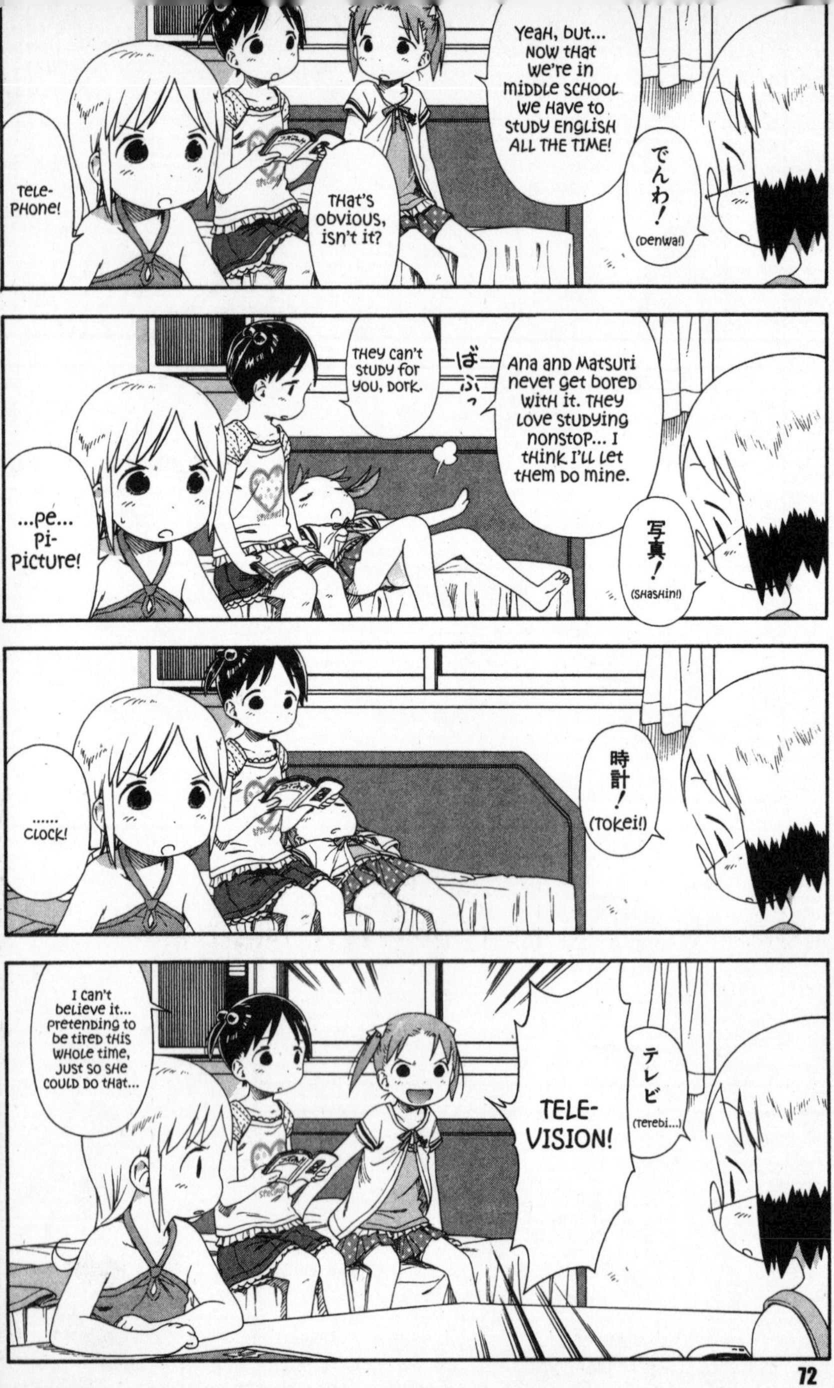
Yeah, but... now that we're in middle school we have to study English all the time!
でんわ!
(Denwa!)
That's obvious, isn't it?
Tele-phone!
Ana and Matsuri never get bored with it. They love studying nonstop... I think I'll let them do mine.
写真!
(Shashin!)
ばふっ
They can't study for you, dork.
...pe... pi- picture!
時計!
(Tokei!)
...... clock!
テレビ
(Terebi...)
TELE-VISION!
I can't believe it... pretending to be tired this whole time, just so she could do that...

Spring	Chika
Summer	Miu
	Matsuri
Autumn	Ana
Winter	Nobue

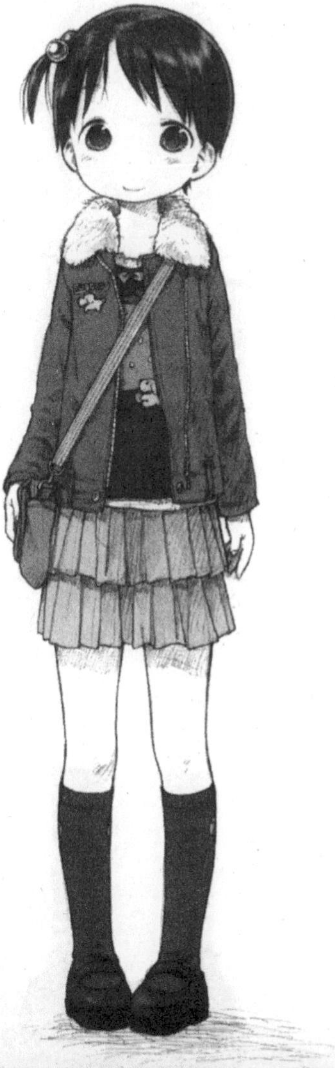

Spring
Summer
Autumn
Winter

Chika
Miu
Matsuri
Ana
Nobue

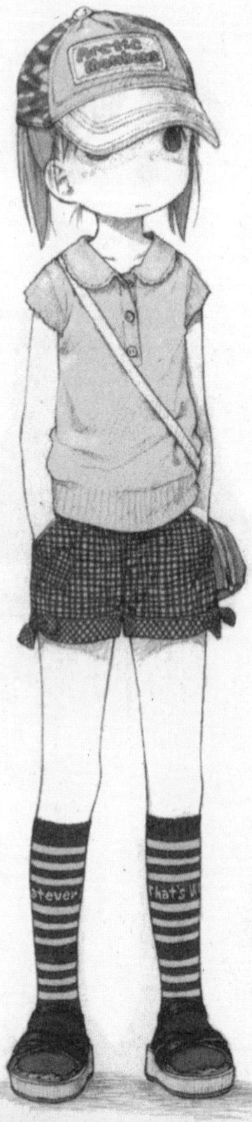

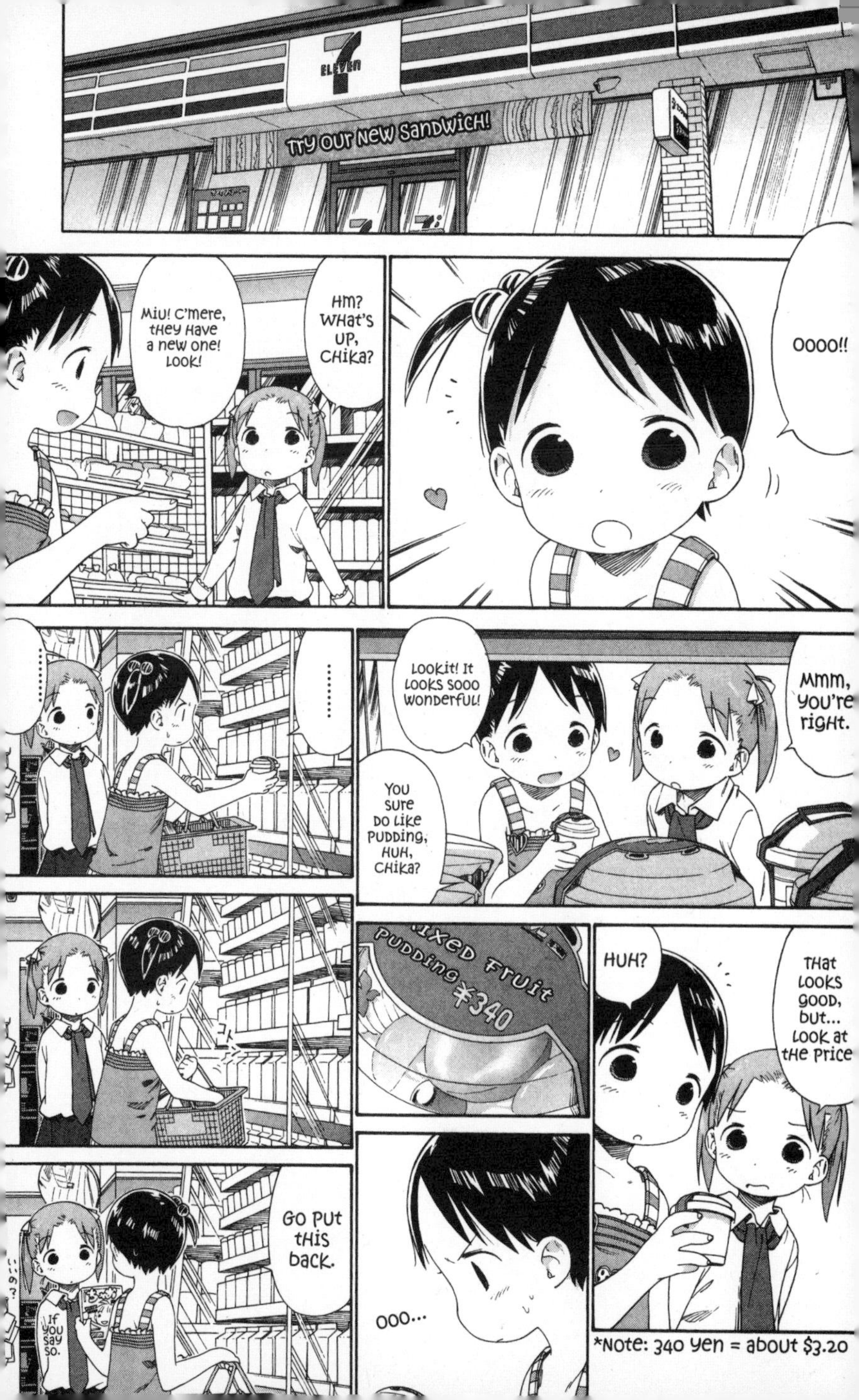
Try our New Sandwich!
OOOO!!
Miu! C'mere, they have a new one! Look!
Hm? What's up, Chika?
Lookit! It looks sooo wonderful!
Mmm, you're right.
You sure do like pudding, huh, Chika?
......
......
Huh?
That looks good, but... look at the price
Mixed Fruit Pudding ¥340
ooo...
コト
Go put this back.
いいの?
If you say so.

*Note: 340 yen = about $3.20

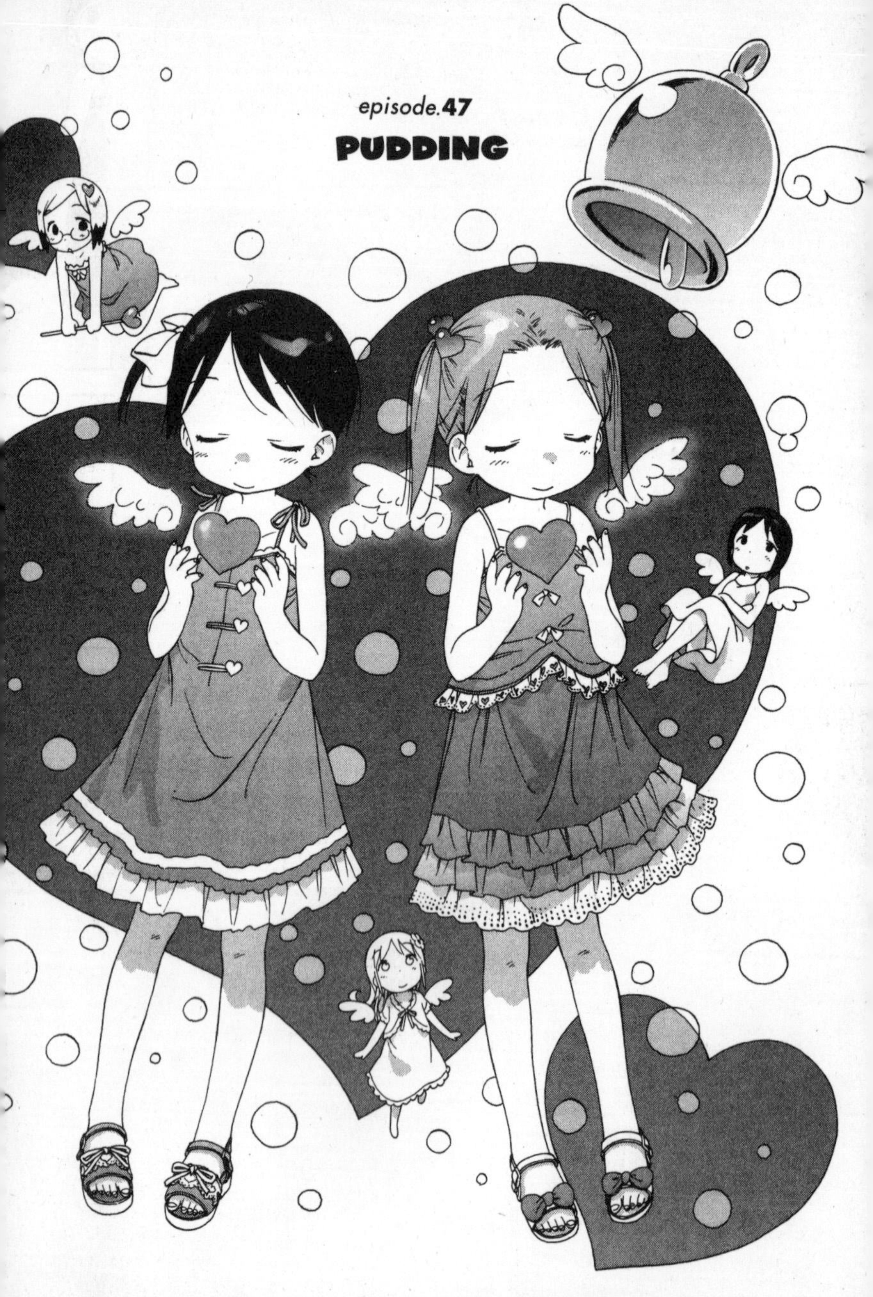
episode.47
PUDDING

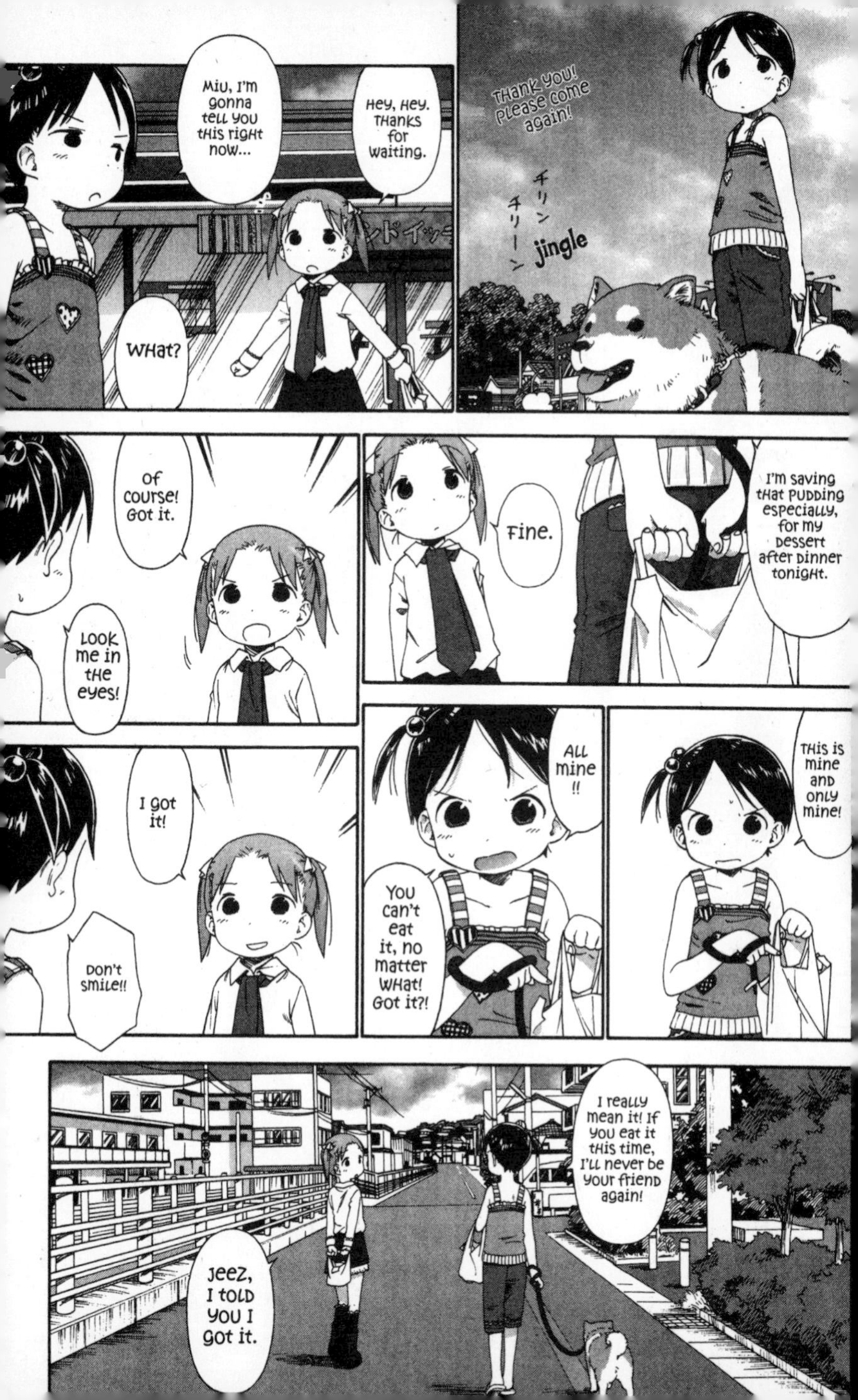
Thank you! Please come again!
チリン
チリーン
jingle
Hey, hey. Thanks for waiting.
Miu, I'm gonna tell you this right now...
What?
I'm saving that pudding especially, for my dessert after dinner tonight.
Fine.
Of course! Got it.
Look me in the eyes!
This is mine and only mine!
All mine !!
You can't eat it, no matter what! Got it?!
I got it!
Don't smile!!
I really mean it! If you eat it this time, I'll never be your friend again!
Jeez, I told you I got it.

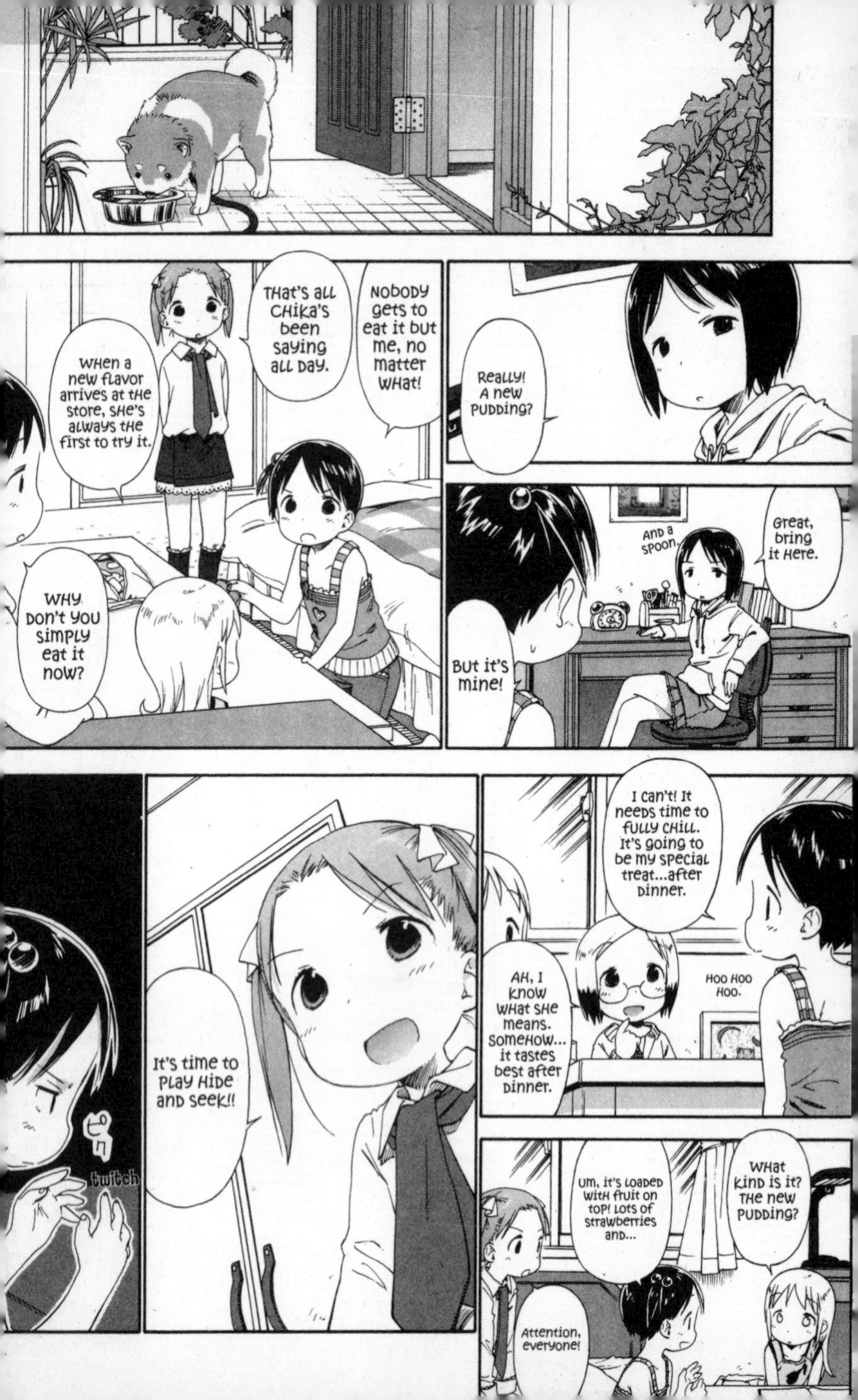
Really! A new pudding?
Great, bring it here.
And a spoon.
But it's mine!
Nobody gets to eat it but me, no matter what!
That's all Chika's been saying all day.
When a new flavor arrives at the store, she's always the first to try it.
Why don't you simply eat it now?
I can't! It needs time to fully chill. It's going to be my special treat...after dinner.
Hoo hoo hoo.
Ah, I know what she means. Somehow... it tastes best after dinner.
What kind is it? The new pudding?
Um, it's loaded with fruit on top! Lots of strawberries and...
Attention, everyone!
It's time to play hide and seek!!
ピク
twitch

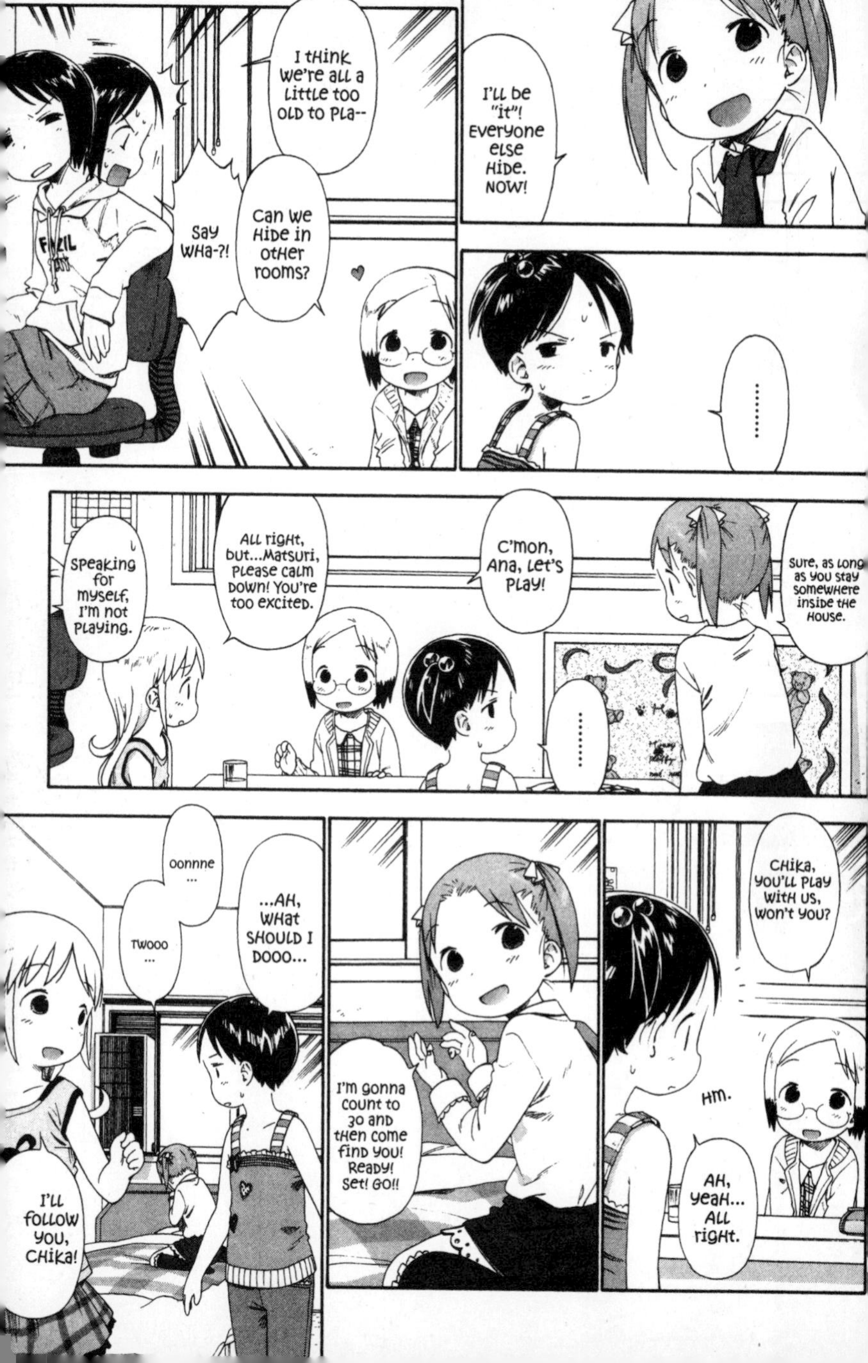
I'll be "it"! Everyone else hide. NOW!
......
I think we're all a little too old to pla--
Can we hide in other rooms?
Say wha-?!
Sure, as long as you stay somewhere inside the house.
......
C'mon, Ana, let's play!
All right, but...Matsuri, please calm down! You're too excited.
Speaking for myself, I'm not playing.
Chika, you'll play with us, won't you?
Hm.
Ah, yeah... all right.
I'm gonna count to 30 and then come find you! Ready! Set! GO!!
...Ah, what should I dooo...
Oonnne ...
Twooo ...
I'll follow you, Chika!

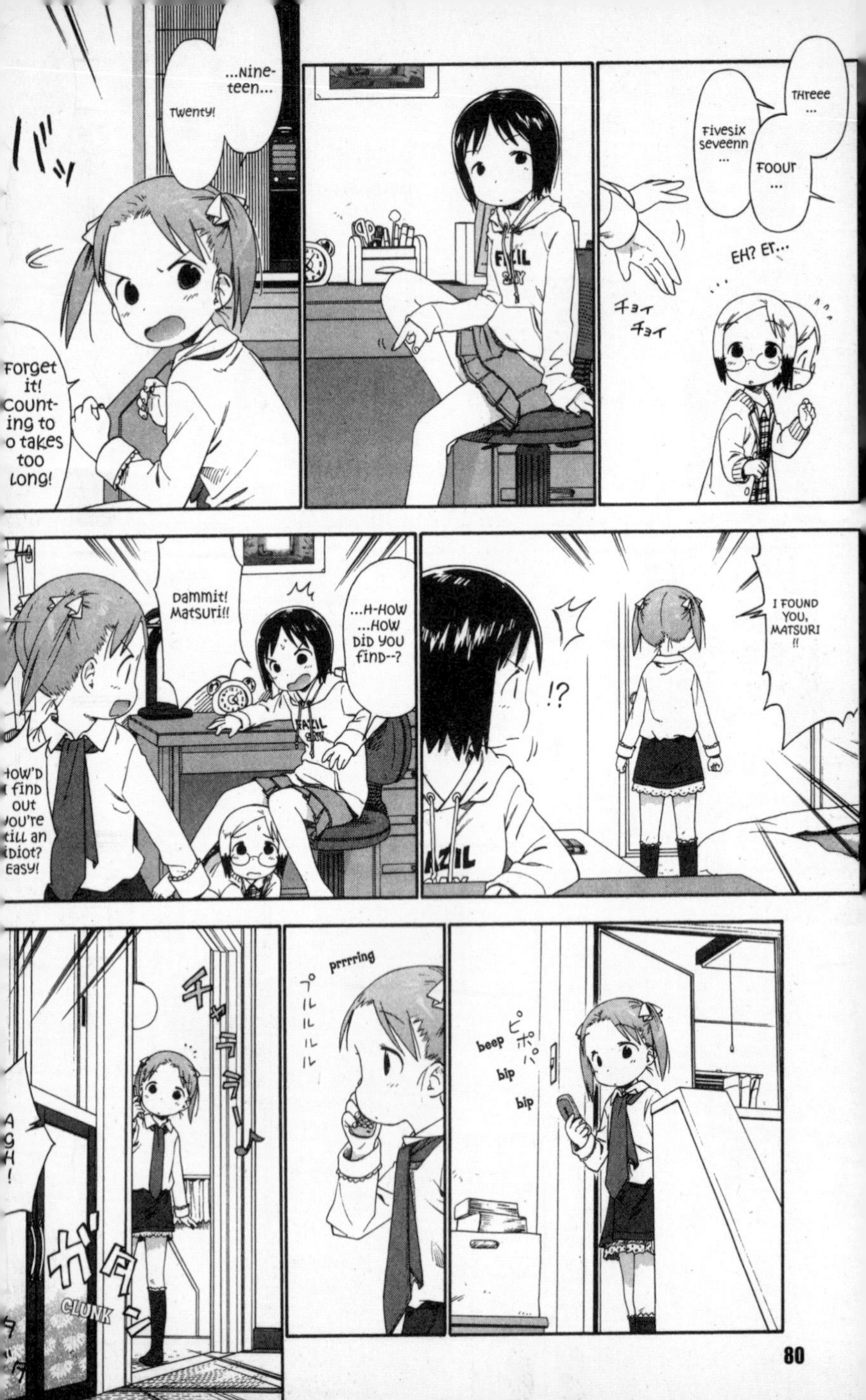
Threee ...
Foour ...
Fivesix seveenn ...
Eh? Er...
チョイ チョイ
...Nine-teen...
Twenty!
バッ
Forget it! Counting to o takes too long!
I found you, Matsuri !!
!?
...H-how ...how did you find--?
Dammit! Matsuri!!
ow'd find out ou're till an idiot? Easy!
ピポパ
beep
bip
bip
プルルルル
prrrring
チャラララー
Agh!
ガターン
CLUNK
タッ

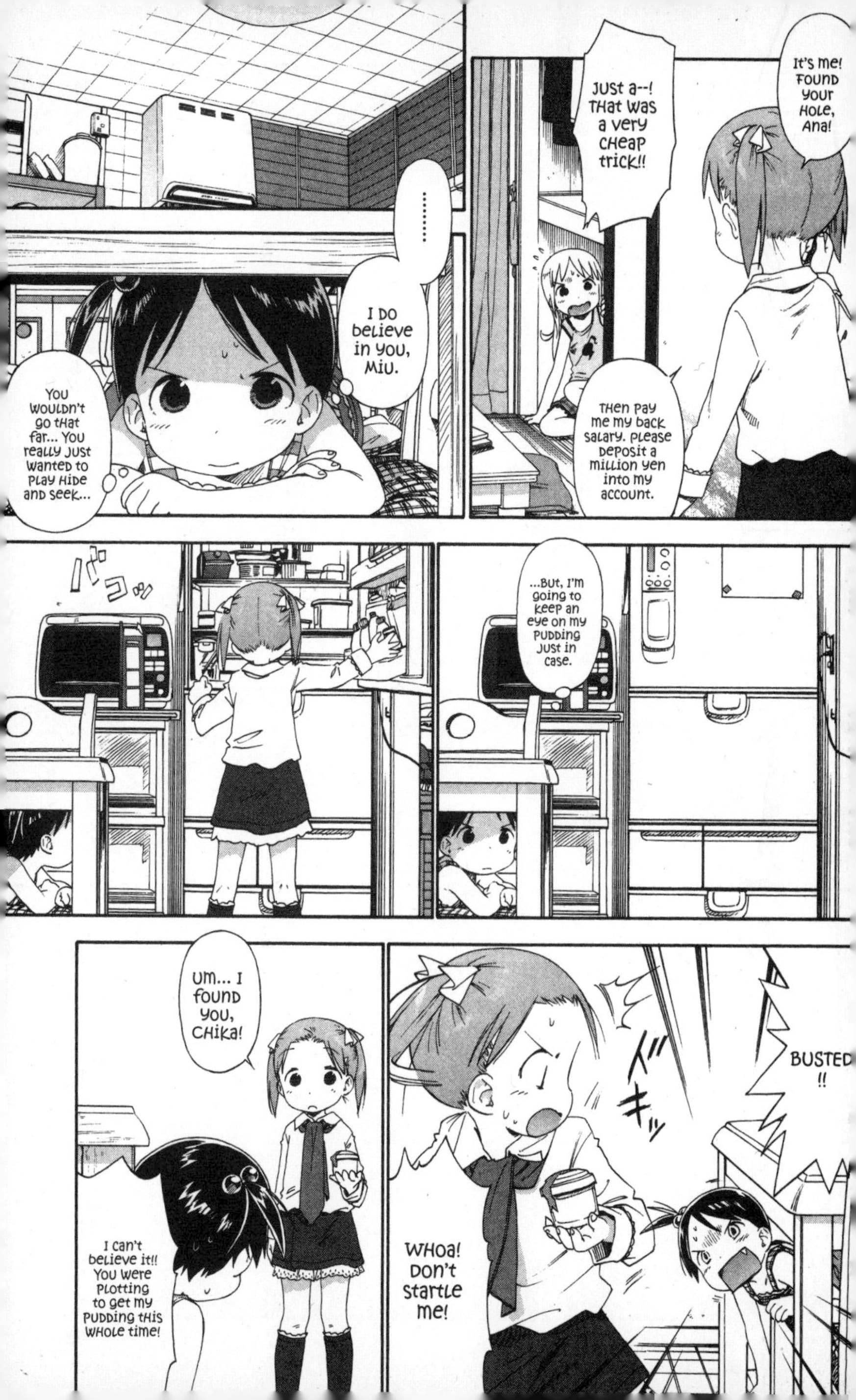
It's me! Found your hole, Ana!
Just a--! That was a very cheap trick!!
Then pay me my back salary. Please deposit a million yen into my account.
....
I do believe in you, Miu.
You wouldn't go that far... You really just wanted to play hide and seek...
...But, I'm going to keep an eye on my pudding just in case.
BUSTED !!
Whoa! Don't startle me!
Um... I found you, Chika!
I can't believe it!! You were plotting to get my pudding this whole time!

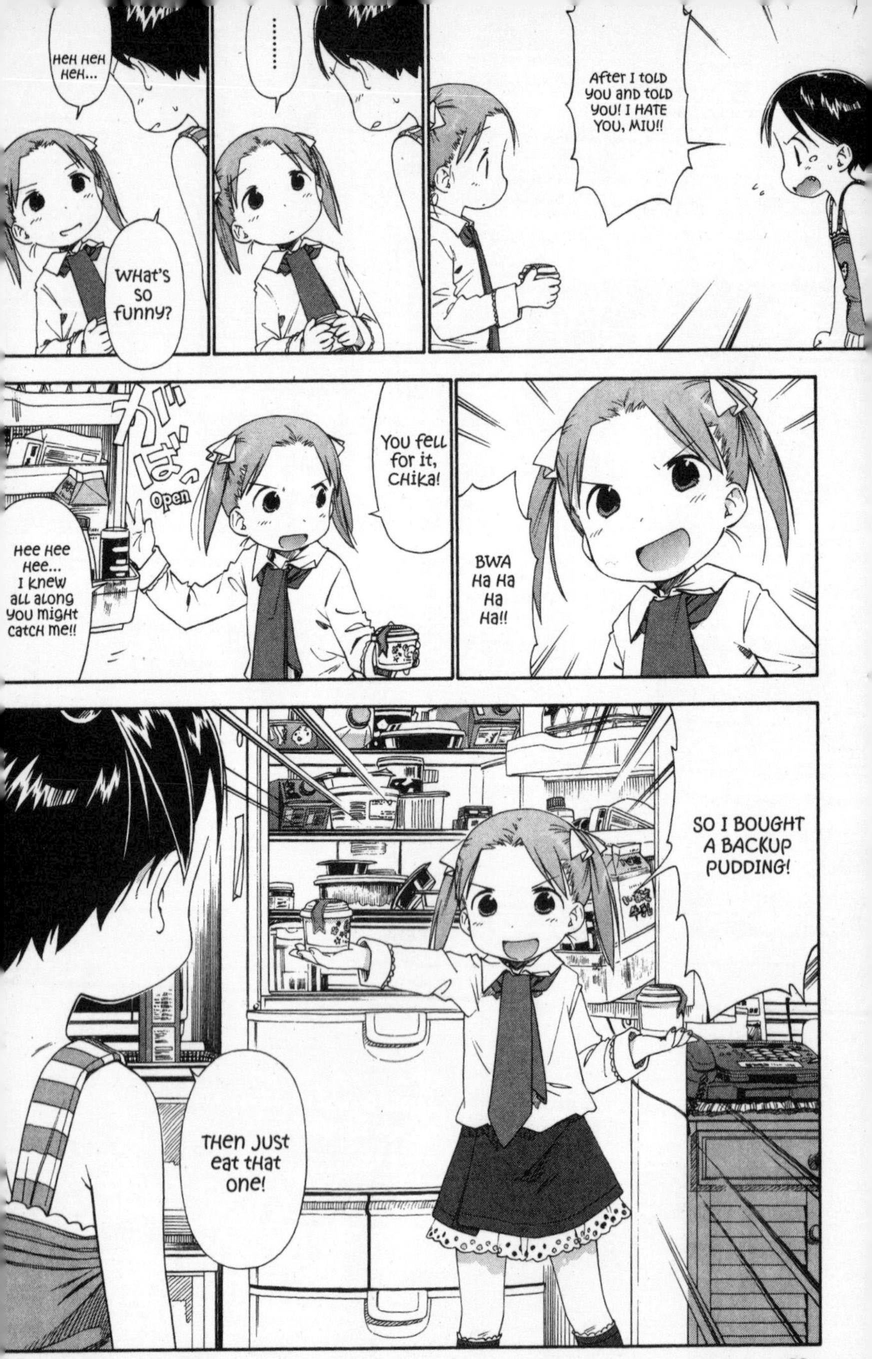
After I told you and told you! I HATE YOU, MIU!!
......
HEH HEH HEH...
WHAT'S SO FUNNY?
BWA HA HA HA HA!!
You fell for it, CHIKA!
Open
Hee hee hee... I knew all along you might catch me!!
SO I BOUGHT A BACKUP PUDDING!
Then just eat that one!

Spring	Chika
Summer	Miu
Autumn	Matsuri
	Ana
Winter	Nobue

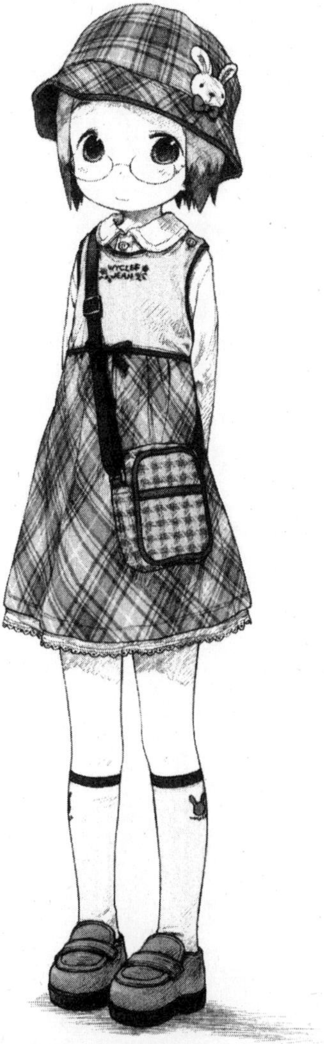

Spring Chika

Miu

Summer

Matsuri

Autumn —— Ana

Winter Nobue

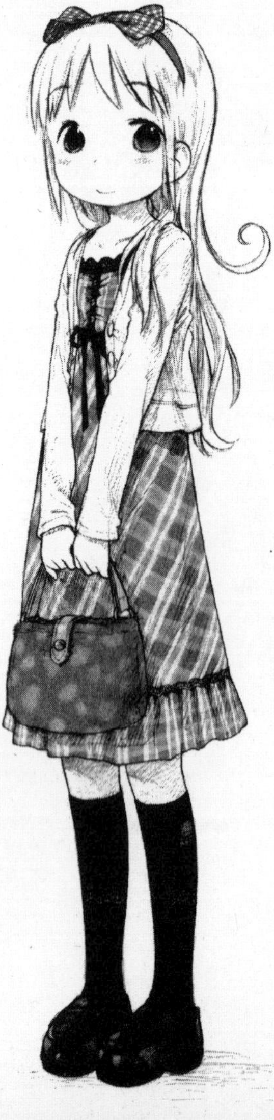

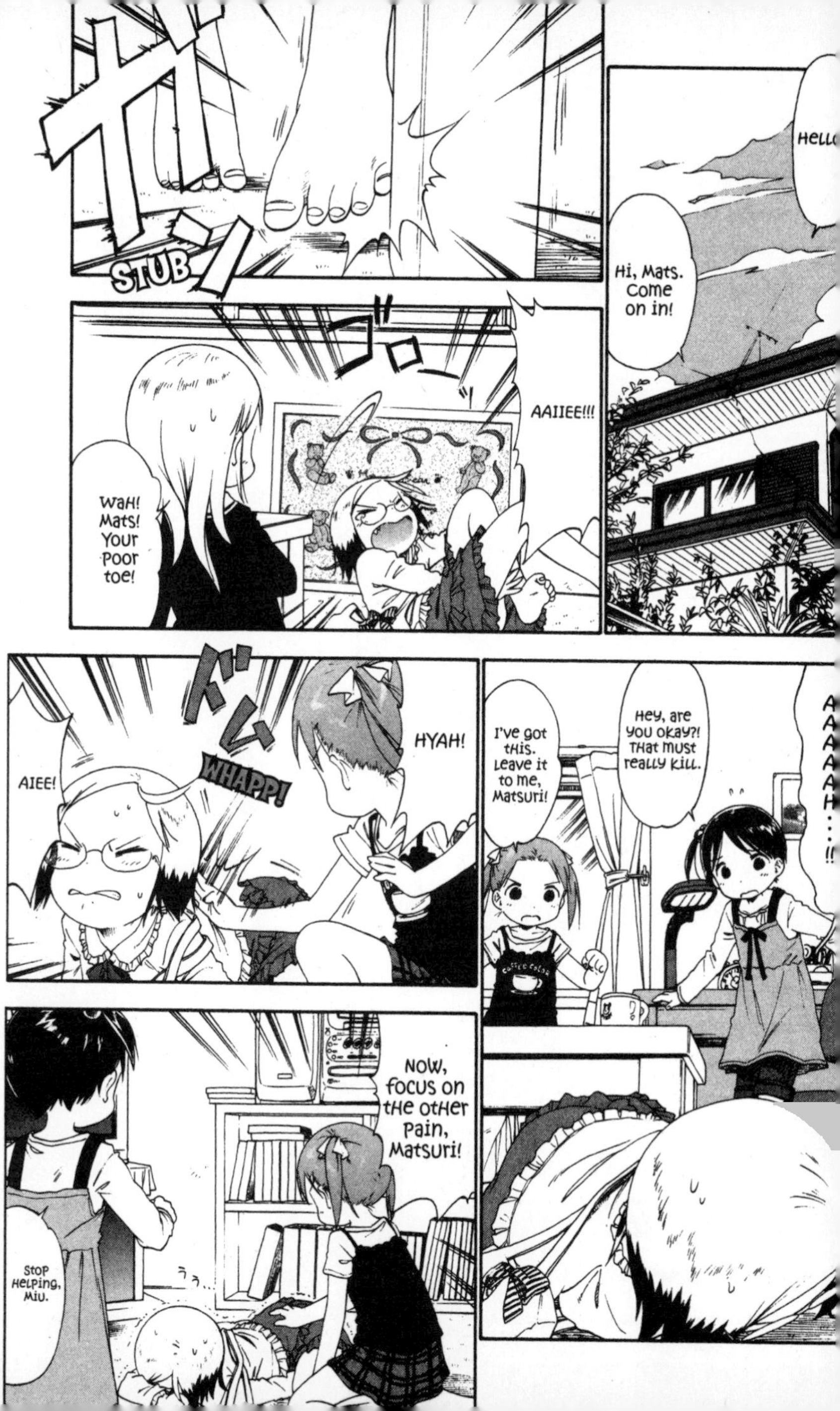

Hell
Hi, Mats. Come on in!
STUB
AAIIEE!!!
WaH! Mats! Your Poor toe!
AAAAAAH...!!
Hey, are you okay?! That must really kill.
I've got this. Leave it to me, Matsuri!
HYAH!
WHAPP!
AIEE!
NOW, focus on the other Pain, Matsuri!
Stop Helping, Miu.

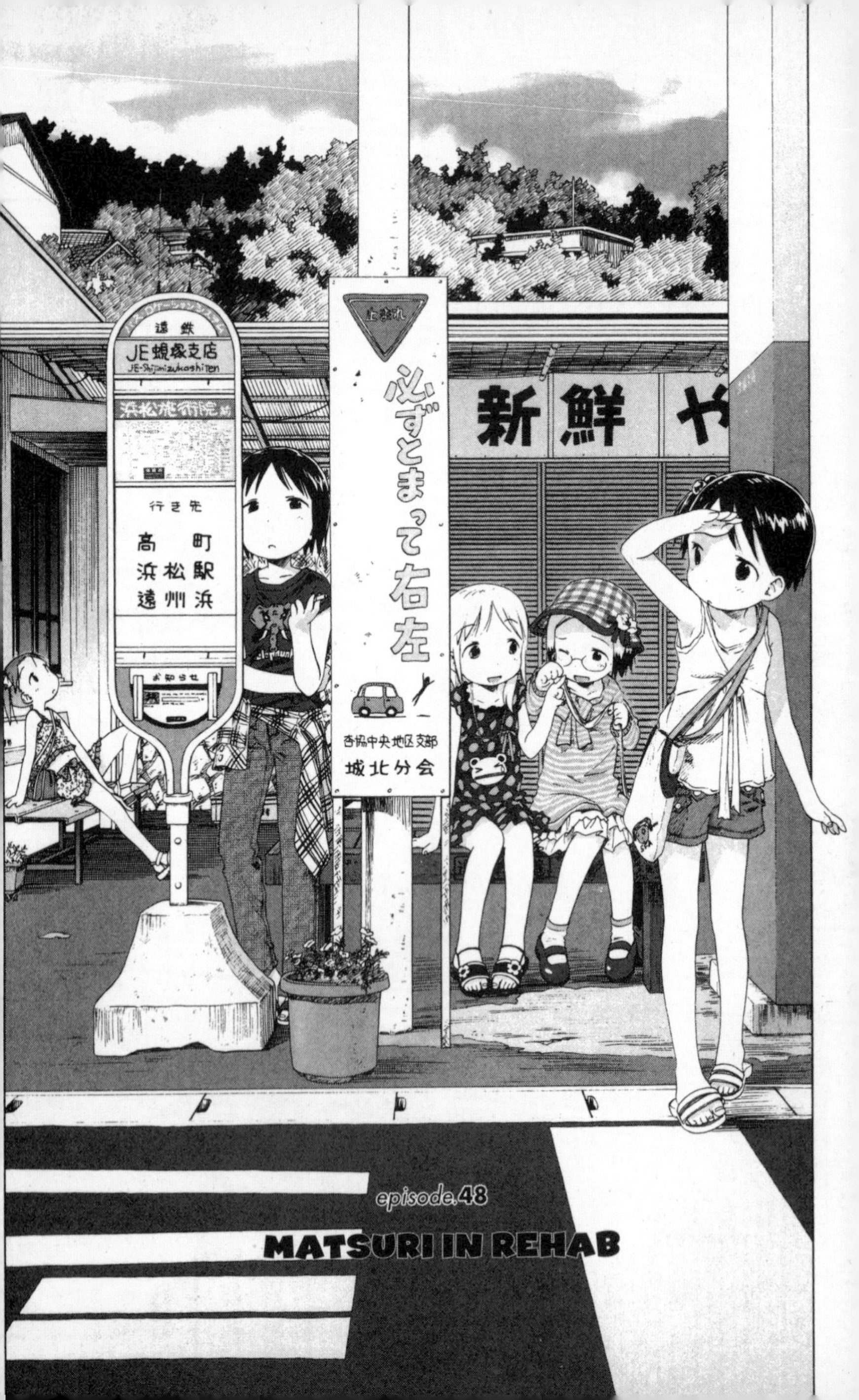
遠鉄
JE蜆塚支店
JE-Shijimizukashiten
行き先
高　町
浜松駅
遠州浜
必ずとまって右左
城北分会
新鮮や
episode.48
MATSURI IN REHAB

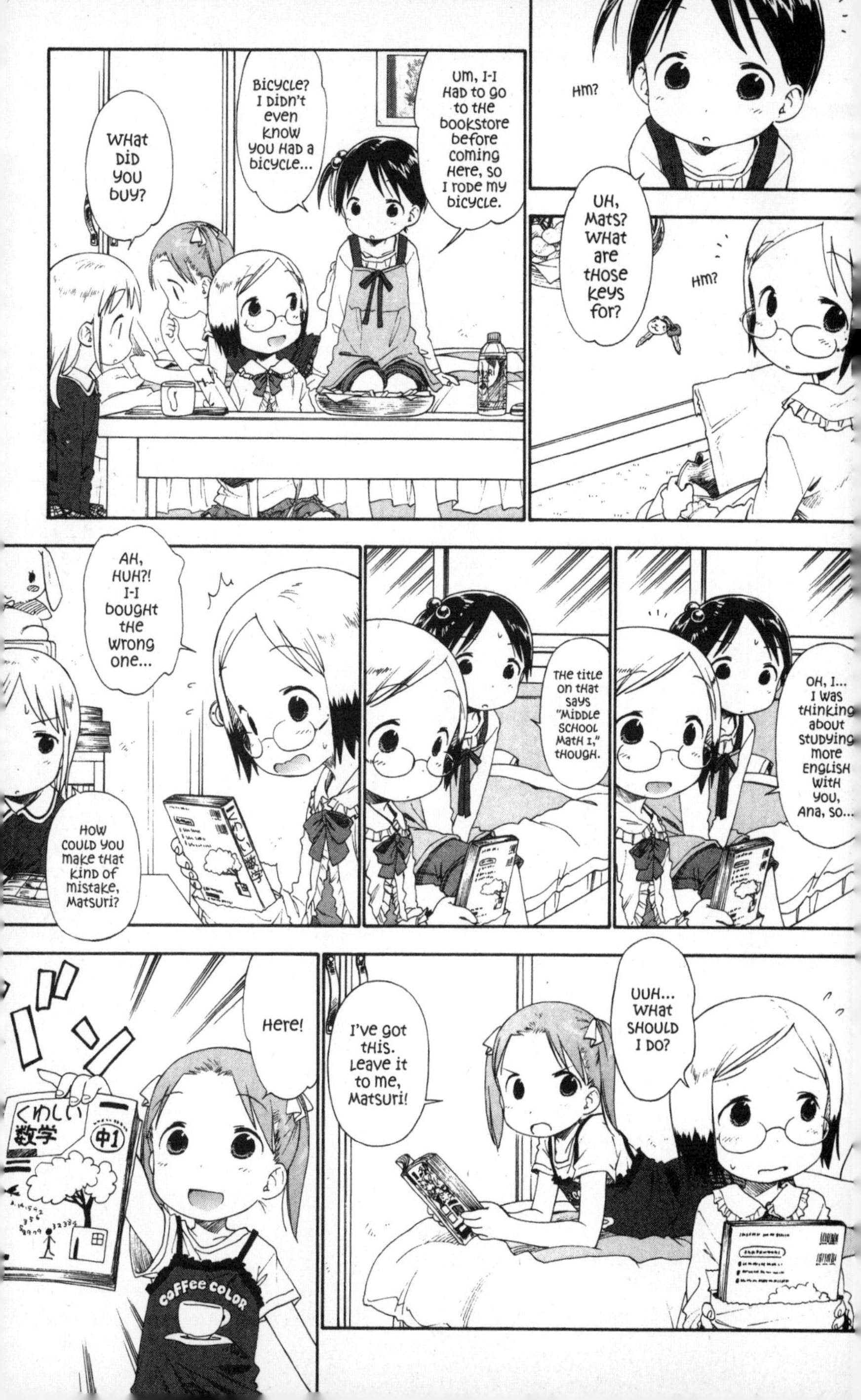
Hm?
Uh, Mats? What are those keys for?
Hm?
Um, I-I had to go to the bookstore before coming here, so I rode my bicycle.
Bicycle? I didn't even know you had a bicycle...
What did you buy?
Oh, I... I was thinking about studying more English with you, Ana, so...
The title on that says "Middle School Math I," though.
Ah, huh?! I-I bought the wrong one...
How could you make that kind of mistake, Matsuri?
Uuh... What should I do?
I've got this. Leave it to me, Matsuri!
Here!
くわしい
数学
中1
Coffee Color

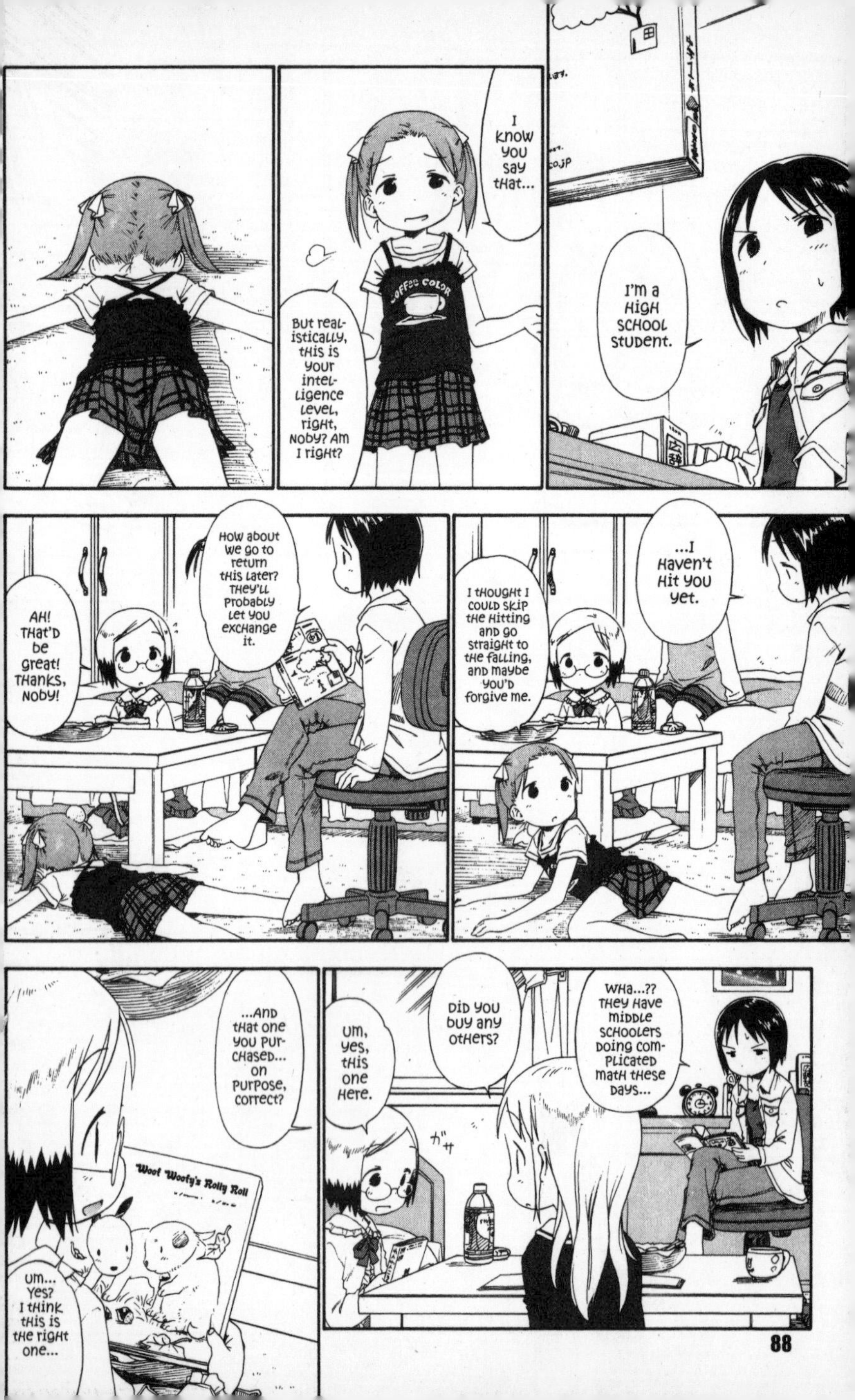
I'm a HIGH SCHOOL student.
I know you say that...
But realistically, this is your intelligence level, right, Noby? Am I right?
...I haven't hit you yet.
I thought I could skip the hitting and go straight to the falling, and maybe you'd forgive me.
How about we go to return this later? They'll probably let you exchange it.
Ah! That'd be great! Thanks, Noby!
Wha...?? They have middle schoolers doing complicated math these days...
Did you buy any others?
Um, yes, this one here.
ガサ
...And that one you purchased... on purpose, correct?
Woof Woofy's Rolly Roll
Um... Yes? I think this is the right one...

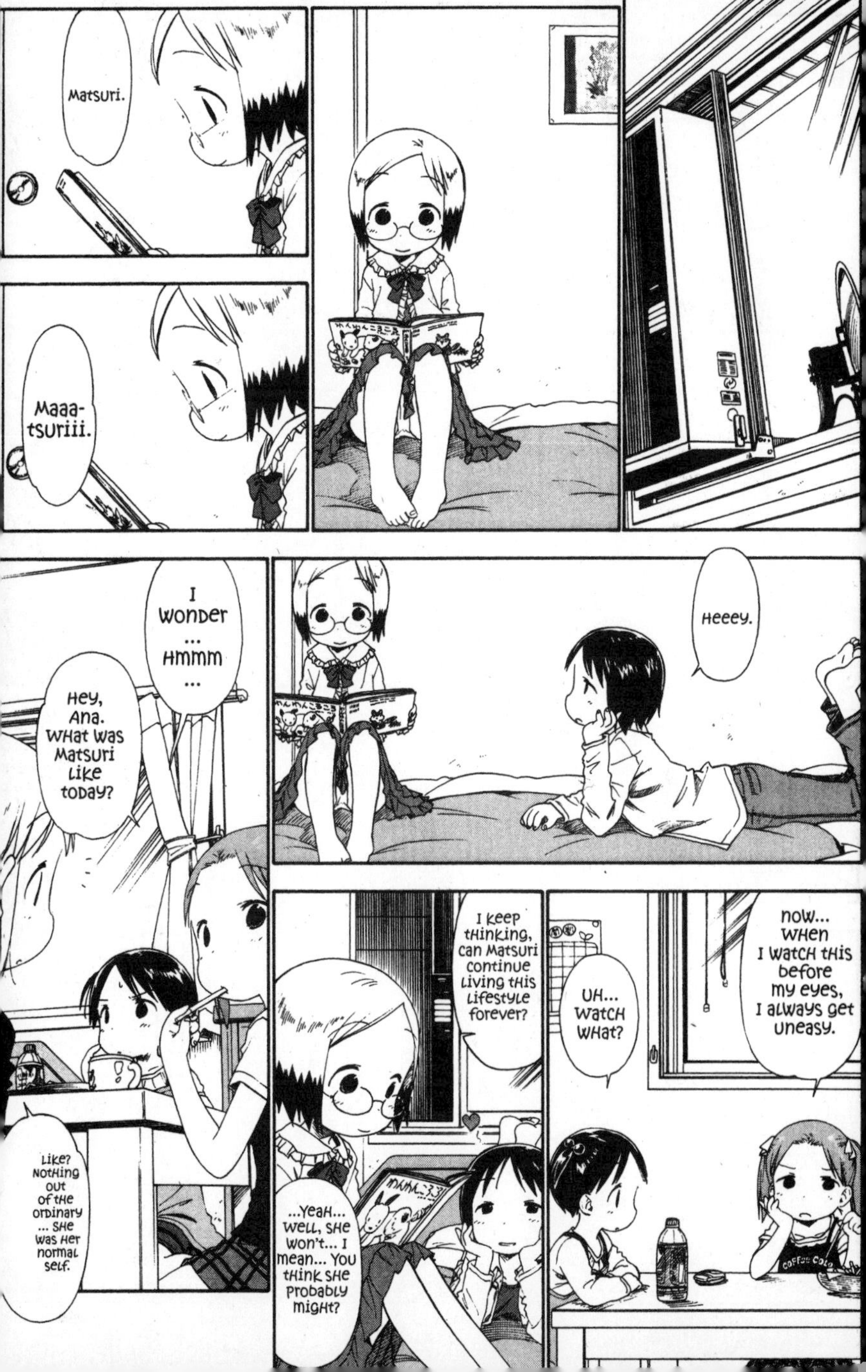
Matsuri.
Maaa-tsuriii.
Heeey.
Now... when I watch this before my eyes, I always get uneasy.
Uh... watch what?
I keep thinking, can Matsuri continue living this lifestyle forever?
...Yeah... well, she won't... I mean... you think she probably might?
I wonder ... Hmmm ...
Hey, Ana. What was Matsuri like today?
Like? Nothing out of the ordinary ... she was her normal self.

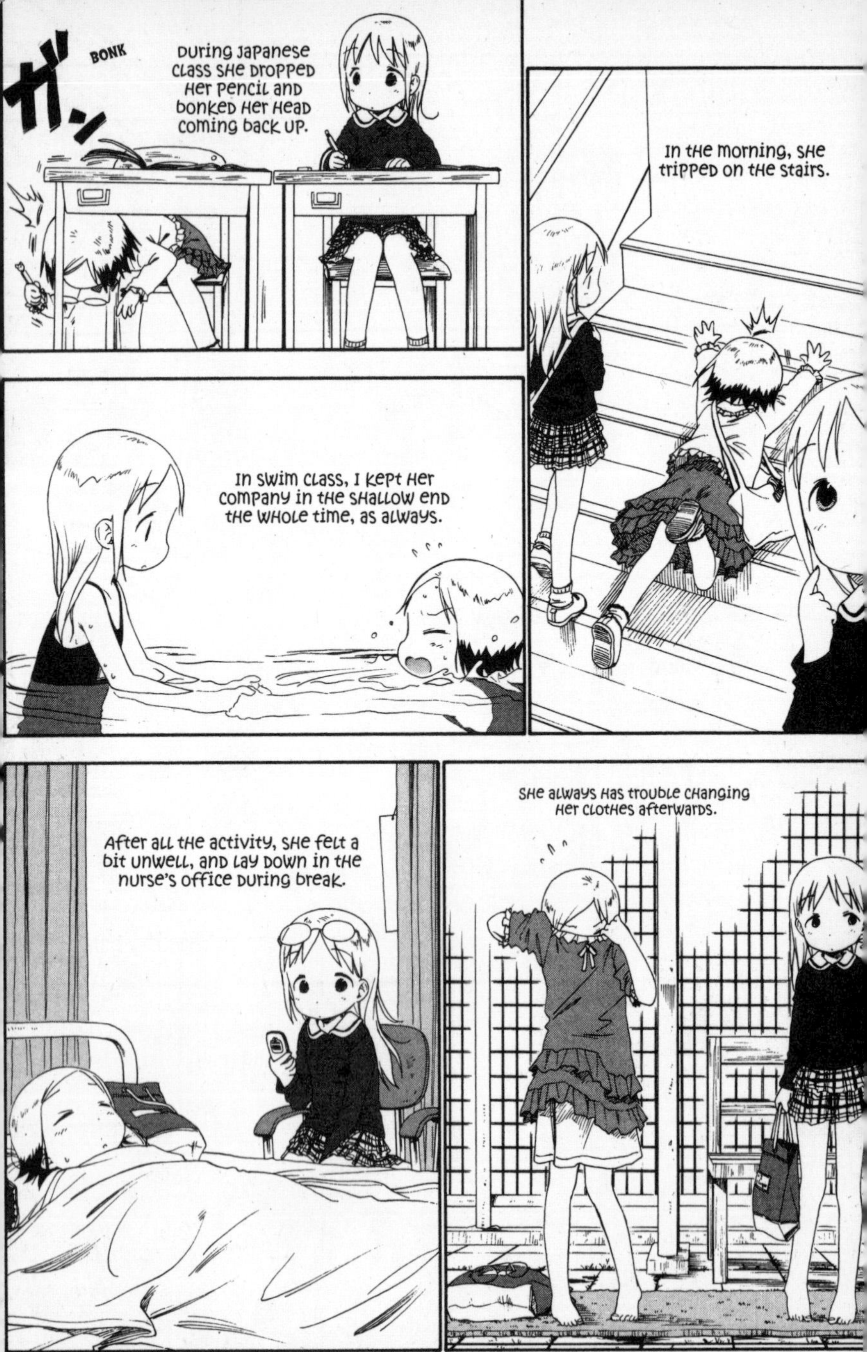
In the morning, she tripped on the stairs.
ガン
BONK
During Japanese class she dropped her pencil and bonked her head coming back up.
In swim class, I kept her company in the shallow end the whole time, as always.
She always has trouble changing her clothes afterwards.
After all the activity, she felt a bit unwell, and lay down in the nurse's office during break.

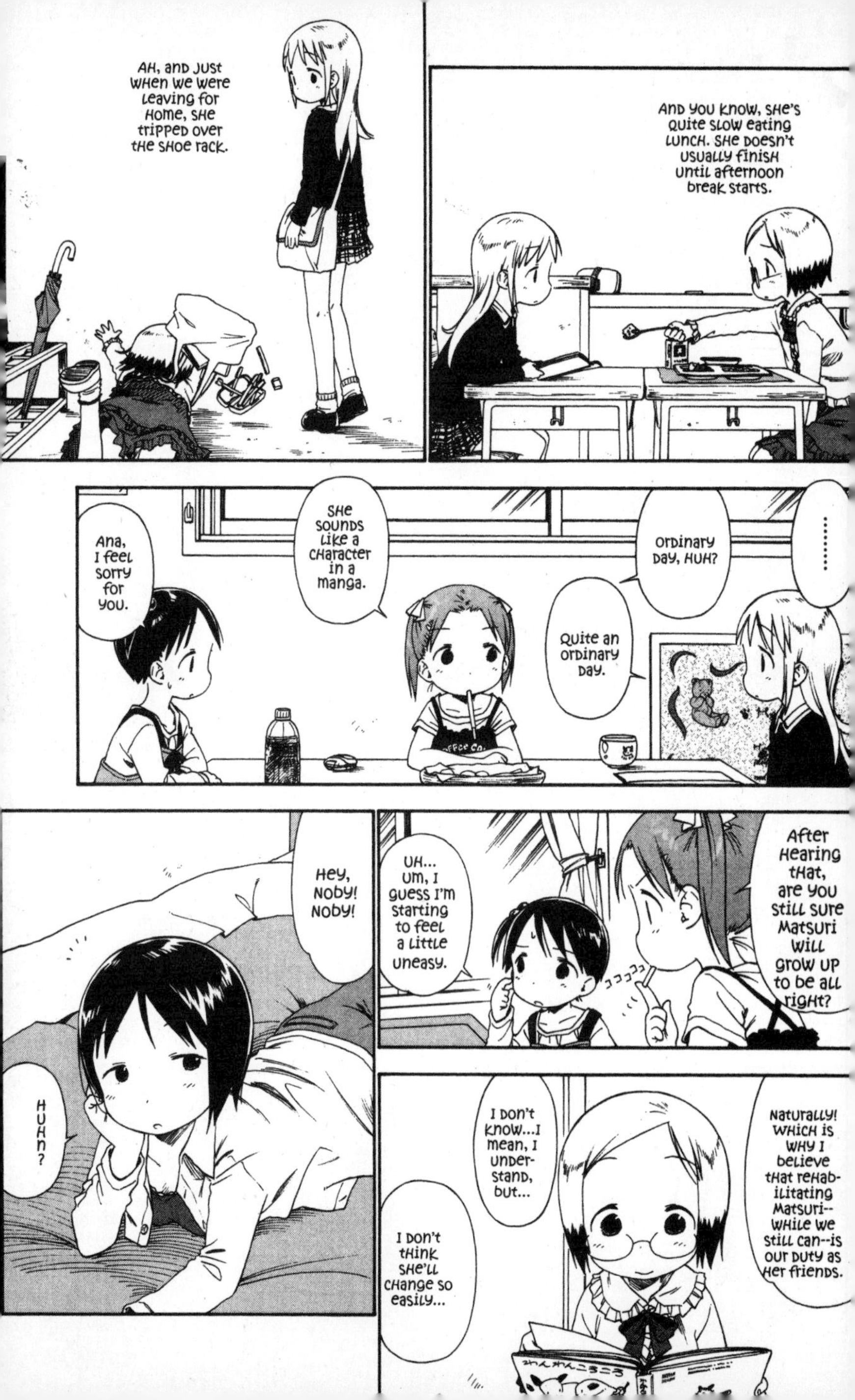
And you know, she's quite slow eating lunch. She doesn't usually finish until afternoon break starts.
Ah, and just when we were leaving for home, she tripped over the shoe rack.
....
Ordinary day, huh?
Quite an ordinary day.
She sounds like a character in a manga.
Ana, I feel sorry for you.
After hearing that, are you still sure Matsuri will grow up to be all right?
Uh... um, I guess I'm starting to feel a little uneasy.
Naturally! Which is why I believe that rehabilitating Matsuri--while we still can--is our duty as her friends.
I don't know...I mean, I under-stand, but...
I don't think she'll change so easily...
Hey, Noby! Noby!
Huhn?

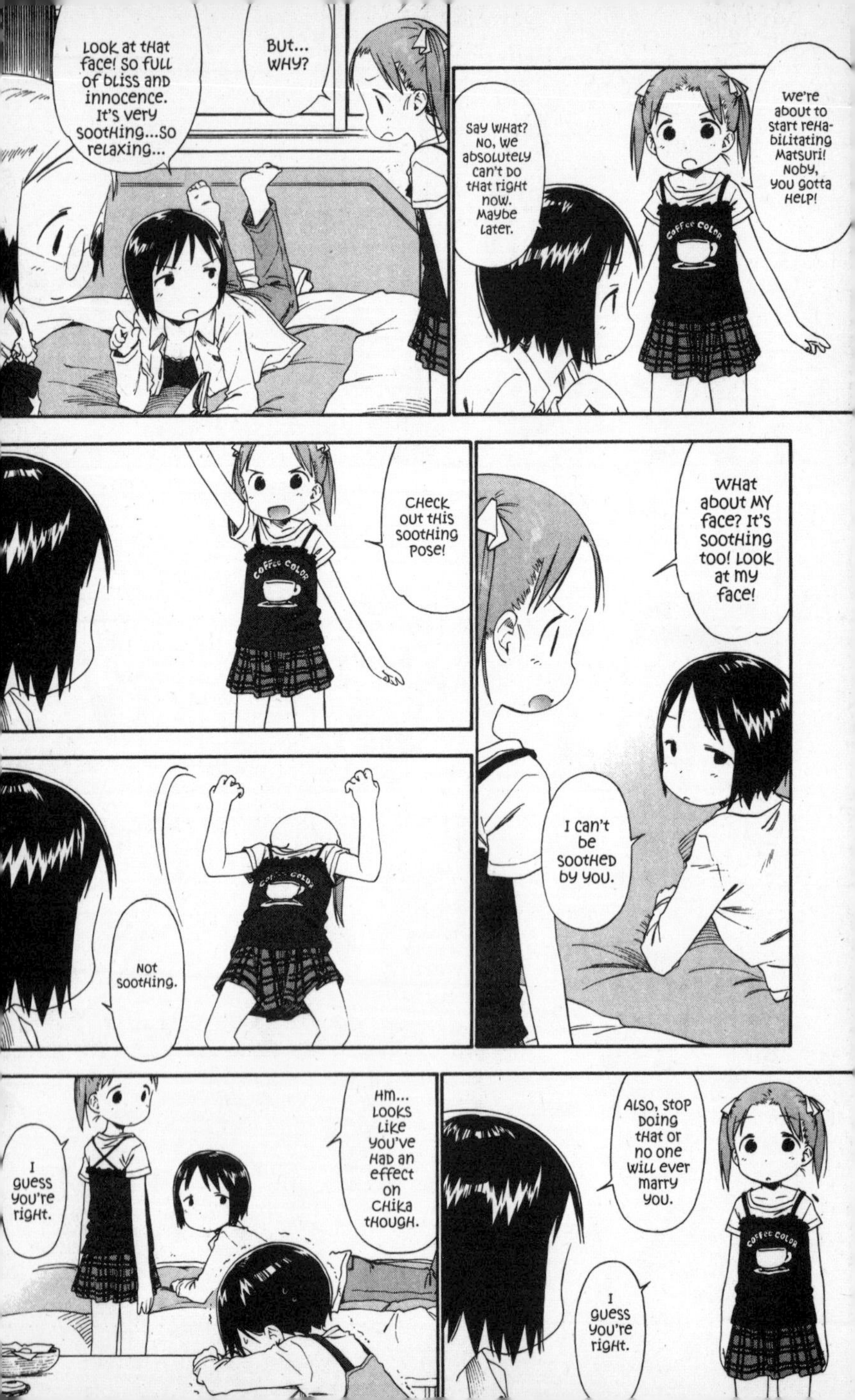
We're about to start rehabilitating Matsuri! Noby, you gotta help!
Say what? No, we absolutely can't do that right now. Maybe later.
But... why?
Look at that face! So full of bliss and innocence. It's very soothing...so relaxing...
What about MY face? It's soothing too! Look at my face!
I can't be soothed by you.
Check out this soothing pose!
Not soothing.
Also, stop doing that or no one will ever marry you.
I guess you're right.
Hm... Looks like you've had an effect on Chika though.
I guess you're right.

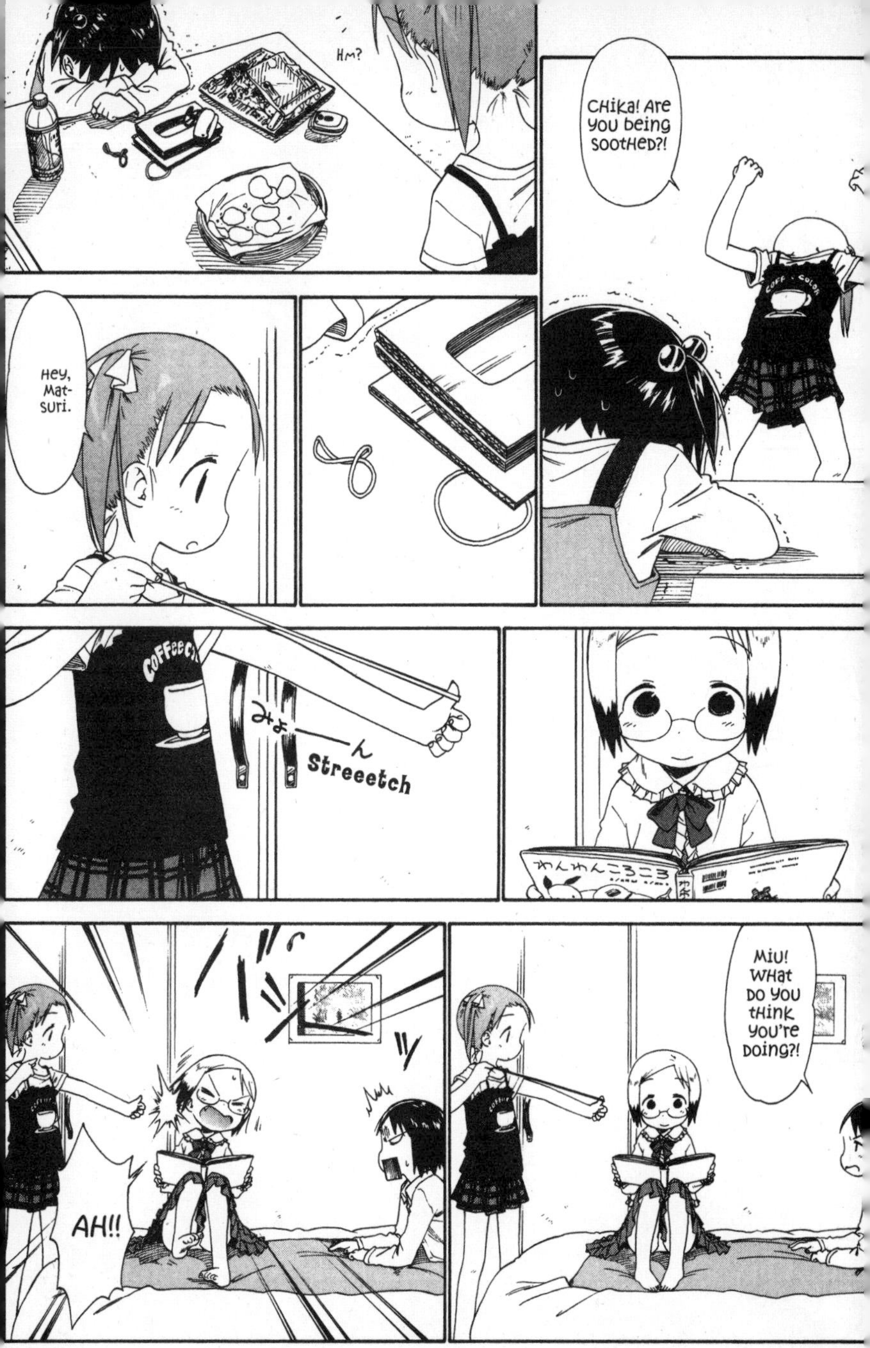
CHika! Are you being soothed?!
Hm?
Hey, Mat-suri.
わんわんころころ
みょーん
Streeetch
Miu! WHat do you tHink you're doing?!
AH!!

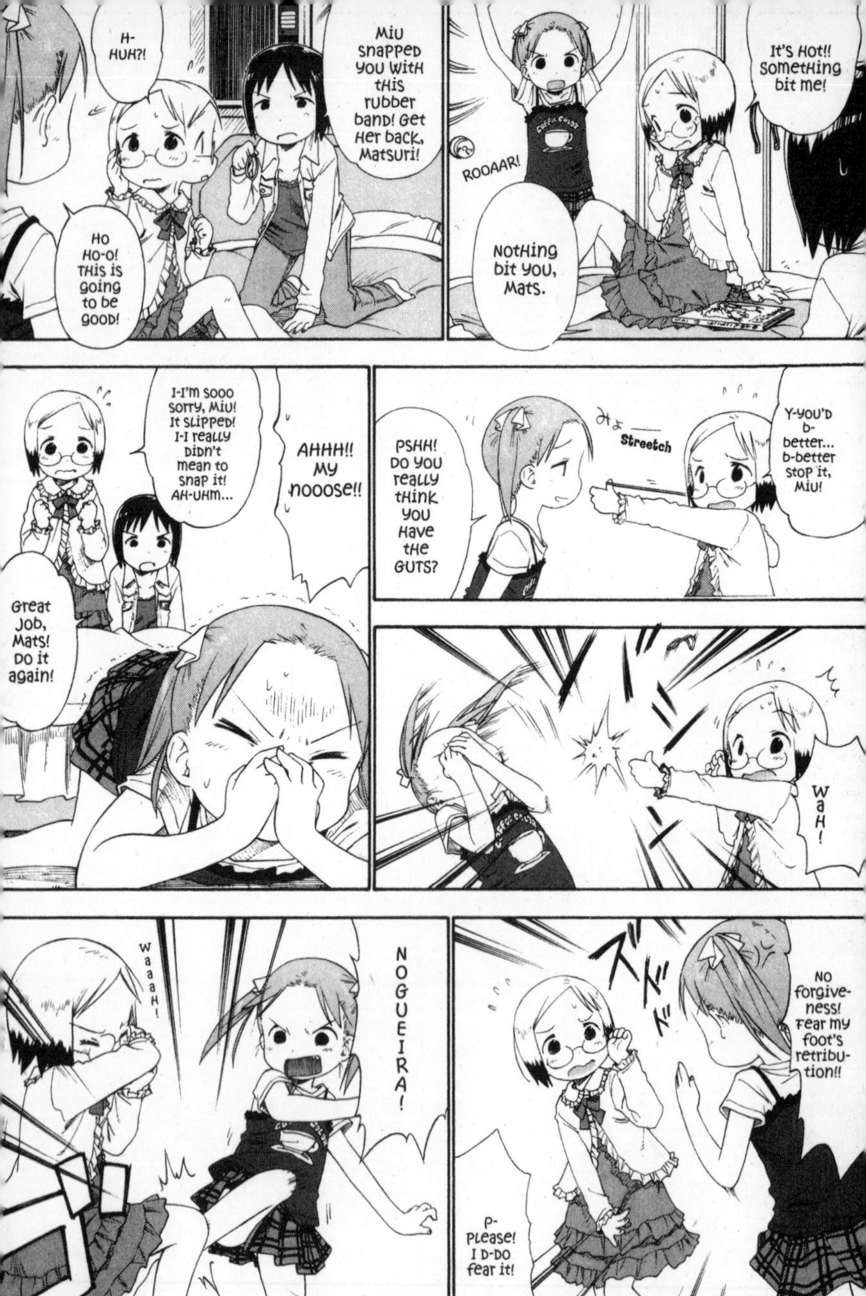

It's Hot!! Something bit me!
ROOAAR!
Nothing bit you, Mats.
H-Huh?!
Miu snapped you with this rubber band! Get her back, Matsuri!
Ho Ho-o! This is going to be good!
Y-You'd b-better... b-better stop it, Miu!
みょ
Streetch
PSHH! Do you really think you have the guts?
Wah!
AHHH!! My noooose!!
I-I'm sooo sorry, Miu! It slipped! I-I really didn't mean to snap it! Ah-uhm...
Great job, Mats! Do it again!
ズドド
No forgive-ness! Fear my foot's retribu-tion!!
P-Please! I D-do fear it!
NOGUEIRA!
Waaaah!

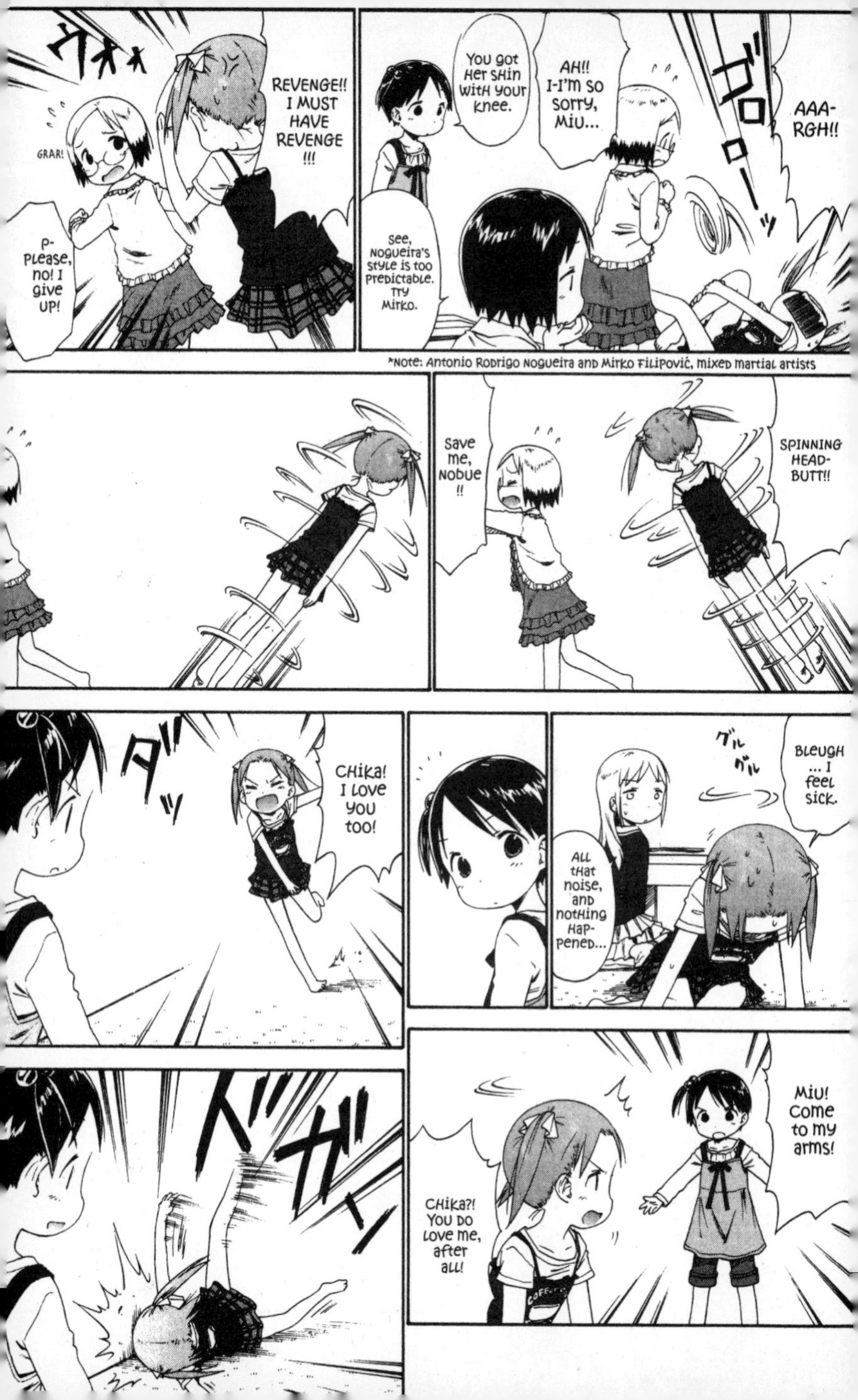
ゴロローッ
AAA-RGH!!
AH!! I-I'm so sorry, Miu...
You got her shin with your knee.
See, Nogueira's style is too predictable. Try Mirko.
ウォォ
REVENGE!! I MUST HAVE REVENGE !!!
GRAR!
P-Please, no! I give up!
*Note: Antonio Rodrigo Nogueira and Mirko Filipović, mixed martial artists
SPINNING HEAD-BUTT!!
Save me, Nobue !!
グル グル
Bleugh ... I feel sick.
All that noise, and nothing happened...
ダッ
Chika! I love you too!
Miu! Come to my arms!
Chika?! You do love me, after all!
ドザッ

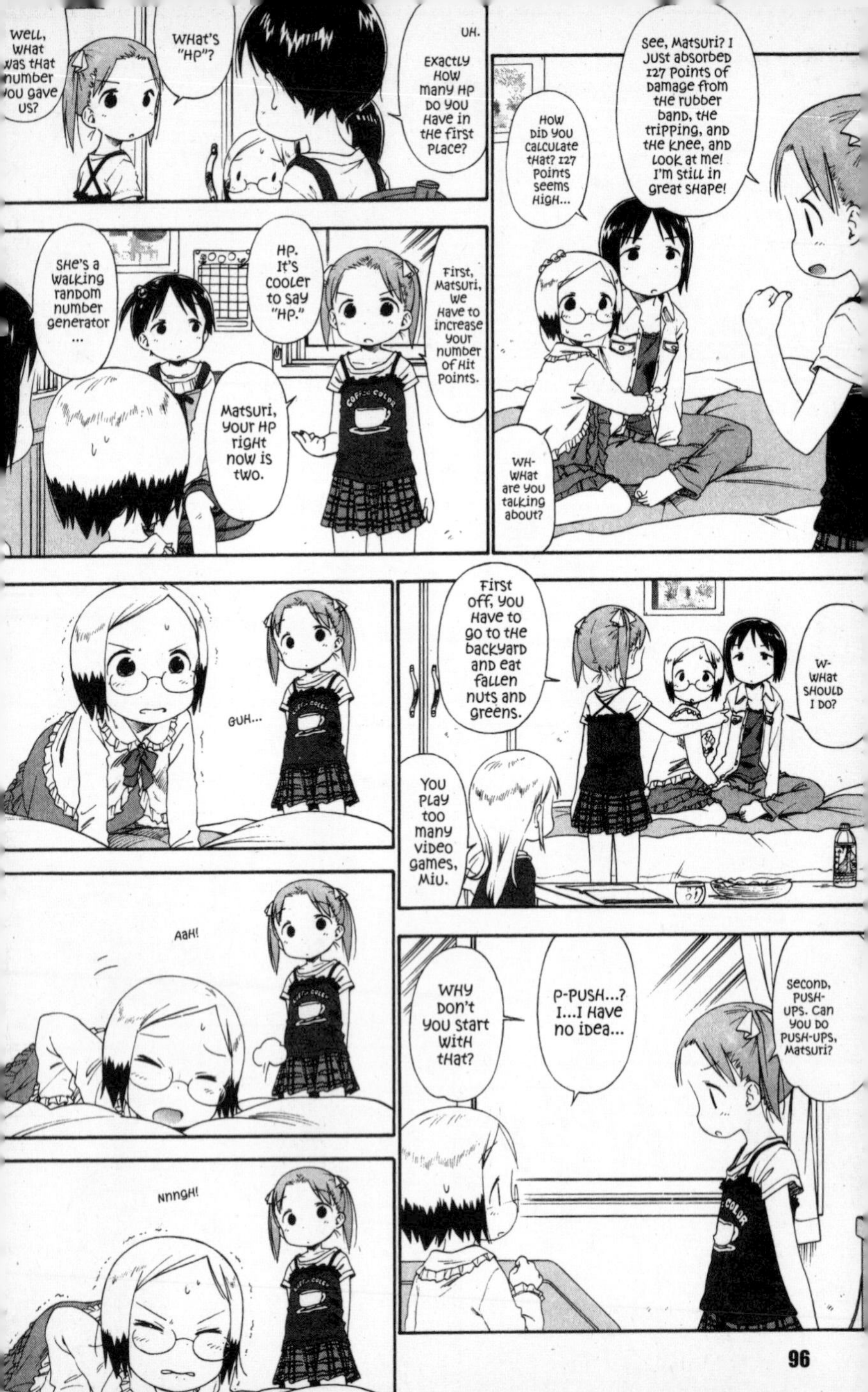
See, Matsuri? I just absorbed 127 points of damage from the rubber band, the tripping, and the knee, and look at me! I'm still in great shape!
How did you calculate that? 127 points seems high...
WH-What are you talking about?
UH.
Exactly how many HP do you have in the first place?
What's "HP"?
Well, what was that number you gave us?
First, Matsuri, we have to increase your number of Hit Points.
HP. It's cooler to say "HP."
Matsuri, your HP right now is two.
She's a walking random number generator ...
W-What should I do?
First off, you have to go to the backyard and eat fallen nuts and greens.
You play too many video games, Miu.
Second, push-ups. Can you do push-ups, Matsuri?
P-Push...? I...I have no idea...
Why don't you start with that?
GUH...
AAH!
NNNGH!

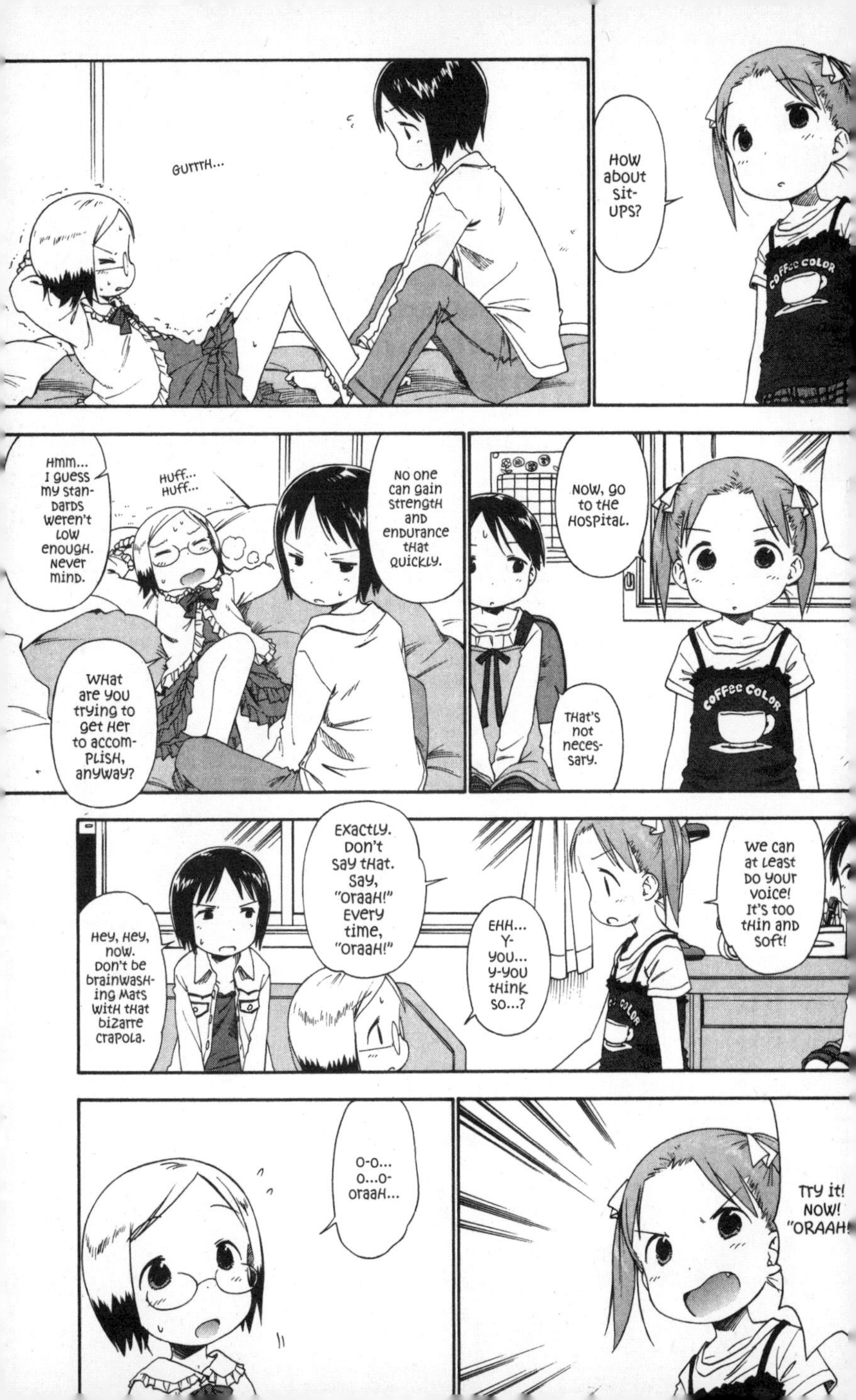
How about sit-ups?
COFFEE COLOR
GURRRH...
Now, go to the hospital.
That's not neces-sary.
No one can gain strength and endurance that quickly.
Huff... Huff...
Hmm... I guess my stan-dards weren't low enough. Never mind.
What are you trying to get her to accom-plish, anyway?
We can at least do your voice! It's too thin and soft!
Ehh... Y-you... y-you think so...?
Exactly. Don't say that. Say, "Oraah!" Every time, "Oraah!"
Hey, hey, now. Don't be brainwash-ing Mats with that bizarre crapola.
Try it! Now! "ORAAH!
O-o... o...o-oraah...

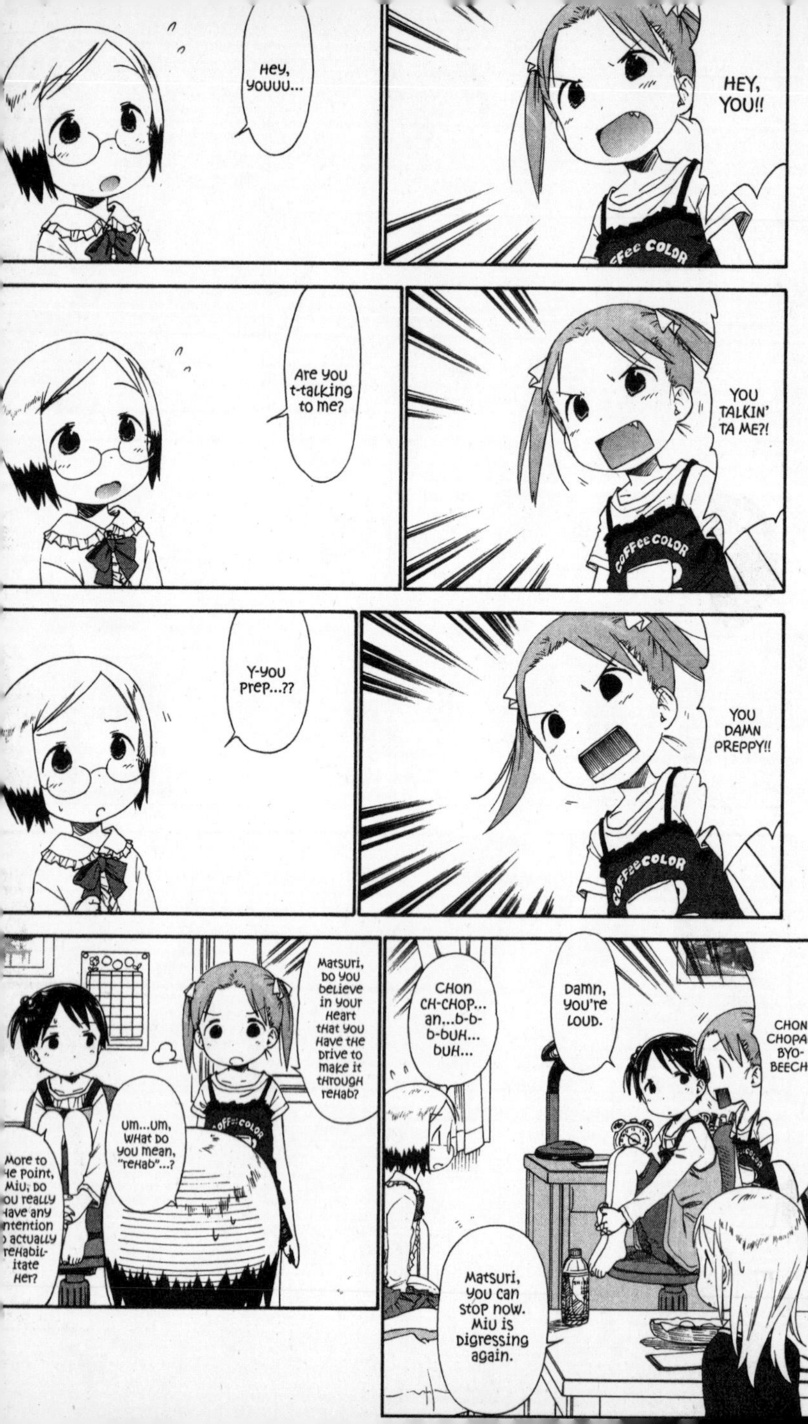
HEY, YOU!!
Hey, youuu...
YOU TALKIN' TA ME?!
Are you t-talking to me?
YOU DAMN PREPPY!!
Y-you prep...??
CHON CHOPAN BYO-BEECH!
Damn, you're loud.
CHON CH-CHOP... an...b-b-b-buh... buh...
Matsuri, you can stop now. Miu is digressing again.
Matsuri, do you believe in your heart that you have the drive to make it through rehab?
um...um, what do you mean, "rehab"...?
More to he point, Miu; do ou really have any ntention o actually rehabil-itate her?

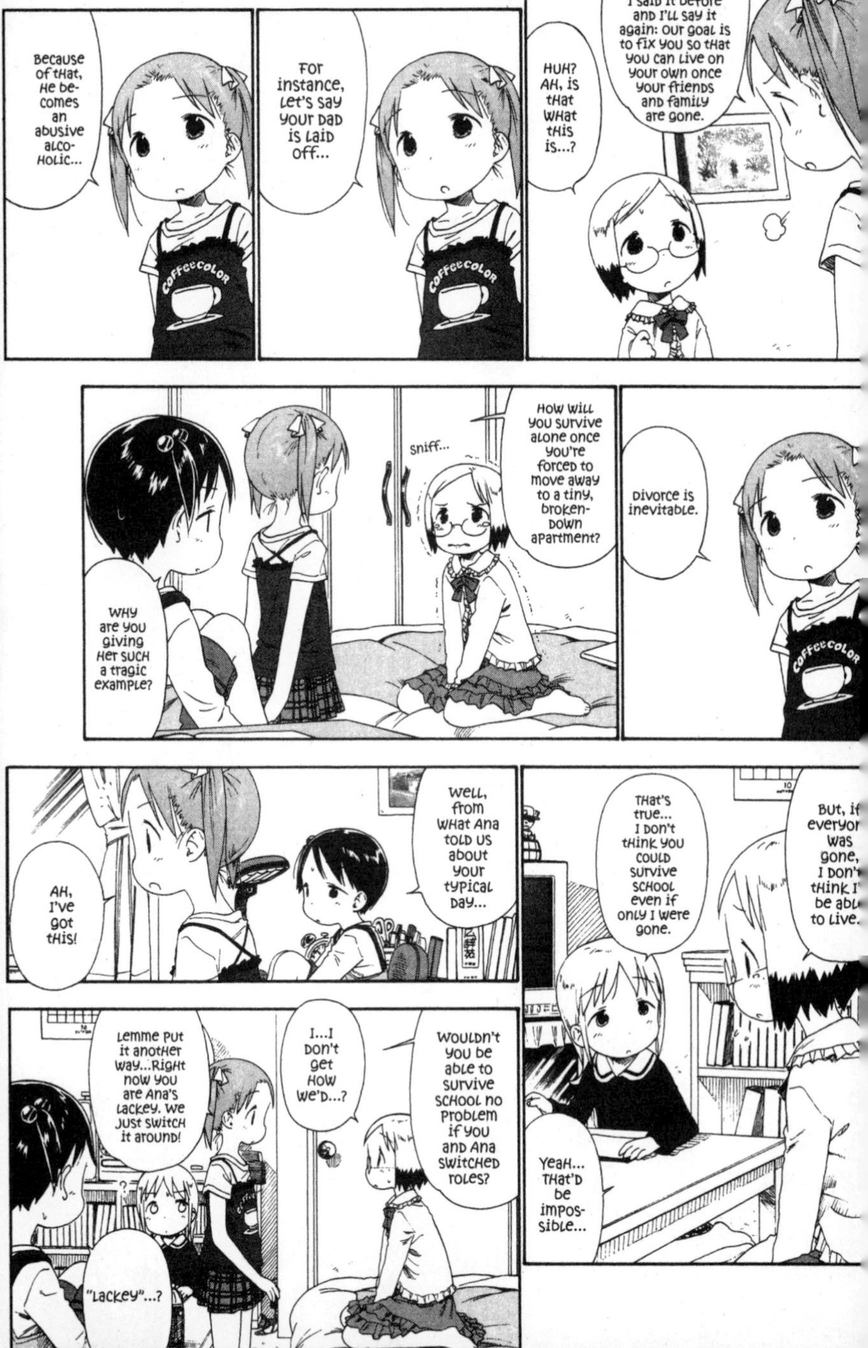
I said it before and I'll say it again: our goal is to fix you so that you can live on your own once your friends and family are gone.
Huh? Ah, is that what this is...?
For instance, let's say your dad is laid off...
Because of that, he becomes an abusive alcoholic...
Divorce is inevitable.
How will you survive alone once you're forced to move away to a tiny, broken-down apartment?
Sniff...
Why are you giving her such a tragic example?
But, if everyor was gone, I don' think I' be abl to live.
That's true... I don't think you could survive school even if only I were gone.
Yeah... That'd be impossible...
Well, from what Ana told us about your typical day...
Ah, I've got this!
Wouldn't you be able to survive school no problem if you and Ana switched roles?
I...I don't get how we'd...?
Lemme put it another way...Right now you are Ana's lackey. We just switch it around!
"Lackey"...?

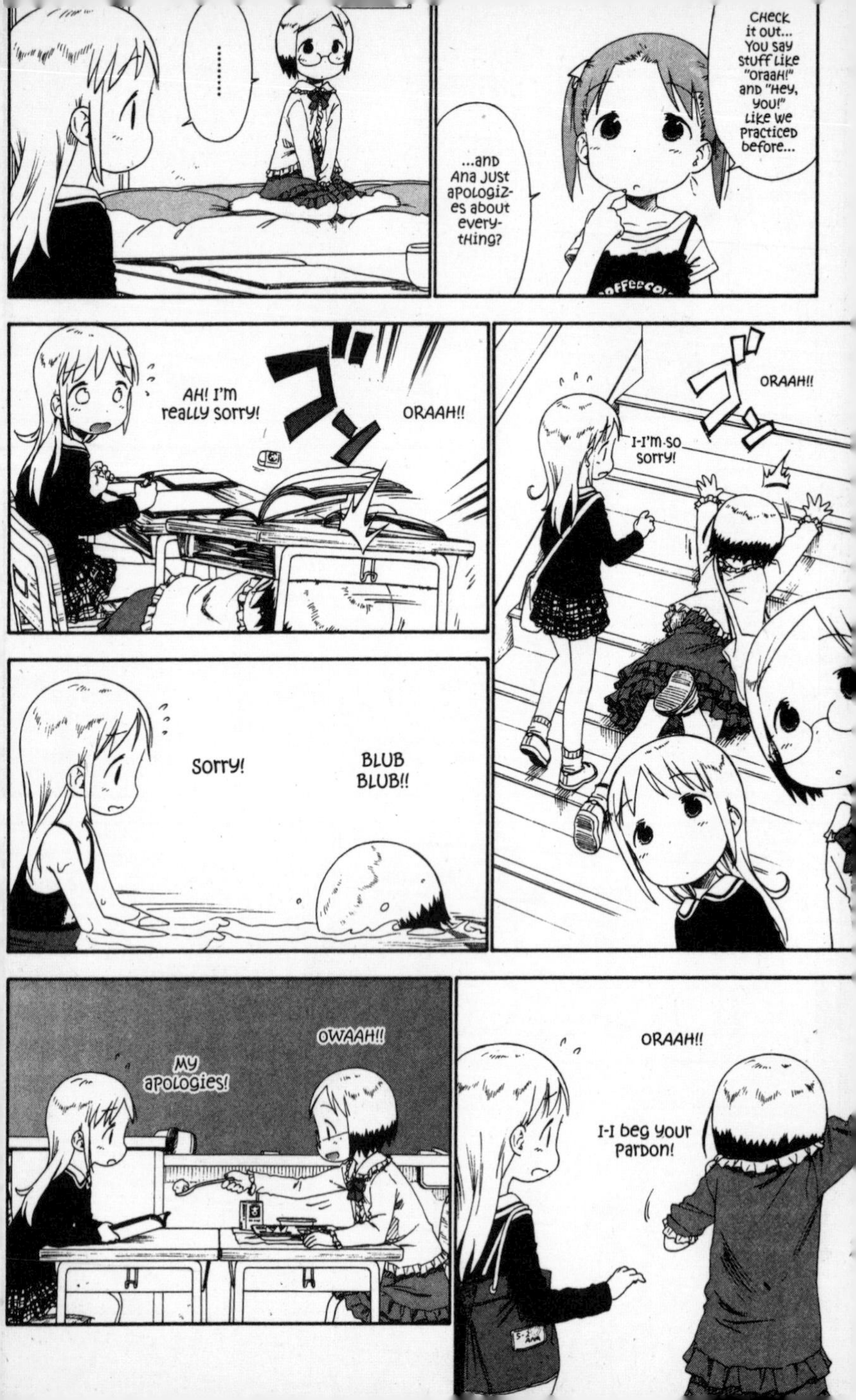
Check it out... You say stuff like "oraah!" and "Hey, you!" like we practiced before...
...and Ana just apologizes about every-thing?
....
ゴッ
ORAAH!!
I-I'm so sorry!
ORAAH!!
ゴッ
AH! I'm really sorry!
BLUB BLUB!!
Sorry!
ORAAH!!
I-I beg your pardon!
OWAAH!!
My apologies!

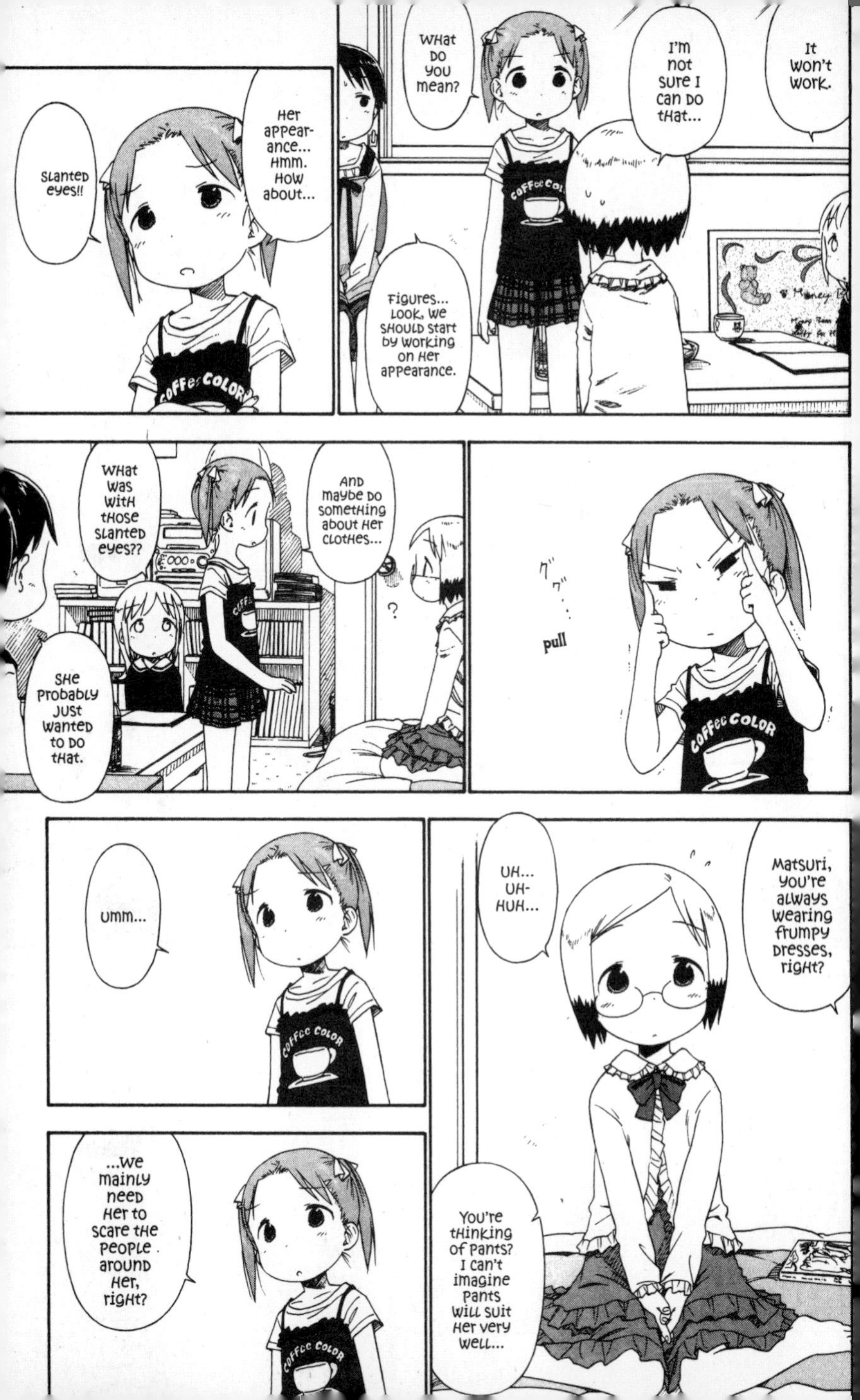

It won't work.
I'm not sure I can do that...
What do you mean?
Figures... Look, we should start by working on her appearance.
Her appearance... Hmm. How about...
Slanted eyes!!
pull
And maybe do something about her clothes...
What was with those slanted eyes??
?
She probably just wanted to do that.
Matsuri, you're always wearing frumpy dresses, right?
Uh... Uh-huh...
You're thinking of pants? I can't imagine pants will suit her very well...
umm...
...we mainly need her to scare the people around her, right?

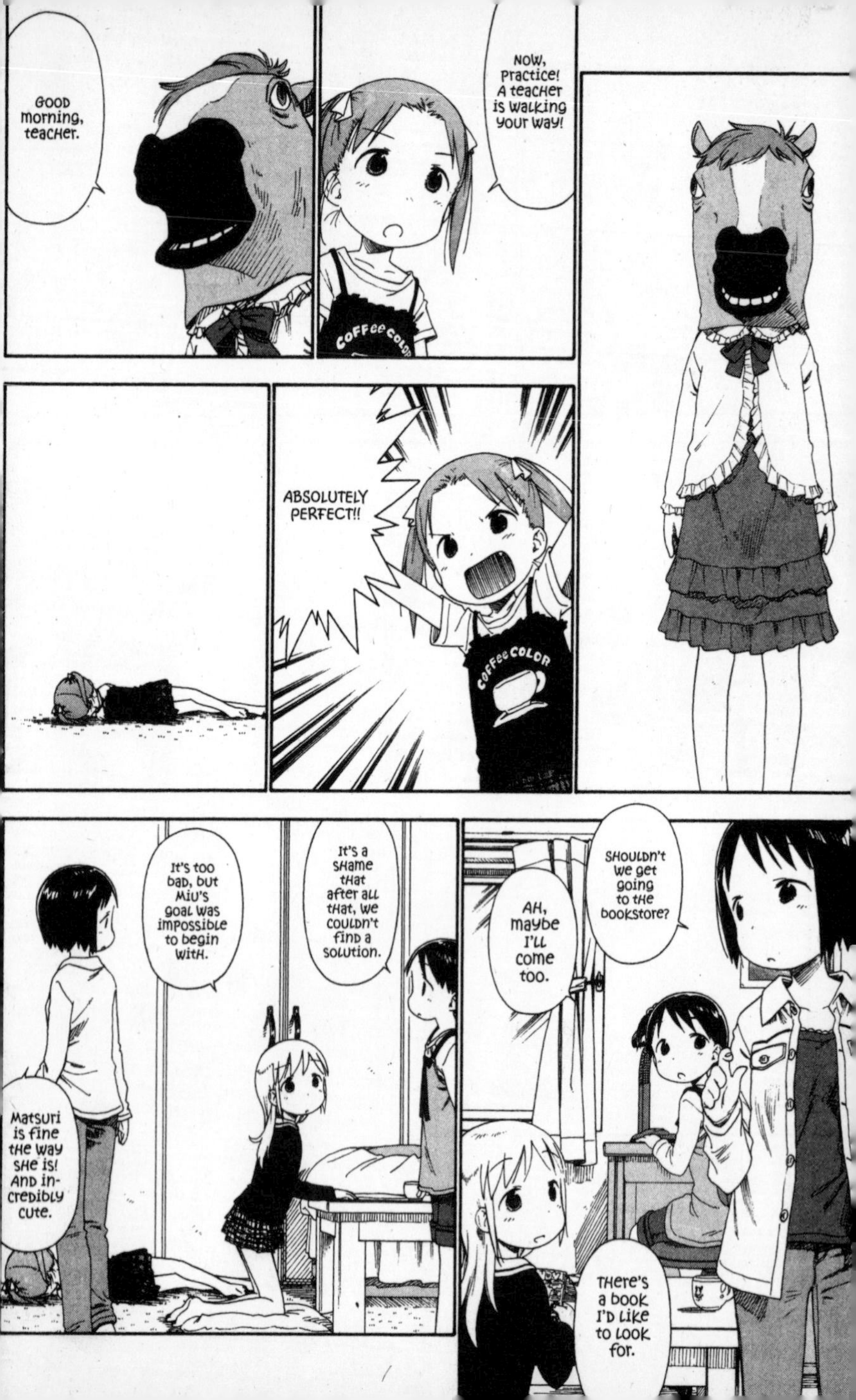
Now, practice! A teacher is walking your way!
Good morning, teacher.
ABSOLUTELY PERFECT!!
Shouldn't we get going to the bookstore?
Ah, maybe I'll come too.
There's a book I'd like to look for.
It's a shame that after all that, we couldn't find a solution.
It's too bad, but Miu's goal was impossible to begin with.
Matsuri is fine the way she is! And incredibly cute.

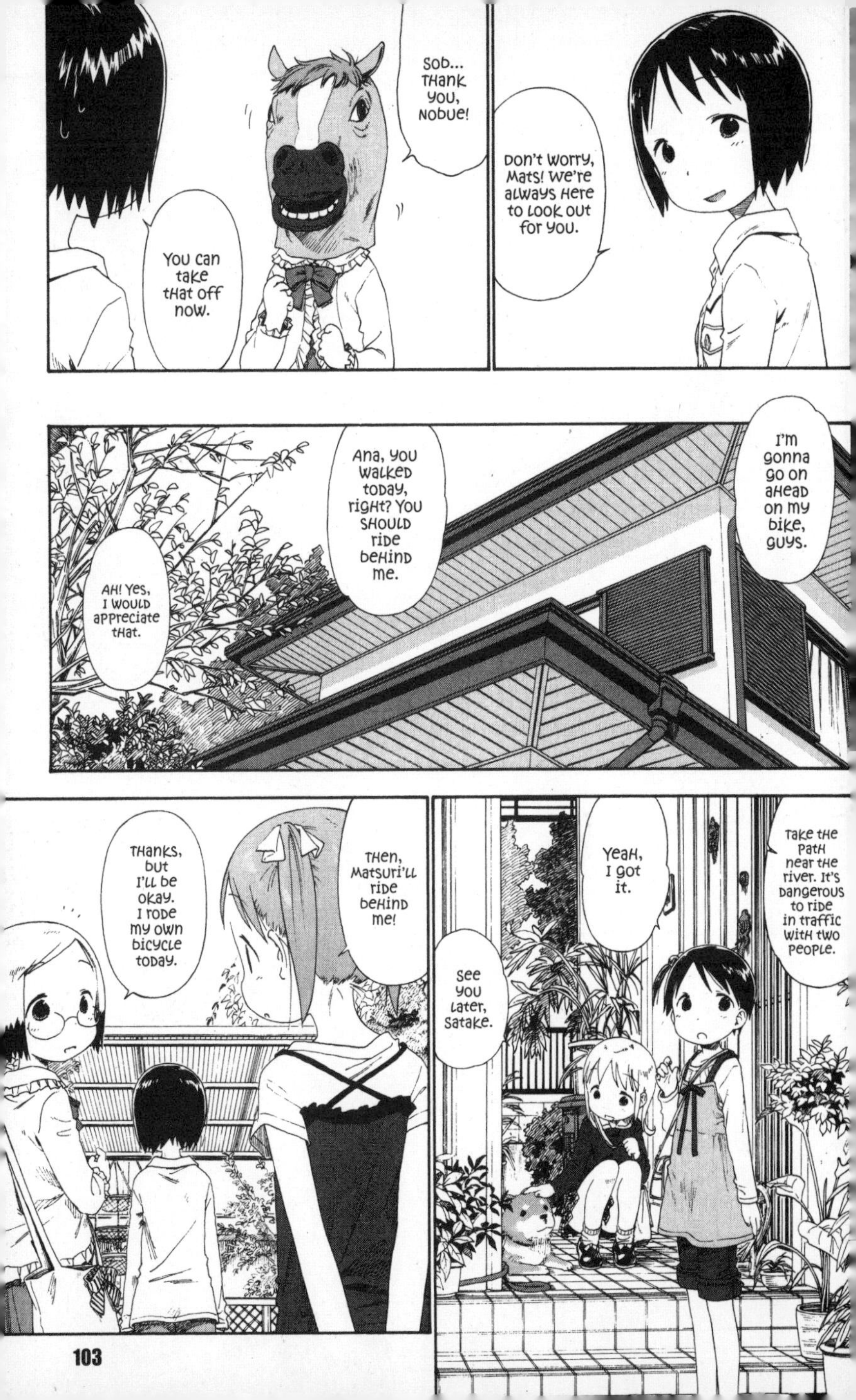
Don't worry, Mats! We're always here to look out for you.
Sob... Thank you, Nobue!
You can take that off now.
I'm gonna go on ahead on my bike, guys.
Ana, you walked today, right? You should ride behind me.
Ah! Yes, I would appreciate that.
Take the path near the river. It's dangerous to ride in traffic with two people.
Yeah, I got it.
See you later, Satake.
Then, Matsuri'll ride behind me!
Thanks, but I'll be okay. I rode my own bicycle today.

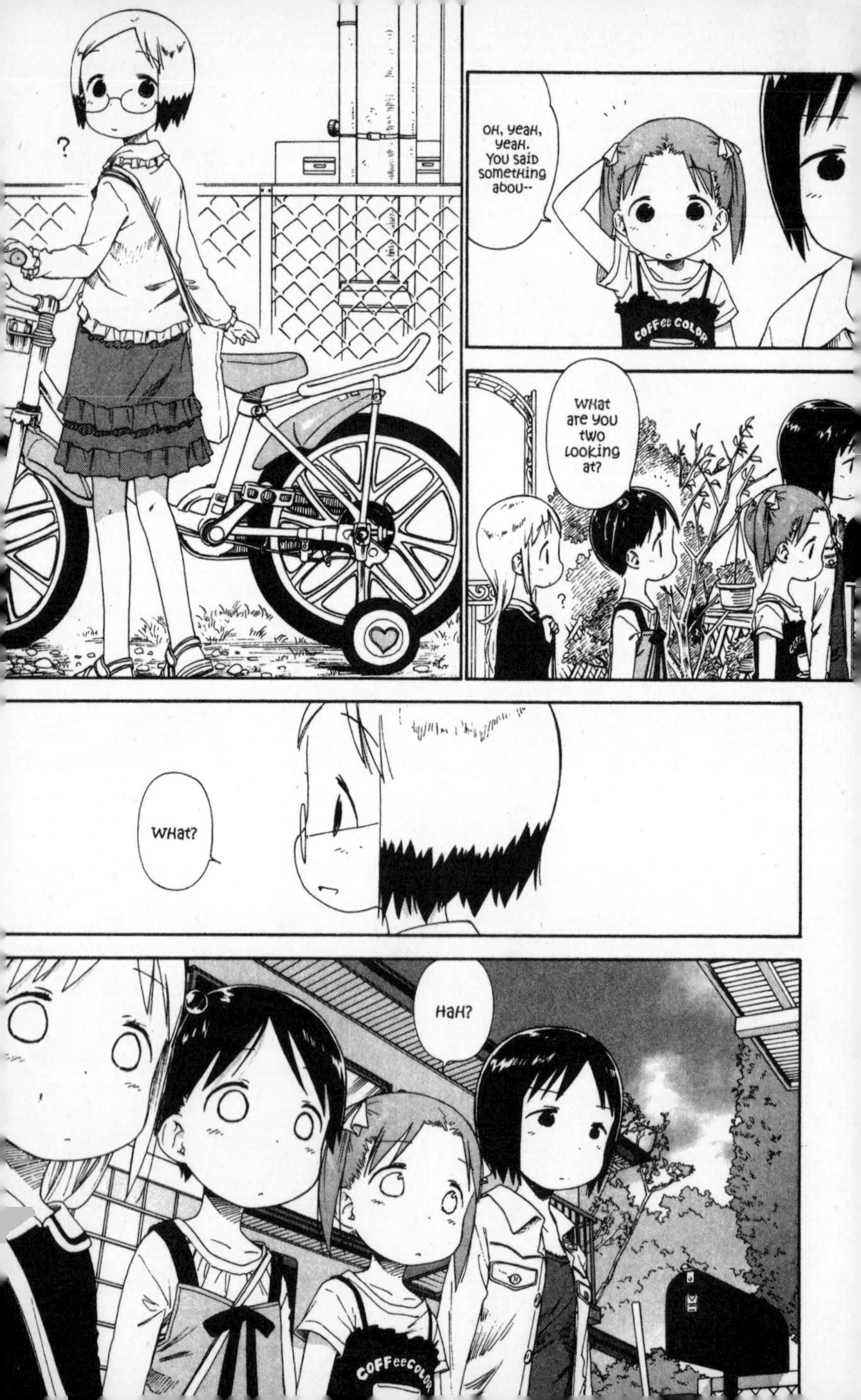
Oh, yeah, yeah. You said something abou--
What are you two looking at?
What?
Hah?

Spring	Chika
Summer	Miu
	Matsuri
Autumn	Ana
Winter	Nobue

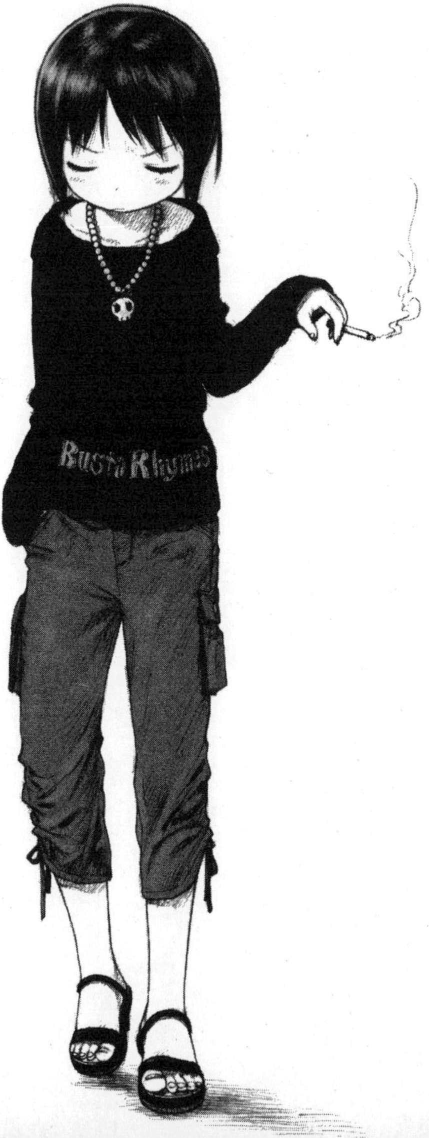
Busta Rhymes

Spring — Chika

Summer — Miu

Autumn — Matsuri

Winter — Ana

Nobue

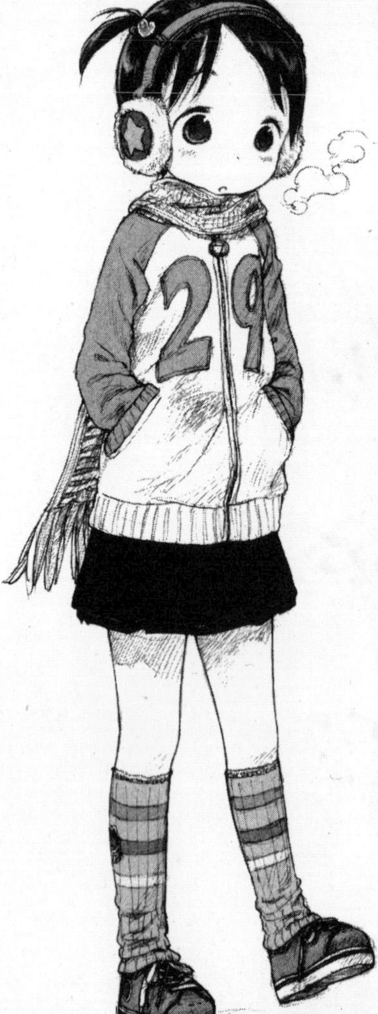

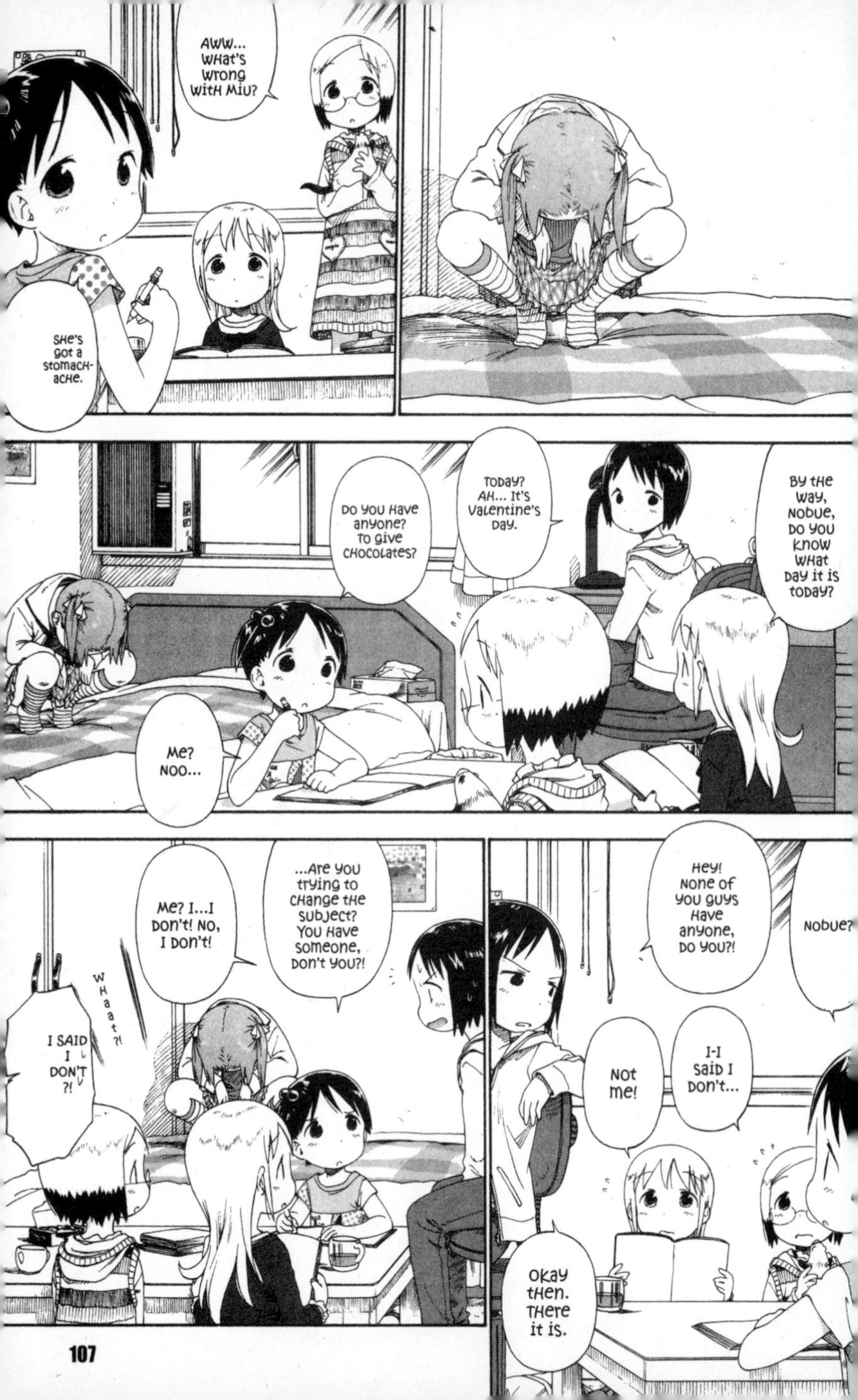
Aww... What's wrong with Miu?
She's got a stomach-ache.
By the way, Nobue, do you know what day it is today?
Today? Ah... It's Valentine's Day.
Do you have anyone? To give chocolates?
Me? Noo...
Nobue?
Hey! None of you guys have anyone, do you?!
I-I said I don't...
Not me!
Okay then. There it is.
...Are you trying to change the subject? You have someone, don't you?!
Me? I...I don't! No, I don't!
Whaaat?!
I SAID I DON'T?!

episode.49

HEART ATTACKS

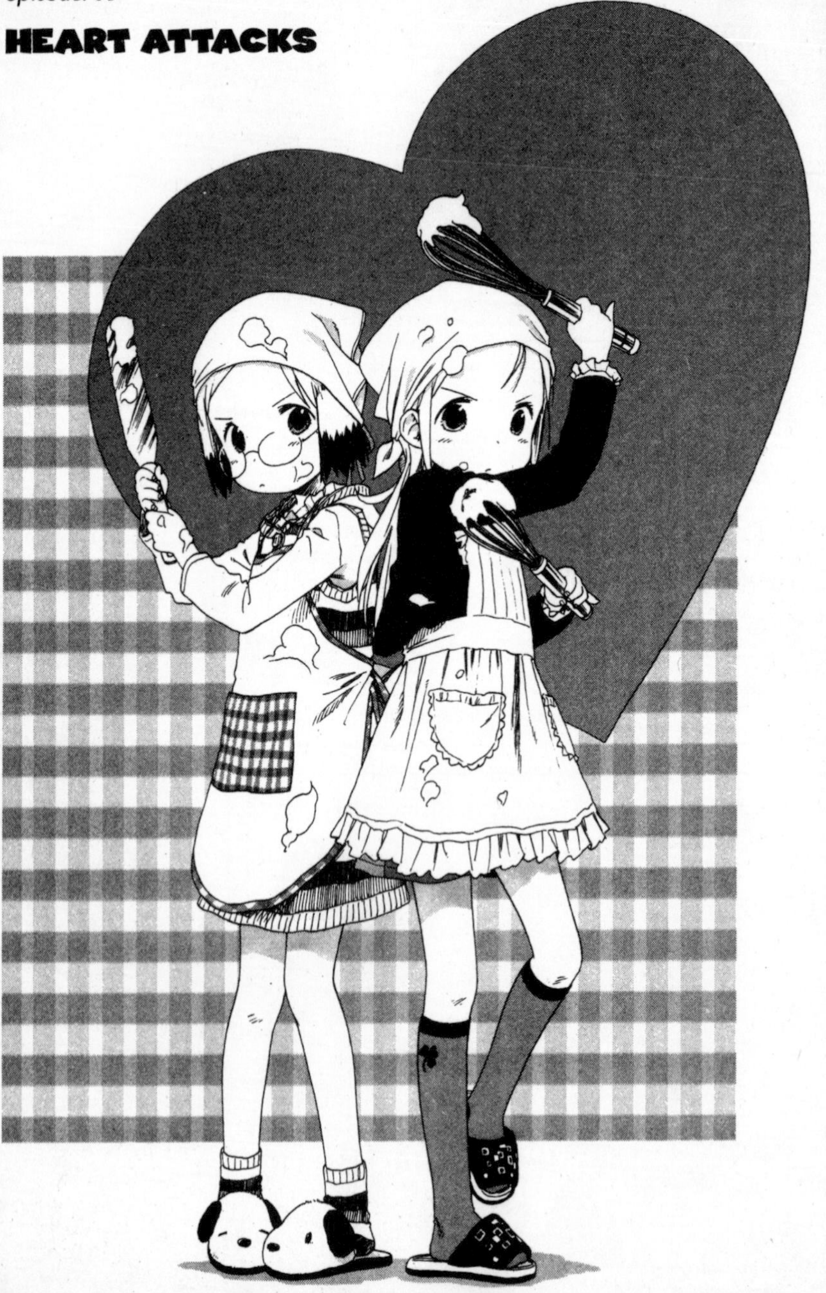

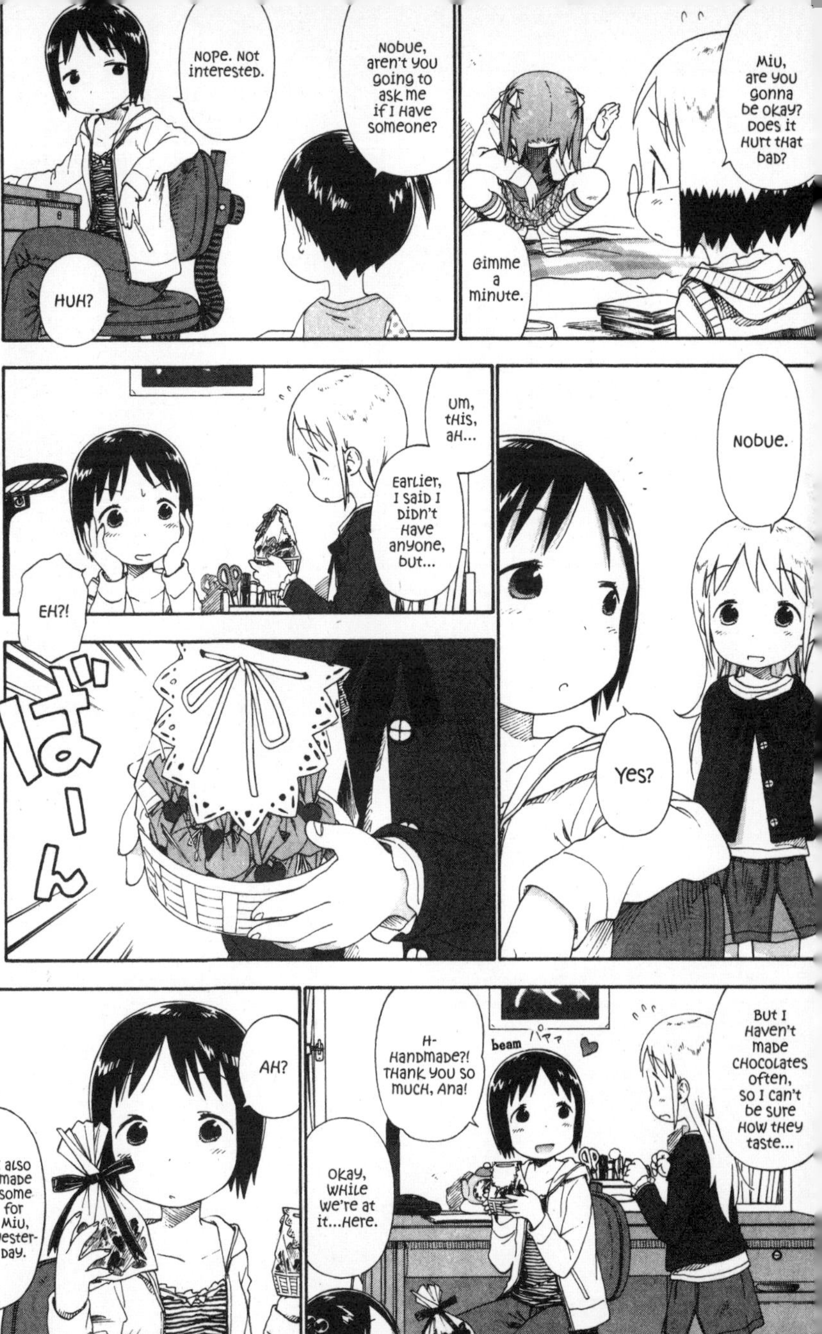
Miu, are you gonna be okay? Does it hurt that bad?
Gimme a minute.
Nobue, aren't you going to ask me if I have someone?
Nope. Not interested.
Huh?
Nobue.
Yes?
Um, this, ah...
Earlier, I said I didn't have anyone, but...
Eh?!
ばーん
But I haven't made chocolates often, so I can't be sure how they taste...
beam パァァ
H-handmade?! Thank you so much, Ana!
Okay, while we're at it...Here.
Ah?
I also made some for Miu, yester-day.

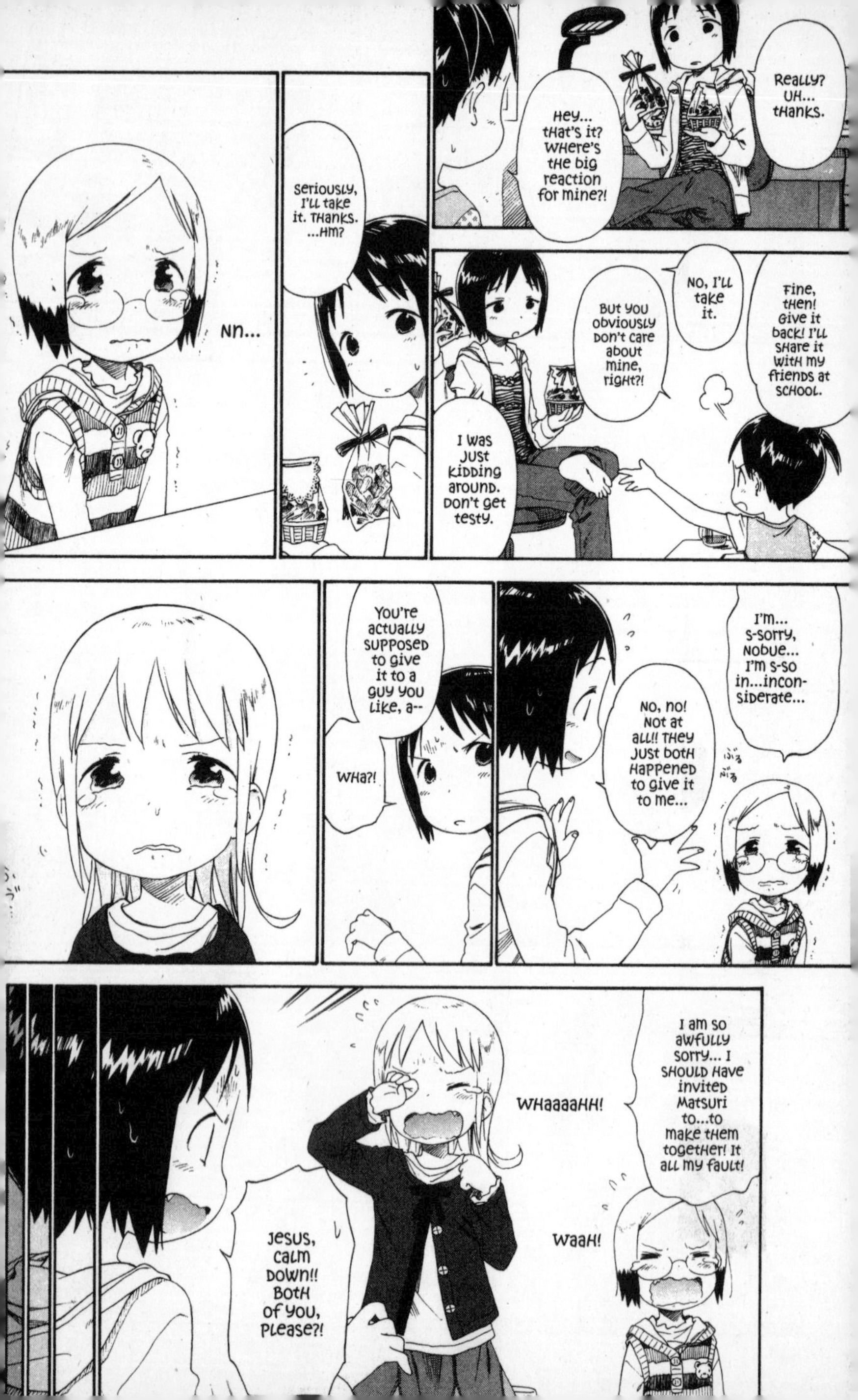
Really? Uh... thanks.
Hey... that's it? Where's the big reaction for mine?!
Fine, then! Give it back! I'll share it with my friends at school.
No, I'll take it.
But you obviously don't care about mine, right?!
I was just kidding around. Don't get testy.
Seriously, I'll take it. Thanks. ...Hm?
Nn...
I'm... s-sorry, Nobue... I'm s-so in...inconsiderate...
No, no! Not at all!! They just both happened to give it to me...
You're actually supposed to give it to a guy you like, a--
Wha?!
I am so awfully sorry... I should have invited Matsuri to...to make them together! It all my fault!
Waah!
Whaaaahh!
Jesus, calm down!! Both of you, please?!

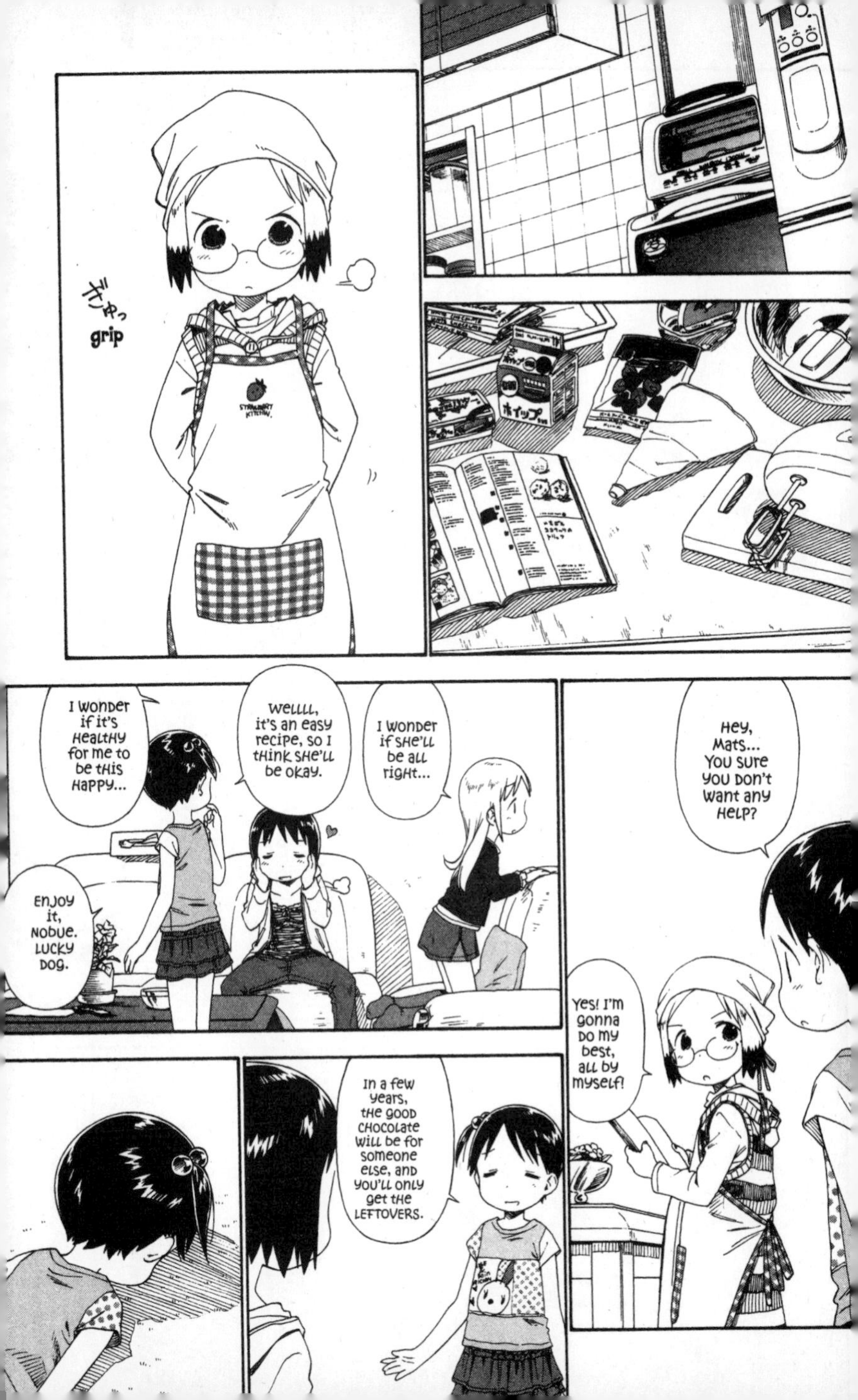
ぎゅっ
grip
Hey, Mats... You sure you don't want any help?
Yes! I'm gonna do my best, all by myself!
I wonder if she'll be all right...
Wellll, it's an easy recipe, so I think she'll be okay.
I wonder if it's healthy for me to be this happy...
Enjoy it, Nobue. Lucky dog.
In a few years, the good chocolate will be for someone else, and you'll only get the leftovers.

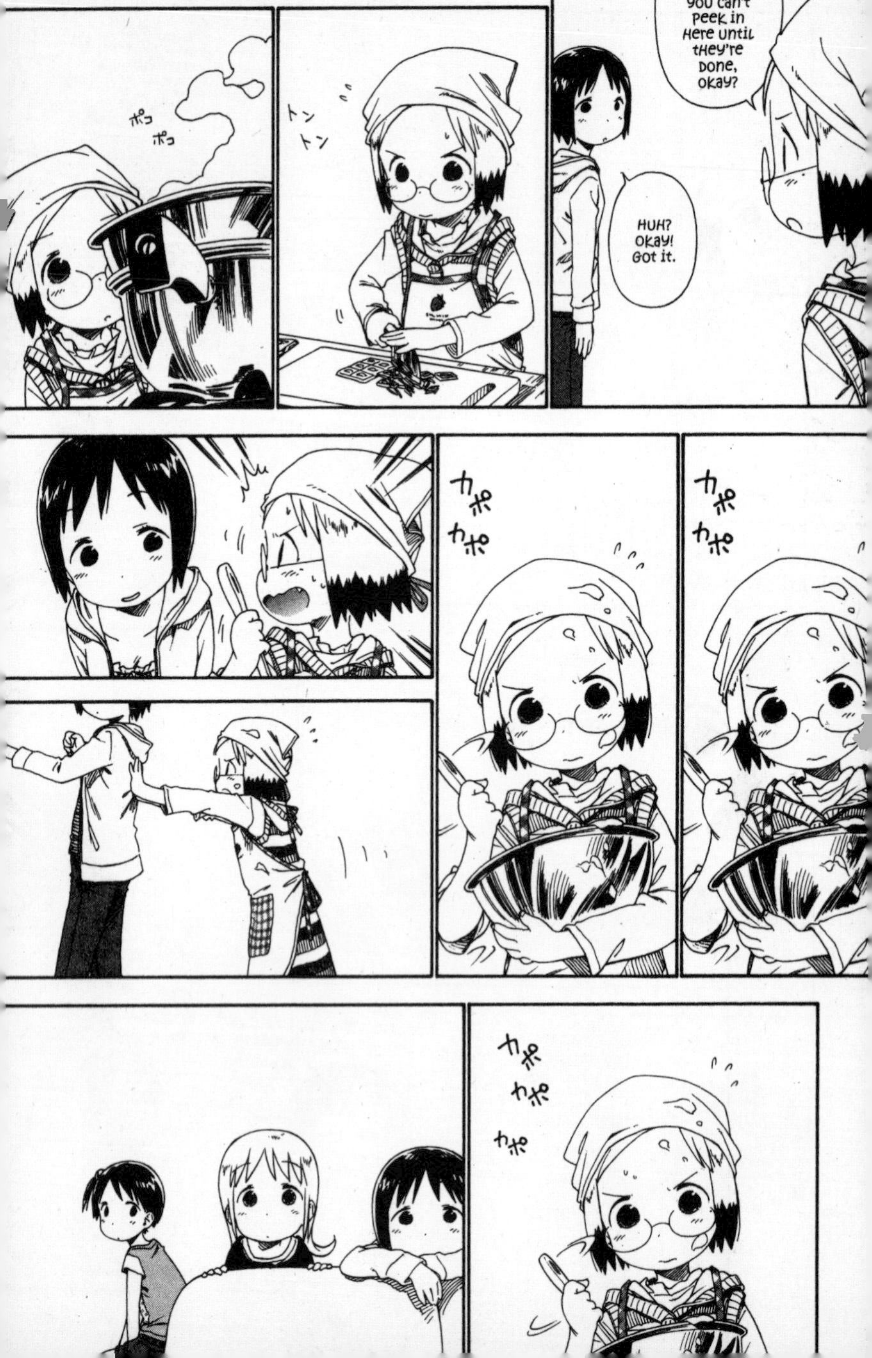
Noby, you can't peek in here until they're done, okay?
Huh? Okay! Got it.
トン
トン
ポコ
ポコ
カポ
カポ
カポ
カポ
カポ
カポ
カポ

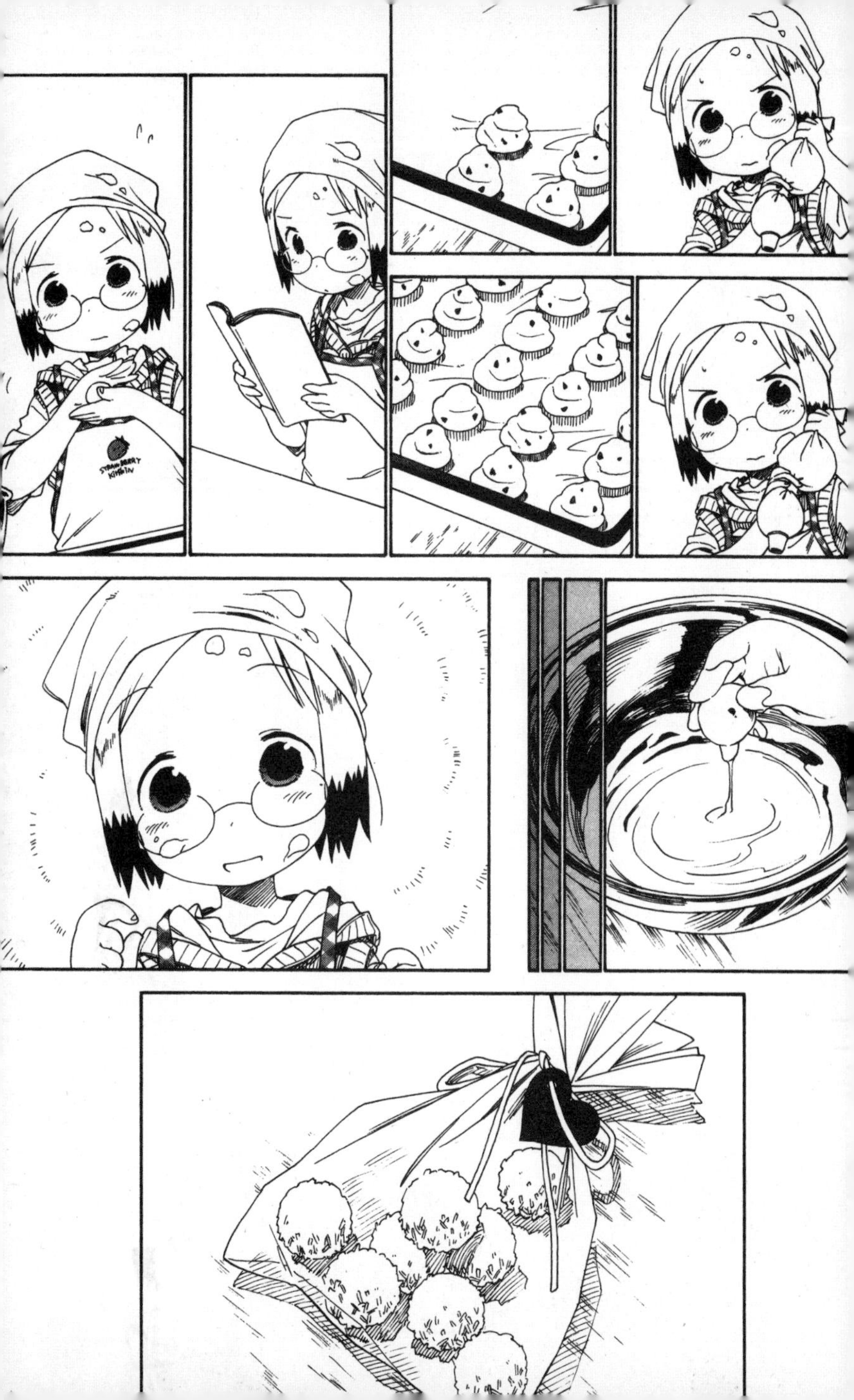

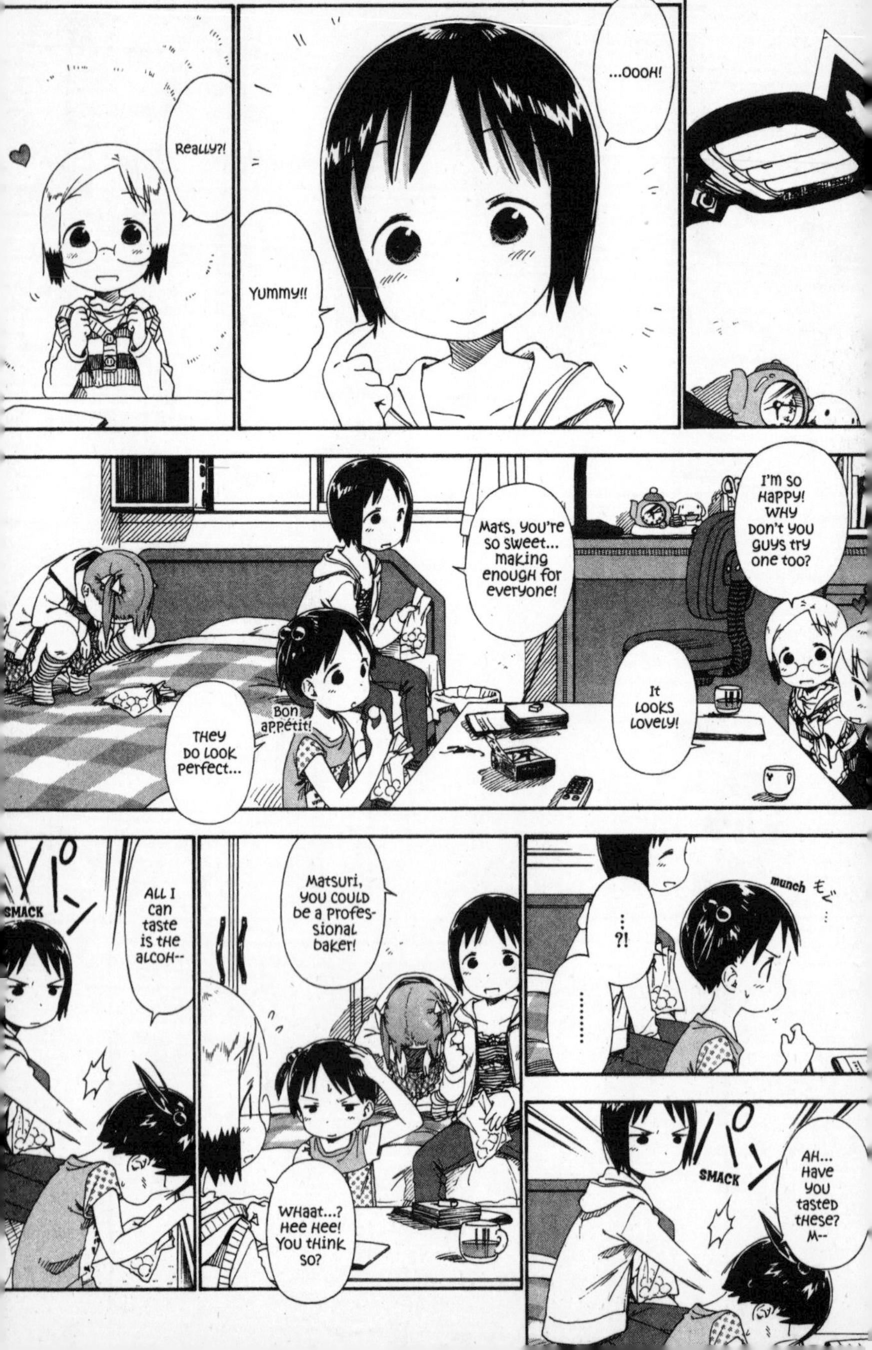

...OOOH!
Yummy!!
Really?!
I'm so happy! WHY don't you guys try one too?
It looks lovely!
Mats, you're so sweet... making enough for everyone!
Bon appétit!
THEY DO LOOK perfect...
munch もぐ
...?!
....
AH... Have you tasted these? M--
SMACK
Matsuri, you could be a profes-sional baker!
WHaat...? Hee Hee! You think so?
SMACK
ALL I can taste is the alcoH--

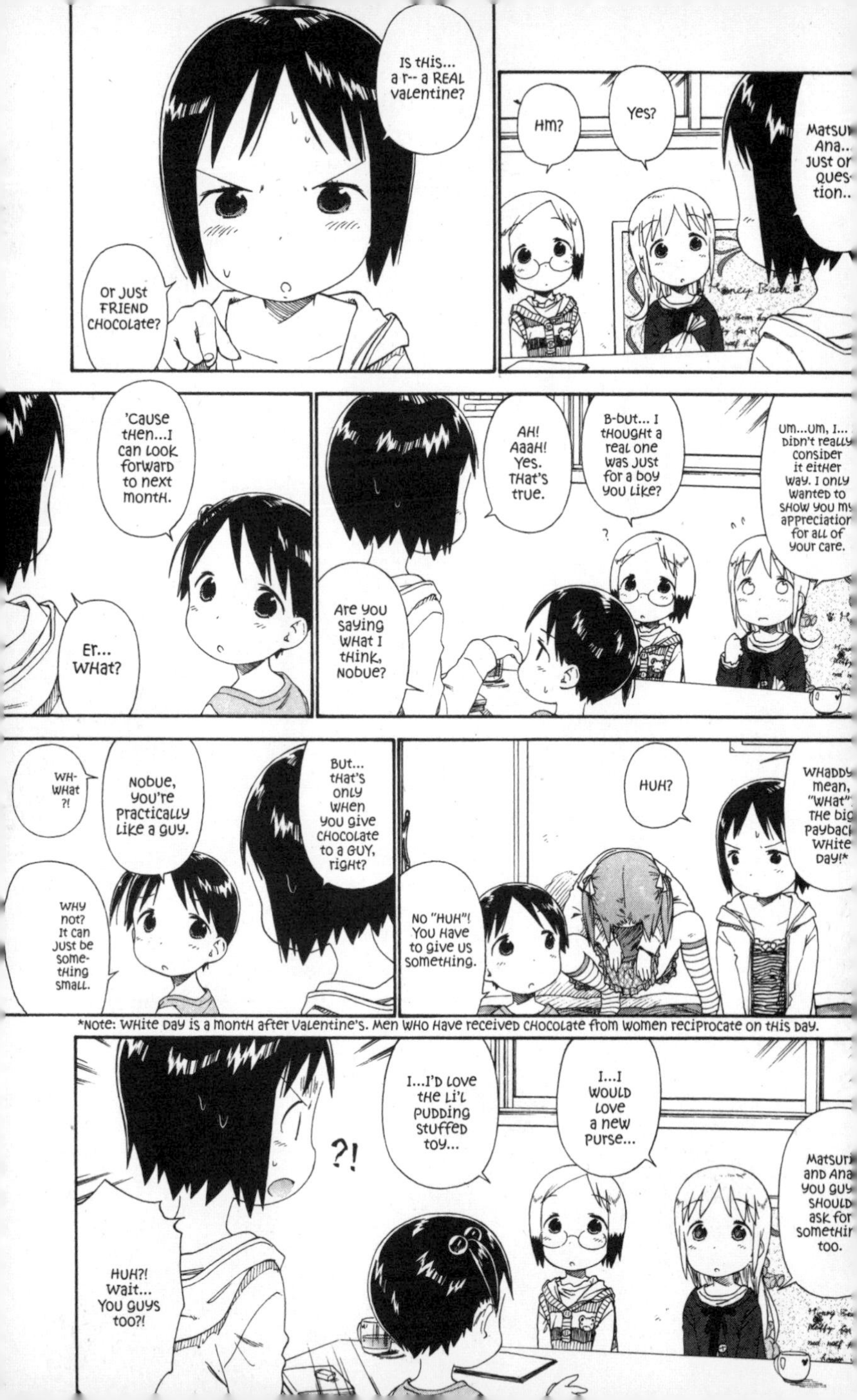
Matsu
Ana..
Just or
Ques-
tion..
Yes?
Hm?
Is this... a r-- a REAL valentine?
Or just FRIEND chocolate?
Um...um, I... didn't really consider it either way. I only wanted to show you my appreciation for all of your care.
B-but... I thought a real one was just for a boy you like?
Ah! Aaah! Yes. That's true.
Are you saying what I think, Nobue?
'Cause then...I can look forward to next month.
Er... what?
Whaddy mean, "what"? The big paybacl White Day!*
Huh?
No "huh"! You have to give us something.
But... that's only when you give chocolate to a guy, right?
Nobue, you're practically like a guy.
Wh-what?!
Why not? It can just be some-thing small.
*Note: White Day is a month after Valentine's. Men who have received chocolate from women reciprocate on this day.
Matsuri and Ana you guy should ask for somethir too.
I...I would love a new purse...
I...I'd love the li'l pudding stuffed toy...
?!
Huh?! Wait... You guys too?!

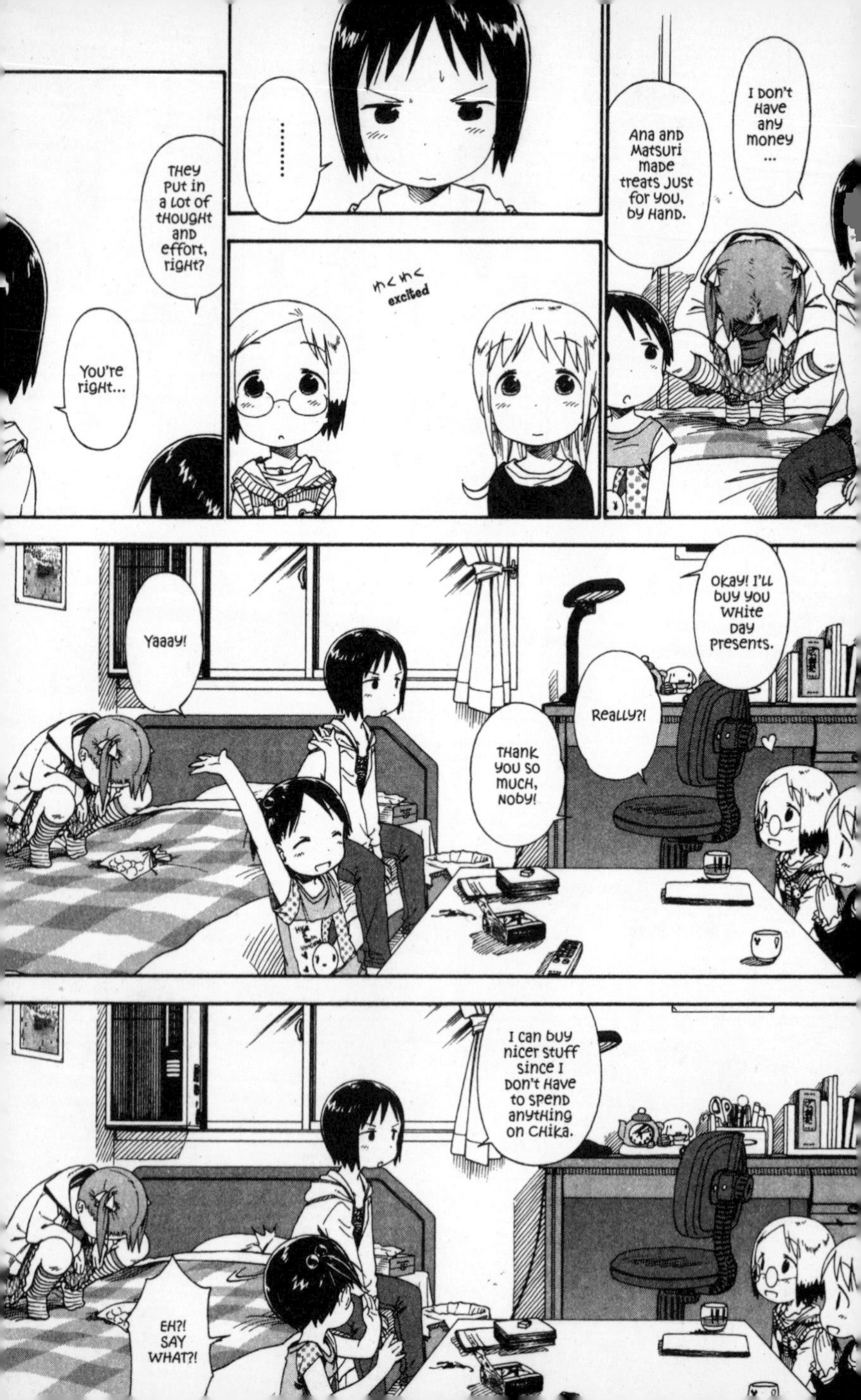
I don't have any money...
Ana and Matsuri made treats just for you, by hand.
......
わくわく excited
They put in a lot of thought and effort, right?
You're right...
Okay! I'll buy you White Day presents.
Really?!
Thank you so much, Noby!
Yaaay!
I can buy nicer stuff since I don't have to spend anything on Chika.
EH?! SAY WHAT?!

Spring Chika

Summer Miu

Autumn Matsuri

Winter Ana

Nobue

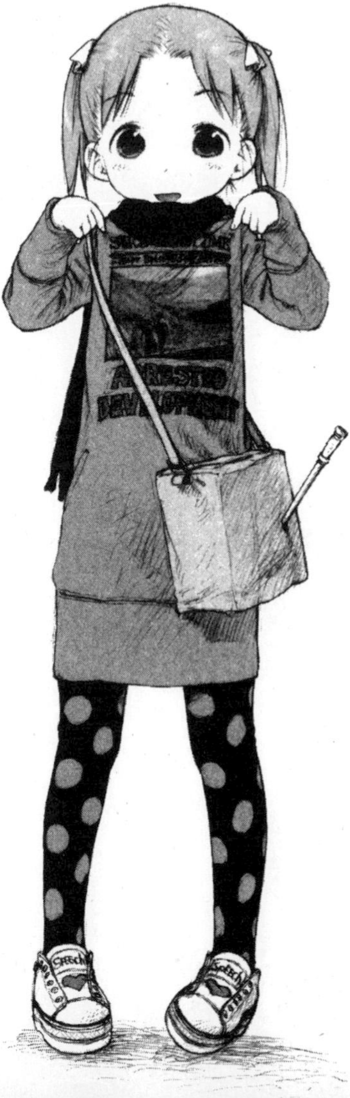

Spring   Chika

                Miu

Summer
                Matsuri

Autumn   Ana

Winter   Nobue

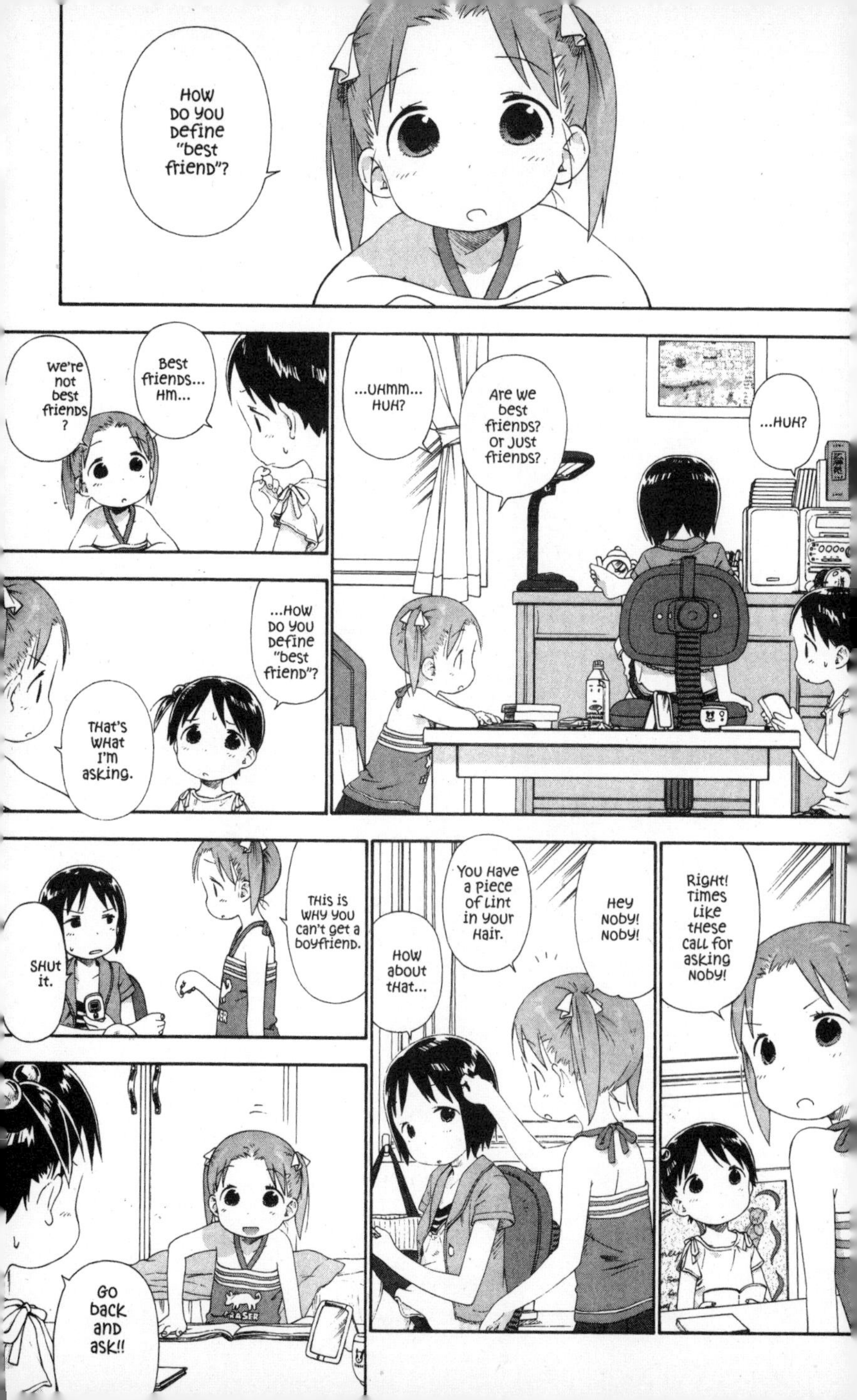
HOW DO YOU DEFINE "best friend"?
...HUH?
Are we best friends? Or just friends?
...UHMM... HUH?
Best friends... Hm...
We're not best friends?
...HOW DO YOU DEFINE "best friend"?
That's what I'm asking.
Right! Times like these call for asking Noby!
Hey Noby! Noby!
You have a piece of lint in your hair.
How about that...
This is why you can't get a boyfriend.
Shut it.
Go back and ask!!

episode.50

FRIENDS OR LOVERS

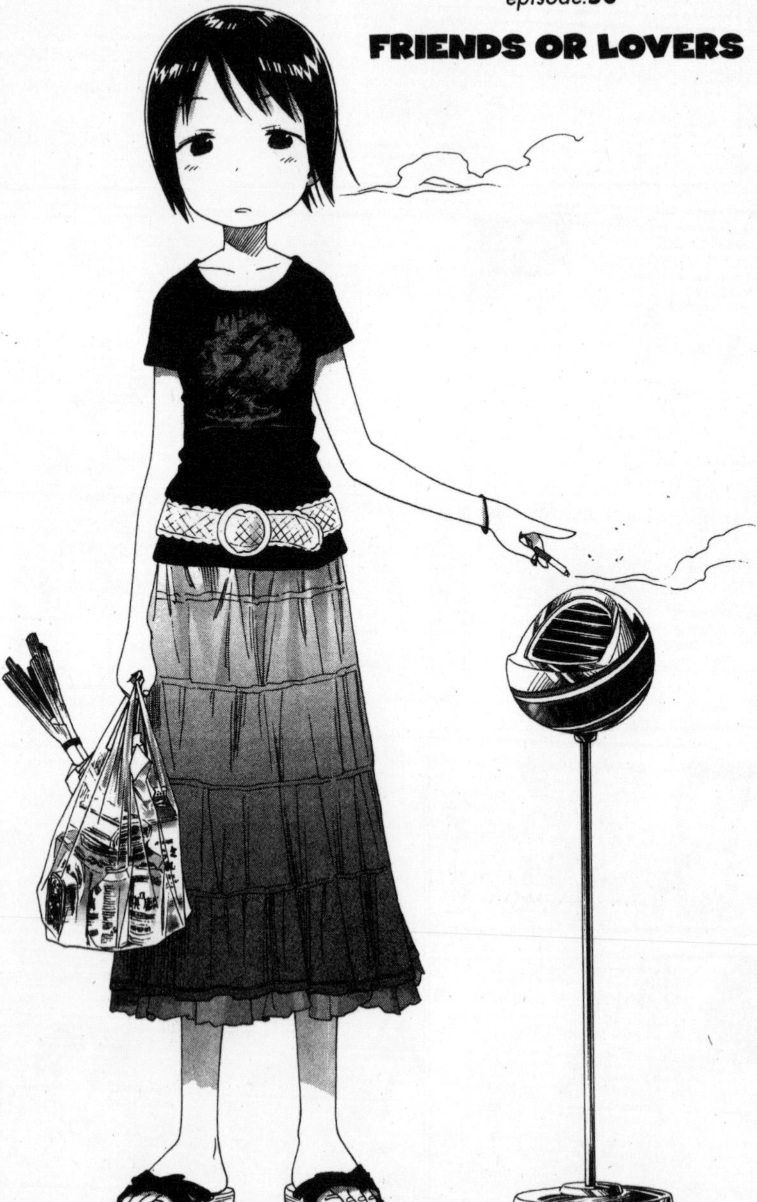

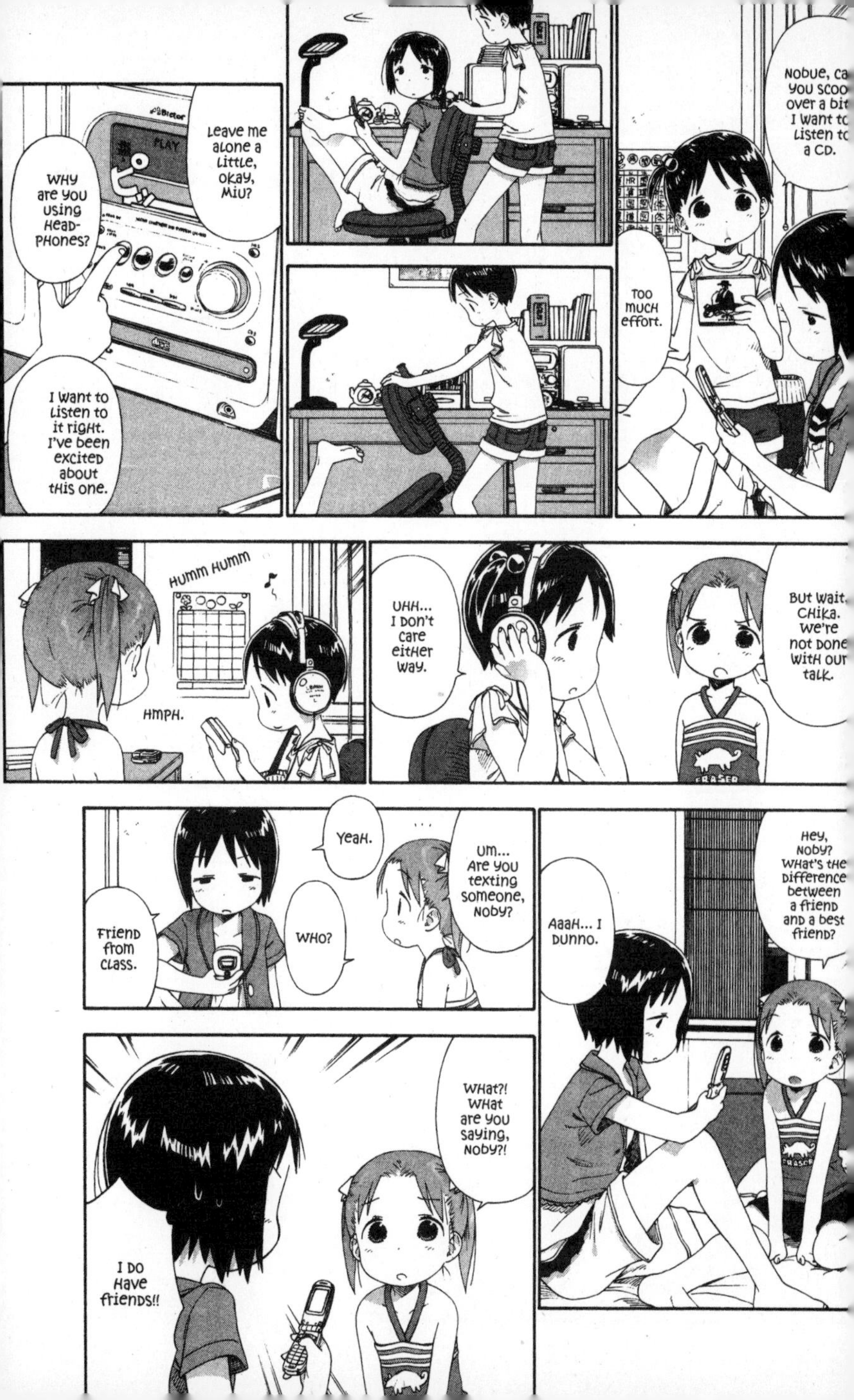
Nobue, ca you scoo over a bi I want to listen to a CD.
Too much effort.
Leave me alone a little, okay, Miu?
Why are you using head-phones?
I want to listen to it right. I've been excited about this one.
But wait, Chika. We're not done with our talk.
Uhh... I don't care either way.
Humm humm
Hmph.
Hey, Noby? What's the difference between a friend and a best friend?
Aaah... I dunno.
Um... Are you texting someone, Noby?
Yeah.
Who?
Friend from class.
What?! What are you saying, Noby?!
I do have friends!!

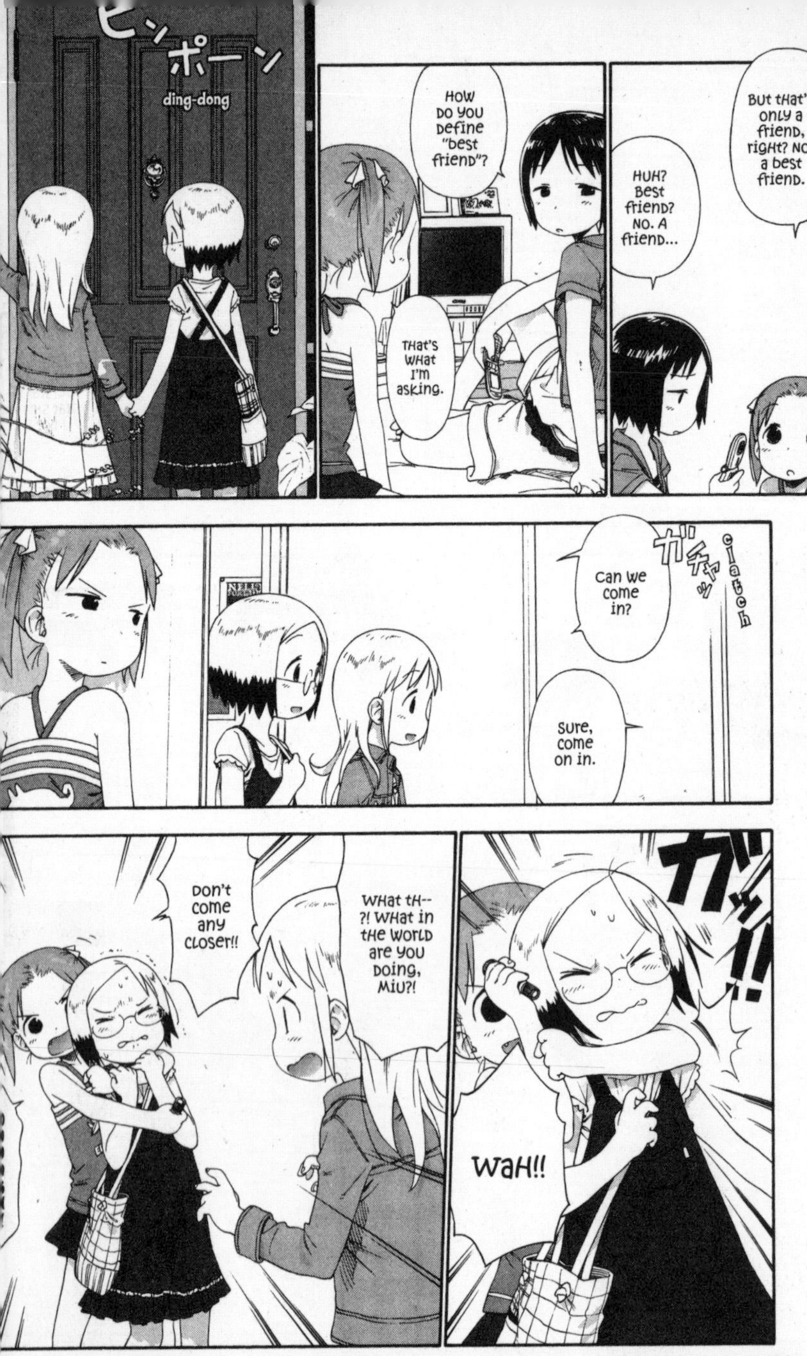
But that's only a friend, right? Not a best friend.
Huh? Best friend? No. A friend...
How do you define "best friend"?
That's what I'm asking.
ヒンポーン
ding-dong
ガチャッ
clatch
Can we come in?
Sure, come on in.
ガッ!!
WAH!!
What th--?! What in the world are you doing, Miu?!
Don't come any closer!!

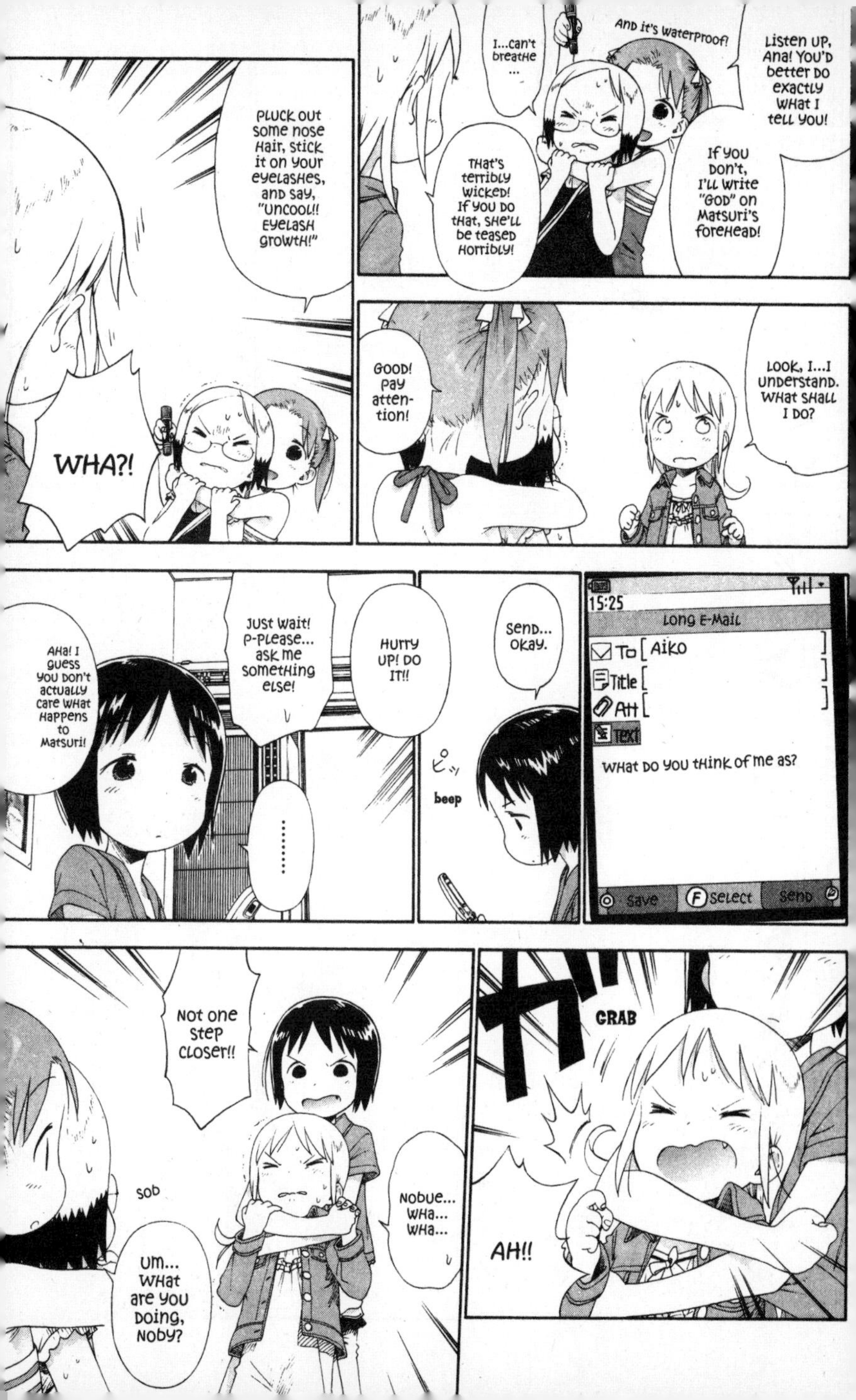

Listen up, Ana! You'd better do exactly what I tell you!
And it's waterproof!
If you don't, I'll write "GOD" on Matsuri's forehead!
I...can't breathe...
That's terribly wicked! If you do that, she'll be teased horribly!
Look, I...I understand. What shall I do?
Good! Pay atten-tion!
Pluck out some nose hair, stick it on your eyelashes, and say, "Uncool!! Eyelash growth!"
WHA?!
15:25
Long E-Mail
To [Aiko]
Title [ ]
Att [ ]
Text
What do you think of me as?
Save
Select
Send
Send... okay.
ピッ
beep
Hurry up! Do it!!
Just wait! P-please... ask me something else!
Aha! I guess you don't actually care what happens to Matsuri!
......
GRAB
AH!!
Not one step closer!!
Nobue... wha... wha...
sob
Um... what are you doing, Noby?

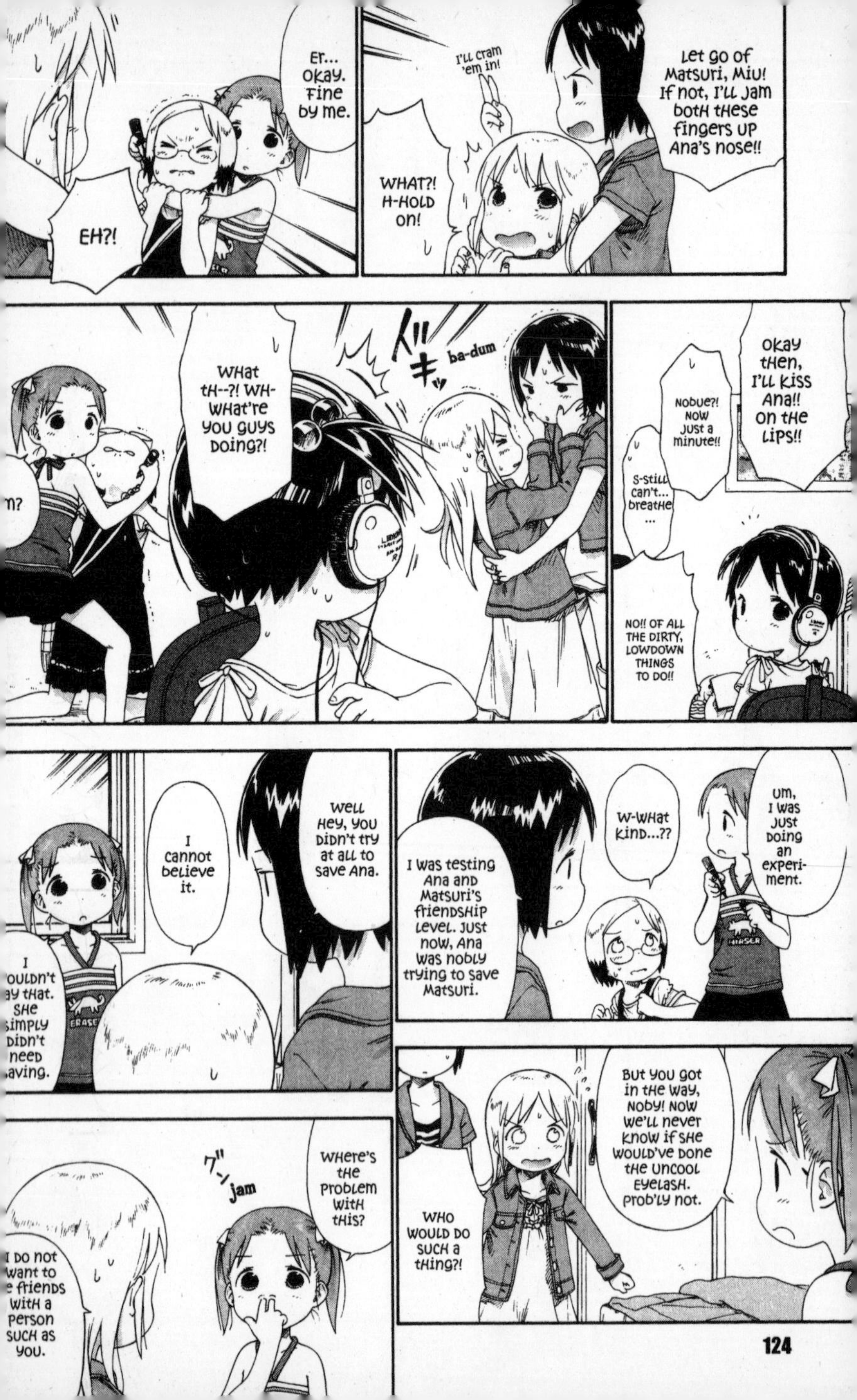
Let go of Matsuri, Miu! If not, I'll jam both these fingers up Ana's nose!!
I'll cram 'em in!
WHAT?! H-HOLD on!
Er... okay. Fine by me.
EH?!
Okay then, I'll kiss Ana!! on the lips!!
Nobue?! Now just a minute!!
S-still can't... breathe...
NO!! OF ALL THE DIRTY, LOWDOWN THINGS TO DO!!
ba-dum
What th--?! Wh-What're you guys doing?!
m?
Um, I was just doing an experi-ment.
W-what kind...??
I was testing Ana and Matsuri's friendship level. Just now, Ana was nobly trying to save Matsuri.
Well hey, you didn't try at all to save Ana.
I cannot believe it.
I ouldn't ay that. She simply didn't need aving.
But you got in the way, Noby! Now we'll never know if she would've done the uncool eyelash. Prob'ly not.
Who would do such a thing?!
Where's the problem with this?
jam
I do not want to e friends with a person such as you.

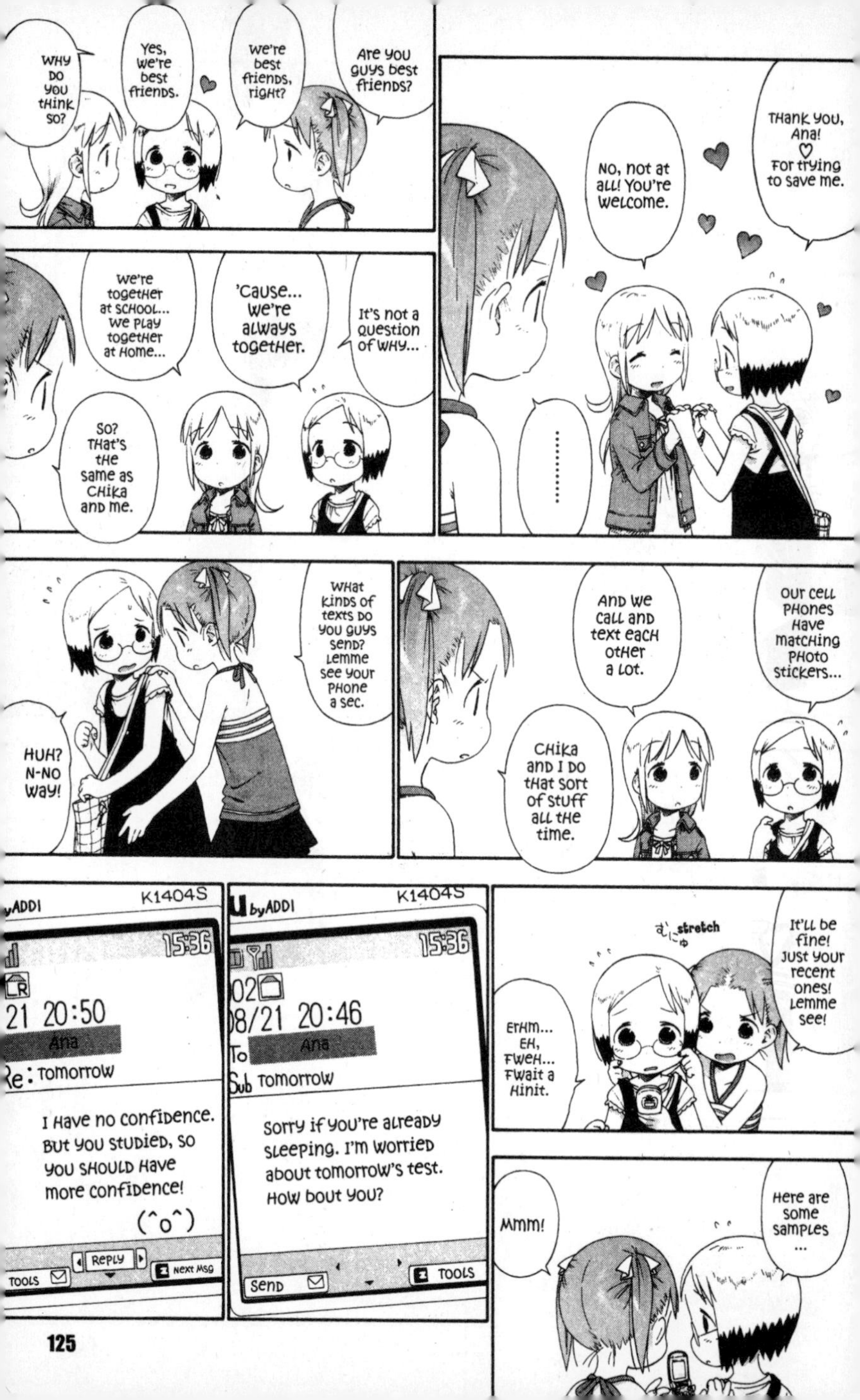
Thank you, Ana! ♡ For trying to save me.
No, not at all! You're welcome.
....
Are you guys best friends?
We're best friends, right?
Yes, we're best friends.
Why do you think so?
It's not a question of why...
'Cause... we're always together.
We're together at school... we play together at home...
So? That's the same as Chika and me.
Our cell phones have matching photo stickers...
And we call and text each other a lot.
Chika and I do that sort of stuff all the time.
What kinds of texts do you guys send? Lemme see your phone a sec.
Huh? N-no way!
It'll be fine! Just your recent ones! Lemme see!
むにゅ stretch
Erhm... eh, fweh... fwait a hinit.
Here are some samples...
Mmm!
U by ADDI K1404S
15:36
002
08/21 20:46
To Ana
Sub Tomorrow
Sorry if you're already sleeping. I'm worried about tomorrow's test. How bout you?
Send
Tools
by ADDI K1404S
15:36
LR
21 20:50
Ana
Re: Tomorrow
I have no confidence. But you studied, so you should have more confidence!
(^o^)
Reply
Tools
Next Msg

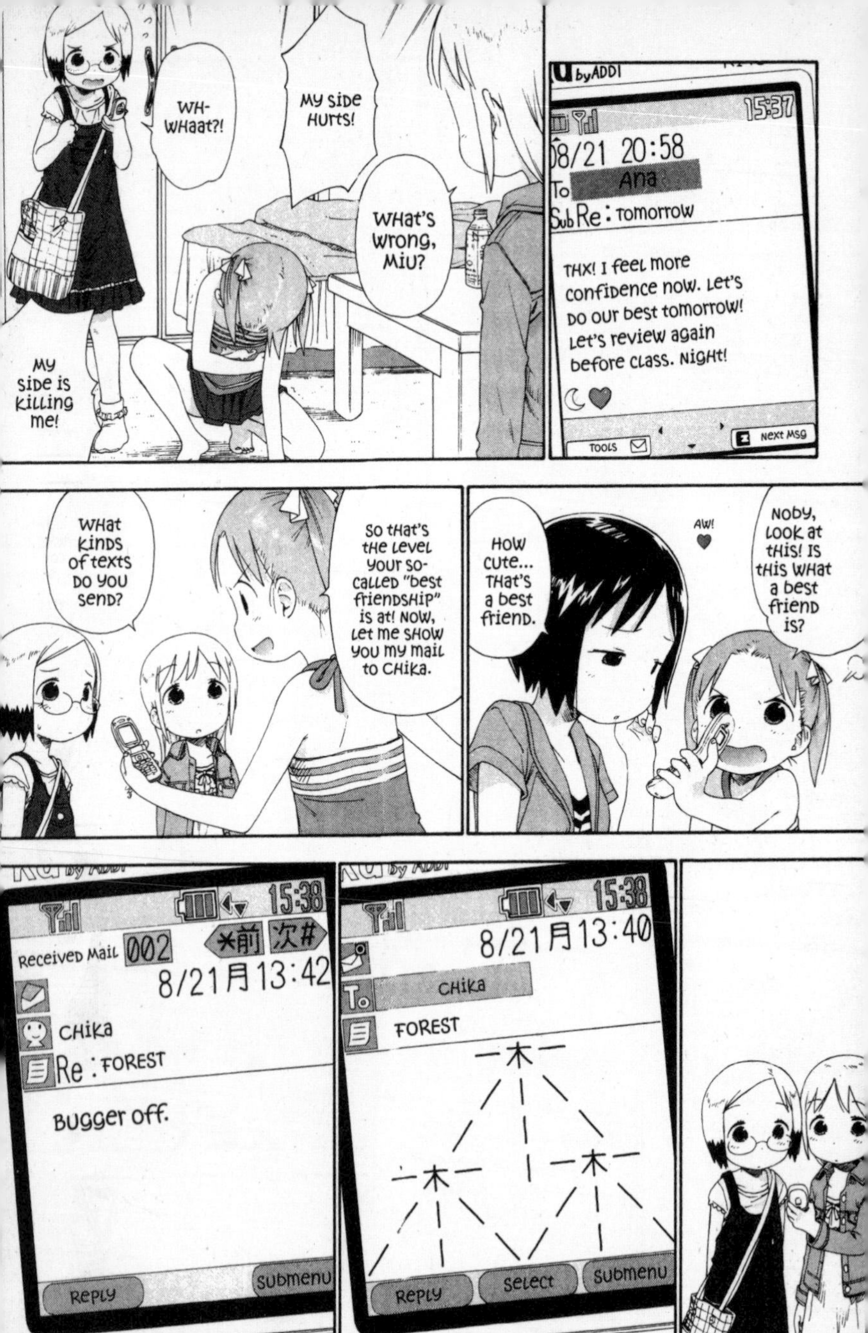
by ADDI
15:37
08/21 20:58
To Ana
Sub Re: Tomorrow
THX! I feel more confidence now. Let's do our best tomorrow! Let's review again before class. Night!
Tools
Next MSG
What's wrong, Miu?
My side hurts!
Wh- whaat?!
My side is killing me!
Noby, look at this! Is this what a best friend is?
Aw!
How cute... That's a best friend.
So that's the level your so-called "best friendship" is at! Now, let me show you my mail to Chika.
What kinds of texts do you send?
15:38
8/21月13:40
To
Chika
FOREST
木
木
木
Reply
Select
Submenu
15:38
Received Mail
002
*前
次#
8/21月13:42
Chika
Re: FOREST
Bugger off.
Reply
Submenu

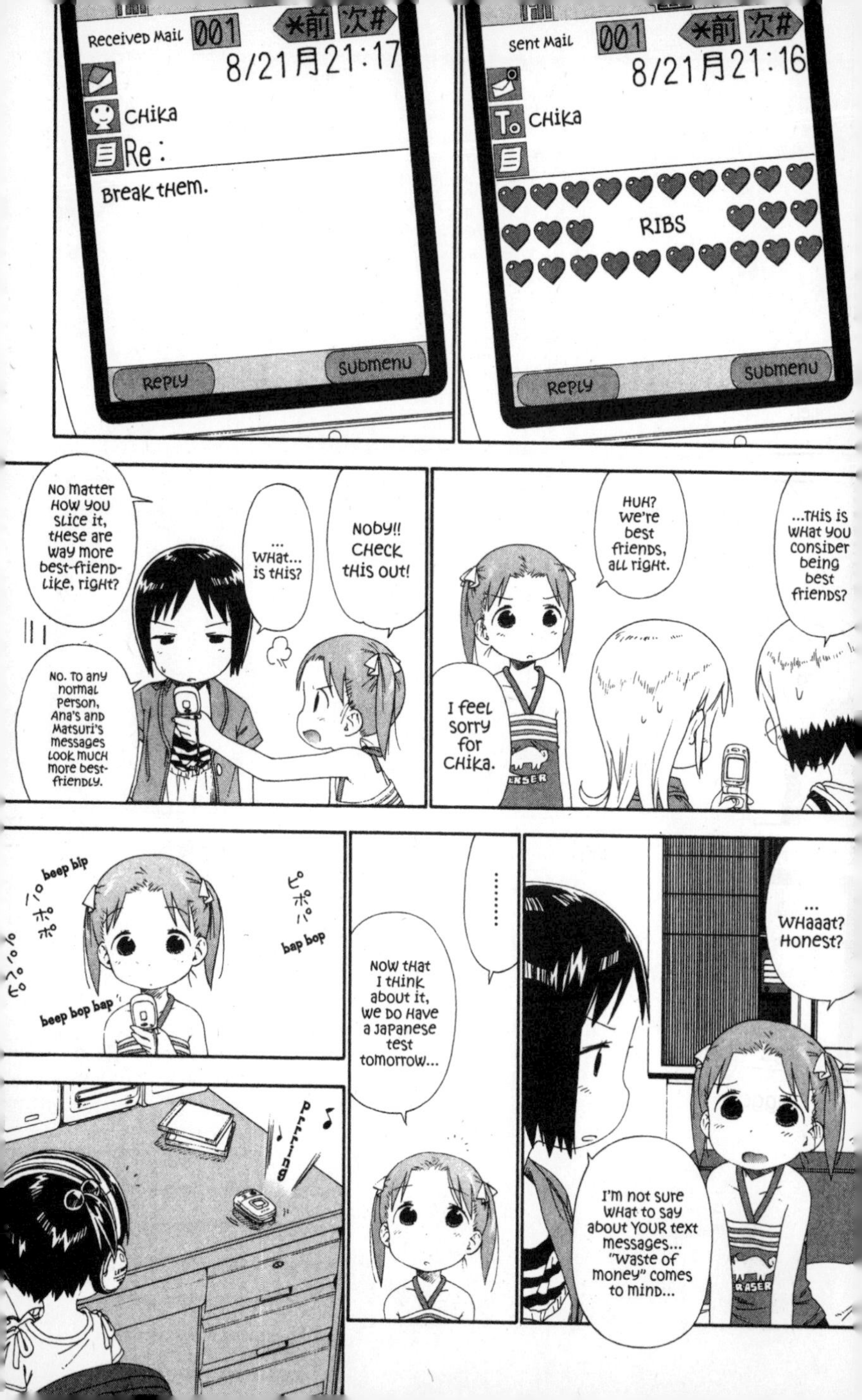

Sent Mail
001
*前 次#
8/21月21:16
To CHIKA
RIBS
Reply
Submenu
Received Mail
001
*前 次#
8/21月21:17
CHIKA
Re :
Break them.
Reply
Submenu
...This is what you consider being best friends?
Huh? We're best friends, all right.
I feel sorry for Chika.
Noby!! Check this out!
... What... is this?
No matter how you slice it, these are way more best-friend-like, right?
No. To any normal person, Ana's and Matsuri's messages look much more best-friendly.
... Whaaat? Honest?
I'm not sure what to say about YOUR text messages... "Waste of money" comes to mind...
....
Now that I think about it, we do have a Japanese test tomorrow...
ピポパ
bap bop
beep bip
beep bop bap
Prrring

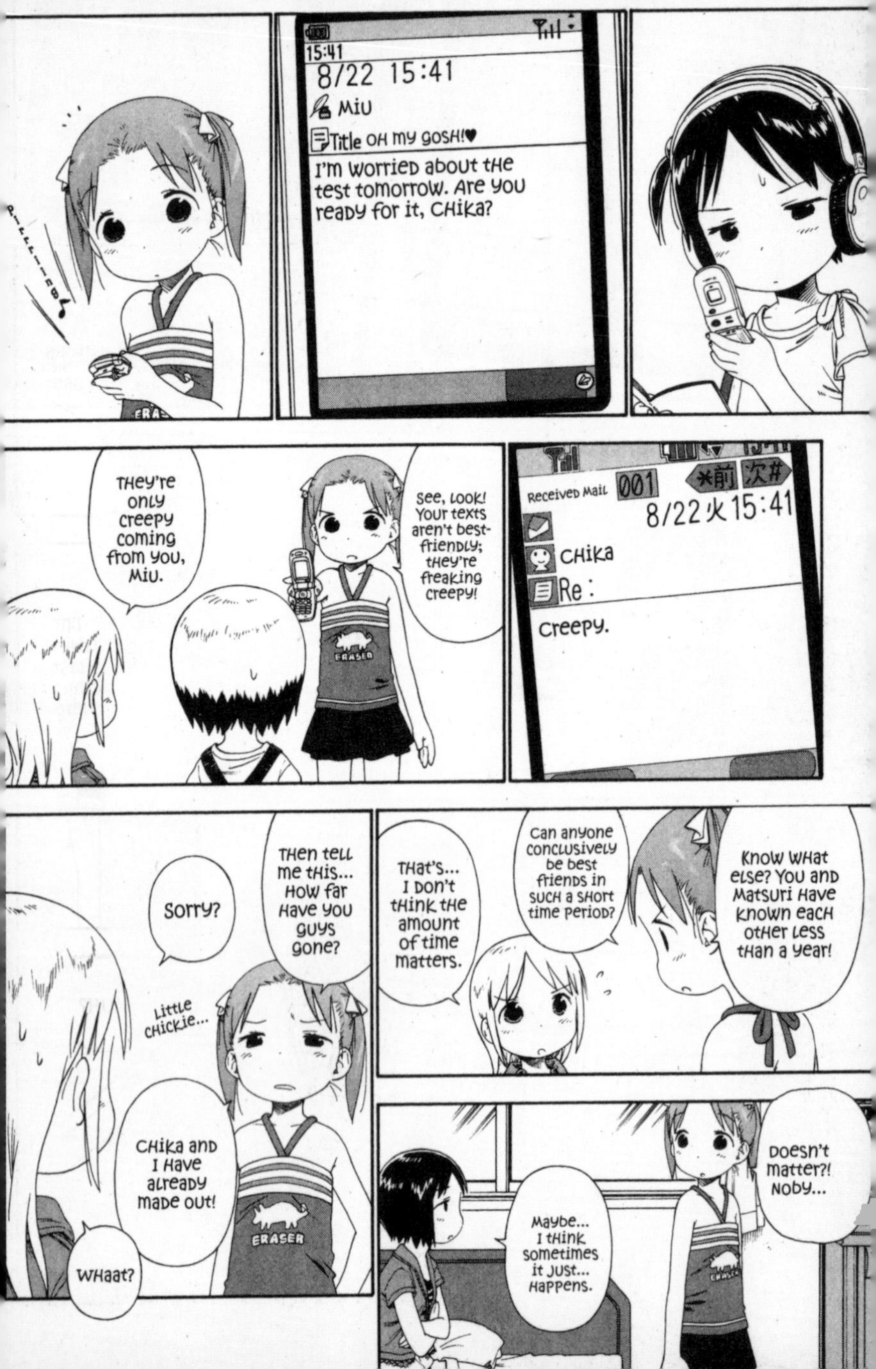
15:41
8/22 15:41
Miu
Title OH MY GOSH!♥
I'm worried about the test tomorrow. Are you ready for it, Chika?
Pirrrriing♪
Received Mail 001 *前 次#
8/22火15:41
Chika
Re:
Creepy.
See, look! Your texts aren't best-friendly; they're freaking creepy!
They're only creepy coming from you, Miu.
Know what else? You and Matsuri have known each other less than a year!
Can anyone conclusively be best friends in such a short time period?
That's... I don't think the amount of time matters.
Doesn't matter?! Noby...
Maybe... I think sometimes it just... happens.
Then tell me this... How far have you guys gone?
Sorry?
Little Chickie...
Chika and I have already made out!
Whaat?

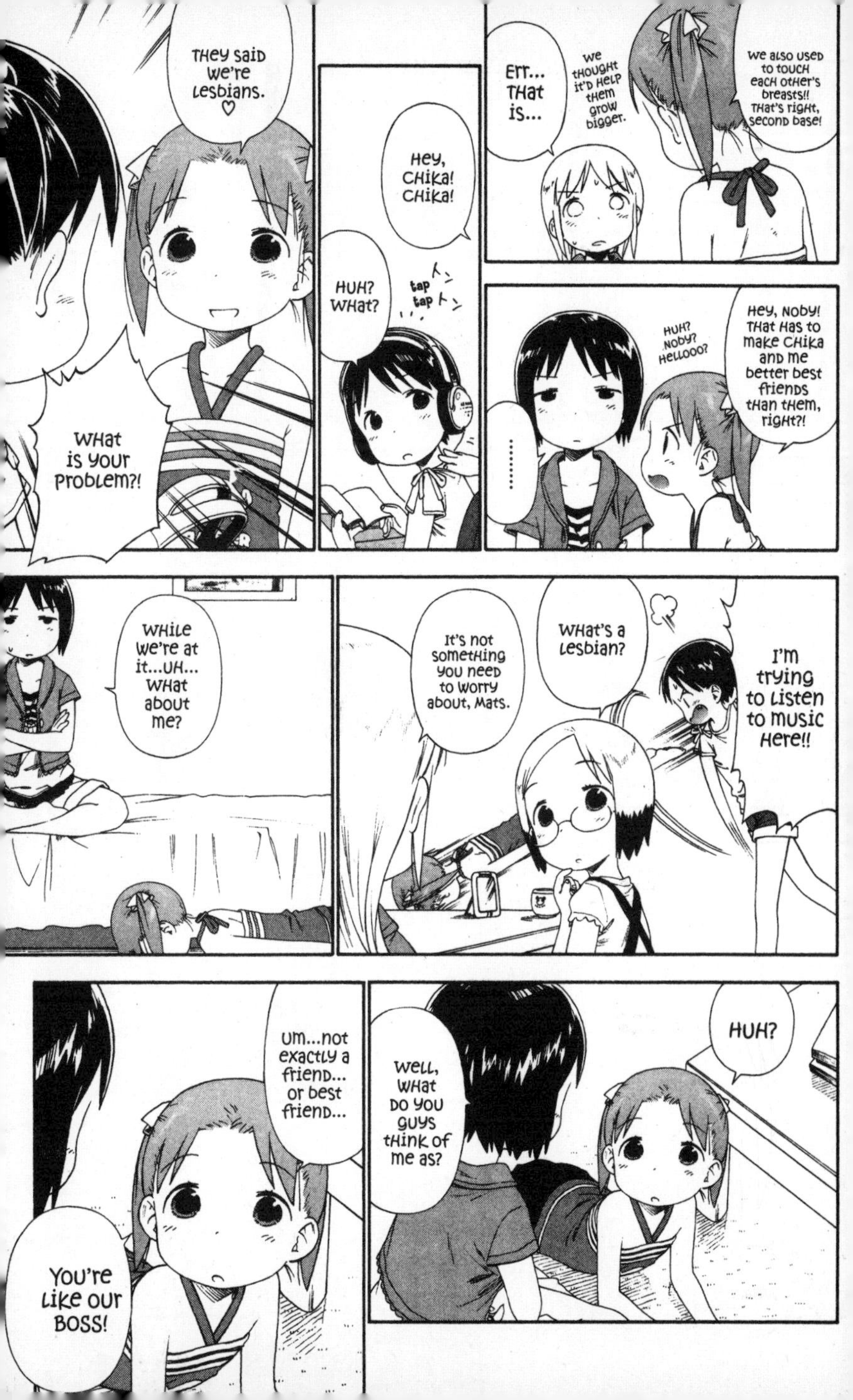
We also used to touch each other's breasts!! That's right, second base!
We thought it'd help them grow bigger.
Err... That is...
Hey, Noby! That has to make Chika and me better best friends than them, right?!
Huh? Noby? Hellooo?
....
Hey, Chika! Chika!
tap tap
Huh? What?
They said we're lesbians. ♡
What is your problem?!
I'm trying to listen to music here!!
What's a lesbian?
It's not something you need to worry about, Mats.
While we're at it...uh... what about me?
Huh?
Well, what do you guys think of me as?
Um...not exactly a friend... or best friend...
You're like our boss!

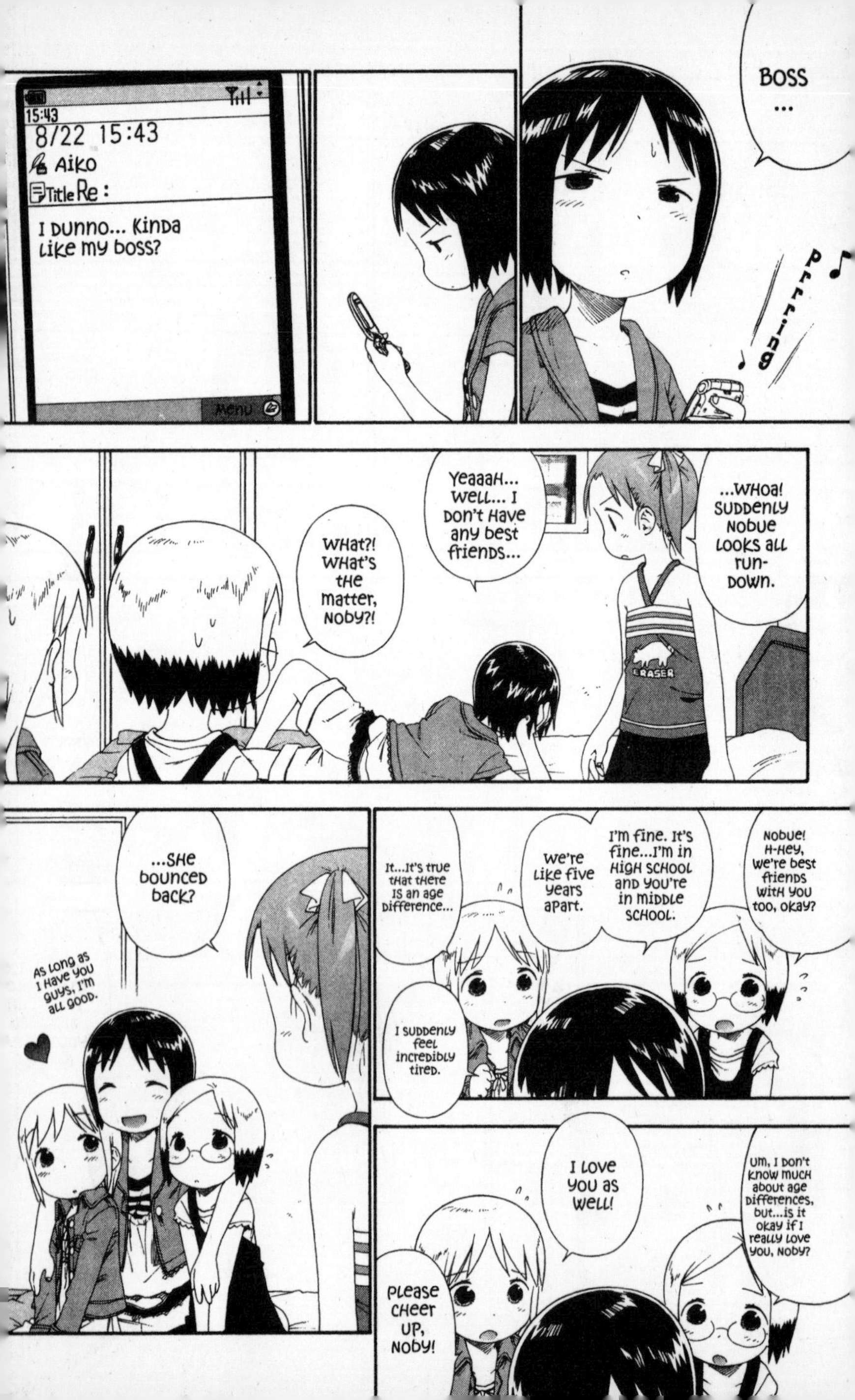
BOSS ...
Prrring
8/22 15:43
Aiko
Title Re :
I dunno... Kinda like my boss?
Menu
...Whoa! Suddenly Nobue looks all run-down.
Yeaaah... Well... I don't have any best friends...
What?! What's the matter, Noby?!
ERASER
Nobue! H-hey, we're best friends with you too, okay?
I'm fine. It's fine...I'm in high school and you're in middle school.
We're like five years apart.
It...It's true that there is an age difference...
I suddenly feel incredibly tired.
Um, I don't know much about age differences, but...is it okay if I really love you, Noby?
I love you as well!
Please cheer up, Noby!
...She bounced back?
As long as I have you guys, I'm all good.

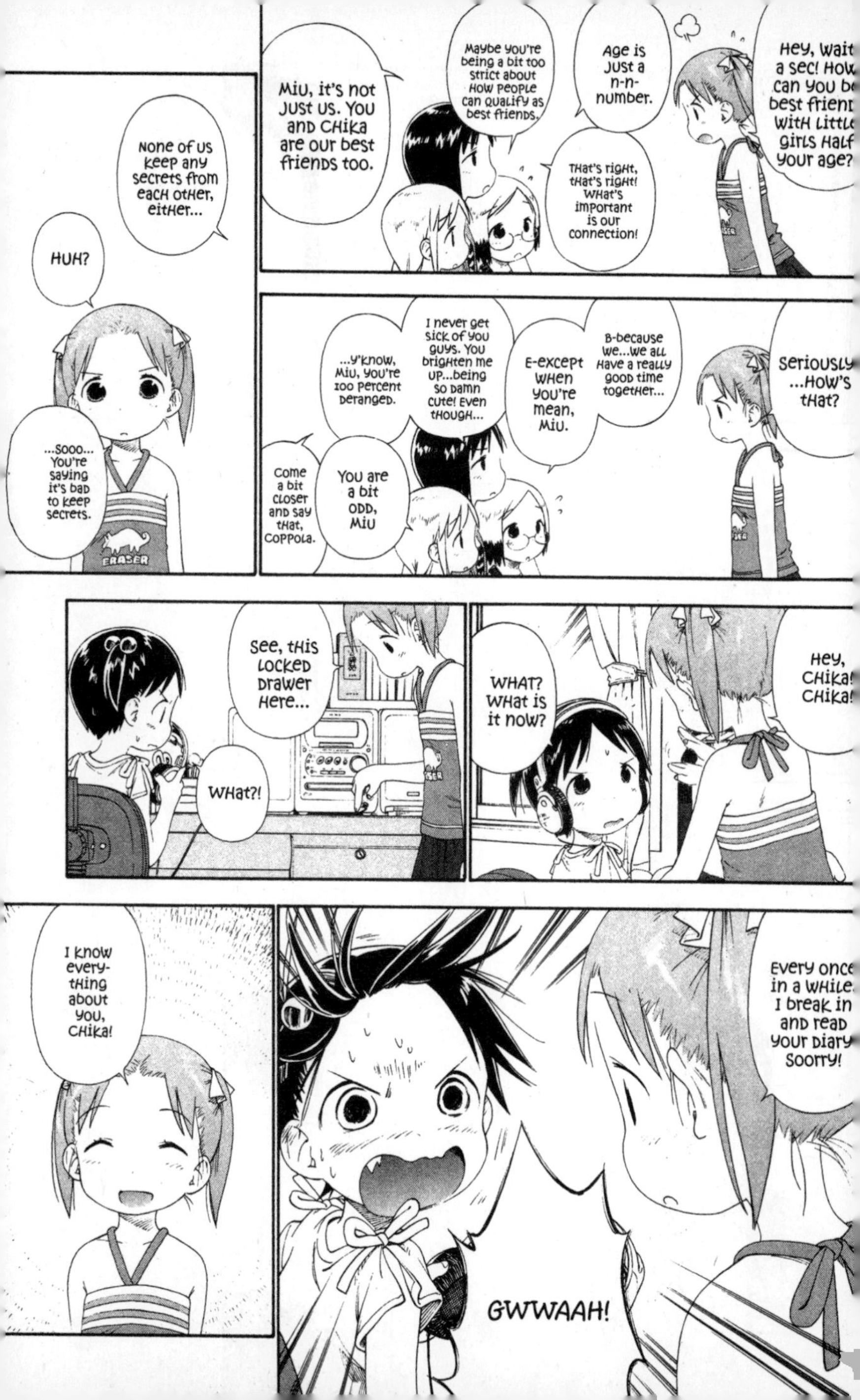
Hey, wait a sec! How can you b best friend with little girls half your age?
Age is just a n-n-number.
Maybe you're being a bit too strict about how people can qualify as best friends.
That's right, that's right! What's important is our connection!
Miu, it's not just us. You and Chika are our best friends too.
Seriously ...How's that?
B-because we...we all have a really good time together...
E-except when you're mean, Miu.
I never get sick of you guys. You brighten me up...being so damn cute! Even though...
...y'know, Miu, you're 100 percent deranged.
You are a bit odd, Miu
Come a bit closer and say that, Coppola.
None of us keep any secrets from each other, either...
Huh?
...Sooo... you're saying it's bad to keep secrets.
Hey, Chika! Chika!
What? What is it now?
See, this locked drawer here...
What?!
Every onc in a while, I break in and read your diary Soorry!
GWWAAH!
I know every-thing about you, Chika!

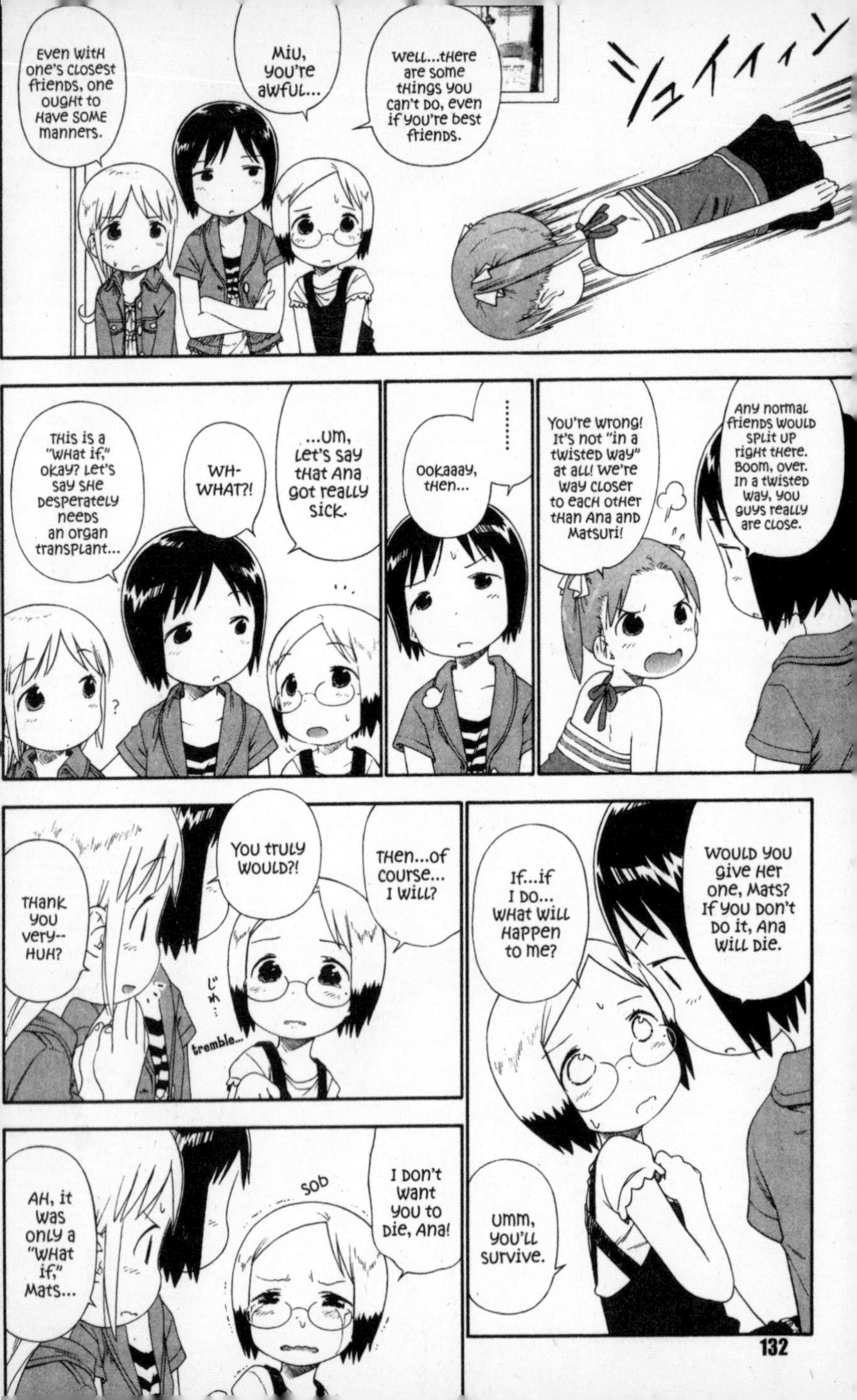

シュイイィン
Well...there are some things you can't do, even if you're best friends.
Miu, you're awful...
Even with one's closest friends, one ought to have some manners.
Any normal friends would split up right there. Boom, over. In a twisted way, you guys really are close.
You're wrong! It's not "in a twisted way" at all! We're way closer to each other than Ana and Matsuri!
....
Ookaaay, then...
...Um, let's say that Ana got really sick.
Wh- What?!
This is a "what if," okay? Let's say she desperately needs an organ transplant...
?
Would you give her one, Mats? If you don't do it, Ana will die.
If...if I do... what will happen to me?
Umm, you'll survive.
Then...of course... I will?
You truly would?!
じわ…
tremble...
Thank you very-- Huh?
I don't want you to die, Ana!
sob
Ah, it was only a "what if," Mats...

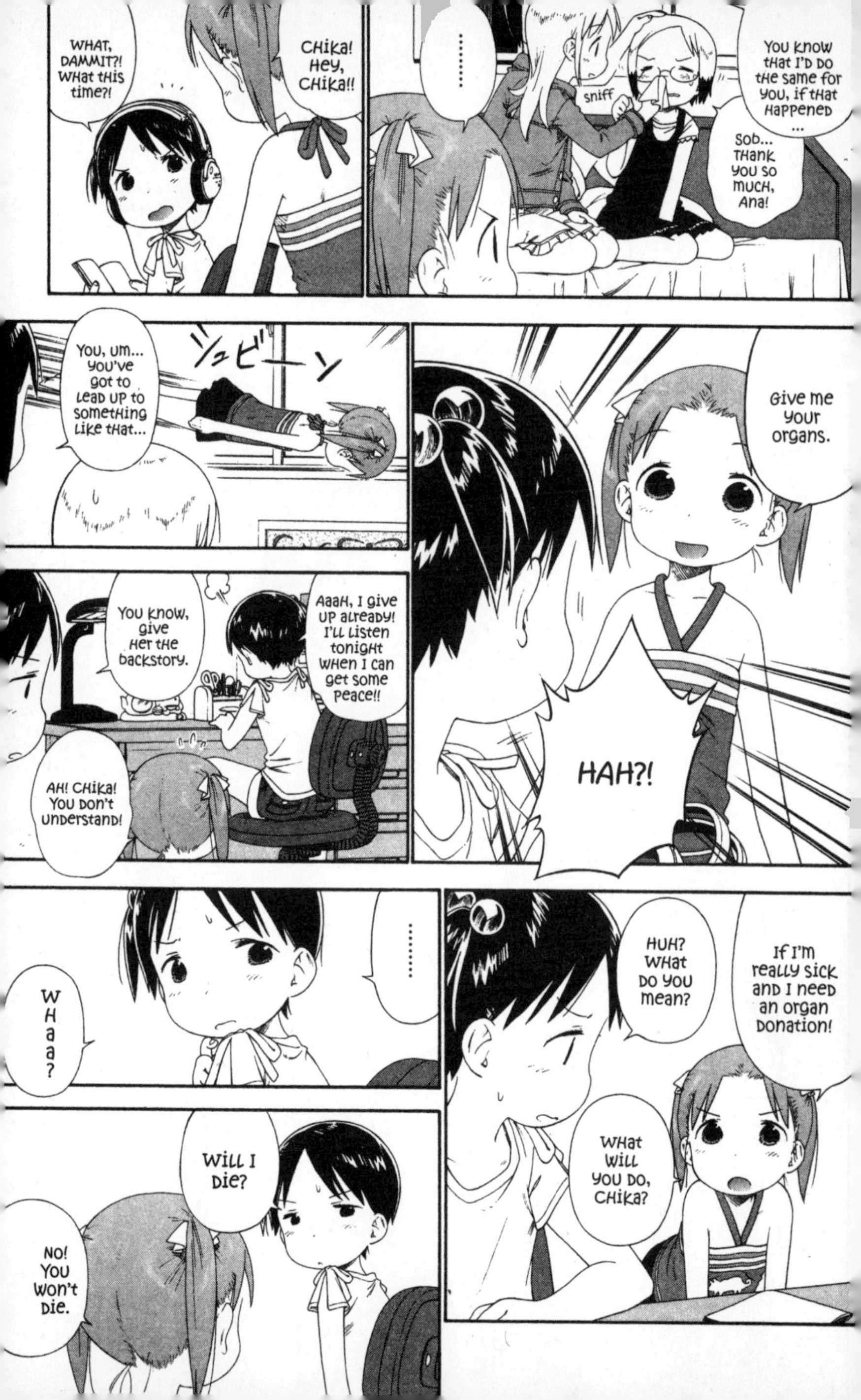
You know that I'd do the same for you, if that happened ...
sniff
Sob... Thank you so much, Ana!
....
Chika! Hey, Chika!!
What, dammit?! What this time?!
Give me your organs.
HAH?!
シュビーン
You, um... you've got to lead up to something like that...
Aaah, I give up already! I'll listen tonight when I can get some peace!!
You know, give her the backstory.
Ah! Chika! You don't understand!
If I'm really sick and I need an organ donation!
Huh? What do you mean?
What will you do, Chika?
....
Whaa?
Will I die?
No! You won't die.

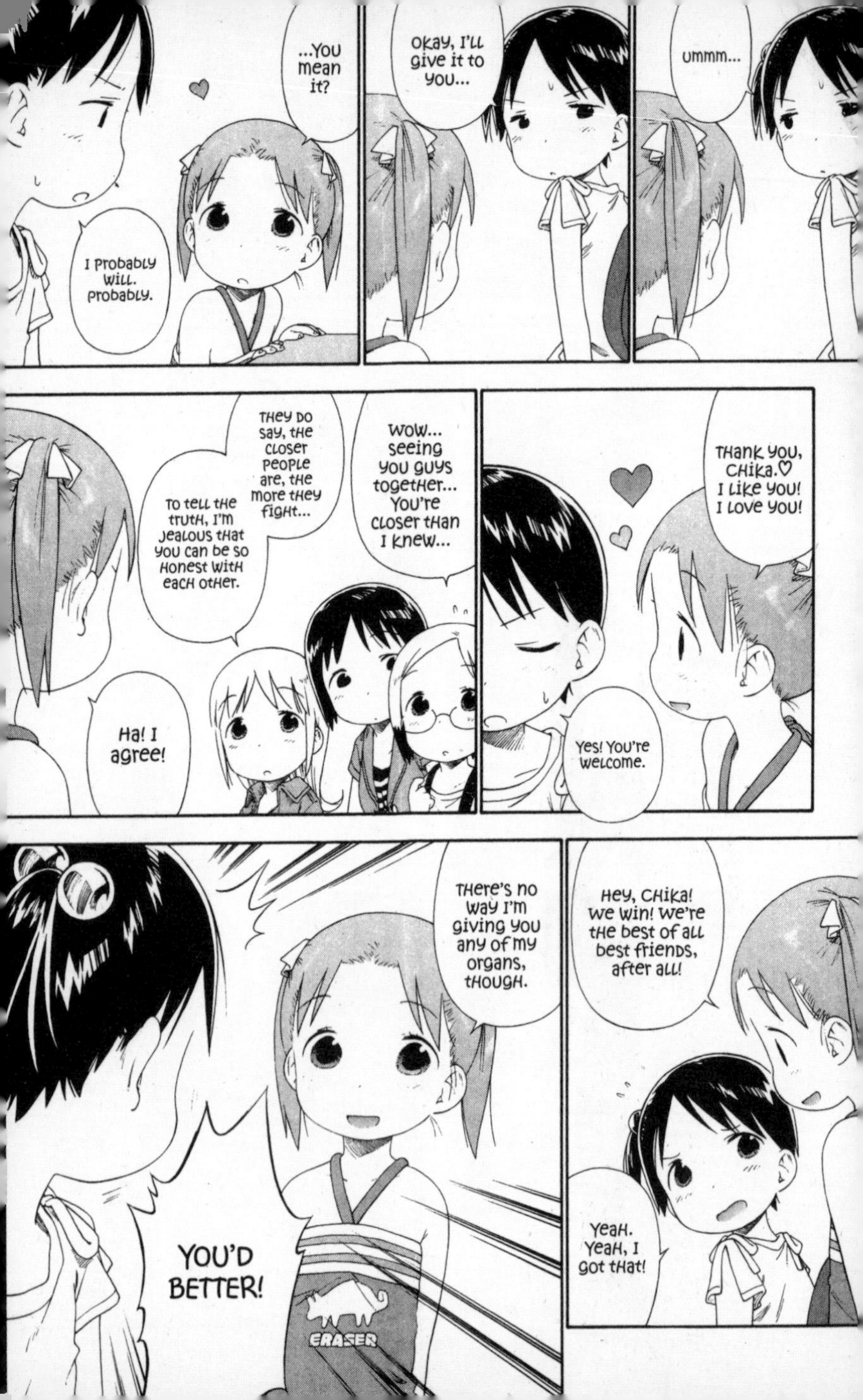
ummm...
Okay, I'll give it to you...
...You mean it?
I probably will. probably.
Thank you, Chika.♡ I like you! I love you!
Yes! You're welcome.
Wow... seeing you guys together... You're closer than I knew...
They do say, the closer people are, the more they fight...
To tell the truth, I'm jealous that you can be so honest with each other.
Ha! I agree!
Hey, Chika! We win! We're the best of all best friends, after all!
Yeah. Yeah, I got that!
There's no way I'm giving you any of my organs, though.
YOU'D BETTER!
ERASER

Spring

Summer

Autumn

Winter

Chika

Miu

Matsuri

Ana

Nobue

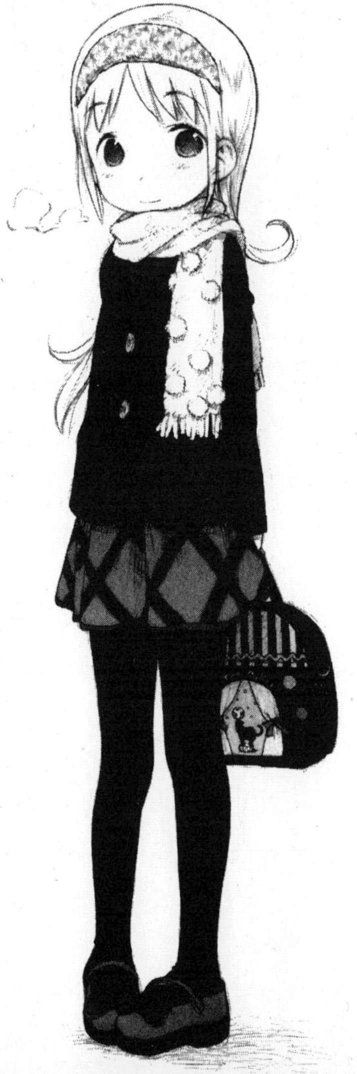

Spring	Chika
Summer	Miu
Autumn	Matsuri
	Ana
Winter ————	Nobue

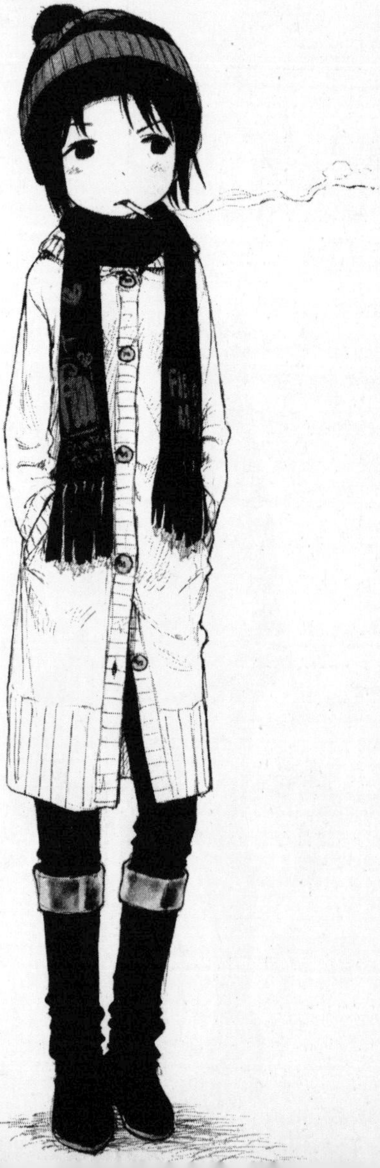

AUM...The Balance of Opposites Resonating in Harmony

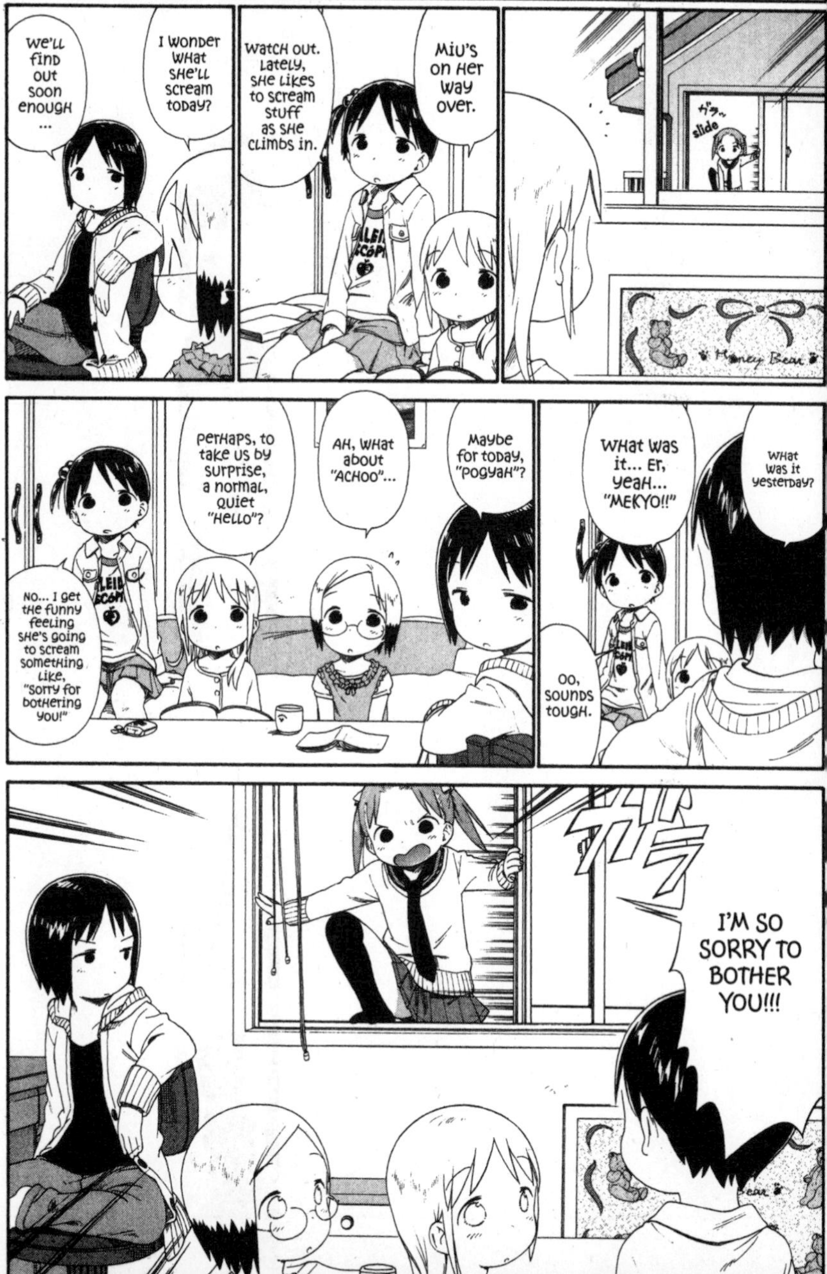
ガラ
slide
Honey Bear
Miu's on her way over.
Watch out. Lately, she likes to scream stuff as she climbs in.
I wonder what she'll scream today?
We'll find out soon enough...
What was it yesterday?
What was it... Er, yeah... "MEKYO!!"
Oo, sounds tough.
Maybe for today, "Pogyah"?
Ah, what about "Achoo"...
Perhaps, to take us by surprise, a normal, quiet "Hello"?
No... I get the funny feeling she's going to scream something like, "Sorry for bothering you!"
ガラ
I'M SO SORRY TO BOTHER YOU!!!

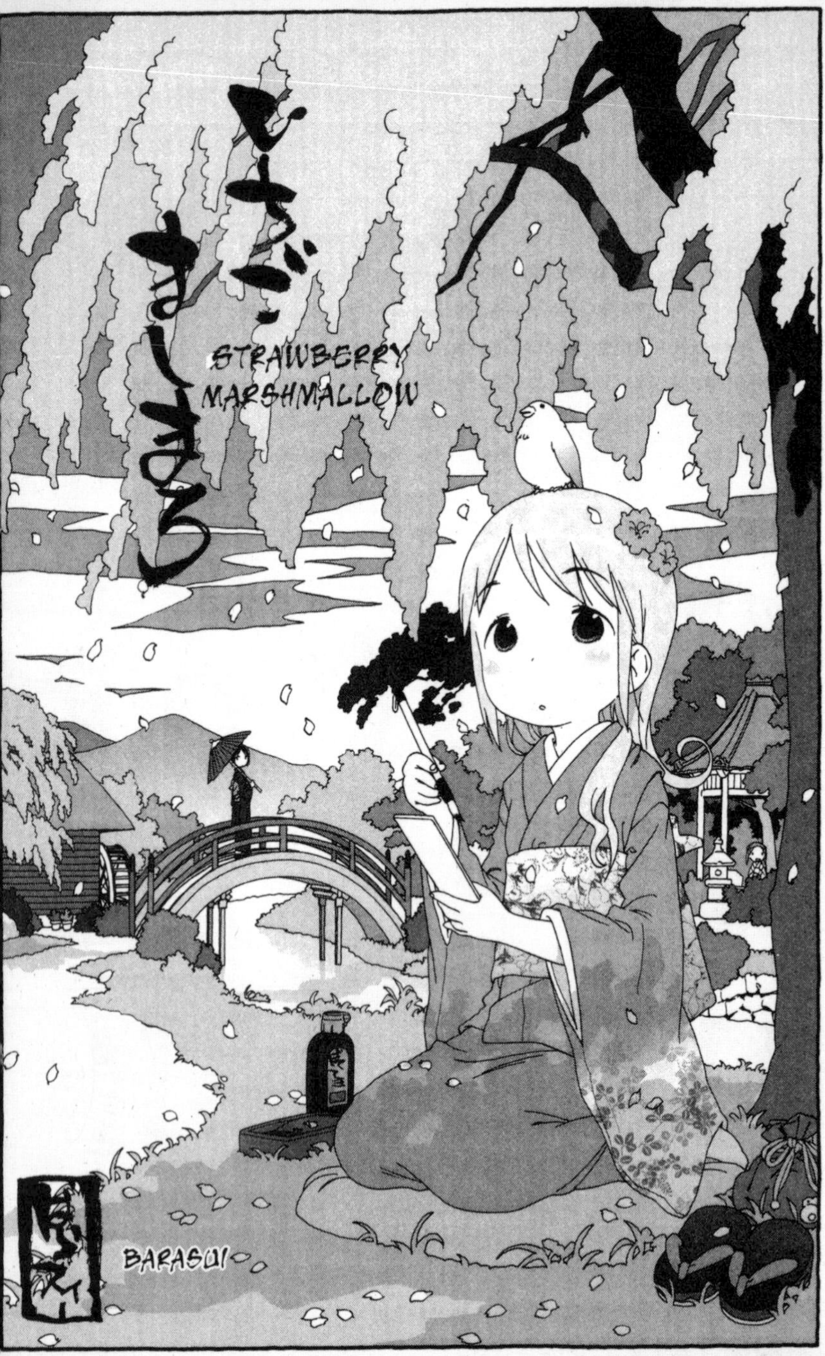
STRAWBERRY
MARSHMALLOW
BARASUI

episode.51 **PROVERBS**

Merely a Member...Present but Useless

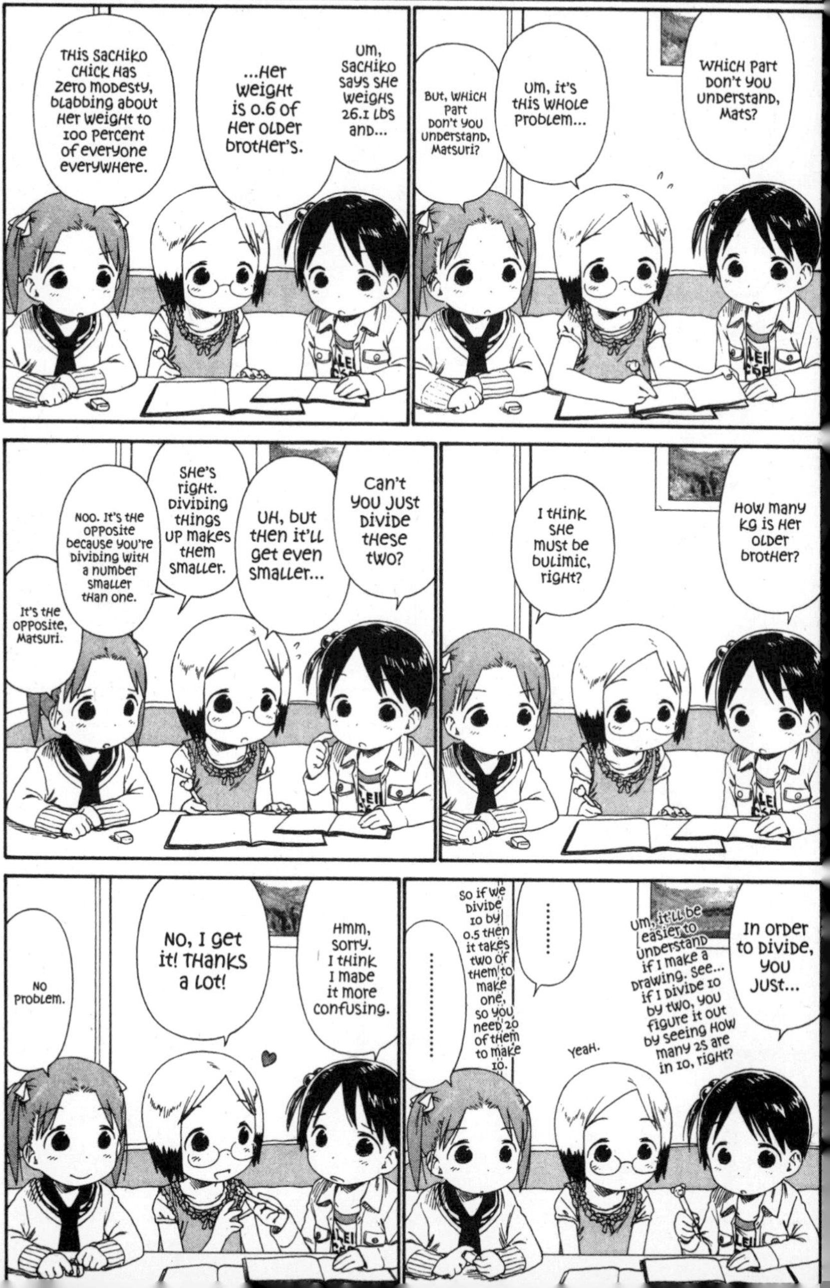

Which part don't you understand, Mats?
Um, it's this whole problem...
But, which part don't you understand, Matsuri?
Um, Sachiko says she weighs 26.1 lbs and...
...Her weight is 0.6 of her older brother's.
This Sachiko chick has zero modesty, blabbing about her weight to 100 percent of everyone everywhere.
How many kg is her older brother?
I think she must be bulimic, right?
Can't you just divide these two?
Uh, but then it'll get even smaller...
She's right. Dividing things up makes them smaller.
Noo. It's the opposite because you're dividing with a number smaller than one.
It's the opposite, Matsuri.
In order to divide, you just...
Um, it'll be easier to understand if I make a drawing. See... if I divide 10 by two, you figure it out by seeing how many 2s are in 10, right?
Yeah.
....
So if we divide 10 by 0.5 then it takes two of them to make one, so you need 20 of them to make 10.
....
Hmm, sorry. I think I made it more confusing.
No, I get it! Thanks a lot!
No problem.

A War Cannot be Fought on an Empty Stomach...You Must Eat First

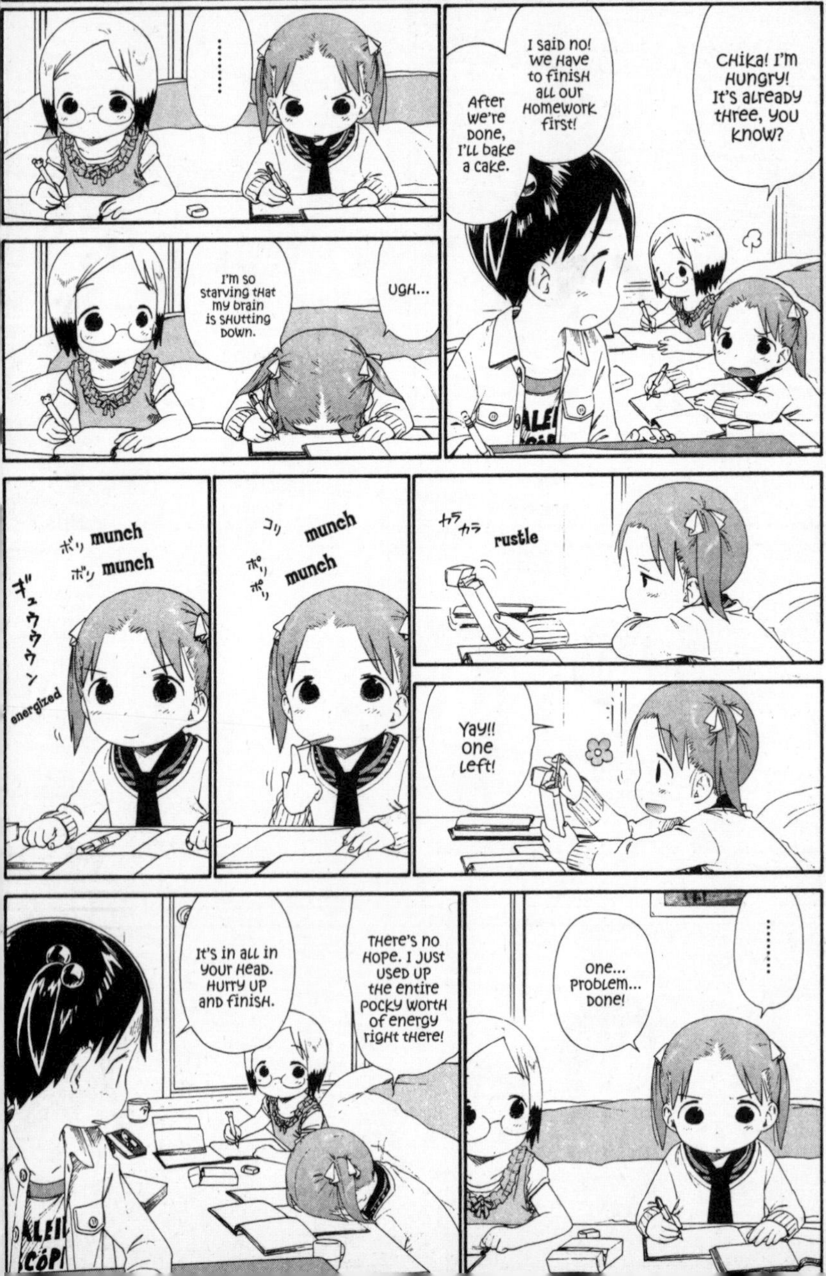
CHika! I'm Hungry! It's already three, you know?
I said no! We have to finish all our Homework first!
After we're done, I'll bake a cake.
......
UGH...
I'm so starving that my brain is shutting down.
カラ カラ
rustle
Yay!! one left!
コリ
munch
ポリ ポリ
munch
ポリ
munch
ポリ
munch
ギュウウウン
energized
....
one... problem... Done!
There's no hope. I just used up the entire pocky worth of energy right there!
It's in all in your head. Hurry up and finish.

The Crow Will Eat the Seeds That Gonbei the Planter Sows...His Work Is All for the Crow

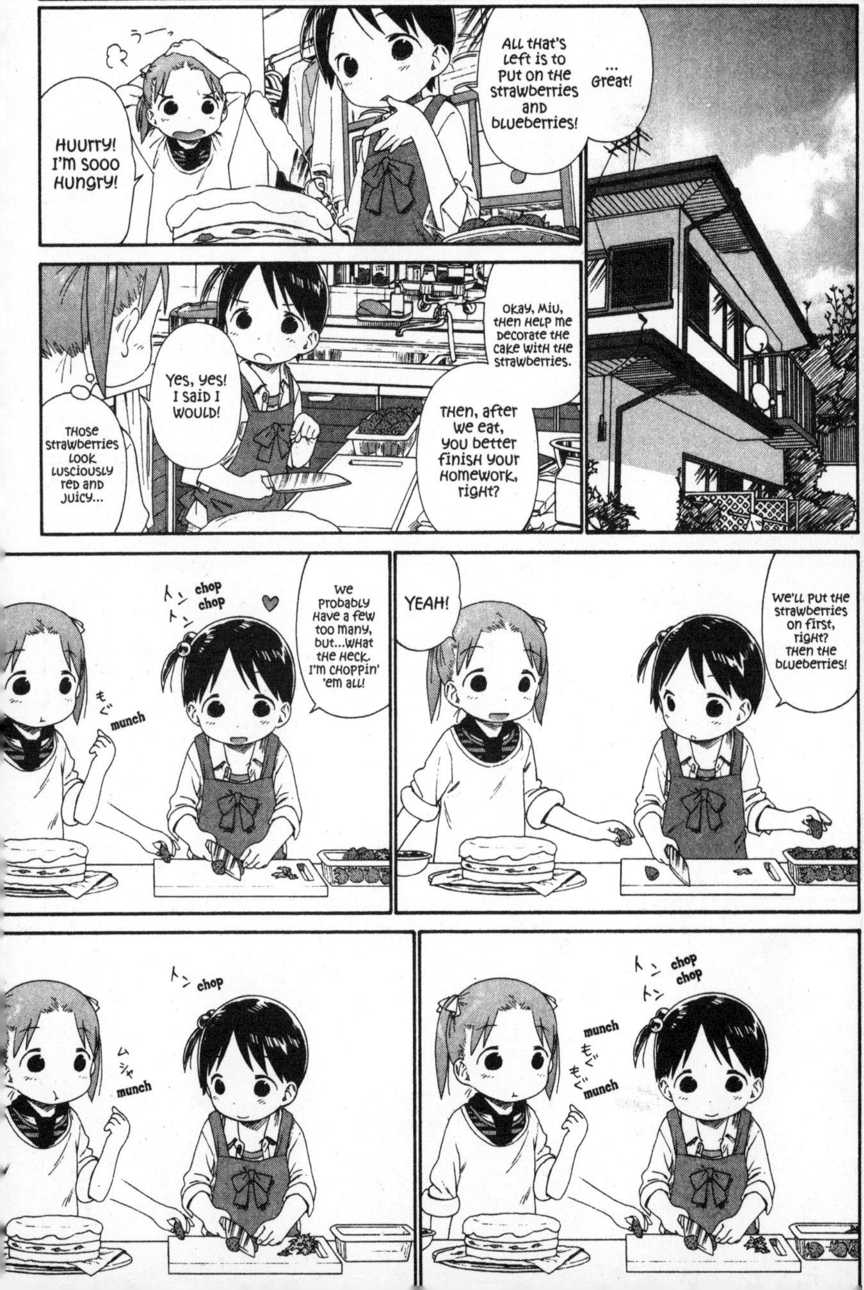
All that's left is to put on the strawberries and blueberries!
... Great!
うーっ
Huurry! I'm sooo hungry!
Okay, Miu, then help me decorate the cake with the strawberries.
Then, after we eat, you better finish your homework, right?
Yes, yes! I said I would!
Those strawberries look lusciously red and juicy...
We'll put the strawberries on first, right? Then the blueberries!
YEAH!
We probably have a few too many, but...what the heck. I'm choppin' 'em all!
トン chop
トン chop
もぐ munch
トン chop
トン chop
munch もぐ
もぐ munch
トン chop
ムシャ munch

Twist the Arm of a Baby...It's a Piece of Cake

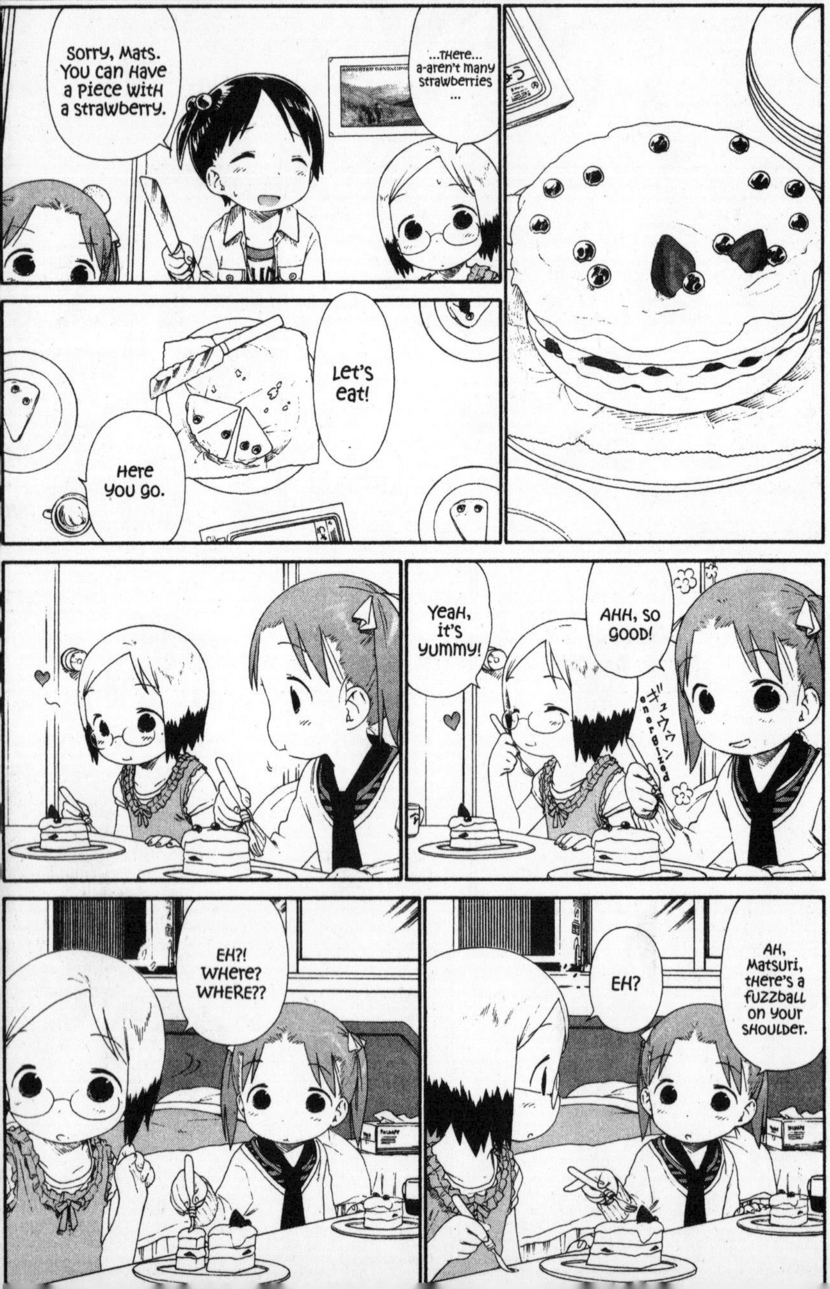
...There... a-aren't many strawberries ...
Sorry, Mats. You can have a piece with a strawberry.
Let's eat!
Here you go.
Ahh, so good!
energized
Yeah, it's yummy!
Ah, Matsuri, there's a fuzzball on your shoulder.
Eh?
Eh?! Where? WHERE??

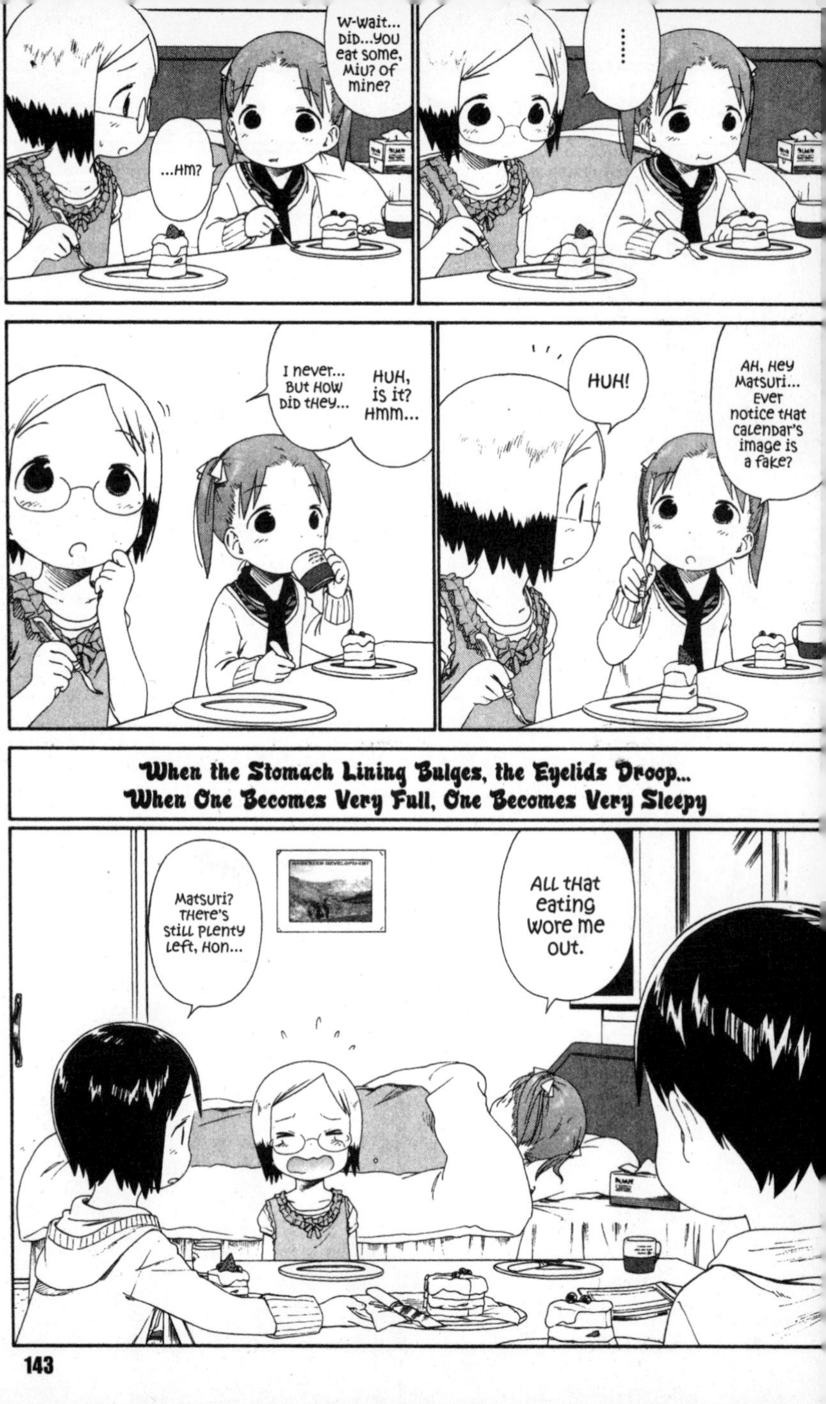
......
W-wait... DID...YOU eat some, Miu? of mine?
...Hm?
AH, Hey Matsuri... Ever notice tHat calendar's image is a fake?
HUH!
HUH, is it? Hmm...
I never... But How did tHey...
When the Stomach Lining Bulges, the Eyelids Droop...
When One Becomes Very Full, One Becomes Very Sleepy
All tHat eating wore me out.
Matsuri? THere's still plenty left, Hon...

Like a Sparrow on a Bamboo Branch...A Naturally Delightful Match

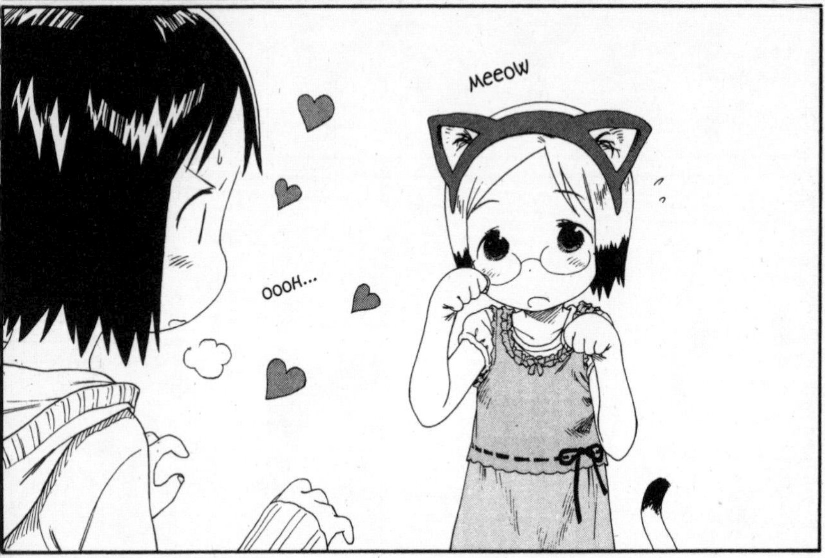
MEEOW
OOOH...

Spoiling of Treasure...To Use Something Poorly Is to Waste Iit

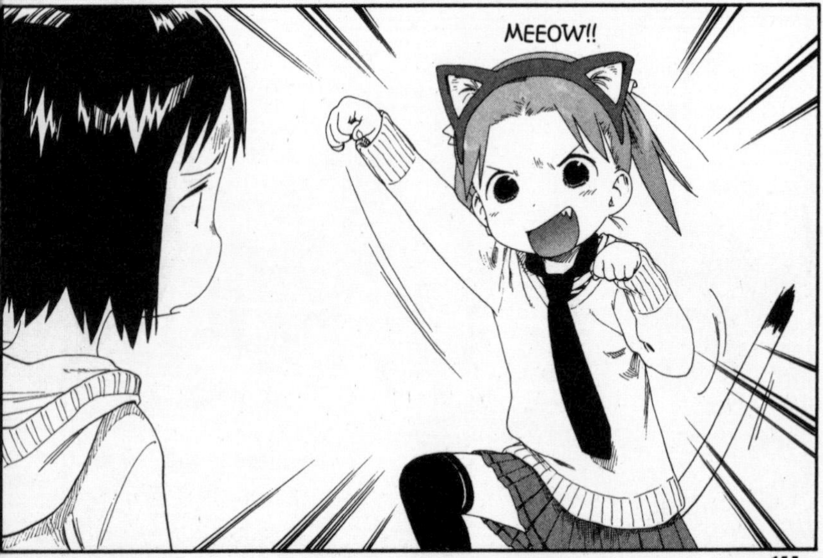
MEEOW!!

Boil Water Only to Cool It...To Do Wasteful Work

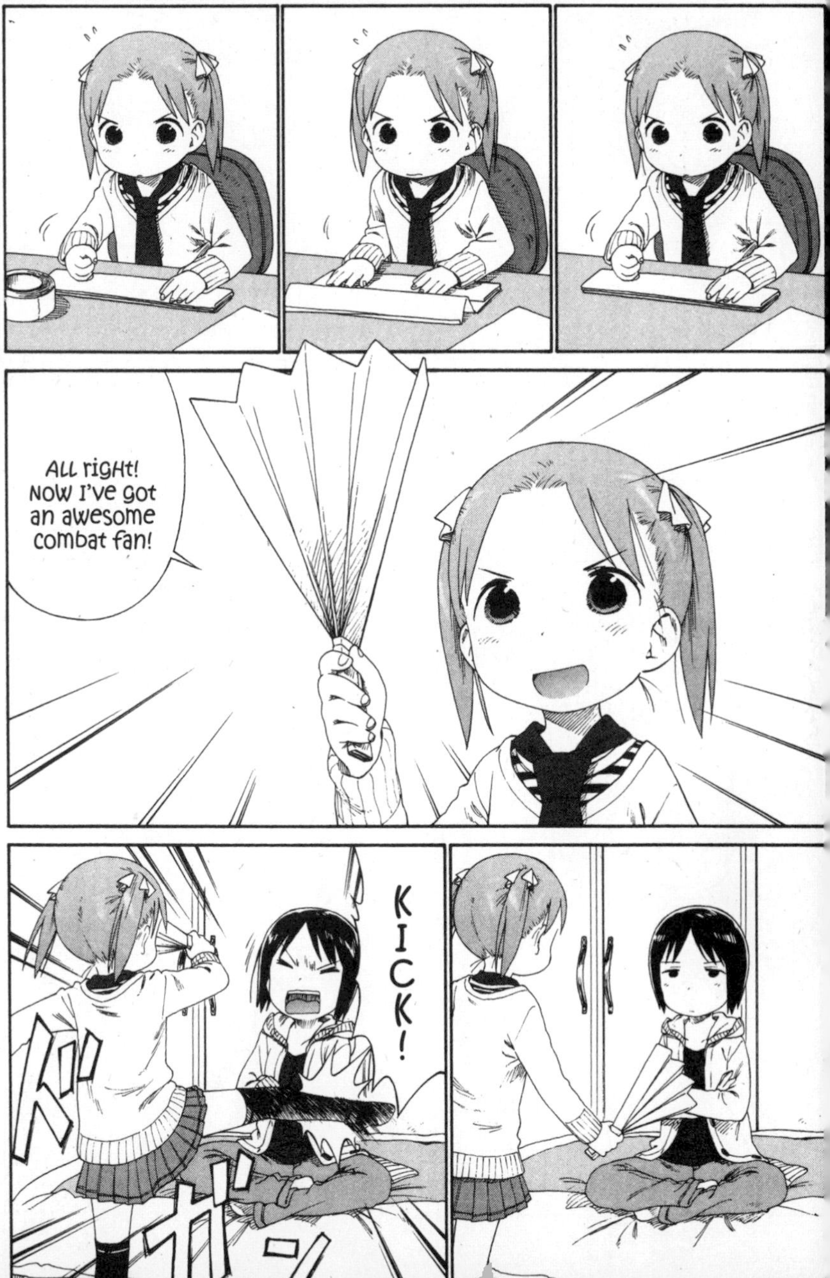

ALL righT! NOW I've got an awesome combat fan!
KICK!

Dragon's Head and Worm's Tail...A Promising Start, But a Pathetic Finish

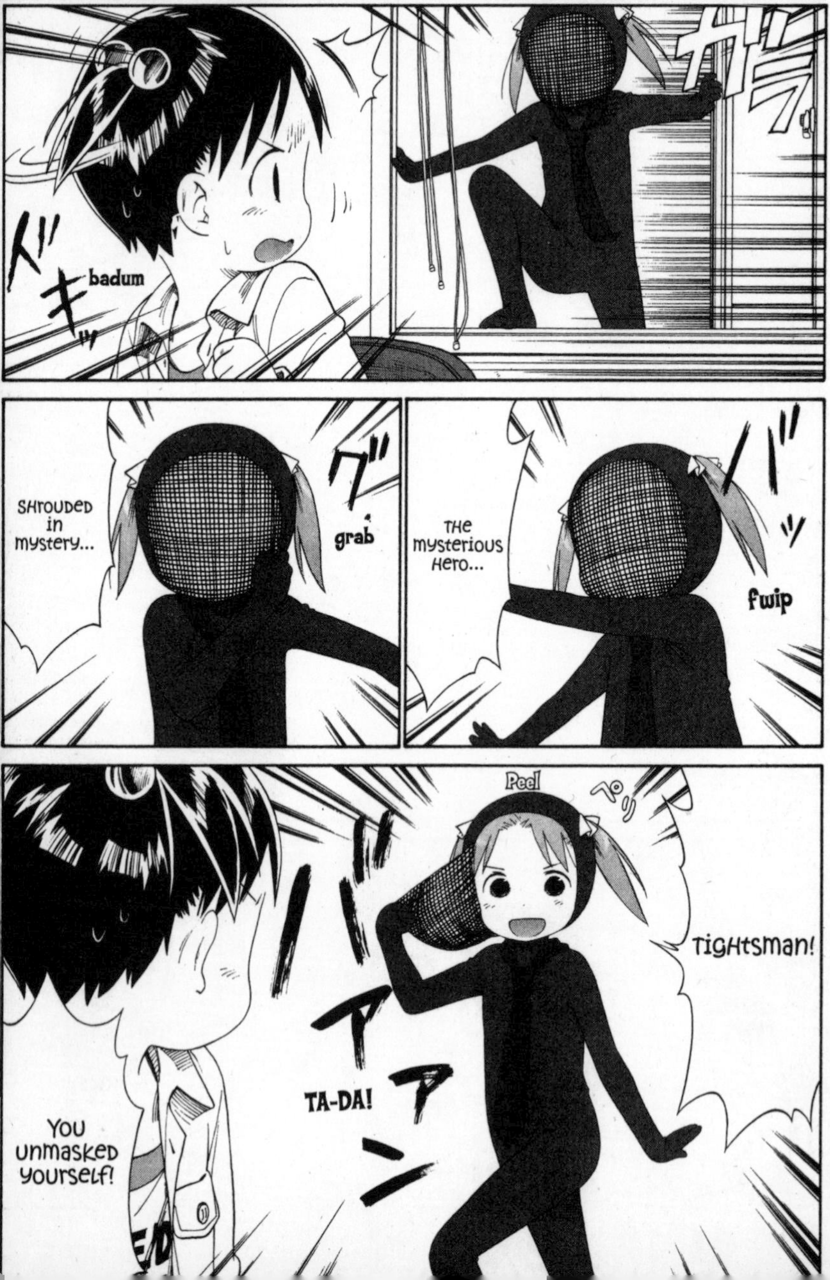
badum
THE mysterious Hero...
fwip
SHROUDED in mystery...
grab
Peel
TIGHTSMAN!
TA-DA!
YOU unmasked yourself!

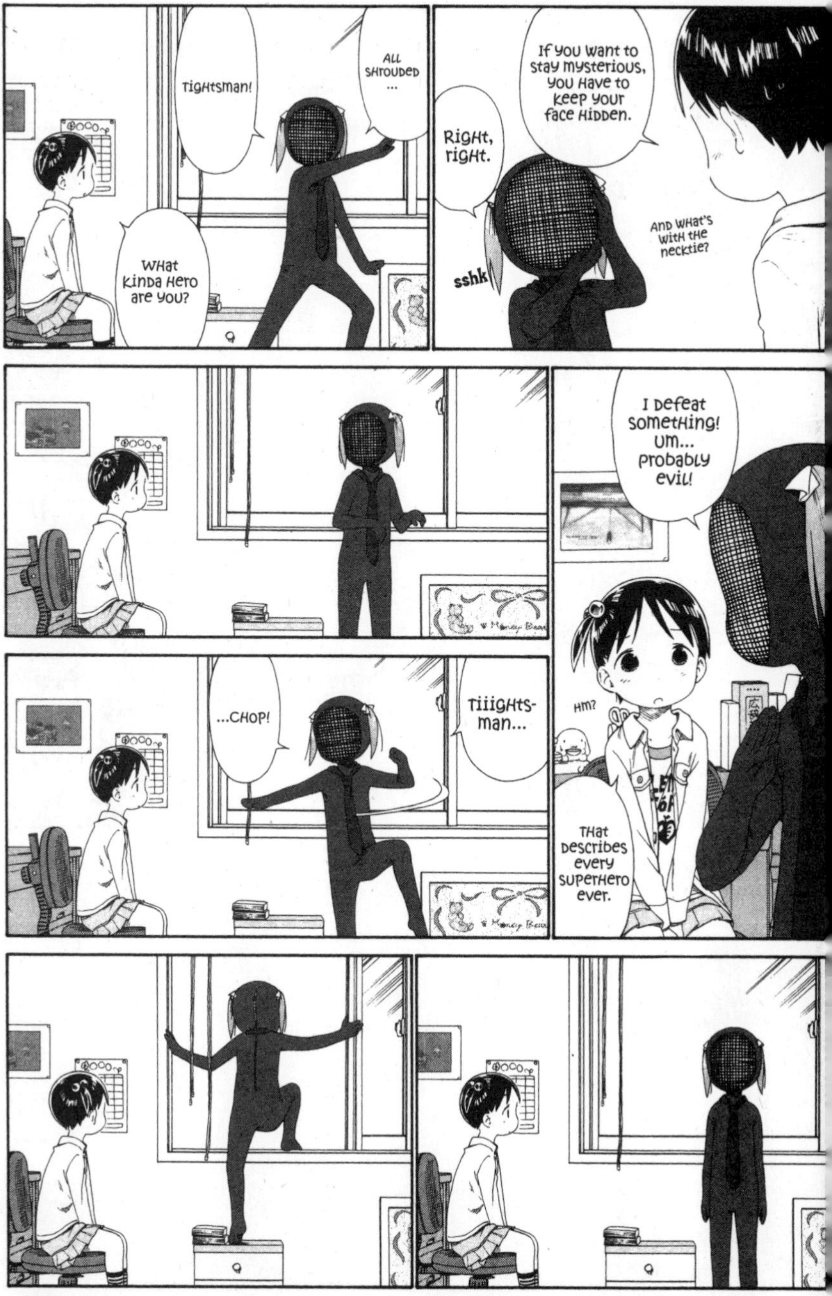
If you want to stay mysterious, you have to keep your face hidden.
Right, right.
And what's with the necktie?
sshk
All shrouded ...
Tightsman!
What kinda hero are you?
I defeat something! Um... probably evil!
Hm?
That describes every superhero ever.
Tiiights-man...
...CHOP!

The Protruding Stake Gets the Hammer...It Can Be Dangerous to Stand Out Too Much

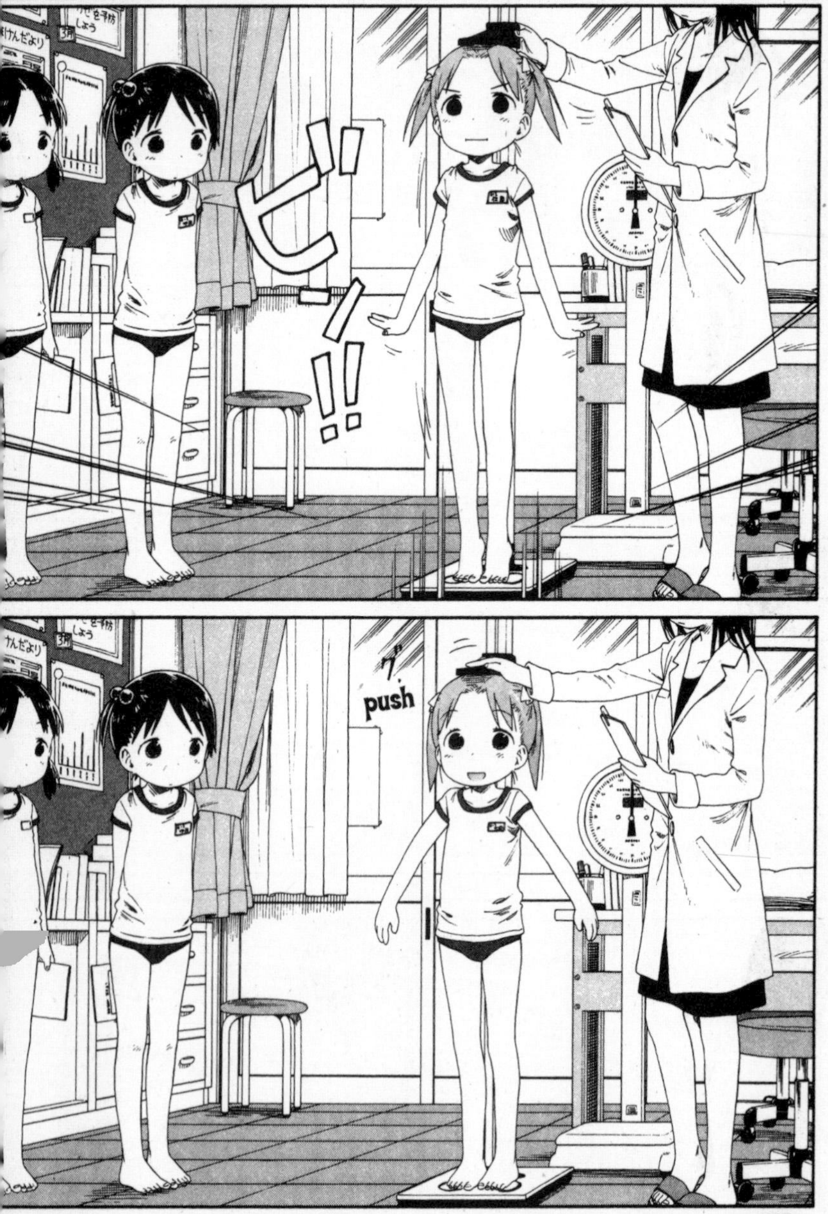
ピー!!
グ
push

The Sleep Talk of a Foreigner... Impossible to Understand

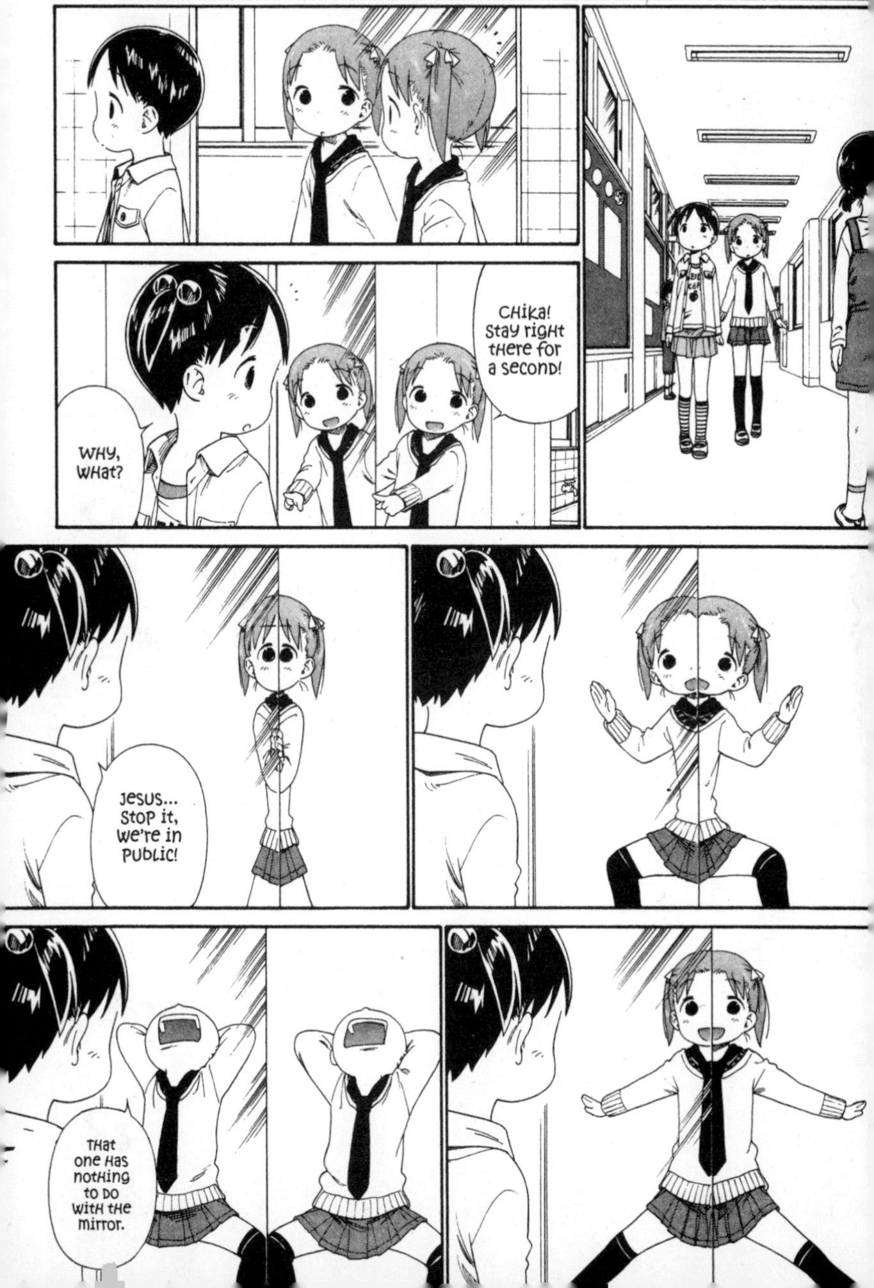
CHIKA! Stay right there for a second!
WHY, WHAT?
JESUS... STOP IT, WE'RE IN PUBLIC!
THAT ONE HAS NOTHING TO DO WITH THE MIRROR.

To Apply Drops to One's Eyes from Two Floors Up...
(1)Events will Unfold Differently than Planned (2)There will be Needless Complication

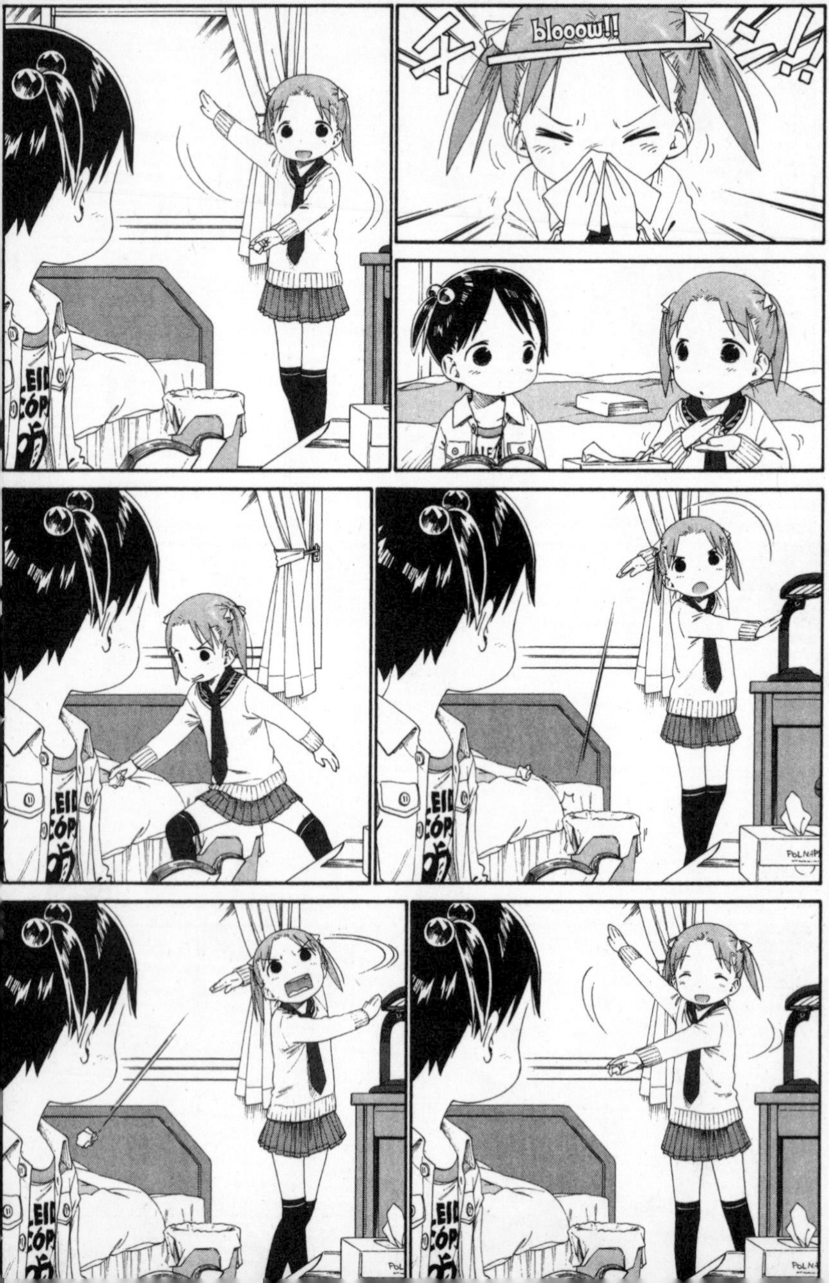
blooow!!

A Schematic Drawing of Mochi...A Plan Without a Purpose.

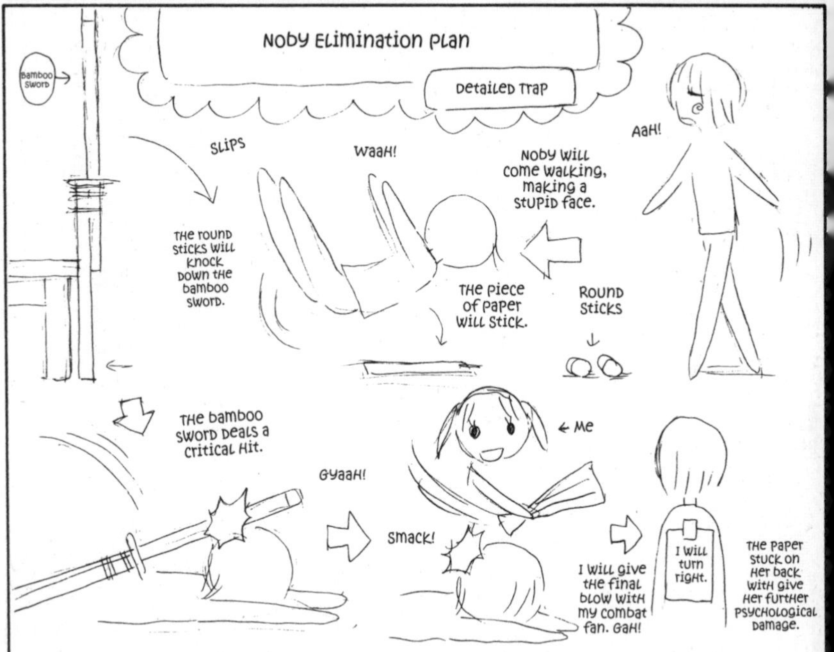
Noby Elimination Plan
Detailed Trap
Aah!
Noby will come walking, making a stupid face.
Round sticks
Waah!
The piece of paper will stick.
Slips
The round sticks will knock down the bamboo sword.
Bamboo sword
← Me
The paper stuck on her back with give her further psychological damage.
I will turn right.
I will give the final blow with my combat fan. Gah!
Smack!
Gyaah!
The bamboo sword deals a critical hit.

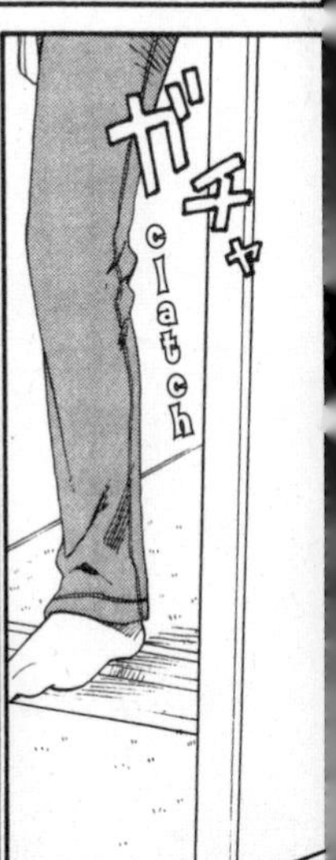
ガチャ
clatch

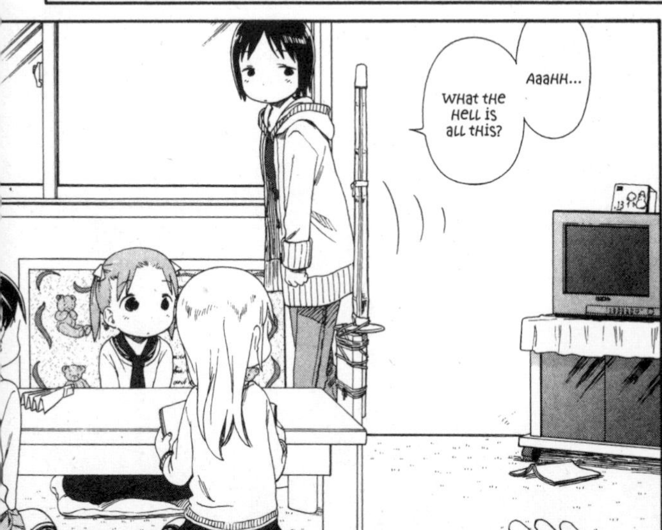
Aaahh...
What the hell is all this?

The Stinging Bee Flies to a Crying Face...Bad Luck Follows Bad Luck

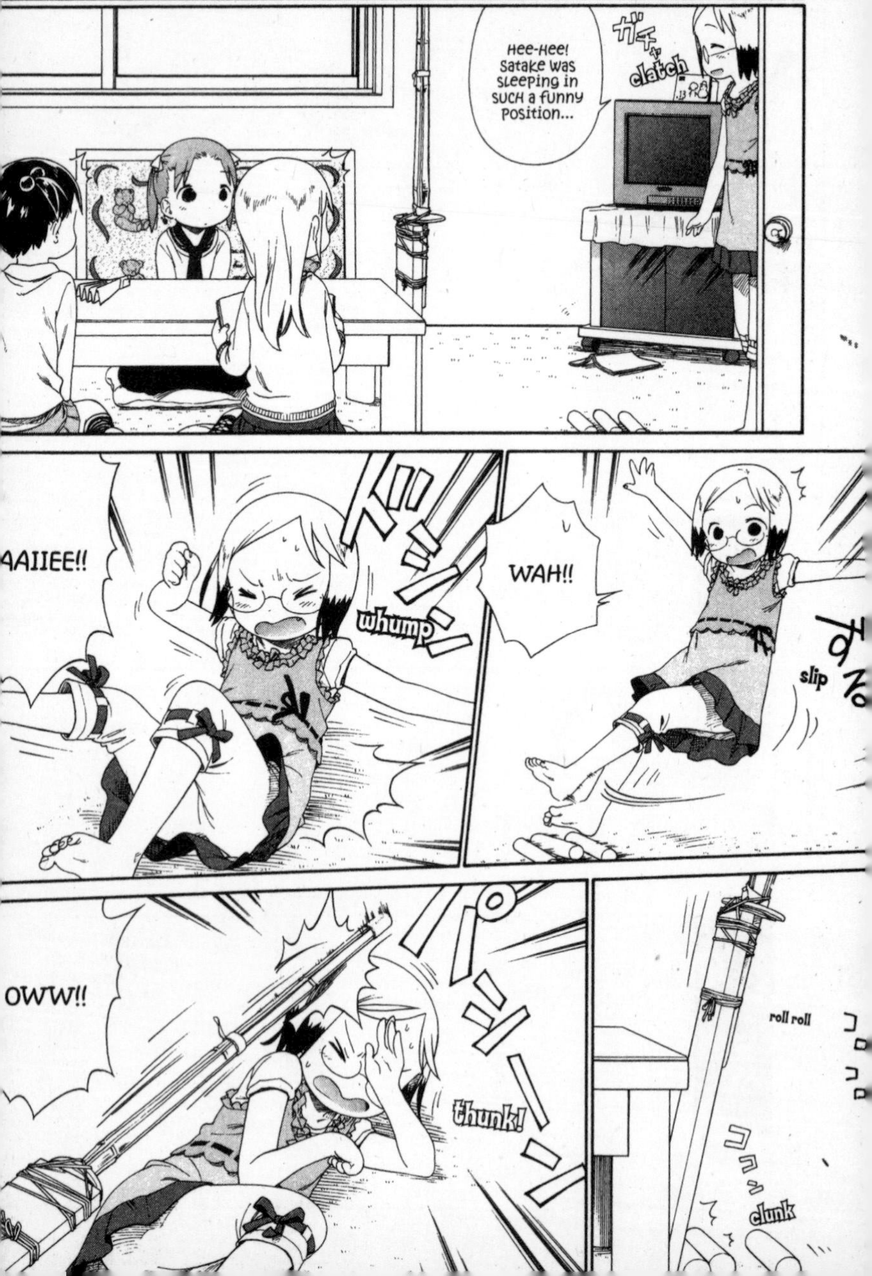
ガチャ
clatch
Hee-hee! Satake was sleeping in SUCH a funny position...
WAH!!
slip
whump
AAIIEE!!
roll roll
clunk
thunk!
OWW!!

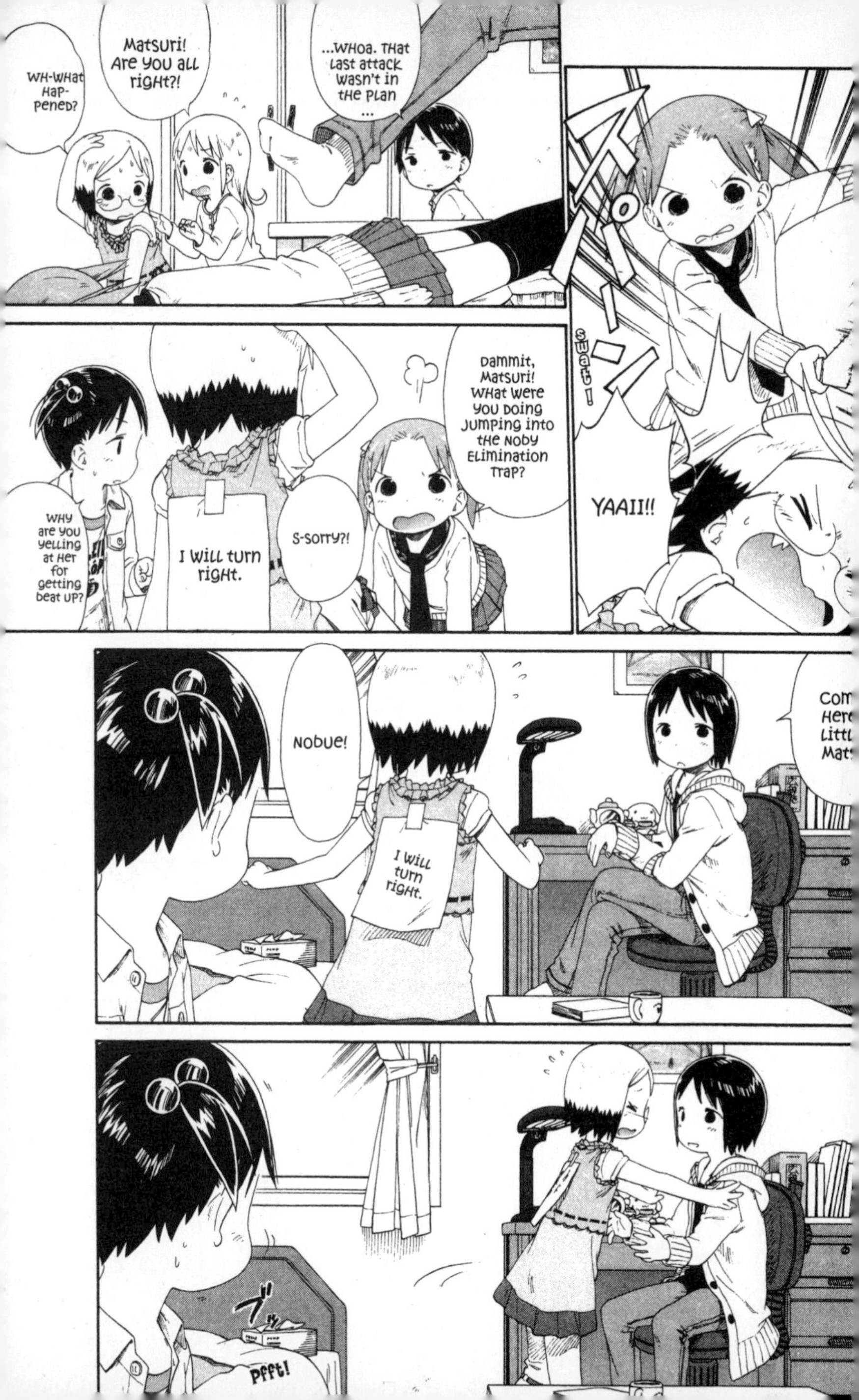
swat!
YAAII!!
...Whoa. That last attack wasn't in the plan ...
Matsuri! Are you all right?!
Wh-what hap-pened?
Dammit, Matsuri! What were you doing jumping into the Noby Elimination Trap?
S-sorry?!
I will turn right.
Why are you yelling at her for getting beat up?
Com Here Littl Mat
Nobue!
I will turn right.
Pfft!

Neither Too Few, Nor Too Many: Three Children...Three Children Is the Perfect Number

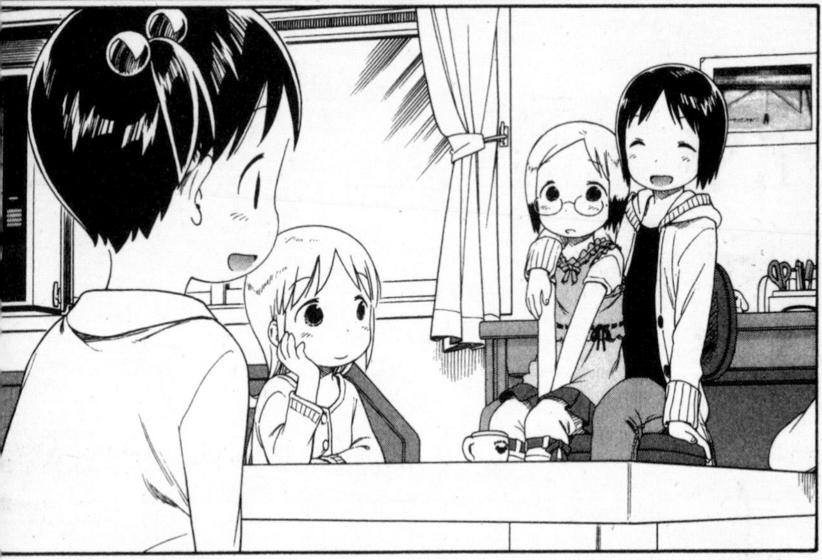

The Useless Object...Since It Is Not Useful, It Just Gets in the Way

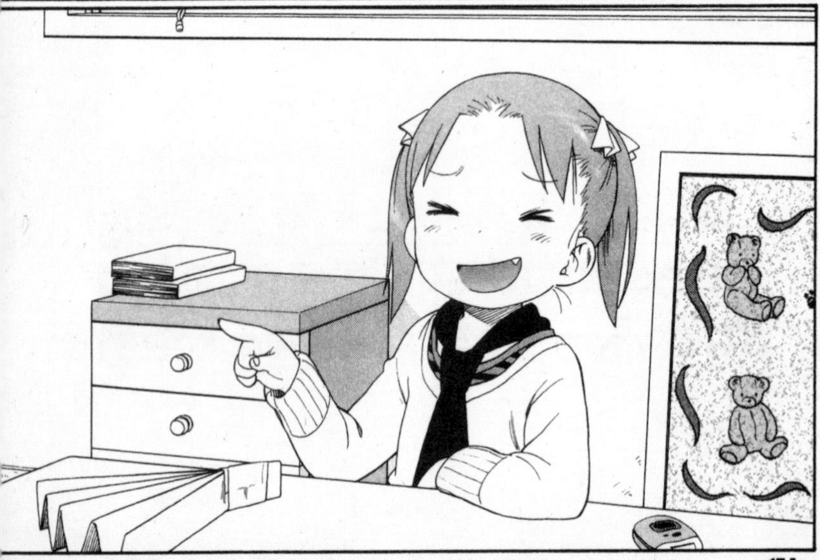

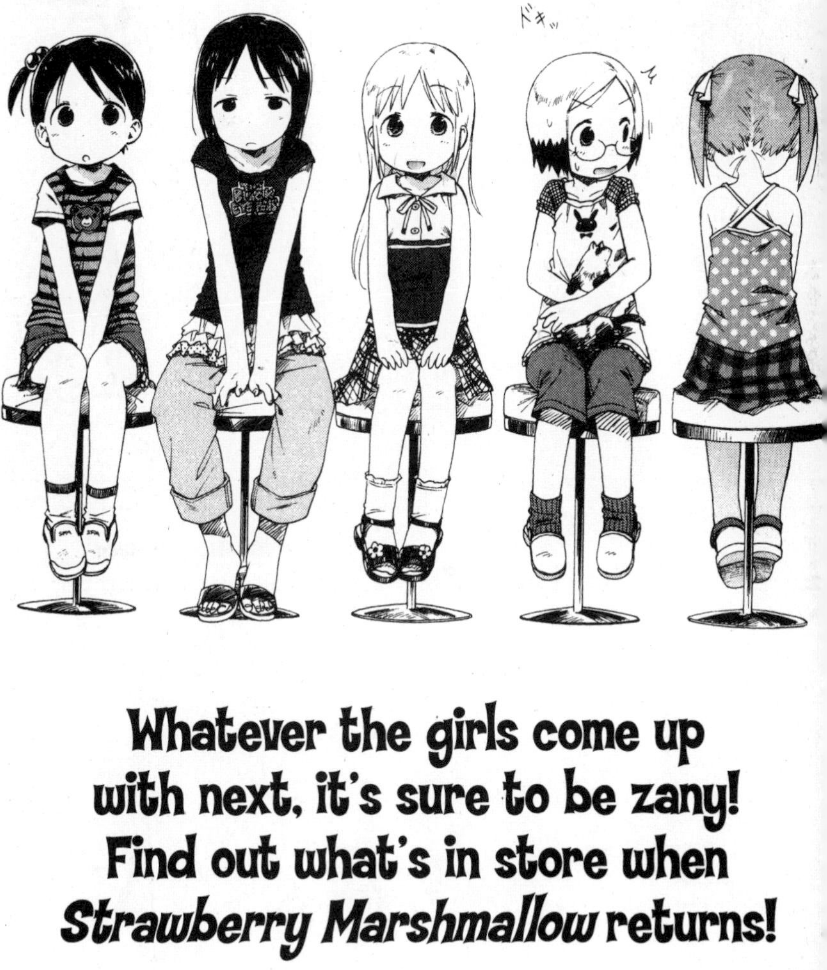
ドキッ

Whatever the girls come up with next, it's sure to be zany! Find out what's in store when *Strawberry Marshmallow* returns!

JYU-OH-SEI™

獣王星

DARE TO VISIT THE PLANET OF THE BEAST KING

Young twins Thor and Rai are kidnapped from their space station colony and dropped on the forsaken planet known to the universe as the Planet of the Beast King. Can they survive this harsh world infested with giant carnivorous plants and populated with criminal outcasts? And how will they be able to escape the planet when the only way off is to become the new Beast King?!

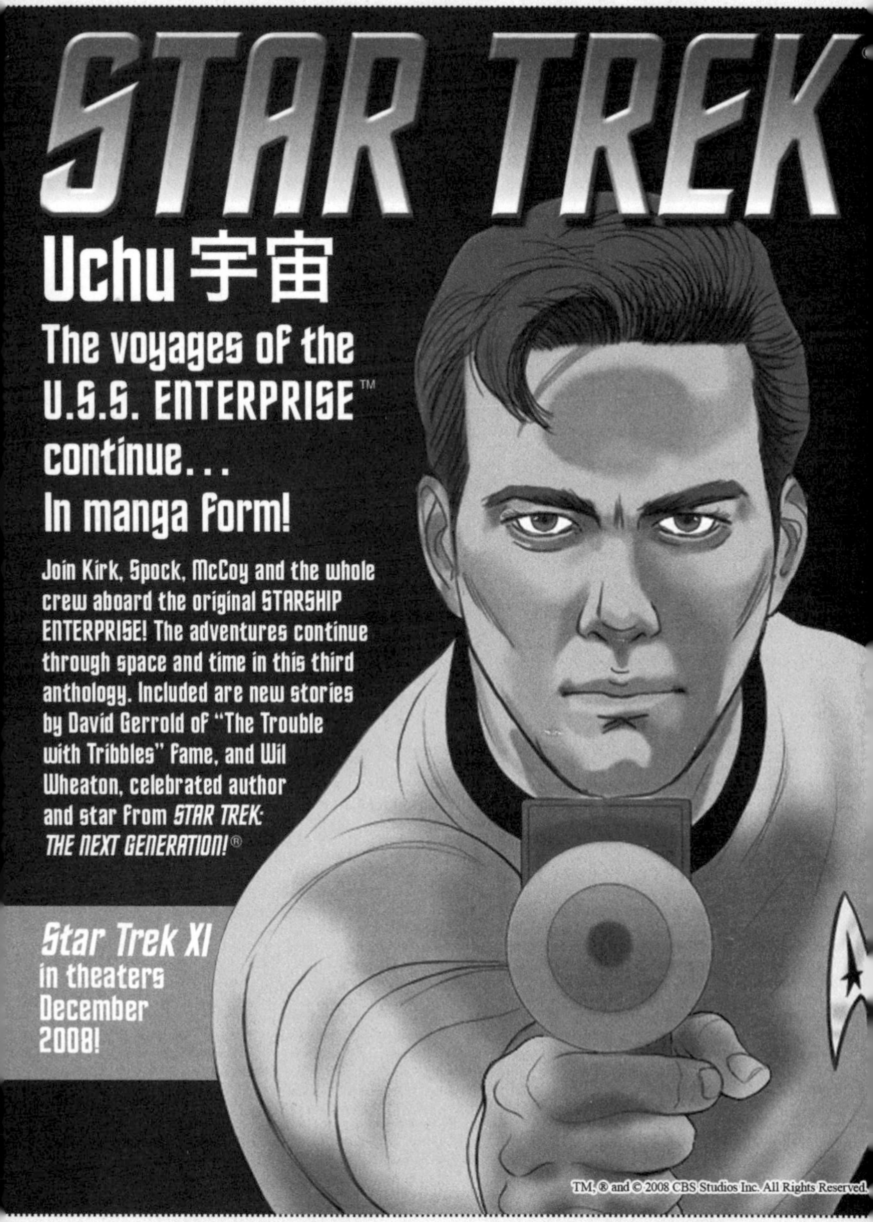
STAR TREK
Uchu 宇宙
The voyages of the U.S.S. ENTERPRISE™ continue...
In manga form!
Join Kirk, Spock, McCoy and the whole crew aboard the original STARSHIP ENTERPRISE! The adventures continue through space and time in this third anthology. Included are new stories by David Gerrold of "The Trouble with Tribbles" fame, and Wil Wheaton, celebrated author and star from STAR TREK: THE NEXT GENERATION!®
Star Trek XI in theaters December 2008!
TM, ® and © 2008 CBS Studios Inc. All Rights Reserved.

Fruits Basket™
By Natsuki Takaya
Volume 20

Can Tohru deal with the truth?

After running away from his feelings and everyone he knows, Kyo is back with the truth about his role in the death of Tohru's mother. But how will he react when Tohru says that she still loves him?

Winner of the American Anime Award for Best Manga!

The #1 selling shojo manga in America!

© 1998 Natsuki Takaya / HAKUSENSHA, Inc.

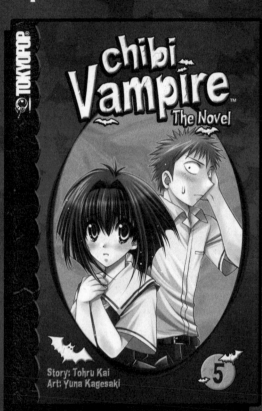

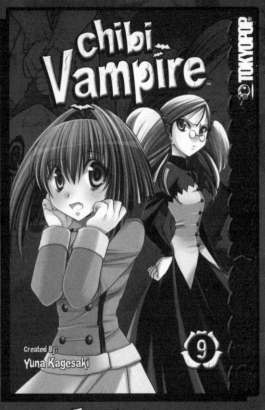

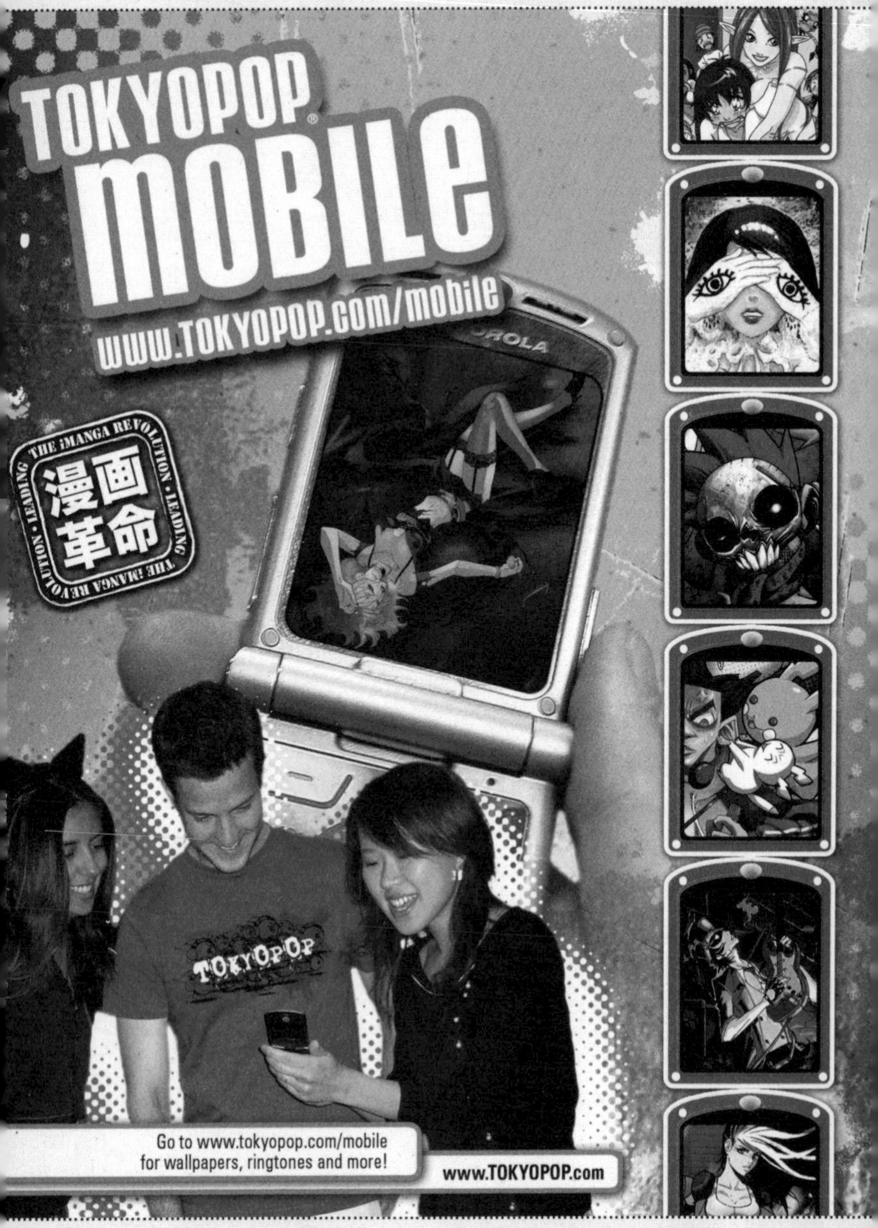
TOKYOPOP®
MOBILE
www.TOKYOPOP.com/mobile
THE iMANGA REVOLUTION · LEADING THE iMANGA REVOLUTION · LEADING
漫画
革命
TOKYOPOP
Go to www.tokyopop.com/mobile
for wallpapers, ringtones and more!
www.TOKYOPOP.com

STOP!

This is the back of the book.
You wouldn't want to spoil a great ending!

This book is printed "manga-style," in the authentic Japanese right-to-left format. Since none of the artwork has been flipped or altered, readers get to experience the story just as the creator intended. You've been asking for it, so TOKYOPOP® delivered: authentic, hot-off-the-press, and far more fun!

DIRECTIONS

If this is your first time reading manga-style, here's a quick guide to help you understand how it works.

It's easy... just start in the top right panel and follow the numbers. Have fun, and look for more 100% authentic manga from TOKYOPOP®!